DIVINE GUIDANCE

Marnie Reilly Mysteries Book One

Second Edition

SHARI T. MITCHELL

Also by Shari T. Mitchell

Marnie Reilly Mysteries Series

Divine Guidance, Book 1
Torn Veil, Book 2
Fatal Vow, Book 3
Vacant Grave, Book 4

Marnie Reilly Mysteries Novellas and Short Stories

The Island
Christmas Eve in Creekwood
Friday the 13th

Praise for Divine Guidance

Divine Guidance is a thriller with personalities that sustain a tightly woven plot that carries it to a hair-raising finish line. Marnie Reilly holds a special talent, and with two of the town's best cops, she sets out to catch a killer. Hidden secrets abound involving the past and present. The sign entering town reads, *Welcome to Creekwood* but perhaps *Beware of Creekwood* is more suitable.
-Chronicles of Crime, Victoria, BC, Canada

It's been a long time since a book kept me up and reading past midnight. I just could not put down Shari T. Mitchell's "Divine Guidance."

Let me be frank: Mitchell crafted a story that scared the bejesus out of me—and it wasn't the paranormal aspects of the story making my heart race! The murders and attempted murders happening around main character Marnie Reilly made me jittery. With ingredients like an abusive ex-boyfriend, a wild ice storm closing the roads, and a stalker-murderer running loose, you certainly have a recipe for a solid creep fest!

But the author doesn't rely on bumps in the night to create a compelling tale. She's also written a sound mystery-thriller with a flawed main character, who despite her rough edges, is good and kind at heart. She's also believable.
-TL Brown, Door to Door Paranormal Mysteries

Dedication

For the ones I love on both sides of the veil.

Table of Contents

Introduction

Hi there! My name is Marnie Reilly, and I am pleased to meet you. My author, Shari T. Mitchell, introduced me to the world way back in 2014 when she wrote Divine Guidance. Here's a bit of trivia: she never intended to write more than one book about my life, but here we are. I guess my traumatic relationship with Ken Wilder and the tragic deaths of my mom, dad, and brother were just too much fodder for one story. Besides, this book has heaps of layers and lots of plot twists to build on.

With four books now in the series and a fifth on the way, a new edition evolved to capture the nuances of the character and narrative arcs in *Torn Veil*, *Fatal Vow*, and *Vacant Grave*. And to be quite honest, the writing needed a zhuzh to make the story a more enjoyable read.

Okay, here's what's been happening. There's a group of psychics and healers here in my hometown who are charlatans. They sell hope to the good folks of Creekwood and surrounds, and I cannot condone their shenanigans any longer. I've made it my mission to shut them down. To be fair, a few of them were kind to me when I escaped my abusive ex, but that doesn't forgive their duplicitous behavior.

Have I mentioned that I am a psychologist and clairvoyant? Anyway, the veil between this life and the hereafter is fragile, and you shouldn't mess with it, like the fraudsters do daily. If you are privileged enough to walk between worlds, you have a duty to protect both the souls of the living and those in the spirit realm. Here's the sticky bit; having psychic abilities is a double-edged sword. It can inspire devotion or breed resentment. I've never considered my gift a moneymaker. I use my *superpower* for good, while many don't. The scammers I told you about don't have a healthy relationship with their abilities and are often afraid of mine. And let me tell you, when fear and greed collide, the consequences can be deadly.

Moving on from that sordid topic, I should warn you that Divine Guidance is not a cozy mystery. I daresay the only warm and fuzzy feelings you'll get will be for Tater, my rescue Border Collie. Now, I am not saying there aren't warm and tender moments—there are. But buckle up. There's a crazed killer on the loose in my little Adirondack Mountains town.

Welcome to Creekwood. Where Thanksgiving is murder.

Warmest,
Marnie

Chapter One

November 17th

5:23 PM, 999 Wildwood Drive, Creekwood, NY

The garrote tightened beneath the man's Adam's apple, and each time he tried to resist the inevitable, his assailant wrenched the wire. Unable to flee or scream, knowing no one would hear him anyway, he fought. Kicking back, he missed his attacker but toppled a music stand, scattering sheet music to the cold white marble floor. With a fierce and jerking twist, his killer sliced through the cartilage, severing his trachea and ligaments with a sickening crunch. As a numbing chill raced through his body, Ken Wilder collapsed, not feeling his skull crack against the blood-soaked stone tiles.

7:18 PM, Station Hall, Creekwood, NY

Marnie Reilly raced through the back door of Station Hall—a redbrick Federal-style structure built in 1831. Her office hours ended at five o'clock, but a client had delayed her.

"Sorry I'm late," she said, shaking hands with Serena, the organizer of the event, who glanced at the stage before checking her watch.

"You're fine. You arrived in plenty of time."

The current speaker's saccharine tone raised Marnie's hackles. She knew him well, but his belief system and ethics were questionable more often than not these days.

She stood in the wings wondering how crumpled her suit was after a day of appointments. A full-length mirror backstage offered her the chance to check her reflection. Her smart black silk jacket and matching trim pencil skirt were presentable. The gray silk camisole that she was wearing gave her eyes the soulful look of the empathetic counselor she knew herself to be. Her understated jewelry and makeup completed the look of a confident, no-nonsense professional.

She peeked through the red velvet side curtains to see the audience. Close to two-hundred women and about a dozen men packed the seats in the front half of the theater. Marnie knew that many of them would bristle at her frank delivery of facts. She was always authentic to herself and to the people who sought her counsel. She would tell them what they needed to hear—not what they wanted to hear. Peering out at the faces, she hoped the audience would trust her candid guidance. Or at least question the drivel they were hearing from the guy on stage, selling hope, not a lasting solution.

He was one of many speakers who made an absolute fortune every year taking people's money. This scoundrel told them what they wanted to hear so they would get hooked. His half-truths and twisted reality and the promise that someday his fanciful nonsense would come true dragged these poor people back for more. The man was what some people would call a sensitive, a spiritualist, or an energy healer. Marnie thought Carl Parkins was a charlatan—a low-life, money-grubbing, soul-sucking trickster who strung people along.

She wrinkled her nose, and her cheeks flamed as he told a battered woman named April that her husband would stop beating her if she sought divine guidance. If she could surround herself with white light, soon her optimism and giving energy would transform her husband into the loving man she wanted him to be. He advised that a change of perspective and positive thoughts would bring encouraging results. He dangled the bait, telling her she had the power to create the relationship she so wanted. Then with a gentle tug, he set the hook.

"April, you have work to do, and I am happy to teach you how to bring change to your life."

Carl's reassuring smile held warmth and confidence. "You can get my contact details at the front desk before you leave. Call me to arrange sessions. I suggest two appointments each week for a few months. I'm sure we can put your life in order in no time."

The woman nodded, smiled and blinked back tears. Marnie knew she was entering a trap. She would buy hope from a man who would sell it to her at a hundred and fifty dollars per session.

When the man finished speaking and stepped away from his microphone, the crowd rose to their feet, offering thunderous applause. The charlatan held out an arm, welcoming Serena to the mic.

"Thank you, Carl. What insightful readings tonight. I am sure your natural gift amazed our audience. I know I was blown away! How did you share things that no one outside of their circle could know? I hope they take solace in your inspiring predictions for their future."

Carl nodded his thanks, turned to his audience, placed his hands over his heart and bowed before exiting the stage.

As he walked to the wings, he caught his first glimpse of Marnie. He bristled and eased toward her as the organizer told the attendees about upcoming events.

"Check our schedule online. You won't want to miss out," purred Serena.

The faint but familiar aroma of citrus and bergamot mingled with cedar undertones crept under Marnie's nose as the charlatan slunk up behind her. She put up her hand to keep him at bay, her eyes remaining focused on the crowd through a slit in the curtain.

Without looking at him, she said, "Surprised to see me? Probably not, eh? But you know me. I like to pop up every now and again to keep everyone honest," she said, pivoting, her eyes locking onto his.

"Ooh! Be careful with your misplaced barbs. No one here is performing. We're all spiritualists who want to help. I don't need to tell you how much your being here will sadden this talented group. These people do righteous work, and your interference ... This is not a group of people you want to upset. Don't make enemies of those who are far more powerful than you."

She leaned in, brushing imaginary lint from his shoulder, and he felt the heat of her breath on his face. "Thanks for the warning, but let's not confuse power with shenanigans. You may not be aware, but there are a lot of folks out there cheering me on, waiting for me to take you down."

He pulled back and attempted a laugh. "You? Come on, Marnie. You're a counselor. You advise the battered, the dreary and the mundane, and yes, you have psychic abilities, but you are not someone any of us need to worry about. It saddens me because you could have been talented, but you gave up too soon. You didn't believe in yourself enough, and your clients knew it. I'm not worried." He sneered, shaking his head.

"I wasn't referring to myself, Carl. I was referring to God, the Universe … the Divine. The souls on the other side of the veil—they are tired of you and your mendacious band of thieves taking money from people who need help of a different kind. Do you believe in Heaven, Carl? People like you don't ascend. They wander in purgatory for an eternity." Nudging him aside with a firm hand, she added, "Get out of my way. I'm being introduced."

His glowering eyes burned into her back as she walked away, and he muttered, "Fuck you, Marnie."

"You're not my type, Carl, but when I finish tonight, you *will* feel screwed. Ciao, ciao. Must go." With a taunting wave, she walked onto the stage.

"Ladies and gentlemen, our last speaker tonight is a leading counselor here in Creekwood. She has spent much of her career donating her time at juvenile detention centers and women's shelters. Many people know her as an angel of mercy, a beacon of light and, yes, a psychic. Please welcome Marnie Reilly."

The counselor walked from the wings and up to the podium, and the crowd clapped as she adjusted the microphone. The other speakers had worn headsets and dressed in colorful clothing with elaborate crystals around their necks. In contrast, she was professional, elegant and not at all what they were expecting.

"Good evening and thank you so much for the warm welcome. I see so many hopeful faces. Please allow me to clear up one thing. I'm not a psychic. I don't like that word. It has such a negative connotation. I don't know about you, but for me it triggers thoughts of trickery, charlatans, and persons of questionable morals who sell hope to good folks like you."

She pulled the microphone from its stand and crossed to the forestage.

"Serena gave you my credentials, so you already know I am trained to help. I am also a clairvoyant, a claircognizant, a clairaudient, and an empath, also known as clairsentient. That means that I see, hear and feel spirits. An empath picks up other people's feelings, emotions, worries, and physical pain. But I'm here tonight as a counselor. I'll listen and offer guidance and share with you places you can go to get help that won't cost you a ton of money. And these will be certified practices where hope isn't sold. There are professional environments where you can talk about where you are now and where you would like to be. Safe places where you can learn about the steps you can take to turn your life around."

Marnie turned to April, who was in the front row, still transfixed after her exchange with Carl.

"Ma'am, I know you are going through a difficult time and what it is like to be in an abusive relationship. Do you feel it's your fault? I blamed myself. And I thought that if I changed, he would too. I can tell you right here, right now, he won't. You need to leave the situation. You need to walk away. It isn't easy, and it will take you time to come to terms with the steps you need to take, but it will be worth it. You don't need a psychic to tell you the situation will not end well if you stay. Common sense is all you need. I have lived it, and I know what I am talking about. It is a gradual buildup, starting perhaps with verbal abuse, criticism that hurts to your very core. And then one day you wake up and you realize it has gone from cutting comments to emotional abuse. Before long, physical abuse rears its ugly head. Then a moment comes when you realize there is nothing left of the person you were—you are an empty shell of emotions and hurt—you feel trapped and fearful. You think if he doesn't love me, then no one else ever will either. It took me two years to escape the man who abused me. Twenty-four months on an emotional roller coaster was enough. I lost thirty pounds and didn't even realize it. My entire world was falling apart, and I couldn't figure out what had happened."

The woman looked up, a sob eluding her throat. Marnie reached back and grabbed a box off the podium, passing it to April, who helped herself to a few tissues.

Dropping the microphone to her side, the counselor dipped her hand in a pocket and handed the woman a card. "Call me tomorrow. I will not charge you anything. We can have a chat, and if you are comfortable, we can put your life back together."

April gave her head a jerk and said, "Thank you."

Returning to the lectern, Marnie spoke with earnest. "Listen, folks. Readings can be fun and helpful. Heck, I give readings to my friends sometimes, but I do not think they are appropriate for people who are going through critical life choices. You need a professional for the tough stuff. Let me ask you all a question. Would you go to a psychic for a cure if you had cancer? No? Then why would you when you're depressed or in an abusive relationship? Critical situations need serious consideration. If you can't find work, don't call a psychic and spend money you don't have. Call a recruitment company. Talk to a career counselor. There are many free services available. Pick up the phone and find one. And if you can't, call my office. My assistant or I will give you a referral. Please don't go to someone who sells hope. Meet a professional who has the skills to help you. Hope is a wonderful thing. It can help us through the darkest hours, but you must work toward finding a long-term solution. A psychic can't help with that unless they are trained in specialized areas like career counseling, psychology, relationship counseling, and services of that sort."

The auditorium filled with chatter as Marnie stepped up to the apron.

"Okay. Who has questions? Throw up your hands. Let's see if we can find answers for some of you. You've paid for the evening. Let's deliver *positive* results for a few people."

A tired-looking woman six rows back in the middle aisle put up her hand, and the counselor skipped down the steps and up the aisle, and handed the woman a microphone.

"Can you please tell me your name?"

The woman stood up. "My name is Helen. I have been raising my hand all night, and no one would call on me." As tears flowed down her cheeks, she took a tissue out of the sleeve of her faded blue cardigan and dabbed her eyes.

"Well, then. I'm the person you were *meant* to speak with. How can I help?"

The woman choked up, struggling to speak through her tears. "My husband died two days ago. There was nothing wrong with him, and no one will give me answers. They did an autopsy, and all they can tell me is that his heart stopped beating, congestive heart failure, and that it was natural causes. But everything was fine. We came home from having dinner with friends, and I went upstairs to get ready for bed. He went out to the yard to lock up for the night, as he always does. I was so tired. I fell asleep before he came up. When I woke up, he wasn't next to me, so I went looking for him. All the lights were still on, and I found him lying on the patio, crumpled up in a heap."

"I'm so sorry you've been through such an ordeal," said the counselor, but before she could ask a question, the woman continued.

"I had two readings the day after he died, and another a day later. A woman, Grace, said he was poisoned. She told me it was at the hands of another—whatever that means, and a man, Bernard, told me my husband took his own life, chewing oleander leaves, and then another man, whose name I can't remember, told me he had given up on life and died. I don't understand, and I want you to talk to him. Please ask him what happened?

The heart-wrenching pain on the lady's face was an angst Marnie had seen before—in her father's eyes—in her own, and in clients'. Tears stung her eyes, a lump caught in her throat, and her chest ached. As an empath, she could feel the woman's pain, and she wanted to do everything she could to help. Reaching out, she took her hand.

"I will do everything I can to help you work through your grief. Please understand that while speaking with the people we love who have crossed over is possible, it is important we don't disturb them. If they want to speak to us, they find a way, but it is inappropriate for us to seek them out."

The woman broke down, dropping Marnie's hand. "I was told that someone here would channel my husband and that he would speak with me! You're the last one! Why won't you talk to him?"

"I don't know who told you that but let me assure you I would never make that promise." The counselor paused, pushing away her anger. "Helen, the veil between the living and the spirit world shouldn't be crossed. My mother taught me that, and I never attempt contact with people who have passed. I am sorry someone made that commitment to you."

She turned around, searching for the organizer, and spotted her walking in the wings backstage. "Serena, can you please come here for a moment?"

The woman peered out—her eyes darting. Marnie glared and made a blunt request.

"I would like to find out who made this ridiculous promise."

Turning back to the woman, she did her best to offer sound advice and comfort.

"I'm going to ask you not to spend any more money on psychics or mediums to speak with your husband. I'll go with you to the medical examiner's office. He knows me, and I am sure we can find out what happened to your husband if we ask the right questions. Can you tell me your husband's first name?"

"His name is Ralph. He is such a loving man. Tall and handsome and a wonderful father," cried Helen, sniffling and dabbing away tears with a worn tissue.

"How old is Ralph?" asked the psychic psychologist, changing tense to match Helen's.

"He will be ninety-two next week."

Marnie reached out and took Helen's hand again. "Have you had a happy life together?"

"Oh, yes. We've had a wonderful life. Our platinum anniversary was last week. All our family was with us. We had a lovely party. Such a wonderful celebration. Our children, grandchildren, great-grandchildren, and dear friends. We danced and sang and danced some more. Oh, it was so lovely."

"That sounds brilliant. If you can wait for me to finish up, I will schedule a time to meet you, and we will work together to find out what happened to Ralph. Does that sound okay?"

"I came here to talk to my husband. What about that?" said Helen, standing her ground.

"You can talk to him anytime you like. I'm sure he's listening. He'll give you signs you can understand. You don't need me to speak with Ralph. You know in your heart that he's listening, and he always will be."

Marnie locked eyes with Helen, hoping she had gotten through to the grieving widow. With a half-shrug, the older woman nodded as the man next to her comforted her into her chair. Meeting Marnie's eyes, he mouthed, "thank you."

The psychologist put a hand in her pocket and held out her card. He accepted it and asked, "Would it be okay if we called in the morning?"

"Yes. That would be fine."

Climbing the steps to the stage, Marnie sensed a presence in the wings, only to see Carl and his psychic friends backstage, scowling at her through the side curtains. Rather than engage in nonsense, she addressed the audience.

"Okay. Does anyone else have a question?"

Hands shot up, and the psychic psychologist beamed with joy. She had them, and they wanted what she was selling — truth, common sense, and a chance for a better life. *Hope is a wonderful elixir if it's the right kind.*

Two figures huddled in the darkness of the theater's wings, glaring at the woman on the stage.

"Your lack of attention to detail screwed us!" said the one wearing a navy-blue baseball cap.

The other, who wore a knitted green tuque, grumbled, "It's not my fault. He promised he'd taken care of it!"

"You didn't think to check? You had the combination," growled Baseball Cap, lips curled back in a snarl.

Green Tuque's face dropped. "Not that easy."

"Nothing ever is with you."

"What do we do now?"

Baseball Cap said, "We stick to the plan."

"Remove her from the equation?"

"Of course."

They leaned against the wall, silent but resolute, as the spotlight lingered too long on Marnie Reilly.

Maps of Marnie Reilly's Home

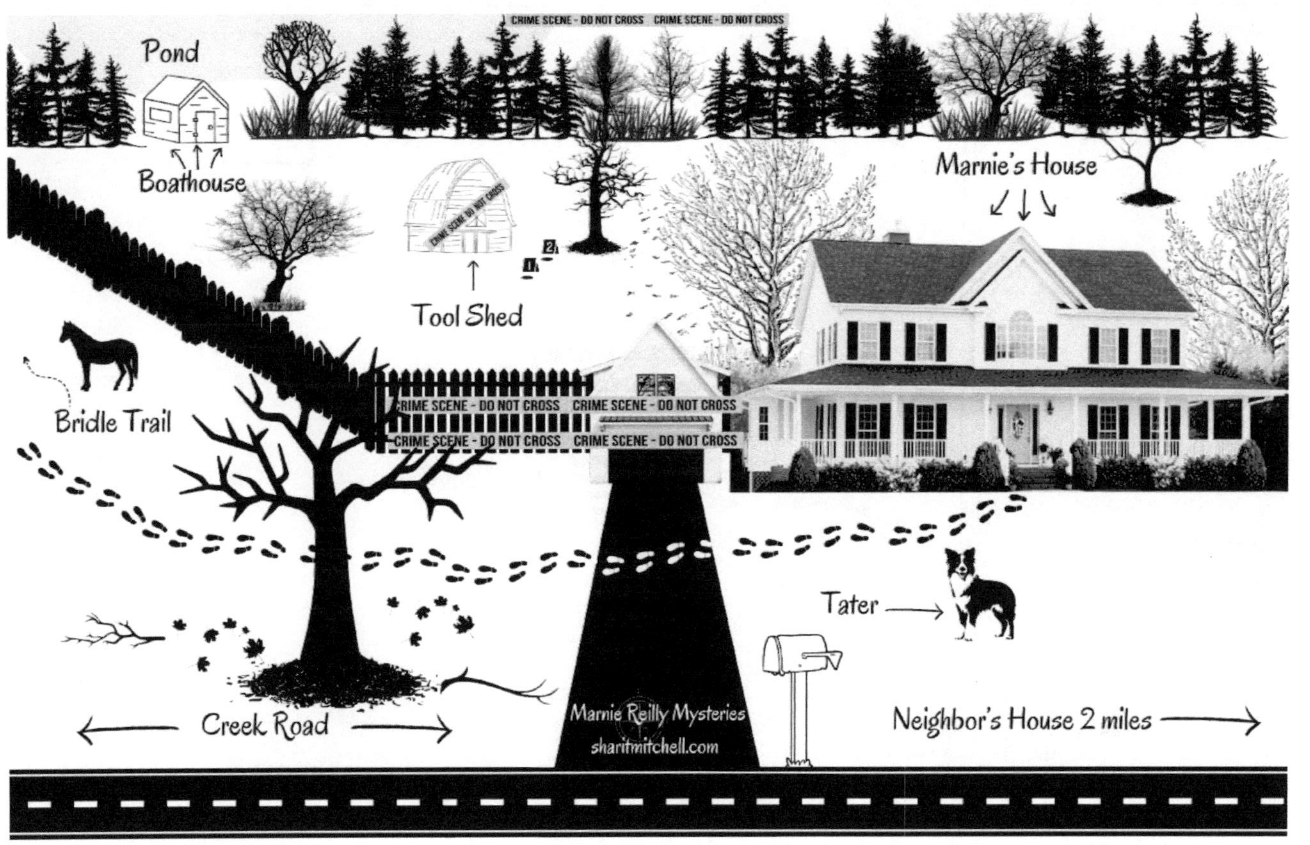

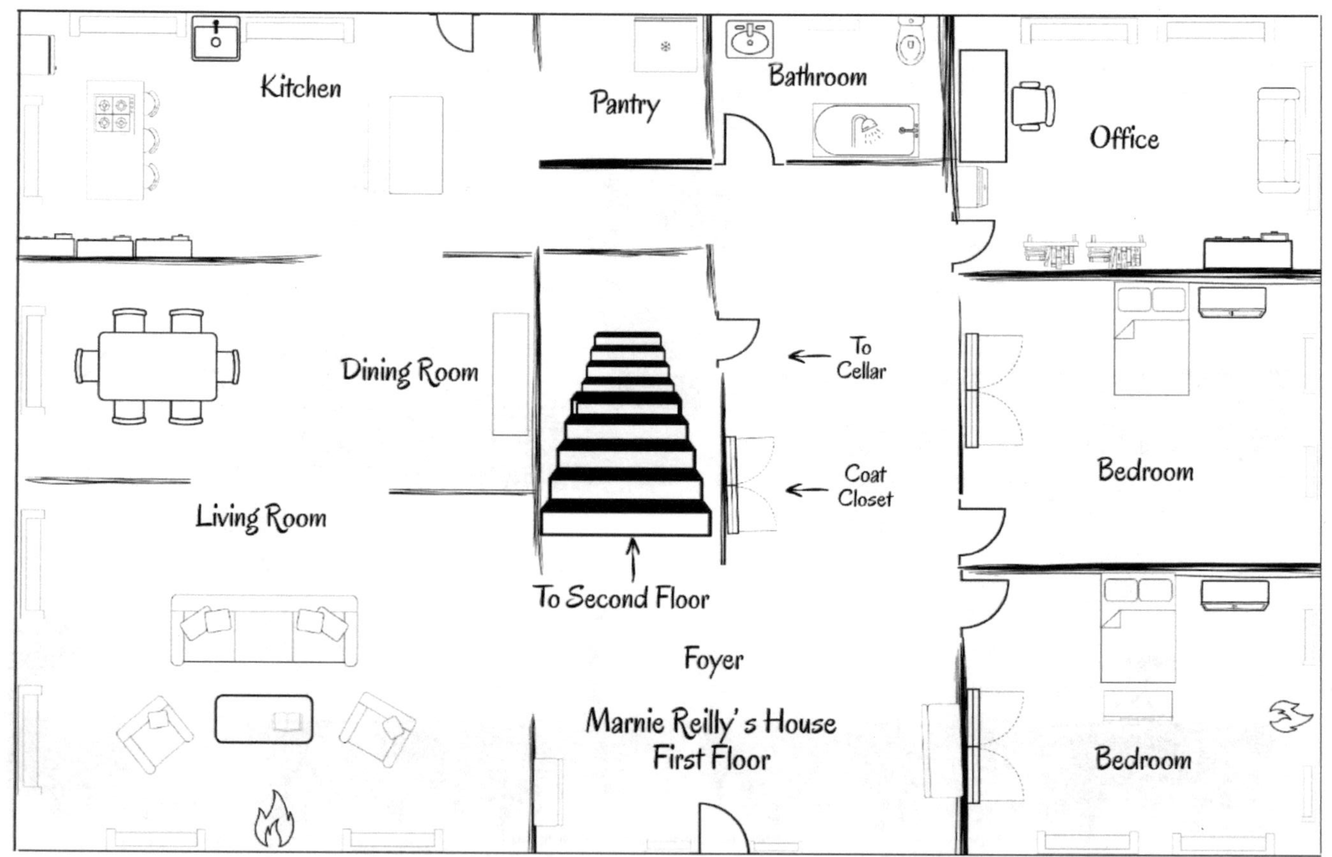
Kitchen
Pantry
Bathroom
Office
Dining Room
To Cellar
Coat Closet
Bedroom
Living Room
To Second Floor
Foyer
Marnie Reilly's House
First Floor
Bedroom

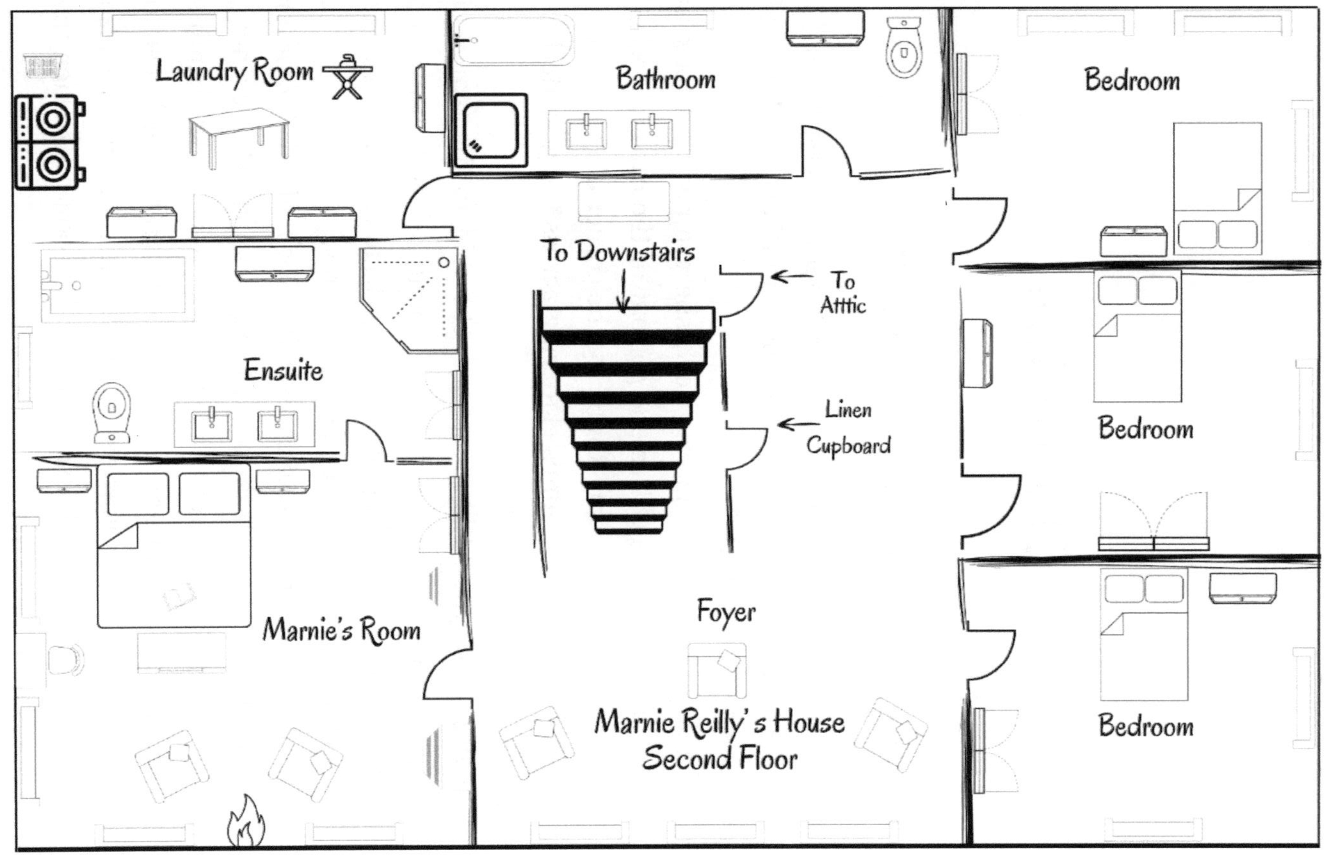

Laundry Room
Bathroom
Bedroom
To Downstairs
To Atttic
Ensuite
Linen Cupboard
Bedroom
Marnie's Room
Foyer
Bedroom
Marnie Reilly's House
Second Floor

Chapter Two

9:27 PM, 404 Creek Road, Creekwood, NY

Marnie pulled into her garage and sat with her head resting on the steering wheel. "Nights like this are why I do what I do. I know I have chosen the best path."

Thankful for where she was now, she grinned and took in the familiar sounds of night as she got out of the car and locked it, tucking it in for the night. Rounding the corner of the house, a kerfuffle of thumps and bumps skittering across the gray deck of her porch told her she had visitors.

"I hear you, you little monsters," she said to the family of raccoons scampering off her veranda, taking refuge beneath the hedgerow. "You'd better stay out of my garbage bins. I've cleaned up enough of your messes, you naughty rodents."

Her memory went back to a time when she had a dog door for her Border Collie Tater. It didn't last long, though. One evening, when she and the pup were out on a stroll, the pesky masked bandits broke into her home, scattering food from one end of the house to the other. With the flap now sealed, a dear friend, who was also a vet, took her four-legged rascal on his afternoon walk when the counselor couldn't get away.

Reaching the front door, keys at the ready, she heard the dog sniffing on the other side of the threshold. "Hello, my little man! How has your evening been?"

It seemed a long time since she had left the horrible man and had found this little ball of fur days later while out for a run one morning. Coming upon a squeaking and squirming burlap bag on the road's shoulder, the thought of someone tossing kittens out of a car disgusted her. But to her surprise, she opened the sack to discover a black and white puppy no bigger than an Idaho potato, hence his name.

Tater's backside wiggled, and he nose-nudged his human for a pat before racing to get his lead, dragging it back and dropping it at her feet.

"Give me a second to change clothes, and we'll go for a run. It's late—no faffing about tonight. Understand me?" she said, scratching him under his chin.

He dropped his leash at the door, and with his tail wagging, followed her upstairs. They had a routine—something his breed loves. Every day, he trailed after her and waited for her to put on her jogging shoes, and then they would run through the forest.

Dressed in sweats, a T-shirt and running shoes, Marnie bounded down the stairs with her pup on her heels. Tater hit the rug at the bottom, and the runner and dog slid across the timber floors, colliding with the wall. Giggling, she patted him and snapped on his lead.

"Are you ever going to learn that the rug moves? Silly boy."

The phone rang as she pulled a sweatshirt over her head.

"Whoever that is can leave a message," she said, opening the heavy door, stepping into the night air.

As an afterthought, she ducked back in and set the alarm. The dog sat, cocking his head.

"I know. I know. There's nothing to worry about with my big, fierce protector looking out for me. But the alarm makes me feel safe," she said, waiting for 'armed' to appear on the screen. "Okay. It's on. Let's go."

A man moved out of the forest and jogged across the street to Marnie's house. He overheard her talking about the security system and knew she must have set the alarm. *That complicates things. Hmm ... Not to worry, I'll improvise.*

Setting a gym bag on the deck of the veranda, he unzipped it, retrieving a mini flashlight, turning it on and holding it between his teeth. The first item he removed from his kit was an amethyst, and he admired the lilac and deep violet gradient of the brilliant crystal point. He tucked it behind the big potted geranium near the front door. Next, he nestled an exquisite blue turquoise in one of the flower boxes, and he tucked a piece of moss agate on the opposite end. Standing on tip-toes, he balanced a clear quartz crystal on the sill over the door, and he hoped it wouldn't fall when she closed it. Last, he placed an Archangel Michael coin under her front doormat and stood back before recalling an item in his pocket.

"One more thing, Marnie," he said, pulling an Archangel Raphael coin from his jacket, placing it under the mat next to its sibling. Gathering his bag, he kissed the palm of his hand and pressed it against the oak door. As he stepped away, he raised his gaze to the inky sky.

"Please keep her safe. I've done what I can. She's in your hands now. Thank you for keeping watch over her. You may not realize it, but she is precious to me."

He stood back and assessed what he had done. "There, Collective, do your worst. She has the angels on her side."

The ring of Marnie's phone as he wandered into the forest made him stop in his tracks. Grimacing, he said, "Hmm … It starts."

In the home stretch, Marnie broke into a sprint, and overjoyed by his human's acceleration, the dog pulled ahead but stopped dead, staring at the treeline. Skipping to a halt, the counselor avoided a collision, and her eyes locked onto the Border Collie's target, digging for grubs at the edge of the forest.

"Leave it," she said, scratching his left ear, and ruffling his long coat. "There will be no skunk chasing tonight. Or ever, for that matter. It's time for dinner and then bed."

The pup whimpered, his ears and nose twitching, but followed her to the veranda with a sigh. She unlocked the door, stepped in and turned off the alarm. As she removed the dog's lead and laid it in a basket, a chill ran up her spine and she paused, glancing behind her. Her scalp tingled, and the hair on the back of her neck prickled. A feeling of dread took hold, and she went back outside, scanning the road where the asphalt met the trees. With thoughts racing, she shivered, feeling like a thousand eyes were watching. She rubbed her arms to chase away a chill and backed into the house, slamming the door and twisting the deadbolt, locking them in.

The familiar shuffle of Tater rummaging in his empty bowl echoed down the hall. She laughed but scolded herself for being late to feed him.

"Okay, boy. Let's share an omelet. Sound good?"

Tater assumed his post at the kitchen window while his mistress dug food out of the fridge. The hair on his scruff stood on end, and his mouth closed tight, his amber eyes intent on the rear of the yard. His low, grumbling growl crescendoed into a roar, and Marnie flinched. She hadn't heard the dog's warning bark since the last visit from her abusive and drunk ex.

Flicking on the back floodlight, she peered out the paned glass. And while she couldn't see anything, the canine could, and she wondered if it was the same presence that had spiked her nerves out front. *Huh ... maybe I'm being paranoid. Nah ... But it could be someone trying to scare me,* she thought, before muttering, "Friggin' Collective."

"What do you think, Mr. Fluffy Butt? Are we imagining things?" she said to her companion, stopping on the way to the fridge to boop his snout. "Suppertime, little dude. How about that omelet?"

The dog woofed once, then settled in front of the door, flashing a toothy smile.

As she cracked the first egg, the phone rang again, and she glanced toward the hall where the phone was sitting in its cradle.

"Leave a message after the beep!" she yelled. "It's late and we're hungry!"

Placing half of the omelet into the dog's bowl, she set it aside to cool and poured juice for herself, buttered crisp toast, and plated up her portion. Prompted by the whimpering of the impatient pup, she cooled his dinner with a splash of milk and set his bowl on his mat with some fresh water. The dog gobbled it up, slurped his beverage, and turned, waiting for his mistress to finish so he could have her leftovers.

Standing at the counter, she picked at her eggs and nibbled the buttery middle bits of her toast—not because she was hungry but for sustenance. With a gulp of juice, she'd had enough, and scraped her plate into Tater's bowl, before rinsing it and popping it in the dishwasher. While wiping up toast crumbs, the phone rang again, and a frown creased her forehead.

"Who would be rude enough to call at this hour?" She scowled down the hallway and crossed her arms with a *harrumph*. "I'm not answering it. They can leave a message."

But her curiosity got the better of her, and she picked it up, dialed into voicemail, and listened. What she heard made all color drain from her face and prickles race up her neck and arms. Slamming down the phone, she rested against the wall, drawing in a breath through her nose and letting it out through her mouth. With a grunt, she pushed herself off the shiplap, trudged back to the kitchen and turned out the light. She stood for a moment in the darkness—the memories the phone call brought back unnerved her, and she trembled.

Hugging herself tight, she let out a sigh and called out to the Border Collie as she walked to the stairs. "C'mon, knucklehead. It's bedtime."

Claws clattering on the timber floors, the canine raced to the stairs, slid across the hall on the rug, got his bearings, and tore up the stairs behind her. Marnie stopped at the top, skipped back down, set the alarm and took the stairs two at a time to the second floor. Once in her room, she paused and looked out the window— her forehead pressed to the cool glass.

"Shit. What have I started?"

Chapter Three

November 18th

5:00 AM, 404 Creek Road, Creekwood, NY

The five o'clock alarm buzzed, and Marnie opened one eye, then the other; and crossing her arms over her head, she giggled. Her Border Collie sat beside her, staring, his cold wet nose inches from her face.

"God, Tater, that is the creepiest thing in the world. Come here, you little freak, and give me a cuddle."

She rolled to the side of the bed, put both arms around the dog's neck and wrapped him in a hug. When she let him go, he sat back and flashed her his trademark smile.

"Ha-ha! You're a cheeky boy!"

A glance out the window revealed ice crystals glistening in the streetlights on the tree branches outside her bedroom.

"Brrr," she said, pulling on a pair of fleece-lined slippers and her bathrobe. "Brace yourself! It's a chilly morning, bud. C'mon, I'll let you out, and then we'll go for a run."

At the bottom of the stairs, she reached to turn off the alarm, but it was already off, and she remembered setting it before going to bed. In fact, she had traipsed downstairs to do it. *Strange. Ah, well.* The dog didn't bark last night, so everything must be secure, but she made a mental note to call the security company today to have it checked.

The sun had yet to poke up its head as she opened the back door for the fluffball. She switched on the floodlight, stepped onto the porch and looked around. All seemed still, but she noticed the shed door swinging in the breeze, its rusty hinges squawking in the frigid morning air. With a tug, she tightened her robe around her waist and went down the steps and into the yard. Tater ran past her, straight for the shack without stopping to pee. He sniffed around a patch of grass outside the door and lifted his leg before sticking his nose inside, but he backed out with a grumble, tail tucked and hackles up.

Eyes darting, Marnie searched for a makeshift weapon and spotted an empty long-neck beer bottle in the grass. A wrinkle creased the center of her forehead, and she thought, *Hmm … That's odd. I didn't leave that there. And no one who drinks beer has been around in weeks.*

With a shrug, she picked it up and carried it by the neck across the yard, approaching the outbuilding with caution. With his nose pressed to the ground, Tater growled, sniffing around the patch of cement on which the building sat. The closer she got, the deeper his bark, and the more rigid his stance.

"Shush, shush. It's okay. What's wrong, buddy?"

The Border Collie planted himself between her and the hut, his gaze never straying from the darkness beyond the open door. Prickles rose on her neck as the dog's snarling intensified, and she whirled around, running back to the house to call for help. As a guttural roar escaped the canine's throat, Marnie quickened her pace—tripping over the threshold, snatching up the portable phone.

Hands shaking, she dialed nine-one-one, but when Tater yelped, she rushed back outside. Teeth bared, the pup limped after a dark hooded figure, scrambling over the fence, and she dropped the phone on the dewy grass and hurried to his side.

"Come here, boy!" she said as he ambled to her.

Other than a frightened stare, he appeared okay—no broken bones or blood. The nine-one-one operator asked for her location as she scooped up the phone. The rumble of an engine starting made her stop and turn toward the sound.

"My name is Marnie Reilly, and I've had an intruder in my backyard, and someone disarmed my home alarm. My address is four hundred and four Creek Road, about two miles west of the Grand Pass turnoff."

Tater gimped through the back door ahead of her, and she scurried in behind, kicking shut the door and twisting the lock.

"Are you under threat, Ms. Reilly? Is the intruder in a position to harm you?"

"What? No, but the bastard kicked my dog. He's limping, and he yipped. The shed door was open, and it's always padlocked. How could someone have gotten in there? I guess the same way someone could have turned off my alarm. Sorry. I'm rambling. Listen. Look ... Geez! Can you have an officer come to my house, please?" She rubbed a hand across her forehead and paused for a breath.

"Yes, ma'am. The police will be with you soon. Please stay on the phone while you wait for the patrol car. My name is Jo, by the way."

"Wait. I think I heard a car out front," said the psychic, jogging to the front room.

"I don't think a patrolman would have gotten there yet. No, I don't see it on the screen. Please don't open the door."

"I'm peeking out the window to see who it is." She pulled the curtain aside and peered out. Throwing back her head, she groaned, "Son of a bitch. Dang it! What the hell is he doing here at this hour?"

"Who is it? Are you all right?"

"Yeah, I'm fine. It's someone I would rather not see, though. The last thing I need is Carl Parkins knocking on my door. Shit! Oh, there's the patrol car pulling up right behind him."

"Okay, Marnie, I'm going to stay on the line until the officer gets to you."

"He's coming up the walk. Thanks, Jo. I'm okay. Bye-bye."

She disconnected the call, turned the latch, and heaved open the large door. Stepping onto the veranda, she welcomed the cop but offered Carl a scowl.

"Morning, Ms. Reilly. I'm Officer Thayer. I hear you've had a bit of excitement." He flashed his badge, glanced over his shoulder, and situated himself between the other visitor and the porch.

She looked at the badge and then over the officer's shoulder to the unwelcome man strolling up the cobblestone walk leading to her front steps.

"Uh ... yes, sir, we've had an intruder in the backyard. He hurt Tater, my dog, then climbed over the back fence and ran away. Sorry. Uh ... I think it was a *man*."

"Is everything okay? I heard you say somebody harmed Tater. Where is he?" Carl's left foot hit the bottom step, and his eyebrows knitted together as he eased up the stairs.

"Not now!" she snapped, before gathering herself. "Please go home."

The officer glanced at her, turned and narrowed his eyes.

"We got a problem here, buddy? The lady doesn't seem so happy to see you."

Hands out, the healer pleaded, "C'mon, Marnie. Give me a break here."

Holding open the door, she said, "Please come in, Officer Thayer. I'll take you to the backyard. Don't worry about Mr. Parkins. He's a nuisance, but nothing more."

Hearing voices out front of the house, the Border Collie made a break for it, scooting around his human and the cop, straight to Carl.

Marnie rolled her eyes as the pup raced past. "You little traitor."

"Hey, mister, how are you? I hear you got hurt, but you look okay, though, huh?" The uninvited visitor roughed the dog's fur and scratched his ears—the pup sucking up the attention with his tail wagging so hard that his whole body wiggled.

She clapped her hands to get the canine's attention. "Tater! Come! Get in the house! Now!"

He galloped to the door, squeezed past the policeman and his mistress, making his way to his bowl. Breakfast was late, and with a hit of his paw, his dish tumbled across the kitchen floor. He sat and smiled—waiting for food.

"Can you give me a few minutes, buddy?" She patted his head on the way to the back door.

Carl followed them into the house and volunteered. "I'll feed him. It's okay. Take your time with the police. I'll keep him company while he has his breakfast. Is his food in the same cupboard?" He flashed a cheesy grin—his eyes dancing with mischief.

Her eyes threw daggers at him, and she gritted her teeth at his display of kindness. "Fine. Yes. His food is where it's always been. Thank you."

She unlatched the back door and led the officer into the yard, and he crossed to the shed, opening the entrance wide. With a hand over his mouth, he muttered an expletive, lurched back, vomiting on the lawn. Digging in his pocket, he pulled out a handkerchief, wiped his mouth, and made a call on his radio. She couldn't hear everything he was saying, but from his reaction and the few words she picked up, it wasn't good.

The officer marched to where she stood, and cupping her elbow with his puke-free hand, he led her to the porch. "Ma'am, please go into the house. This is a homicide investigation, and I need to protect the integrity of the crime scene and wait for the detective in charge."

Eyes wide, her knees wobbled.

"Homicide? No, are you serious? There's a body in there? Are you telling me there's a corpse in my shed?"

She took a step forward, but the officer hooked a hand around her arm and escorted her to the house. She glanced back—mind racing.

"Who the hell is in my shed?"

Chapter Four

6:43 AM, 404 Creek Road, Creekwood, NY

Marnie rested her folded arms atop the sash and stared out the living room window. A crease deepened between her eyebrows as she assessed the crime scene tape stretched from a huge maple to the mailbox to the garage door, blocking access to the driveway and gates. Officer Thayer stood guard, awaiting the homicide detective and forensics team. She dropped her chin onto her arms and drew in a shaky breath.

The sun poking up over the horizon painted psychedelic bat wings across the sky in hues of red, orange, yellow, and violet. The sky told her to expect foul weather today. Her sixth sense screamed that a big, bloody storm loomed and it would shake the little mountain town of Creekwood.

"Red sky at night, sailor's delight. Red sky in the morning, sailors take warning," she said.

Straightening the curtain, she paused, stealing another peek at the yellow tape flapping in the breeze. Then, her thoughts pulled her back to the corpse. *What the hell is happening? Who's in my shed and how did they get there?*

As she turned the corner to her kitchen, she frowned, remembering that she had a visitor. Technically, he wasn't a guest. She hadn't invited him, and he wasn't welcome. She sighed, knowing that she was as much a pain in the ass to him as he was to her.

Coffee mug cupped in his hands, he leaned against the kitchen counter and glanced up as she entered the room. "What's going on out there?"

"There's a bloody body in the shed, Carl! A corpse." Her face clouded over, considering the predicament. "What are you doing here?" Wrapping her arms around herself, she rested a hip on the counter.

"Ah, I'm sorry. I guess I picked the wrong morning to have a calm, rational conversation with you about last night. But you pissed off The Collective. Your stunt at Station Hall was a terrible mistake. You shouldn't have said the things you did, and you know better than to fuck around with the people who supported you when your life was a pile of shit."

Her body tensed, and her eyes sparked. "The Collective? What's that? A crew of thieves? A group of misguided, soul-sucking, narcissistic phonies with the shared consciousness, decency, and intellect of a gnat? Argh! What do you want, Carl?"

He dragged a palm down his face, knowing he had to diffuse the bomb he lit by coming here. Every single inch of her five-foot-ten frame rippled with indignation. The first time he had seen her angry, it had shocked him. He never knew a person's fury could take over their entire being—except in movies and comic books.

Marnie Reilly had a long fuse—but when she reached her limit, she would explode. First came the tightened jaw, then with clenched fists, her aquamarine eyes would flash with an intensity that could burn through the soul. And if anyone was stupid enough to shove her past the point of no return, she'd plant her feet like a boxer, take a swing, and connect. Her left hook was legendary.

Carl put up his hands in surrender.

"Okay ... okay. Calm down. I didn't come here to argue or to have you punch me. I came with a warning. You know the people in The Coll ... Uh... the group are sensitive, and they deal with things in their own way, so you need to work with me. If you stay away from them, they will leave you alone. That's all. It's easy. Don't take their clients. Stop calling them names. Don't speak at events where they are, and everything will be fine. Cross the line, though, and you know what they're capable of, don't you? Are you listening to me?"

She took a deep cleansing breath, and when she exhaled, her eyes were no longer filled with anger, just sadness and pity.

"Carl, you were once an amazing psychoanalyst. The world was in the palm of your hand. And then you got caught up in a nuisance complaint, and ... Well, it doesn't matter why, but how did you let yourself get sucked into this hoodoo voodoo bullshit? Last night, you told a battered woman to change her behavior so that her husband would love her. What happened to the doctor who told me it wasn't me? Or the guy who encouraged me to remove myself from the violence and toxicity and who told me I could be anything if I believed in myself. Where did that man go? I have always been thankful that you were there when I needed help. God, Carl, you were brilliant. You helped me change unhealthy patterns, my negative beliefs, my ... my life. I couldn't have pulled my world back together without your guidance, but now this. What the hell happened to you? Back then, I trusted you with my life, and now you're here threatening me—telling me to fall into line or your friends are going to get me. Are they going to get my little dog, too?"

Movement in her periphery caught her attention, and she peered outside at the crowd gathering around the shed. Eyebrows furrowed, she swung back to him.

"So which member of The Collective has been hiding bodies in my yard? Is it their way of getting back at me?"

"For God's sake, Marnie, no one from the group would do something like that. Is your gut telling you they did it? No?" He pursed his lips, waiting for an answer—knowing one wouldn't come.

"They have more creative ways of messing with you. You and I both know that the collective powers of The Coll..., well, you know, they could scare you, terrorize you, or ruin you. They are far more imaginative than dumping a body in your garden."

He looked past her into the backyard. Four investigators in white jumpsuits gathered bits and pieces and placed the items into plastic bags. Evidence markers scattered the lawn, and fingerprint dust dotted the back veranda railing and the toolshed.

A loud bark greeted a heavy knock on the back door, and Tater raced to his mistress's side as she opened it. The detective who entered was a hulk of a man. He was tall, broad, imposing and handsome in a rugged sort of way.

Holding up his gold shield, he said, "I'm Detective Daniel Gregg. Are you Miss Reilly, or is it Ms. Reilly?"

"It's Ms., and Marnie is fine. Come in, please."

Holding out her right hand, she looked up at the man's face, and with a firm grip, she shook his warm and calloused fingers. His haunted eyes offered a strange contrast to the dimples book-ending the curled-up corners of his mouth. The psychic saw kindness in his features, which surprised her. Frowning, she wondered, *why kindness? Why did I think that?*

"Ms. Reilly, I've spoken to Officer Thayer, and he shared the details of your nine-one-one call with me. We need you to come to the station this morning to make a formal statement."

The professional and aloof tone of the detective was neither kind nor warm.

"Okay. I have a few appointments today. I'll need to move things around. What time suits?" she asked, checking her watch.

"I suggest you postpone everything, Ms. Reilly. I'm heading to the station in ten minutes and would like you to meet me there."

His gruff reply elicited a snarky response.

"Well, I'll just rush upstairs and get dressed then, shall I? Or should I go into my office and grab you a copy of the video from my security camera first? I assume an astute detective like yourself noticed the surveillance equipment on the property." She smirked, not masking her sarcasm. "There's an alarm system, too, that's linked to the local police station."

"We saw the cameras. In fact, we have a warrant on the way to search the house. My people will gather up everything and bring it to the station," he replied with a smug grin.

"Fine," she countered, stomping to the stairs with Tater following on her heels.

Trudging up the steps, she wondered what the detective's problem was—she was the one with the dead body in her shed. She wasn't a victim, but she wasn't a suspect either. Her eyes widened, and she stopped short.

Holy shit! Am I a suspect?

The detective frowned and turned to Carl. "Are you the boyfriend? Lover? Ex-husband, perhaps?"

The man laughed and held up his hands. "Whoa! God, no! Marnie and me? That woman would be the death of me. Oh ... uh, that was an unfortunate choice of words. Um ... no, she is a... well, a colleague... and a friend, and I dropped by this morning to discuss a business proposition."

"Which is it? Officer Thayer told me she didn't seem happy to see you. Colleague or friend. Which is it, Mr. Parkins?" He narrowed his eyes and waited for an answer.

"Both." Carl did a double take, raising his eyebrows. "How do you know my name? Marnie didn't introduce us."

"I know everything, Mr. Parkins." He leaned in close, enunciating every syllable. "Ev - ry - thing. I'll be back in fifteen to collect your colleague and friend."

Chapter Five

7:03 AM, Marnie's Home

Marnie returned to her living room, her strawberry blonde hair pulled up in a ponytail, revealing a flawless angular face with minimal makeup. She wore a navy-blue V-neck T-shirt, a white and blue-checked scarf, faded jeans, a tan belt, and matching boots. A cognac leather jacket was draped over her arm, and a ring of keys dangled from an index finger.

The detective took in her perfume as she walked past. She smelled like sheets from the line on the first warm day of spring. Breathing in, he realized he was staring.

Carl noticed and edged closer to him. "She's like a breath of fresh air, isn't she? Bet you're glad she isn't my girlfriend. Oh, but wait. There's nothing you can do about it, is there? That body out there makes her either a suspect or a witness. What a shame."

Ignoring the taunt, Daniel Gregg turned to Marnie. "Do you need a ride to the station, or can you make your way there?"

"Yes, my car is in the garage. Or is it part of the crime scene, too?" Her question dripped with sarcasm.

"Uh, no. Sorry. The car remains here. Forensics will want to run some tests. They'll have it towed. Looks like you're riding with me."

"Uh ... I'll get a lift from Carl. He's going that way anyway, aren't you? We can finish our conversation in the truck."

Smoothing her ponytail, she shot him a conspiratorial stare. He knew the 'look' and thought it best not to argue.

"Sure. I'll drop you at the station on my way."

"On your way where, Mr. Parkins?" The detective pivoted his attention to the healer.

"Nowhere in particular—errands and groceries." He clapped his hands in front of himself and turned his head, hiding a grimace. "Let's go, kid. You ready?"

"Yup. Detective, when will they finish? I don't want to leave the house unlocked."

"They'll be here for a while. They can secure it."

"I'm not comfor..."

The detective held up a hand to stop her, closed his eyes and raked fingers through his thick hair. "Ms. Reilly, there are police everywhere. What could happen? I'll ask Officer Thayer to take care of it."

His steely glare made her think twice about arguing the point.

Eyes on the ceiling, her jaw clenched and through gritted teeth, she said, "Fine."

Then she remembered her dog.

"Hang on. What about Tater? I'm not leaving him here. I need him to come with me."

The pup stood next to her, bumping her hand with his nose. He picked up his paw and placed it on her leg as she looked down into his smiling face.

She tapped Carl's arm and asked, "Can Tater come in your truck?" Her eyes met the detective's. "I'm bringing him. He's no trouble. He'll behave. I can't leave him here alone."

He scoffed, "Tchah! Ms. Reilly, dogs are not allowed in the station."

With a hand on her hip, she countered, "Oh, really? Don't you have a canine unit?"

"He can't come."

Her glance bobbed from one man to the other, her eyebrows woven together.

The healer gave in. "The knucklehead can come with me. Call me when you're done, and we'll pick you up at the station and take you wherever you need to go."

"Thank you!" she said, giving his arm a warm squeeze. Then she pulled on her jacket, grabbed her handbag, and headed for the door, glaring at the detective over her shoulder.

"Well, let's get this over with."

Tater jumped into the back seat of Carl's pickup and rested his head on the console. Marnie got into the front passenger seat, slamming the door. The detective threw her an icy stare when she peered out the window to see where he was—she volleyed back with a sneer.

"The story of the damsel in distress continues as I, the handsome and daring prince, take you off on my trusty steed for a rendezvous with the evil sheriff."

"Shut up, Carl," she said, head pressed against the window.

He grinned, started the engine and drove off into the sunrise.

Chapter Six

7:36 AM, Creekwood Police Station, 818 North Main Street

Marnie hopped out of the truck, gave Tater a pat, and told Carl that she would call as soon as she was done. The Border Collie barked when she closed the door, and she glanced back to see her pup's nose art on the back window, bringing a smile and chuckle to the dreary day.

The station was an older sandstone walk-up featuring huge canary-blue double doors with the police shield adorning each window. She checked her watch and looked up and down the street. Deserted. But at seven thirty-seven on a chilly Saturday morning, you would expect that.

She trudged up the steps, opened the big door, and walked into the station. A duty sergeant sat behind an enormous desk, engaged in a chat with a wobbling man wearing a filthy coat. The officer looked up when he heard the door, nodded, and continued his conversation. She approached the desk, wrinkling her nose. The man reeked of alcohol, and he swayed from side to side. She was certain he was going to tip over. The duty sergeant asked him to sit down and told him someone would help him soon.

The sergeant straightened his tie before licking his fingers and smoothing his thick, unruly sideburns. "Yes, ma'am. What can I do to help?"

Spying his desk tag, she said, "Um … Sergeant Beaumont. My name is Marnie Reilly. I'm here to see Detective Gregg."

"Yeah. Hang on a minute. He's up in the squad room. Have a seat." The cop eyed the drunk bobbing his head in a drunken stupor. "Second thought, wait right there. I'll call up for you."

A handsome detective walked into the station as the sergeant picked up the phone and a smile spread across Marnie's face. The man was her lifelong friend, Tom Keller, and his violet eyes lit up when he saw her.

"Marn, what are you doin' here?"

Grasping his arm, she said, "Oh my gawd. I've never been so happy to see you. It's a long story. I'm waiting for Detective Gregg so that I can make a statement."

Giving her a hug, he said, "Hey, Beau, I'll take her up. She's a friend."

Tugging her sleeve, he led her to the stairs as the sergeant waved them on and answered another call.

"What the hell, Marn? A homicide? One of your clients? Why didn't you call me?"

"Because I've cried on your shoulder more than enough. Anyway, the police found a body in my shed."

"Are you fucking kidding me?"

"Nope. And that's all I know, except the detective gave me a warrant and now they're searching my house. I would have been happy to let them look around," she rambled.

Her friend smirked. "No, you wouldn't have. Who are you tryin' to kid?"

"Ha-ha! Yeah, okay. You're right. I would have told them to fuck off."

They were still laughing when they reached the squad room.

Detective Gregg stood inside the door and greeted them with an icy stare and a tone to match. "Good to see you can laugh. You've got a corpse in your backyard, and you're having a chuckle."

With a protective hand on his friend's shoulder, Detective Keller said, "C'mon, Danny. Marn and I go way back. We were talking about old times. Give her a break. She's had a rough morning."

"Yeah, and not to sound clichéd, but it's about to get a lot rougher. The body we found in her shed is that of Ken Wilder. He's an old *friend* of yours, isn't he, Ms. Reilly?"

"Ken?" she said, but her face turned gray and she gagged. Throwing a hand over her mouth, she pivoted left, then right. Her friend grabbed her arm and led her to the ladies' room, though too late. She threw up in a wastebasket in the squad room. Wrapping an arm around her, Tom scowled over his shoulder at his colleague.

Without noticing his workmate's admonishment, the detective growled, "Pull yourself together. We'll get a statement when you're ready."

She accepted the handkerchief her pal was offering and wiped her mouth on the way into the lavatory. Returning to his desk, Tom got a tube of toothpaste and a bottle of mouthwash from a drawer, backtracked, and knocked. He peeked in, handed in the items, and backed out. His fellow officer followed his movements, considering him with amusement.

Keller caught the smugness and shook his head. "What's your problem? Why are you enjoying this?"

Rolling his eyes, Danny said, "Are you telling me you don't remember the saga of Ms. Reilly and Ken Wilder?"

"Yeah. Of course I do. Look, Marn and I grew up together. She is honest as the day is long. She says Wilder abused her, and I believe her, and not just because I witnessed the bruises. I saw the downhill slide from the moment they met. That piece of shit isolated her from her friends and family. Convinced her to move in with him so he could control her. About twelve months into their cohabitation, I run into her at the diner up the street and don't recognize her. She faded away into nothing. The guy was sick and twisted. He gaslighted and beat her," said Tom, nostrils flared, and cheeks flaming red.

"*Not* the story he told. He said she dove into a deep depression and became reclusive after her father died. He said he couldn't speak to her and that she would sit in the dark and cry for days. She accused him of cheating on her, and she would call him non-stop throughout the day. In the end, he had to throw her out of his house because he couldn't deal with it anymore. He told me she made it all up to get attention and ruin him." He turned his head and quirked up one corner of his mouth—challenging Tom to counter the story.

Shaking his head, his eyes grew stormy. "No way! That is not how it happened. She walked out on *him*. He stalked her, and I *caught* him." His voice grew louder, and a vein threatened to pop out of his forehead.

Danny gestured with his hand, telling his colleague to calm down.

Lowering his voice, he continued, "She was hiding from him. He didn't know she'd inherited her father's place because she kept it a secret. Anyway, Marn had been looking for a way out, so when he left on a business trip, she called me, and I got a bunch of our friends together, and we swooped in. We filled up our cars with her stuff and helped her disappear. A couple of weeks later, I was going over to install security cameras. I drove up, and he was racing off. He'd kicked in the front door, smacked her around and terrorized poor Tater. The only good to come out of it was that she broke his nose and fractured her hand doing it, but hey, collateral damage. He tried to press charges until I got involved. No one can say it didn't happen. He's a liar. *I* saw him speed off. *I* saw the damage to the door. Shit, Danny, I took her to the hospital to have her hand X-rayed, and the cuts and bruises checked. Wilder was a low-life woman-basher!"

"Why didn't she press charges?"

The detective's smugness made the color rise in Tom's face.

"She did. Wilder's uncle is ... *was* a dirty judge. He started threatening her. I tried to protect her, but he came after me, too. When the judge retired, there was no point worrying about it because Wilder hadn't bothered her in a while."

Hearing the latch squeak, he lifted his chin toward the ladies' room door. "Here she comes. Be nice."

Chapter Seven

8:04 AM, Creekwood Police Station, 818 North Main Street

Detective Gregg held open the interview room door. Marnie entered, but she stood waiting for him to close the door. The room was the bland institutional gray one would expect in a police station. A chipped metal table filled most of the space. Four steel straight-back chairs surrounded it. She followed the detective's eyes and noted which seat he wanted her to take, so she chose the opposite. Giving in to her power play, he moved to sit opposite, tossing down his pad and pen. He turned the chair sideways, sat, and stretched his long legs toward the door. She sat with her back straight, hands resting on the table, and her eyes on the man.

"Where should we begin?" she asked.

"Let's start with some questions," he said, matching her intense gaze.

"Okay. Do you know how long he's been dead?"

"I'll ask the questions, Ms. Reilly. You can give me answers."

Detective Gregg's authoritative tone irked her, and she jutted out her chin in response.

"No problem," she said, pulling her ponytail over her shoulder and cocking her head.

"When did you last see Mr. Wilder?"

"It's been a few months. We ran into each other at the deli near my office. I was with a client, and Ken was alone. He kept staring at me, and I ignored him. When my client left, he came to my table and asked if he could join me. I told him I was leaving. He grabbed my arm. I pulled away. He clutched my arm again. I stomped on his foot and walked away. He called me a bitch. I paid my bill and left. He followed me to my office. I called Tom." She rattled the wooden response, never losing eye contact with the detective.

"Ms. Reilly, the police discovered your ex dead on your property this morning. The severity of the situation and your lack of emotion are ringing some warning bells," he said, searching her face for some sign of remorse, but saw none.

"Well, if you spend two years with a man who isolates you, insults you, beats you and tells everyone you're crazy, you force yourself to stop feeling. You get numb and protect yourself from the pain—from what's coming next, which from experience, was him throwing me across a room or slapping me. He used to grab my arms so tight that I would have bruises for weeks. Then there's the time he hit me for putting the wrong mustard on his sandwich. I'll never forget it because it gave me a concussion and ringing in my ears for a week. Oh, and I vomited for two days. You tell me, Detective, how would you be feeling right now?"

She raised her left eyebrow and lifted her chin—cheeks reddening.

"Why aren't there any reports in the system? Nothing. There's not one domestic abuse filing anywhere," he said, arching his right eyebrow—mimicking her.

"There are reports. Call and ask for Judge Wilder's archived files. Talk to Tom. He'll tell you everything. On the occasions I tried to get help, I was told that police don't involve themselves in domestic issues. Keep digging, Detective. You'll find the proof you say isn't there. Contact the hospital and ask them for my records. Ring my friends. Speak to my doctor. I'll give you his name and permission to take copies of the files and X-rays."

She sat back in her chair, stretched her neck and looked at the ceiling before turning to face him.

"I'll do that. Now, tell me where you were yesterday."

"When yesterday?"

"All day."

Rolling her eyes, she said, "Pfft! I got up at five, went running, got home around five-thirty, made tea, and got ready for work. I left the house at six-thirty and arrived at the office at seven. The deli delivered breakfast around seven-fifteen—I have a standing order. Then I read and answered e-mails until eight. My assistant arrived about that time, and we had a quick meeting. My diary was full all day. I ate lunch at my desk, left the office for Station Hall around seven to speak at an event, and departed there around nine, and I was home at nine-thirty. Then. I changed my clothes. Tater and I went running, and we were back by ten-thirty. We had some dinner; I showered and was in bed around midnight."

"Can anyone else confirm your whereabouts during those hours?" He jotted down a note and then glanced up.

"Okay. You know, I think this is a little more than giving you a statement. Before I answer anything else, I'm going to give my lawyer a call. Under normal circumstances, I would be happy to answer questions, but something about this stinks."

"You're not under arrest, Ms. Reilly. We're just having a chat."

He sat up and swirled the pad around the table with his index finger.

"Hmm ... yes, well, then you won't mind if my lawyer sits in, will you?" she asked, appraising her interrogator.

"That's not a problem. I thought you were happy to cooperate," he replied, shrugging.

"I was, then I remembered the search warrant. Now, the language you're using isn't you asking me a few questions or us having a chat. It's an interrogation," she said, placing her hands flat on the table and glaring at him.

"Suit yourself. Lawyer up."

He grabbed the pad and pen and stood, leaving the room with the door ajar. Marnie took her phone out of her pocket. Eight missed calls. She listened to the messages, saved the important ones, and deleted the rest. Helen's grandson had called ten minutes ago and April twenty minutes earlier, but they would have to wait until later.

Dialing her lawyer, she got voicemail. "This is David Bennett. I can't take your call at the moment. Please leave a detailed message after the tone, and I will call you back as soon as I am available. BEEEEEP."

"David, it's Marnie Reilly. SOS."

She called April and asked if she could meet with her on Monday morning at eight. April confirmed, and Marnie told her she looked forward to seeing her. Next, she called back Helen's grandson, Michael. He said his grandmother had calmed down, and that he didn't feel a trip to the medical examiner's office would be necessary. He thanked her and told her he would call if they needed anything.

Her phone rang, and David's name lit up the screen.

"Thanks for calling me back," she said.

"Hey, what's happening? SOS? That's serious. You haven't used that since you left Ken."

"David, can you meet me at the police station? I need your help," she said, glancing up to see if the detective was listening to her conversation.

"Uh ... right now? I've got to be back in court in about ten minutes. I've got an arraignment and won't be free until 11:00. Is that okay, or is this urgent?"

"The police found Ken's body in my shed this morning."

"What? Ken? Are you okay? What happened?"

"Yeah, I'm fine, and no, I didn't do it."

"Geez! I know you didn't. If you were going to kill that bastard, you would have done it long ago. I'll talk to my assistant and see if he can manage things. It's not a biggie. I'll call you back in five."

Alone with her thoughts, she remembered she had scheduled a late lunch with her friend Kate. They had been pals since second grade, when Marnie had gotten glasses. Everyone picked on her except for her new buddy and Tom. At recess one day, her girlfriend told everyone that if you wore spectacles, you were super smart. It's what she believed. Her grandfather had them, and he was the smartest person in the world.

Pulled back to the present by the ring of her phone, she answered, "David?"

"I will be there in ten. The case was dismissed. See you soon."

"Perfect," she said, hanging up. Then she called her friend and got voicemail.

"Hey, Katie, it's me. I know we have a lunch date. Wondering if we could postpone or catch up tomorrow instead. Something's come up, and I can't tell you over the phone. Chat soon."

Danny stood in the doorway as she disconnected her call. Walking in, he sat and sighed.

"Ms. Reilly, I may have been ... Look, I... You don't need a lawyer. If you tell me what happened, I'll take some notes and record your statement, and then you are free to go. I'm sorry about earlier. Listen, Ken gave a lot of money to a charity that's helped so many people in Creekwood. He was known in the community for being generous, and I had heard rumors about the two of you. I shouldn't believe gossip, but hey, I'm human. I see a guy who does charitable work, and I expect him to be a decent human being. It's not always true, and I know that. I dug deeper, and there were reports sitting out there that should have been followed up. Tommy showed me. Now, him, he's an honorable guy. He's had my back a few times. What I'm tryin' to say is, he trusts you, so I gotta open my eyes wider. Okay?"

"Tom is as loyal and honest as the day is long. But I have already called my lawyer. He's going to be here in a minute, so if it's all the same, I'll let him sit in for moral support, if nothing else."

"Suit yourself," he said, getting up to leave. "You want a coffee?"

"No, thank you. I don't need caffeine. I'm already wound tighter than a drum. Do you have tea? If not, I would appreciate water."

"I'll check."

He started out the door, turned back around and leaned in—his hands grasping the door jamb.

"I apologize. I was a prick," he said as he walked away.

"Men! Just when you think you've got one pegged, they do a one-eighty. Impossible creatures!"

Chapter Eight

8:38 AM, Creekwood Police Station, 818 North Main Street

David Bennet arrived at the station and met Marnie and Detective Gregg in the interview room. He requested a moment with his client. The detective hesitated, but conceded, saying he would be back in a few minutes.

The lawyer glanced at his client, got up, closed the door and sat.

"What is going on? Give me the five-minute breakdown."

She took a deep breath and reported the events of the last twenty-four hours. He listened without comment, and then he exhaled, put his chin on his chest and peered at her over the top of his glasses.

"Okay. They only want a statement. You had a full schedule yesterday with people around you who can verify your whereabouts. You were only alone in your car and at home. Let's find out what they've got, then we'll write your statement. Let's not trip up. Have you told me everything, and I mean everything?"

"Yeah. I think so. God, David, I wasn't expecting that I would have to remember every single detail of my day. If I'd known, I would have kept notes."

Leaning her chin in her palm, she curled her lip.

"Okay. Here's some free advice. Put the smart-ass away for the next hour. Let's get this done."

Opening the door, he flagged down the detective and sat next to Marnie.

The cop returned, shut the door, and sat across from them. His eyes dropped to his notepad before focusing once again on the interviewee.

"Ms. Reilly, do you mind if we record your statement?"

David shook his head and responded for her.

"No, Detective, I will take notes, and my client will sign the document when we have completed the interview."

"Okay. Let's get started then. Ms. Reilly, can you please recount your movements yesterday?"

Nodding, she said, "Yes. Tater and I went running after I woke up at five. I made myself a tea, took it upstairs, got ready for work and left the house about six-thirty. I arrived at my office around seven. The delivery guy dropped off my breakfast around seven-fifteen. From seven to eight, I answered e-mails, and that's when my assistant Andrea arrived. We discussed my schedule, and I had meetings in the office all day. We ordered lunch. Andrea picked it up at the deli, and I ate at my desk. I left the office at seven to go to Station Hall to speak at an event. The event finished around nine. I packed up, drove home and got there about nine-thirty, at which time I changed my clothes, took Tater out for a run, and we were back by ten-thirty. We had dinner. I showered and was in bed by twelve."

"That's it?" he asked.

"No," she said, recalling last night's voicemail. "Some strange things happened."

"Tell me," he said, leaning forward, readying his pen above the notepad.

"Well, when we were leaving for our run, I had a weird feeling. I never set the alarm when I am going to be out for a few minutes, but at the last moment, I ducked back inside and armed it. When we came home, Tater was pulling at his lead and staring off into the woods. It was odd because that's not typical behavior. Anyway, it was eerie—like someone watching us. Then, when we were in the kitchen, he stood on his hind legs—looking out the back window. His bark was funny, too. I can't explain it. It's how he used to be when Ken would show up in a drunken mess. He would panic, and his scruff would bristle. He did that last night. The phone rang a few times, too. I ignored it because of the hour and let it go to voicemail. When I listened to the messages before going up to bed, it was the same message both times. Someone playing music down the line. A haunted song..."

Her voice faded, and her eyes drifted to the corner of the room. She stared as if she were looking into someone's faces, someone's eyes. The silence in the room grew heavy.

"Ms. Reilly, are you okay?" the detective asked, peering over his shoulder.

He saw nothing, but she remained transfixed, and tears had welled up in her aquamarine eyes.

"Marnie?" David turned his attention to the corner, following her gaze but could see nothing. He frowned and brushed her arm. "Marn!"

Eyes darting back, she apologized. "Sorry. I was ... I was thinking about... Sorry. Where was I? Um ... the song. It rattled me. I haven't heard it since Ken and I were together. He loved Johnny Cash, and he used to play that damn song every time, every damn time … After he would hit me, he'd put it on the stereo." Tears rolled down her cheeks, and she wiped them away with her sleeve.

"Do you want some water?" The detective leaped to his feet. "I'll get you a drink." *I need some air too,* he thought. *Spooky…*

When he left the room, David put his hand around hers, waiting for her to meet his gaze.

"Kiddo, you're scaring me. You were staring at something in the corner, or more like someone. What's going on?"

Ignoring the chill running up her spine, she said, "Just a ghost, David. I'll be fine."

The detective returned, balancing a bottle of water, a steaming paper cup, and a box of tissues. Smiling, he placed them on the table. She looked up and noticed how kind his face was when he smiled. Nodding her thanks, she sipped the water.

"God, I feel like an ass. I never cry in front of people." She sucked in a breath, exhaled and locked eyes with the detective. "Okay. I'm good. Let's keep going." She took another deep breath, ready to go on with the interview.

"You said there was a song playing down the line. Johnny Cash. What song was it?"

"Do you know the song 'Hurt'? It's very … um… it's dark and lonely. It always makes me feel cold when I hear it."

"And you say Ken used to play it after hitting you?"

"Yes, he played Johnny Cash a lot, but that one song he reserved for…" Her face hardened and she looked away, a blush creeping across her cheeks. "He played it … He played that damn song after hitting me. Then he'd tidy up his mess and go out for hours."

Tears stung her eyes, and she clenched her jaw and sighed. Rubbing the bridge of her nose with her index finger, she drew in a shaky inhale, blowing it out through pursed lips. "Last night, it frightened me that Ken would turn up on my doorstep again. I locked up the house, set the alarm and we went upstairs. I didn't hear a thing, and Tater didn't bark, and if someone was near the house, he would have. He growls at squirrels, possums, skunks—even leaves. He would have howled if a person had been on the property."

"Okay. What happened this morning?"

"The alarm was off, but I remember setting it. It's crazy because I had gone back downstairs specifically to arm it."

"Has that happened before? The alarm malfunctioning?" he asked, rolling his pen over his knuckles.

Eyes wide, she said, "No. Never. We can check with the security company. They'll have a record."

"Thanks. I'll call them. Can you continue, please? What happened next?"

"We went downstairs, and I let Tater out. I walked out onto the back porch and noticed the shed door ajar, swinging in the breeze. It was strange because it's always padlocked. I've got a lot of my father's tools and the lawn mower in there. Anyway, he ran over to investigate, and his scruff bristled. I looked for something to protect myself and picked up a beer bottle lying in the grass. I thought it odd that it was there—I don't drink it often. Anyway, I walked across the yard, and Tater warned me away from the building. The closer I got, the more he growled. I got scared, ran into the house, grabbed the phone and called nine-one-one. But I ran back outside when my boy yipped and I saw a man climbing over the back fence. Then, an operator answered, and I told her about the guy wearing a hoodie."

"No need to go into that. We have the recording of the nine-one-one call. We will have to check evidence for the beer bottle.

I don't remember seeing it at the scene. What do you remember about the man?"

Marnie said, "He wore black or navy-blue, I think. I believe he had on a hat or hoodie. I couldn't see his hair. Not tall, but not short. An inch or two taller than me. He favored his left arm. I noticed that when he scaled the fence. Um ... I guess an athletic build. Like a distance runner."

"Did he speak?"

Recalling the moment, she said, "No."

"Okay, anything else happen before Officer Thayer arrived?"

"No, Carl arrived right before your officer drove up. Then I took the patrolman to the backyard. He looked in the shed, threw up, said something into his radio, and walked me to the house."

"Detective, can you share information with us? Marnie told you everything she knows. What have you got?" asked David.

"Not much. We know it was Ken Wilder's body in the shed because we all recognized him. He's well-known to most cops and has been generous, donating to the Police Benevolent Association and to other charities I work with. A group of us attended a fundraising event with him yesterday evening. Toys for Tots. I'm sure you are aware of it."

The lawyer smiled. "Of course, we are. Marnie contributes..."

"David, stop!" she screeched, anger flashing in her eyes.

"What? You do." He glanced sideways, holding up his hands.

Her jaw jutted forward, her face red. "That's private! I make those contributions anonymously."

"Sorry. I thought the detective should know."

Marnie slumped her shoulders, mouth agog, and huffed out a breath.

"Geez, David. You're my lawyer. Stop sharing personal information that isn't relevant."

"I'm sorry."

Narrowing his eyes, the detective asked, "Why don't you want people to know?"

With a deep sigh, she replied, "I helped set up that charity with Ken. Geez! Look. I didn't want him to know about my donations. I didn't want to associate with him, and I *did not* aspire to be invited to events."

"Okay. Well, thank you," said the cop, nodding at the reasonable explanation. "So … anyway, we all know the event finished at four-thirty, and Mr. Wilder left when I did because I walked him to his car. We were discussing the volunteers we would need to shop, wrap, and deliver. Thanksgiving is only a week away. We need to get the ball rolling to meet the Christmas Eve deadline. He drove away around four-forty-five. I checked my watch when I got in my car."

Marnie's attention drifted back to the corner, and the detective followed her gaze, but saw nothing. David squirmed, wondering what the cop thought of his client's trance-like demeanor. As he reached out a hand to nudge her, she spoke, startling both men.

"Was he heading home?"

"I'm not sure. I didn't ask. He drove up Banks Avenue and turned right," replied the detective, jotting in his notebook.

"Has anyone checked with security at the gates?"

"Sorry?" The cop wrinkled his forehead.

"He lives in a gated community. The guards will know when he arrived."

"I'm heading over there soon to inform his wife of his death. I can speak to security then."

"His wife? I didn't know he'd married. Why wasn't she at the event?" she asked, eyes still focused behind him.

Craning his neck, the detective looked over his shoulder. "Ms. Reilly? What's so interesting in the corner? You keep looking over there."

"Nothing. I'm thinking."

David interrupted, "Have you found a murder weapon yet?"

"Yes, but I can't share details at this stage of the investigation," he said, standing to leave.

Marnie jerked her head, her eyes locking on the cop's.

"I heard Officer Thayer on his radio. He said the words 'garroted' and 'wire.' It was piano wire, wasn't it?"

The detective's jaw dropped and his eyebrows shot up.

"What? How did you know?"

She untied her scarf and moved the collar of her jacket, revealing her neck. The detective grimaced at a pink, razor-thin scar.

"Who did that?" he asked, leaning forward, examining her healed wound.

"Ken Wilder wrapped piano wire around my neck when he tried to kill me because I threatened to leave him. It happened right before I escaped."

Her eyes drifted to the corner again, and the detective dared a look, turning back as an explosion of thunder and lightning shook the building.

"Here comes the storm," she whispered, her eerie tone matching the haunted depths of her aquamarine eyes.

Chapter Nine

9:42 AM, Creekwood Police Station, 818 North Main Street

Detective Gregg returned to the squad room, searching for Tom before spotting him engaged in a discussion with another detective. Waving a hand, he caught his colleague's attention, gesturing that he needed to speak with him. Detective Keller held up his hand, displaying five fingers, and mouthed, 'five minutes.' When he finished his conversation, he joined Danny in the interview room with a cup of coffee.

Closing the door, he leaned against it and asked, "What's up?"

Propped against the back wall, the detective said, "Tell me more about Marnie Reilly."

"Okay. We grew up in the same neighborhood, went to school together, and college. I've known her my whole life and only lost touch with her when she was with Wilder. She works hard. Comes from a wonderful family. Mr. Reilly was a carpenter—an incredible craftsman. Her mother was a lawyer and a judge. She died about eight years ago. Tragic accident. We don't talk about it. Her father passed a few years ago on a sailing trip with his boat buddies. She was close to her parents, and she had a brother, too. Sam. He was a great guy, a brilliant athlete, and he was smart. Man, he could debate on any topic. He finished university cum laude and signed up with the FBI, but he died in the line of duty."

"Geez. So much tragedy. Okay, family history is important but tell me about *Marnie*."

Tom nodded his understanding. "She finished college with a business degree, started working for a tech firm in DC right after college and moved back here when her mother died. She was worried about her father taking care of himself. He was fine, but she always fussed over her old man."

Tom took a sip of coffee, gathering his thoughts.

"Anyway, she took an interest in her dad's business and helped him build it up so he would focus on something other than her mom's death. She bought a house a few miles up the road from the family home and sold it when she and Ken got together. I remember Mr. Reilly was furious. They'd done a lot of work on it. He did not like Ken. He kept it to himself, but he told me that if he ever got the chance, he would straighten Ken out. Her father didn't know about the abuse. Marn hid it from him well. They talked every day, and she would visit him on the weekends if she didn't have visible bruises. Ken didn't like it. A lot of their arguments were about her visiting her dad. After she got away from Wilder, she told me she had taken up martial arts six months into their relationship to have an excuse for the bruises. She told me that Ken had argued with her about it. When she told him she was tired of explaining away her injuries, he shut up. I know she was trying to leave him. We discussed it, and I offered to get her outta there more than once, but she was terrified of what he would do to her if she left."

Danny pursed his lips, shaking his head.

"Yeah. Now you're gettin' the picture, but there's more," said Tom, taking another sip from his mug. He continued, "Once when he found her bags packed, he tried to kill her. He was supposed to be out of town but came home early and accused her of trying to sneak off. That time, he wrapped some kind of wire around her neck. When he broke through the skin and she bled, he backed off. He took her to the hospital and told the doctor it had happened during a break-in. They didn't buy it and called the police. He talked his way around it. She told me about it when Sam died. We got drunk after the funeral, and she spilled her guts to me. Anyway, what else do you wanna know?"

"When did she become a counselor?" asked Danny, crossing his arms across his broad chest.

"After the Ken crap, she saw a shrink, and he told her that sometimes when you help other people who have been through similar things, it can be cathartic. She took some courses, loved it, and that's it."

"Tommy, she seemed spooked when she was in here earlier. I don't mean the normal nervousness that people feel when they give a statement regarding a homicide. I mean *spooked*. She kept staring off into the corner over there. Her lawyer and I both tried to see what she was looking at. There was nothin' there. She appeared ... Hmm ... What is the right word?" Dragging his hand down his face, he searched for an apt description. "*Haunted.* That is the only way I can describe it."

"Well, when tragic deaths take so many people from your life, maybe that's what happens. You sit and think about it. It would scare the shit out of most people, don't you think?"

He shrugged one shoulder and frowned.

"Yeah, I suppose so. Give me the scoop about Carl Parkins." Danny pushed himself off the wall, rubbing his hands together.

"Ah, Mr. Parkins." Tom reflected for a moment. "Well, he was the shrink who put Marn back together. He's a decent guy—but he hangs out with strange people. You remember the Henry Jackson murder? Big time restaurateur. I think you'd joined us around the time it happened."

"Vaguely. Tell me." Danny motioned with his hand for Tom to keep talking.

"We discovered Henry Jackson's body with two bullet holes in the back of his head. It was behind Elliot's. You know the restaurant on Plaza Avenue? It was a professional hit, and we were scrambling to find answers. Nothin' like that had happened here in years. Anyway, we started digging for information when this woman, Grace Wilmot, comes to the station tellin' us she can help. We think it's great. Woo! Hoo! Someone saw something. Then she tells us she's psychic and gets flashes. We're thinking more like hot flashes."

Tom rolled his eyes and took a slurp of his cold coffee, wrinkling his nose.

"She then says she can help us. She says Henry came to her during a séance and told her stuff. We're all lookin' at her like she's loony when she tells us a few things that weren't released to the press, like the shooter got him at the base of his skull. We hadn't told that to anyone, so we take her to the scene. She does all this mumbo-jumbo bullshit, walkin' up and down the alley chanting and shit. Finally, she says the gun is on the roof of The Amsterdam two blocks down. We haul ass over there, get up on the roof, and there's a pistol. Tests show it's the same one used in the murder. No prints, and the serial number is filed off, but we've got the murder weapon. A week goes by, she turns up again and tells us a bit more.

Next thing we know, there's shit in the press about how this psychic is helpin' us solve Henry Jackson's murder. Makes us look like a bunch of idiots."

Danny scratched his forehead and grinned. Tom smirked and continued his recount.

"Yeah, I can tell by the look on your face that you remember this one. She comes back a few days later and shares a couple of details. Then she's feeding us dribbles on a daily. Meanwhile, this woman's makin' buckets of money from people calling her to help find their cats. This goes on for a month or two when I get a call from Marn. She tells me she's overheard this woman telling another woman what she's been up to. This Grace Wilmot is trying to get herself a following as the psychic to the cops. Truth is, she did witness the murder but was holding out information so that she could capitalize on the situation. Anyway ... Marn comes in and makes a statement. Tells me that Carl introduced her to a group of psychics and that they are building a business around their collective gifts. Once she knew what they were up to, she cut and ran. She didn't want any part of it. They gave her a hard time for a while, but somehow, she and Parkins have remained friends."

"What happened to Wilmot?"

"Fined for obstruction of justice for withholding vital information. She told us she was afraid the shooter would find out who she was and where she lived. Wilmot testified to get a suspended sentence for cooperating. Then they sent her on her way into witness protection. The shooter was a junior gang member trying to make a name for himself. He killed Jackson for his watch, wallet, car keys, and street cred. The DA and the Feds figured his cronies would get to Wilmot and deliver payback. Personally, if it had been up to me, I would have let her live in fear for the rest of her days." Tom reached for the ceiling, stretching his long, lanky frame.

"Okay, so Marnie was hanging out with a group of psychics. Why? Because her friend Carl introduced her? Sounds like there's more to it than that. Is he a psychic?" asked Danny, pulling a face.

"Nope. Well, I don't think so anyway. He's a spiritualist and not a bad guy. He loves meditation, crystals, and all that shit. I've heard he's a brilliant energy healer, too."

"Pfft! Give me a break."

"Hey, the guy is the real deal. Doctors send people to him all the time. He's not a psychoanalyst anymore, though. I don't know the full story, but he lost his license. Marn can tell you. I know he hangs out with a questionable group, but he's not bad."

Lips pursed, Danny cocked his head and said, "Okay, I'll ask again. Why was she hanging out with those people?"

"Well, she's clairvoyant, but uses her powers for good. Unlike that whacky crew at Station Hall. For the last few years, she's knocked them down every chance she gets. She turns up at their events to keep them honest. You should see her speak. She wipes the floor with those loons. It's very entertaining, but she gets mad when I say that. I go along sometimes to watch her squash them. Ha-ha! You should come with me next time. She is a sight to be seen."

"No. Thanks. But try this on. You think Carl hid the corpse? Being her shrink, he'd have knowledge of the piano wire, and as you say, she taunts him and his colleagues. Is it possible?"

"I don't see it. He's not a violent guy. Wait a minute." He stopped. Eyes wide. "Did you say Wilder was killed with piano wire?"

"Yeah. Garroted. Marnie and her lawyer don't know this piece of information yet, but whoever killed Wilder didn't kill him in the shed. They moved the body. There wasn't enough blood. He bled out somewhere else and was placed in the shed after he died. Marnie said her dog was barking last night when they got home from a run, and that the dog behaved like he did when Ken used to come calling. She said she turned on the floodlights in the yard, but nada. No one was there. We have to watch the security footage to see who comes up. Oh, and someone disarmed her alarm overnight. She remembered setting it, but it was off this morning. We'll have to talk to the security company and check here as well. She said it's wired through the station." Danny stretched his neck until it clicked before dropping his shoulders with a satisfied smile.

"Yeah, I told her to have that done so that I could monitor it."

"Listen, I know there might be a conflict of interest, her being your friend and all, but I could use your help. She's clear. There is no way she could have done it with the timeframes, and I don't think she's the type to hire a hit. Do you?" he asked, moving to open the door.

"No, I don't. Let's check with the captain and see what he says about me working this one." Tom turned to walk out before reeling around. "Oh, and by the way, if Tater was asleep in Marnie's room last night, he wouldn't have heard anything in the backyard. Her room is at the front of the house. Double-glazed windows. Big house. Her room is a long way from the backyard, and I'll bet the windows were closed. It was cold."

Danny steepled his fingers, considering the next steps, and turned to watch the storm through the barred window. Thunder rumbled as rain slashed against the glass. He saw Marnie below, standing in the rain on the steps to the police station. She looked small, lonely, and drenched. He wanted to rush downstairs, wrap her in a towel, and hold her in his arms. That was his impulse. He knew he shouldn't, but he couldn't help it. The counselor bewildered him, and he didn't welcome the uncanny attraction.

Pivoting back to Tom, he asked, "You and Ms. Reilly? Anything there?"

"Nah. We had a thing in college, but it never got past kissing, and we realized it was weird. We laugh about it, but no, she's like a sister."

Danny grinned. "She shot you down, didn't she?"

Tom grinned back. "Yup. No hard feelings, though. It was awkward for a bit, but she's my wingman now. She's the perfect icebreaker."

Opening the door, Danny announced, "Time to pay a visit to the Widow Wilder. Hope she'll be cooperative, and we won't need a warrant. It hasn't come through yet. Come with?"

"Right behind you. I'll check in with the captain and catch up. I'll meet you there. You got the address?"

"I got it! I'll get a head start and question the guards at the gate."

"Ah, yes, the ivy-draped community of the rich and famous. The house is enormous. Formal gardens, a tennis court, a ten-car garage, two pools—one outside and another in. I was behind the grand gates a month ago questioning one of the rich kids. Drove past Ken's house and I saw a canopy set up outside and a party goin' on. There were hundreds of people there, easy. Anyway, I'll go speak with the captain and see you soon."

Chapter Ten

9:58 AM, Creekwood Police Station, 818 North Main Street

Marnie huddled close to the building, shifting from foot to foot, trying to stay warm as pouring rain lashed out, driven by the force of an icy north wind. Dark as night at ten in the morning, streetlights shone on Creekwood's soggy streets as Detective Gregg pulled up his collar and pushed through the door. He was greeted by the growl of thunder and streaks of lightning pulsing across the sky. Headlights and streetlamps glistened on red and orange leaves sailing down the road and into the storm drain.

"Ms. Reilly, you can wait inside, you know. You'll catch cold out here in the rain."

Danny jogged down the steps and stood below her. She turned away, wiping rain away from her face with a sleeve, but it could have been tears with the telltale red blotches dotting her cheeks.

"I'm fine, Detective. The rain doesn't bother me. It's the chill in the air. I've felt cold all morning. Death does that. When someone you know dies, you can feel it in your bones," she said, her beautiful and haunted eyes fixed on the street.

The strain of sadness on her face overwhelmed him. Reaching out a hand to comfort her, he pulled back, putting it in his pocket to hide his awkwardness.

"Yes, it's hard to lose someone. Can I give you a lift home?"

"No, thank you. Carl and Tater will be here soon," she replied, looking past him to the street.

"Okay. Well, I need to go. If you think of anything else, call me." He walked back up the steps and handed her his card. "Here's my number. You can call anytime."

He started down the steps again.

She called out, "Detective Gregg, can I go home? Are they done there?"

"Yes, of course, you can go home. I'll call the team and let them know you're on your way. Please don't clean around the outside of the house, though, in case we need to come back. The tape will remain around the yard. Please don't go out there, okay? We'll have an officer inside and another out for the next forty-eight hours."

On the verge of tears, she bobbed her head, and he wasn't sure if the gesture was acceptance or the start of a crying spree.

He added, "I know it's an inconvenience. It's for your safety and to maintain the integrity of the scene."

With a half-hearted nod, she waved, and Danny turned to see the healer pulling up in his truck. Tater sat in the front seat, looking out the window, and when he saw Marnie, his tail began wagging. As Carl opened his door, the pup leaped past him and up the steps to his mistress. Sitting on the wet steps, she pulled the fluffball into her lap and sobbed. The Border Collie nudged her with his snout and licked away her tears.

Carl frowned at the detective. "What the hell happened? She's crying. She never cries."

"I think that's a lifetime of tears, Mr. Parkins. Get her out of the rain, and stay with her, please. There are officers at the house, but a friend would be better. You're her shrink. Look after her."

With the storm gathering around them, the detective rushed down the street, disappearing into the fog rising from the pavement.

Chapter Eleven

10:10 AM, N. Main Street, Creekwood, NY

They drove along in silence; Carl focused on the road as the wind and rain whirled around the truck. Marnie rested her head against the window, listening to the thunk of the wipers and the slosh of the big tires on the wet road. Tater laid his chin on the console between the seats, waiting for someone to pay attention to him. Impatient for affection, as pups often are, he nudged his mistress's elbow. She turned to see his smiling face and shifted in her seat to pat his head.

Carl glanced over at her.

"Are you going to tell me what's happened?" he asked, leaning to turn up the heater. "Are you warm enough? There's a blanket under the back seat if you want it."

"No, thanks. I'm warming up. Uh ... I don't know where to start. It's been a shit of a day, and it's just after ten."

A yawn escaped as she pressed her back against the seat. She turned her head to face him. "It was Ken. In the shed. Ken is dead, and he died in my shed."

"Okay, there, Dr. Seuss." He couldn't help but laugh.

"It's not funny, Carl! Geez! You are such an asshole!" She glared at him and punched his arm.

He continued laughing. "You said, 'It was Ken. In the shed. Ken is dead, and he died in my shed.'" He paused. He waited.

Her scowl became a lopsided grin as she considered the childlike nature of her statement and started laughing too. She tried to speak, but the giggling returned.

"This is impossible. Someone dies in my backyard, and you crack a joke. How can you find this funny? Worse, why am I laughing along with you?"

"I don't find the situation humorous. The way you put it is. Admit it, Marnie; it is comical."

She tried to stifle her amusement, but couldn't, breaking into a titter. "You're still an asshole."

"Yeah, well, we established that fact many years ago. Now, tell me what's happening." He patted her leg, encouraging her to go on.

"I'm not sure. The detective was scant with details. I know the murder weapon is piano wire. He was garroted, Carl."

Alarmed to learn the murder method, he looked at Marnie. Her wide-eyed gaze made the seriousness of the information take hold. The truck hit the rough edge of the road. He grabbed the steering wheel to correct, but they skidded, throwing Tater across the back seat with a thump. Marnie's head bounced off the passenger window with a dull thud as he righted the truck and pulled to the verge.

"Geez! Are you okay? Marnie?" Carl leaned across the seat and peered into her face.

Giving her noggin a shake, as if to clear water from her ears, she nodded, and they both turned around to check on the dog. He scrambled up onto the seat, got himself situated and smiled—his tail thumping in time with the wipers.

"Shit, guys, I'm sorry. I wasn't paying attention. Are you sure your head is okay? You cracked it pretty hard." Running his fingers over her scalp, he checked her pupils.

"Yeah, I'm fine. I've got a thick skull," she said with a snicker, knocking her knuckles against her noggin.

"You do," he said with a grin, and pulled back onto the road.

"Let's get you and Mr. Smiley home. I need coffee. A lot of coffee."

"Can we stop at the grocery store? I'm almost out of tea and milk, and I'd like a bottle of whiskey and soda, too."

"Isn't it a bit early in the day for a drink, Ms. Reilly?" he asked, raising an eyebrow. "But sure. We can make a couple of stops. Do you want me to drop by my place and pick up an overnight bag? I can stay with you tonight."

She glanced out the window, considering his offer. An evening alone with the police did not give her a warm or cozy feeling, and despite their spats, the man sitting to her left was a comfort to her. "It couldn't hurt. Besides, I prefer not to drink alone."

"So that's a 'Yes, Carl. I would like you to stay with me tonight. Thank you, Carl. I will feel safe with you watching over me?'"

Offering him a sheepish grin, she said, "Yes, Carl. Thank you, Carl."

"Okay. It's settled. Pajama party at your house tonight. What are you making me for dinner?"

"How about a roast chicken? Or beef? Or pork? How about a pot roast?"

"A pajama party with a gorgeous blonde and a pot roast. All in one day. I am a lucky, lucky man." He looked at Tater in the rearview. "So are you, buddy. So are you."

The Border Collie smiled, wagging his tail in agreement.

Chapter Twelve

11:30 AM, Marnie's House

Carl pulled up at the curb outside the Reilly house, and Marnie gawked at the streamers of police tape flapping in the wind. With a deep frown, she cursed the deep, muddy tire tracks on her lawn where the forensics truck and coroner's van had parked. The front porch light was on, and an officer held vigil, his rain slicker shielding him from the storm.

Opening the truck door, the counselor summoned her courage and stepped down onto the pavement as Tater leaped past her to the torn-up grass, lifting a leg on a shrub. He zoomed from one end of the yard and back again, burning pent-up energy and looking for bunnies to herd.

The psychic and healer got the groceries from the back and started up the walk as the front door opened, and another cop joined her colleague on the porch.

"Ms. Reilly, I'm Officer Davis. I'm not sure whether you remember me. I was a friend of your father. Joan Davis."

"Yes. Yes, of course. It's lovely to see a friendly face. This is my friend Carl, and the little guy is Tater."

The policewoman shook the man's hand and then introduced the pair to her colleague. "And this is Officer Stewart. He and I are here until four. Two replacements will relieve us for the night shift, and then two will arrive at midnight."

Marnie's eyebrows shot up. "That's an awful lot of taxpayers' dollars being spent. I thought the department was understaffed. How can they afford to do this?"

"Ha-ha! We came over from Hudson Hollow, where the victim, Mr. Wilder, has his office. The two departments are working together. There's no shortage. We move around to suit needs." She reached out a hand to help with the groceries. "Let me give you some help with those bags."

Marnie handed a satchel to Joan and called out for her pup, who was peering into the brush. When she whistled, he ignored her.

"Come on, boy! Let's go in where it's warm."

The dog snuffled the ground before lifting his leg on a fallen red maple leaf, ignoring his mistress.

"Tater! Come! Now!" barked the shrink, before giving a shrieking whistle.

The Border Collie turned and galloped toward them, jumping all the steps in one flying leap to sit at the man's feet.

"Just because he fed you this morning, it doesn't make him the boss," scolded the psychic.

The dog nudged Carl with his nose, hit him with a paw, and then woofed at Marnie.

The healer laughed. "He thinks it does," he said, before entering the house with the black and white fur ball close on his heels.

Making her way to the door, Marnie stopped to speak with Officer Stewart. "It doesn't seem fair that you are stuck out here in the damp. How about some hot coffee?"

He nodded his appreciation as he turned up his collar and adjusted his cap.

The psychic kicked off her boots at the door, shrugged out of her coat, hanging it on the newel post. Her cozy home smelled of lemon furniture polish, toast, and the faint scent of wet dog. She glanced around at the mess the police had left behind, drew in a breath and rolled her eyes. Fingerprint powder lingered on surfaces. Drawers hung open, their contents scattered. And couch cushions in piles, tossed out of place. Her shoulders slumped, and she let out a huff.

"Geez! Like I don't have enough to deal with," she whinged, trudging to the kitchen, where she found Joan and Carl unpacking groceries.

Tater whimpered, patting the door with his paw, looking to his mistress to set him free.

"Nope, sorry, bud. You can't go out there. Police orders."

She petted his wet head, and with a harrumph, he turned in circles before plopping onto his mat and dropping his head onto his front paws.

"I hope you don't mind that I made some toast. I didn't have time for breakfast. The call to Creekwood came early," said Joan, putting a loaf of sourdough into the breadbox.

Marnie waved a hand. "Goodness, it's fine. Make yourself at home, please. I'm hungry too. I haven't eaten since last night. Has Officer Stewart had breakfast?"

"Yes. I took some toast out to him and would have made coffee, but I couldn't find a coffeemaker," she said, holding up a pottery mug with a hopeful grin.

"I don't have one, but Carl here is a whiz with a French press. Would you mind?" she asked.

He nodded. "Not at all. I'd like one myself. Would you like a pot of tea?"

"Yes, please. I'm going to run up and get out of these damp clothes. Back in a sec," she said, scooting around the corner and jogging up the stairs.

She slid to a stop outside her bedroom, mouth agape. The cops had left this room in a similar condition to her downstairs space. Cosmetics lay scattered across the top of her dressing table. Her closet door was ajar—her clothes rumpled and pushed to the sides, and the shelf above displayed shoeboxes in disarray. She ran a hand over the fingerprint powder on her dresser and nudged closed a drawer with her hip as tears stung her eyes.

"Let it go, Reilly," she told herself, falling back onto her bed with a growl, the comfort of the soft mattress easing her angst. She lifted her head at the patter of paws on the timber floors and wrapped her arms around her pup when he hopped onto the bed, settling beside her.

"Good boy," she said, running a hand over his silky coat, both falling asleep, safe from the storm raging outside.

1:45 PM, Marnie's House

Raindrops pelted the darkened windows, startling Marnie and yanking her from sleep. She leaped out of bed but sank back onto the mattress to regain her equilibrium. Groggy after a daytime sleep, she rubbed her eyes and glanced at the clock on the nightstand: one-forty-five.

Flames flickered in the fireplace, casting dancing shadows about the room. The coziness of the fire did nothing to mask the eeriness of the howling wind whipping around her house. As the gale whistled through the eaves, she did her best to forget the morning's tragic event. The warmth of the fire did little to soothe her, and she got up and went into her ensuite to shower away the chill and the feeling of dread creeping into her bones.

"Shit. I look like crap," she said, looking in the mirror.

Wrinkling her nose at her reflection, she got undressed, turned on the shower, and tiptoed inside. As she focused her energy on imagining bubbles of white and pink light surrounding and protecting her, the stream of water worked out the knots in her back. Inside the steamy cocoon, she washed her hair, and once rinsed, turned off the tap and grabbed a bath sheet. Stepping onto the bathmat, she heard the familiar scratch of Tater's paws on the door. With her hair wrapped in a towel and her robe cinched at her waist, she twisted the knob and greeted the pup.

"Hello, little man." Stooping to scratch his ears, she glanced up at the sound of approaching footsteps, and Carl appeared with a teacup and saucer.

"I heard the shower and thought you might want this." He set the china down on her dresser and turned to leave.

"Hey, Parkins?"

He stopped, glancing back.

"Thank you for being a friend. I know we've had our differences, but it's decent of you to be here when I need you." With a wink, she picked up the cup and took a sip. "Oh. I appreciate the fire, too. It was nice to wake up in a cozy room."

"So, I'm not an asshole?" he asked.

"Not right now." Her eyes crinkled as she shot him a cheeky grin.

"Ha-ha! Others don't understand our relationship. It's weird, and we know it is, but you'd do the same for me. And I know my current situation isn't ideal, but a guy has to pay his bills."

"I know, but there must be a better way. Anyway, I'll be down in a sec to get that pot roast going. Dinner will be late. Is that okay?"

"Yup. I'm not hungry. Joan made a snack for us. Besides, it's only two-fifteen. Still early." He left, shutting the door behind him.

At her dressing table, she put moisturizer on her face, applied mascara, brushed her hair, and stepped back.

"That's better," she said to her dog, putting her cosmetics in their rightful drawers, nooks, and crannies.

A pair of black leggings, an oversized fisherman knit sweater, and her slippers completed her comfy outfit for an evening with Carl and her furry pal.

"That'll do, huh, buddy? I don't need to dress up for you, do I?" she said as they padded down the hall and headed downstairs. At the top landing, the dog mumbled and grumbled, and she looked over her shoulder twice before taking eight more steps. She couldn't shake the presence. This one was creepy—not like the spirits at the station. With a shudder, she hopped from the landing down to the main floor, and the dog shot past her, making his way to the kitchen.

In the living room, a flickering fire spit sparks up the chimney as Carl leaned an elbow on the mantel, a coffee in one hand and a pipe in the other. The smell of cherry tobacco drifted through the house, and Marnie breathed in the scent as she walked past. Her grandfather had smoked the same brand, Sutliff Black Cherry Cavendish Tobacco. The scent conjured memories of her granddad sitting in his rocking chair with her in his lap, telling her stories as he drew on his pipe. She could still hear his voice and the way the pipe clicked on his teeth when he placed it in his mouth.

"I love that smell," she said, sniffing the air, fanning the smoke to her nose with her hands.

"That's your olfactory gland working its magic," he said with a wink.

"I'll try to return the favor. I'm off to put the pot roast in the oven."

Entering the kitchen, Marnie found Joan at the table, writing in a notebook and sipping from a mug.

"Sorry. I shut my eyes for a minute and slept for hours. My plan was to make lunch. Did poor Officer Stewart get some hot coffee at least?" she asked, putting her cup in the microwave to warm her tea.

"We're not houseguests. I'm here to work. Not that drinking coffee looks like it, but that's why I'm here. You don't need to take care of us." Pointing outside, the officer said, "I've been watching the yard. No movement. No noise. I had forgotten how lovely this spot is. Your father would sit on the back veranda at night and stare into the woods. I asked him once what he was looking at, and he told me nothing. Then he would laugh and say, 'Joan, the woods are lovely, dark, and deep, but I have promises to keep and miles to go before I sleep. And miles to go before I sleep.' It sounded familiar to me, then I recalled *Stopping by Woods on a Snowy Evening* by Robert Frost. I remember hearing it again when you read it at his memorial. It's a wonderful poem, haunted and lovely, like your father."

"He was both, wasn't he? Mom's death did that to him. But thank you for sharing fond memories." Marnie walked across the kitchen and gave the cop an impulsive hug. "I know that was out of line, but you brought back so many memories."

"That's okay. I don't mind getting a hug. Most people spit at me. Ha-ha!" Joan's forehead creased as she took in a shaky breath. "You know it's going to get worse before it gets better, and you need to prepare for that. That's a bit of friendly advice from an old friend of your father's." She patted Marnie's arm.

"Yeah, as soon as I heard it was Ken, I figured as much. I don't understand. After all these years, he turns up dead in my backyard. Who would even think to...?" Her thoughts trailed off onto another path. "What was he doing in my backyard to begin with? Why did he come here last night? We ended things years ago. He didn't drink beer. Did he drink beer? No, he drank Scotch. Sometimes wine. Red. But never beer." Her brain jumped from one thing to another as she tried to put the pieces together.

Joan pulled a face. "He didn't drink beer. Marnie? Why did you say that?"

"There was an empty bottle near the back door. I picked it up in case I needed to protect us this morning. I remember wondering at the time where it had come from."

"Did you give it to Detective Gregg?"

"No. I didn't even think about it. Was it in my statement? I don't remember."

"Don't worry. I'll call him and see if it's with the evidence. Do you remember what kind of bottle it was? The label? Longneck, stubby?"

"I am certain it was a longneck, but I don't remember the brand—sorry," said Marnie with a shrug, before turning her focus to dinner preparations.

Chapter Thirteen

4:40 PM, Marnie's House

Officers Webb and Jalnack took over guard duty at four o'clock. The former manned the veranda, the latter performed another investigative sweep of the backyard, hoping for clues. Marnie recognized both men, having seen them out and about in downtown Creekwood.

Carl strolled into the kitchen, sniffed the air, and rubbed his stomach. "That pot roast smells amazing! I can't wait to eat. Do you want a drink? I was thinking a Cabernet Sauvignon or a Shiraz might be nice."

"Sure. Help yourself," she said, gesturing to the wine rack in the back corner of the kitchen.

"Yes. My choice. What do you recommend?" With a finger on his chin, he perused the bottles.

"How about a Shiraz? Whatever one you want," said the counselor, scrubbing potatoes at the sink.

He slid out several options until he found what he was looking for.

"Here we go. A Coonawarra Shiraz. I knew you'd have an Australian red. This one okay?"

"Yeah. That's great," she said, grabbing glasses from the cupboard.

He opened the bottle with a twist and a dramatic pout. "I miss corks. It takes away from the grandeur of opening an exceptional vintage."

"Ha-ha! Yes, but it tastes the same, and that's what matters."

The clunking of metal on timber flooring alerted them to a canine presence, and Tater pranced in with his lead dangling from the corner of his mouth. He dropped it at Marnie's feet, sat and flashed his pearly whites.

"Hey there, beautiful boy. Let's go out front for a sniff and a wander," she said, snatching up his leash on her way to the door.

"Want me to take him?" asked Carl.

"Thanks, but fresh air would do me good. I'm still groggy after my nap."

She snapped on the dog's lead, pulled on her boots and rain jacket, and heaved open the front door. Out on the porch, she greeted Officer Webb with a nod.

"I'm taking the fluffball for a walk. We won't be gone long."

"Don't go too far, ma'am."

She cocked her head, raising an eyebrow. "We usually go to the bridle trail. Is that too far? Am I under house arrest or something?"

"No, ma'am. Detective Gregg gave strict orders that you aren't to be out of sight. It's not safe out there," he warned, scanning the darkening forest surrounding the trail.

"He thinks I'm under threat, does he?" Her pulse quickened as she looked into the trees, seeing nothing but murky outlines of bare limbs and the conical peaks of pines.

"I didn't say that. But we are taking every precaution to keep you safe and to protect the integrity of the scene."

"Okay. We'll stay close then." The psychic pulled up her hood, and she and her energetic Border Collie jogged down the front path to the road.

"Appreciate it," he said, watching them set off in the rain. The sights and sounds of the forest met his keen eyes and ears—birds chirped, squirrels darted for the safety of home, and a white-tailed doe chewed on a bush. And while he spotted nothing worrisome, he had a bad feeling in the pit of his stomach.

Tater and Marnie walked up Creek Road, the dog's head down, sniffing the grass. He stopped at a gnarled sugar maple, lifted his leg and moved on to a white birch.

Checking the sky for signs of another storm, Marnie grimaced. Its green tinge told her they were in for foul weather again. The current drizzle and the north wind snaking around them made her teeth chatter, and she wished she'd brought gloves and an umbrella. But neither would have helped tonight. The frigid gusts would have turned one inside out, and the rain would have soaked her gloves, so she put her free hand into her pocket and shivered.

"C'mon, boy. Are you finished? Let's go home," she coaxed, giving his lead a gentle tug, and this time, he followed her without an argument.

"Thank goodness the rain has stopped?" said Marnie as she and her dog trotted back to the house. The pup pulled at his lead, eager to chase the neighbor's cat as it sauntered up the sidewalk, tail twitching. Before he could lunge, she tightened her grip.

A familiar pickup rumbled past, the driver giving a quick beep of the horn, and she smiled, happy to see Tom Keller pulling to the curb. But as a blue Jeep drove in behind him, her hackles rose. Detective Danny Gregg was not on the guest list. To be fair, neither was her childhood pal, but he didn't need an invitation.

She and the dog strolled to the truck, the psychic side-eyeing the detective. Her friend got out of his vehicle and waved, nodding his chin toward Danny. He mouthed, "It's okay."

The counselor gave a curt nod, and her shoulders relaxed. Feeling the leash tighten, she dropped her eyes to Tater, who sniffed the grass at her feet and began digging at the lawn.

"Hey! Stop that, you knucklehead. The grass has been dug up enough for one day."

Detective Gregg unlatched his seatbelt, opened the door, unfolded his legs, and stepped out of his car—his dimples on display.

"Evening, Ms. Reilly," he said, acknowledging her with a nod.

"Hello," she said, offering a stilted smile.

Tater, who had been busy snuffling in the dirt, picked up his head and barked when he saw Tom, and pulling at his lead, he wagged his tail, and trilled.

"Hey, buddy!" said the visitor, holding out his arms.

Marnie let her dog off his lead, and he ran to her friend, who stooped and gave the pup a scratch behind his ears.

"C'mon, Tater-Tot. You're wet. Let's get you inside, and your favorite uncle will dry that fluff."

On his way to the house, he stopped and gave Marnie a one-armed hug, wrapping it around her shoulders, leading her and the soggy canine up the walk and into the cozy home.

Detective Gregg followed, pausing to speak with Officer Webb before joining the others in the house.

Tom's eyes lit up when he entered the living room. "Something smells good in here! Is that pot roast teasing my olfactory senses? Ha-ha! New word in my vocab. I've been waiting to use it."

Marnie snorted, patting him on the arm. "Well done, weirdo."

Carl joined them, rubbing his hands together. "Indeed, it is, Detective Keller! It's my reward for being her fearless protector. We're having a pajama party, you know." Flashing a toothy grin, he turned to his hostess. "I'm not sure where the napkins are to set the table."

Pulling a face, she replied, "Check the top drawer of the hutch. There should be some there."

Tom smirked at her discomfort, knowing the healer's comment about a sleepover might be taken the wrong way by his partner. "Hehe! What's the matter, Marn?"

"There is way too much testosterone in this house tonight," she said, glancing over her shoulder as she went to the kitchen.

The detectives and her houseguest followed, taking in the savory aroma of the stewing beef wafting from the oven.

"Join us for dinner? There's plenty for everyone," she said, checking on a pot of potatoes boiling on a back burner.

Tom clapped his hands. "I would love to. Danny, you cannot miss out on the best pot roast in the world. Marn has perfected her mother's recipe. It is so good; it will make you weep when you take your last bite. You'll stay?"

"Uh, no. I can't. Thank you for the offer, though. I still have reports to file. I came to collect the beer bottle and to speak with Mr. Parkins." The detective cocked an eyebrow at his suspect, who shifted with unease as all eyes fell on him.

"Sure thing. What can I help you with?" Carl glanced up, aware of the other man's stature.

At six-foot-five, the cop stood with the confidence of a guy who tamed hardened criminals for a living. The healer narrowed his eyes and opened them again. "Anything I can do to help. No problem."

"Let's go in by the fire." The towering cop gave a chin nod toward the living room, and Carl followed him.

Tom turned to Marnie, shrugged, seated himself at the island and helped himself to a piece of cabbage from the chopping board.

She leaned across the counter, calling out, "Dinner's in fifteen."

Chapter Fourteen

5:40 PM, Marnie's House, The Living Room

Carl took his pipe from a tray on the mantel, opened a satchel of tobacco, and fiddled some into the bowl. He knew what the detective wanted to discuss, and the activity calmed him. Nothing he had done last night was nefarious. He was only trying to shield Marnie from potential harm.

"Mr. Parkins," boomed the detective, his deep timbre startling the psychoanalyst, who jerked, spilling the black cherry Cavendish. "I've got some interesting video of you sneaking around Ms. Reilly's house last night. You wanna tell me what you were doing?"

The healer shifted his stance, rested his elbow on the mantel, and lit his pipe. "Detective Gregg, I did nothing ominous, if that's what you mean."

"That thought had crossed my mind. Setting up an old *friend,* perhaps?" He raised his eyebrows and looked down his nose at Carl.

The suspect chewed his bottom lip, considering his answer. "No. It's not like that. I was here to protect her. She *is* a friend, and that's all."

"We found some stuff you left behind. Wanna explain these to me?" The detective held up evidence bags containing several items.

"Yes. I am a spiritualist, and these are tools I use in my work. Archangels Michael and Raphael are for protection and healing; the amethyst is for positive vibes and to ward off negative energy; and the agate balances yin and yang. It has several purposes, but that's why I placed it. The turquoise is Marnie's birthstone, and it's used for defense, power, and wisdom. The clear quartz point is so the divine can hear her if she needs help. It opens the mind and heart to a higher vibration. Divine guidance, you could say. I had wanted to place the items in the house, but she set the alarm and I didn't know the code. I left everything outside to protect her on entry and exit."

"You're tryin' to tell me that these little trinkets are supposed to keep her safe? I don't get it." The cop shook his head, studying the bag in his hand.

"Detective Gregg," said Marnie, entering the room.

He half-turned, offering her a blank stare. "Yes, Ms. Reilly."

"Carl is right. Those *trinkets*, as you call them, have special attributes. He was correct when he told you what the stones are for, and Archangels Michael and Raphael—well, he was right about them, too."

"Well, thanks for confirming, but I'm not finished. Can you please give us a moment?" he glanced between the psychic and healer, the line of his jaw hardening.

"No, dinner is ready. We are all hungry and tired, and I think we should sit down and share a meal. I'm sure Carl wouldn't mind answering your questions while we eat. He'll be honest with you, *especially* if I'm sitting with him. I know when he's lying, and he won't do it in front of me." Face tight, her eyes traveled between the men, landing on the detective's steel-blue gaze.

Considering his other option of cold cuts and week-old bread at home, he conceded. "Fine. Let's have dinner, and … well, thank you for inviting me. I haven't had pot roast in years. It's always been a favorite."

"Great. Make your way to the dining room and I'll be right there," she said, leaving them.

6:03 PM, Marnie House

The men gathered in the dining room; the detectives discussing the deer Danny had picked up from the butcher Friday afternoon.

"I'll cook up a batch of venison chili soon, and we'll get the guys over for a game," he said.

"Sounds good to me," replied Tom.

"You don't hunt, do you?"

"Nah. But I love to fish."

"Fishing is good. Parkins, what about you?"

"Small game mostly, but I haven't been this year."

"What's the topic of conversation?" asked the cook, carrying a deep, oblong platter filled with beef, gravy, carrots, and baby potatoes. The men ogled the food and took their seats after she placed the main course on a trivet at the center of the table.

"Hunting," said Danny, standing behind an empty chair.

"Ah. I make a mean venison chili. But anyway, since you've never been to one of my dinner parties, Detective, let me give you a rundown." Pointing to each of the bowls, she explained, "The blue bowl is cabbage salad. That little green dish is horseradish, and the flowery casserole has mashed potato. Umm … the white one—that's steamed veggies. Oh, I forgot the extra gravy," she said, disappearing into the kitchen, returning in moments with a steaming pitcher.

"Okay. Let's dig in."

She reached for her chair, but Danny scooted behind her and pulled it out, pushing it in as she sat. Surprised by his gesture, her mouth lifted at the corners.

"Thank you," she said, cheeks blushing.

"You're welcome," he replied, sitting to her left.

Tom, who sat on her right, pounded his fists on the table. "I'm starving! Please pass the pot roast," he said, kicking her under the table as she slid the platter to him. Eyes darting to Danny, he waggled his brows. Her pursed lips and tight jaw delivered a non-verbal 'knock it off' to her lifelong friend.

The detective rubbed his hands together. "Marnie, this looks amazing."

Everyone turned to him with mild surprise at his change in attitude and his use of the psychic's first name.

Unaware he had caused a stir, he dropped a napkin into his lap and said, "Can you pass the roast when you're finished, please?"

Tom loaded up his plate before handing it across the table to his partner, who grabbed it with both hands. Turning, he held it out to the chef.

"You'd better fill your plate while you can. I've seen Keller eat," he said with a good-hearted snicker.

Side-eyeing him with a goofy grin, she said, "Thank you again." When she had taken a healthy serving, she took the china tray and returned the favor. "Here, let me help."

Tom and Carl exchanged glances while Danny beamed, helping himself to meat and veggies.

"Wine. Who wants a drink?" the healer called out, getting up from his seat at the head of the table, opposite the hostess. "I know

I do." He excused himself and returned with a bottle and extra glasses. Holding up the Shiraz, he said, "Anyone? "

"No, thank you. I have to go back to the station," said the detective.

"Yes, please," said Tom.

Marnie took a sip of her water, shaking her head. "No, thanks. I'm exhausted and want a decent night's sleep. Every time I drink wine, I'm restless."

"Okay, Mr. Parkins, if you're ready, let's have that chat." Danny glanced up, wiping his mouth on his napkin.

Carl made direct eye contact and said, "Sure. What else can I tell you?"

"There's video of you in the backyard. What were you doing out there? You walked up on the back step and down again." The interrogator appraised the trespasser, eyebrows arched.

Setting his silverware aside, the healer explained, "Before Marnie left for her run, I checked the back door. I had hoped she would unlock it when she arrived home. My plan was to sneak in the back, hide the items while she and Tater were gone. I knew I could get in and out without a problem, but she didn't unlatch it, so I walked around the front and waited in the woods. When they left, I settled on the front porch." He picked up a forkful of beef and brought it to his mouth, his hand steady.

Considering the man's calm demeanor, Danny pushed, hoping to rattle him. "Okay. Why didn't you knock on the door and tell her what you were doing? You're here now, playing the faithful guardian. Why didn't you do that last night, and why did you think she needed protection? Am I missing something?"

"That is more complicated. Uh ... To be frank, she has pissed off my colleagues because she doesn't like them, and she revels in making them look unsavory. We were both at an event last night, and she told the audience that my associates in The Collective … that's what they call themselves … are charlatans. I know these people. They could go after her. Not in the way you may think, but they would deal with her, well, on a spiritual level. It would be a psychic attack." Knowing that the detective may not find his statement credible, he glanced at Marnie, hoping for backup.

The detective snorted. "What does that mean? This sounds like a bunch of hoodoo-voodoo crap to me."

"It may sound like that to you, but trust me, it's not. The things I placed around the front porch have a positive charge. The Collective could put negative things around her home. They might meditate on unfortunate things happening to her. There are spells, potions, and a myriad of things they could do to weaken her or make her sick. I was only trying to protect her. Marnie is what we call a sensitive. Is everything I just said weird? Sure. Unbelievable? Perhaps to you." Scooping up a forkful of potatoes, he sighed and rested it on his plate. "But I'd rather appear a fool than suffer the consequences."

The detective quirked up one side of his mouth. "Pfft! Sounds like bullshit to me."

The psychic grasped his arm and gazed into his steely blue eyes. "Detective, it's not BS. What he's saying is true. I know many people don't believe in this sort of thing, but it is real. I took The Collective to task at an event, and I damaged their credibility *and* made them look like idiots. They may seek retribution. Carl and I had words last night before I went onstage, and he wasn't immune to my reproach, but he takes it on the chin. He wouldn't have knocked on the door because I would have bitten off his head. I was angry and gave him an earful this morning, but it would have been worse last night. He knows it irks me when people try to shield me from harm—emotional, psychic or physical. It pisses me off. It feels to me they are saying I'm weak. After everything that happened with Ken, personal power is important to me, and he would have, in my mind, taken that away from me if I had known he was trying to protect me." She released Danny's arm and had a drink of water. "He wouldn't hurt me, Detective. Never. He wouldn't let anyone else either."

"Is there something going on between you two? Are you covering for him?"

"No, and there never has been. He was my therapist. No way," she replied, her surprise genuine.

Turning his attention back to Carl, Danny asked, "What time did you arrive home last night?"

"I left the house around eleven but waited for Marnie to get inside. And her phone was ringing when I stepped off the porch. People in The Collective would do that—call to give her a hard time. My housemate can confirm I got home around eleven-thirty. Her name is Michelle, and yes, there is something going on there," he said with a satisfied sneer.

"Okay. Now, I want to finish my dinner before it gets cold. Thank you for answering the questions." The detective picked up his fork and dug into a pile of mashed potatoes and gravy.

They savored the rest of the meal with small talk about the weather, Creekwood gossip, and current events. Tater settled beneath the table, his tail thumping as he waited for someone to drop him a scrap out of his mistress's view.

"Hey, Marn, did you make dessert?" Tom raised an eyebrow as he scraped up the last morsel of his second helping of pot roast.

"Uh ... I've got pie. Does that work?"

"What kind?"

"Raspberry."

"My favorite. I wanted to know so I could save room!" he said, setting down his fork and winking at her.

"Do you have ice cream? You can't have pie without it," said Danny, glancing up from his plate.

"I think so," she replied with a grin, relieved the tension had passed.

"Well, that settles it! This is the best dinner I've had in forever!" said the detective, wiping his napkin across his lips.

Chapter Fifteen

7:48 PM, Marnie's House

The clatter of dishes led the detectives to Marnie, who was rinsing plates and chatting with Officer Jalnack as he finished off a slice of pie. Shoulder pressed to the back door, the cop had a plate in hand, spooning pastry and ice cream into his mouth between words.

"Not a bad gig if you can get it, huh, Jalnack?" said Danny with a chuckle.

The cop saluted with his spoon and grinned.

Tom dropped a kiss on top of the counselor's head and said, "We came in to say goodnight and thank you."

Giving him a one-armed hug, she pointed to two brown bags on the counter and said, "There are leftovers for you both. Lunch tomorrow, perhaps."

"Marn, you are a legend. Is there pie in there too?" said her friend, opening a packet to have a look.

"Yup. And pot roast." She rolled up the top again, handing one to each.

The detective accepted the sack and peeked inside. "I love leftovers. Thank you."

Squeezing her shoulder, her friend asked, "You gonna be okay?"

A step behind them on the way to the door, she said, "Of course. Carl is here, and he's going to stay up and wait for the next shift of officers to arrive. I'm heading off to bed after I take Tater for a quick walk."

She took her jacket from the coat rack and clipped the lead to the pup's collar.

Tom pulled open the door with a dramatic bow. "Age before beauty."

"Hardy har har," she said, stepping outside.

Marnie froze in place for a silent breath, then shrieked from her core, throwing her hands over her face. She lurched back into the men as Tater skittered sideways with a growl. The detectives peered over her head—confronted by a gory sight. Officer Webb lay in a pool of blood on the light gray decking, his head at an odd angle. Tom grabbed the psychic and dragged her into the house, while Danny snatched hold of the dog and slammed the door.

Carl and the on-duty cop rushed into the front hall as the Border Collie paced low and slow in front of the door, grumbling and mumbling with discontent.

Danny snapped, "Jalnack, call it in. We've got an officer down. I want an ambulance. Damn! Hang on a sec." He stepped back outside, returning a few seconds later, his complexion green. "Call the coroner and forensics. Shit! Three cops sitting right inside! Damn it!" He slammed his hand into the wall, clattering knick-knacks on a nearby whatnot. "Gawd! Webb's nearly decapitated!" He closed his eyes and grimaced, remembering civilians were present. "Uh, sorry."

Tater barked and back-walked to his mistress, who shivered, and sank to the floor, pulling the dog into her lap. "Is he ... is he..." Her voice quaked with fear.

Tom patted her shoulder. "How 'bout that drink now?"

Face ashen, she nodded, and Carl excused himself, returning a few minutes later with a glass of rye and ginger ale. He handed it to her and settled beside her and the pup. She put her head on his shoulder as the jarring ring of the phone made everyone jump.

Tom snatched up the living room extension. "Hello." He listened. "Uh … Kate, hi. Yeah, it's Tom. Umm … She's kinda busy. I'll have her call you back in the morning." Jutting out his jaw with a sigh, he continued through clenched teeth. "Look, I can't talk. A lot has happened today. Listen to me. Ken is dead. I can't get into it now. I'll call you tomorrow with an update. She is…" He stepped toward the kitchen, not wanting Marnie to hear him. "She's a mess, and I gotta go. We'll speak later."

"Tommy, come with. We need to check around the house to see if there's anyone out there," said Danny, reaching for the doorknob.

"Don't go! Please! It's not safe." Marnie's terrified eyes locked onto Danny's and then her friend's.

Squatting down next to her, Danny kept his voice calm. "We gotta go out there. We have to find the person who did that to Webb." He brushed her cheek with the back of his hand and mustered a smile. "Hey, we're cops. It's what we do. We have each other's backs. Carl and Officer Jalnack will be right here with you and Tater. Okay? It's gonna be fine."

He stood and nodded to his partner, who returned the gesture, and they stepped onto the veranda, pulling their sidearms from their holsters.

The detectives stooped to inspect the body of Officer Webb.

"What the fuck is happening?" growled Danny.

Tom let out a low whistle. "This is friggin' freaky. Is that piano wire?" He glanced at the corpse, wondering how long it took blood to coagulate in cold temperatures. With an involuntary shiver, he turned away.

"Yeah, that's exactly what it is," replied his colleague, swallowing the taste of bile rising in his throat.

"Let's grab a flashlight and have a look around. Whoever it was is probably long gone. Or they could be in the woods, waiting for us to leave," said Tom, jogging down the steps.

Or waiting to take us out, thought Detective Gregg. Catching up to his partner, he asked, "When you say Marnie is clairvoyant, what does that mean?"

"Ah ... well, she sees and hears spirits," he replied, scanning the road and surrounds, allowing his associate time to process his friend's gift.

"So, she sees and talks to dead people."

"Ha-ha! Yeah, I guess so," said Tom, pivoting on the path, hoping to end the discussion. He didn't enjoy talking about the paranormal—it made his skin crawl.

The entrance to the bridle trail loomed ahead, and the detectives switched on their Maglites, the beams catching misty rain. Pulling up their collars, their teeth-chattered against a wild breeze ripping the last of fall's leaves from their branches.

"How long is the path?" asked Danny.

"A couple of miles. It goes down to the pond and winds around to the equestrian park," said Tom, stopping and turning his head, holding up his hand. "Wait. Did you hear that?"

"What?"

"Screaming. It's Marn!"

The men doubled back, sprinting to the house, and racing up onto the porch. They rushed through the door where the psychic sat frozen on the stairs, her face as white as a ghost. Carl was seated a step below, bracing to catch her if she fell. Tater's eyes focused on the darkness above them, a warning snarl on his muzzle.

Tom clapped his hands. "Shush. Sit, boy."

The dog sat, grumbling and mumbling to himself.

The healer moved up a step and sat next to her. "Marnie, what did you see? Tell me."

He glanced up at the detectives, shook his head, and shrugged.

The Border Collie whimpered, growled again, bounded forward, then back, before breaking into a vicious snarling bark.

"It's Ken," she said, coaxing her dog into her lap, massaging his ears to calm him.

"What? It can't be Ken. He's at the morgue," said Danny, moving closer and staring into her tear-stained face.

"I saw him upstairs in the hallway. He was looking out the front window, and he turned and glared at me. Dead eyes … his throat … Oh, gawd! It was horrible!" Her lips trembled, and she wiped away tears with the back of her hand. "I've seen spirits before, but not like this. He's tortured. He's in pain, and he's confused. Spirits often appear bewildered, but he … It's horrifying!" She buried her face in her sleeve, choking back sobs.

Kneeling next to her, the detective said, "Marnie, I'm having trouble with this, okay? I don't believe in what you're talking about, or that ghosts are around us, and I find it hard to fathom that people see them."

"Danny!" Tom shouted, fixing a glare on his partner. "I can't see them either, but she wouldn't be saying this if it weren't true."

She lifted her head, her eyes locking onto Danny's with defiance. "Just because you doubt me, Detective, doesn't mean it isn't true. Your wife and mother are here." Her voice softened. "They stand beside you all the time and gaze into your face when you look sad, wondering why you allow sorrow to suffocate any joy that comes into your life. Is it because they suffered from depression or that you couldn't save them? Why do you feel responsible for their deaths? They want you to live your life and move on because you had nothing to do with them committing suicide. You couldn't have stopped them."

Face drawn, the detective sucked in a breath, placing a protective hand against his stomach, readying for another gut-punch.

"Sarah is telling me you were always the sunshine of her life, and your mother, Carol, has a message too. It was your father's preoccupation with his job, and her inability to cope that sent her over the edge. She also said she loves that you carry her tiger in your pocket every day."

Sirens blared in the distance as the detective tried to stand, but he sank to his knees, tears stinging his eyes. His voice filled with anger, and he shuddered, grabbing the newel post. "How do you know those things? What is this?! How dare you dig into my life?! How dare you?!"

"I didn't dig into your life. It dug into me. Your mother and your wife were there with us today in the interview room. They were asking ... No! They were pleading with me to help you. I didn't go looking for them. They sent you to me so that I would tell you to hear what they have been trying to communicate for years, but you won't listen. They saw an opportunity this morning, and they sent you. You weren't even supposed to catch this case, were you? It was supposed to be another detective's call, but his car broke down." Marnie shook with frustration and anger, a mirror to Detective Gregg. "They sent you here, so do not fucking accuse me of interfering!" She choked back a sob as fury and exhaustion overwhelmed her.

The squawk of the sirens grew closer, and flashing lights shone through the windows.

Danny stood and glanced at Tom. "I gotta go for a walk. I just … I need to get out of here for a minute."

Tom nodded before looking back at Marnie, sitting on the stairs with Carl's arm around her shoulders. He blew her a kiss and left to meet the forensics team and coroner.

Chapter Sixteen

8:20 PM, 404 Creek Road

A gust of sideways rain whipped up the road, splattering the bloody crime scene. Cringing as he zipped his jacket, Tom quickened his stride, eager to get away from the grisly sight. He found Danny leaning his back against a van, talking to two officers and a man in a white jumpsuit. He grabbed his partner's sleeve and pulled him away from the group.

"How much of that stuff did you tell her?" asked Danny, snatching his arm from his colleague's grip.

Tom studied the deep bags under the detective's eyes, noticing his low, gravelly voice was hoarse with an edge of gruff.

"I didn't tell her anything. Not a word. Besides, I knew nothing about your wife or mother. I'd heard Sarah was dead, but I didn't know how. Look. Marn is spooked. I've seen her pick up stuff before, but not like that. It gave me the willies," he said with a tremor.

With his lips pressed in a straight line, the detective said, "Something's not right here. How did she find out things about my personal life? Stuff I don't share. People in the squad know some details, but they wouldn't repeat it. She had to research me. Somebody must have fed her that shit. Sarah's obit was in the papers. Cause of death was not. Only people close to me knew about it. I moved here to leave it behind. The raised eyebrows, the looks of pity and blame—it was too much. First my mother, and then my wife. You can't imagine the crap people were saying." Avoiding eye contact, he zippered his jacket and shoved his hands in his pockets.

"I can only assume it wasn't a good time for you." Tom shifted from one foot to the other. "Look, we need to focus on catching the killer. Marn didn't do this. We know she didn't. We were right there with her. I know she freaked you out with the ... well, you know. She didn't say it to upset you. That is not how she rolls. Let's go for a walk and see if we can find order in this mess. Let me grab a couple of flashlights." Tom gave his partner a push forward and walked off into the rain.

A pang of dread knotted in the pit of Danny's stomach as he watched him leave. He pulled his hand from his pocket and brought out a tiny gold tiger. Its green eyes glistening in the patrol cars' swirling lights.

"What have you got there, Detective?" asked a tall, willowy woman with long chestnut hair, falling in waves around her angular face. Tipping her bright blue umbrella so he could see her, she shoved a microphone in his face.

Angered that she had startled him, he tightened his fist around the tiger and peered down into her cold, mocking fawn eyes. "Who are you?" he growled.

"Carrie Sutherland, Nightly News," she said, offering her hand.

The detective ignored it, setting his steel-blue eyes on the cameraman standing behind her.

"Ms. Sutherland, this is a crime scene. I want you off the premises now." Arms out, he herded them to the road. "Move back, now!"

"Can you tell us what happened here tonight, Detective? We've received information that Ken Wilder was murdered on the property this morning, and now you have discovered a slain officer. What can you share?" Staring into the camera, she pressed him for information—faux compassion plastered on her Botoxed face.

"I can't tell you a damn thing! Get off my crime scene now, or I will arrest you for trespassing and interfering with an investigation! Move it! Both of you!"

He called out to two uniformed officers to assist, and as the cops escorted the reporter and crew under the tape, they continued filming from the road. Danny ducked beneath the flimsy barrier, tore the camera out of the man's hands, snatched the SD card, and handed the equipment back. "This is a private road, and you are still trespassing. Return to your van and go!"

The cameraman charged forward, reaching out to grab the card. "Hey! You can't take that! We have a right to film!"

The detective waved him off and flagged down the officers again. "Get them outta here and block off the road in both directions."

The policemen took charge, guiding the press to their van, ignoring their protests and threats. Waiting for the news crew to leave, they called for backup before driving off to set up the roadblocks.

Danny returned to the house to find the forensics team gathered around the body. He looked around for Tom and saw him running toward the house.

"We've got tracks down by the bridle trail. The guys have gotta get over there fast before the rain washes the evidence away." He bent to catch his breath and added, "Looks like fresh four-wheel-drive tires."

Detective Gregg jogged to the porch where the head of forensics, Doctor Rick Price, was working alongside his team.

"Hey, can you get a couple of guys over to the trail? We've got tracks."

"Yeah. We're done here. Not much to go on other than the obvious. No prints. Nothin'. The coroner will do a morgue drop, and I'd guess Dr. Markson will autopsy tomorrow. But I can tell you the estimated time of death is six PM," he said, his white suit crackling as he stooped to fasten a case.

"Thanks, Rick," said the detective, scowling at the sky. "What's with this weather? It's gonna be a slippery drive home."

The precipitation segued into sleet, and the wind shifted direction with a furious gust, ripping crime scene tape from its anchor of an oak tree branch. It flailed with wild abandon before settling on the spiked leaves of a holly bush, sparkling with a thin blanket of freezing rain.

Icy arrows stung the forensics specialist's drawn face. He had been here twelve hours earlier, pulling a body out of the back shed. He called out to his team. "Guys, zip up the bag and get it into the coroner's wagon. Let's pack up here and head over to the trail. I'll grab a tent. Could one of you bring the plaster kit?"

A tech nodded as he secured Officer Webb into a black cocoon, hefting it onto a cart with the help of a colleague.

Wrapped in her jacket, Marnie stepped onto the veranda, and Danny shook his head, waving for her to go back inside.

"Tater needs to pee. He's crying at the door. Can I please bring him out for a minute?"

He assessed the scene and turned back. "Yeah, okay, but don't let him off his lead."

She ducked back in and reappeared moments later with her dog. He pulled her down the steps, relieved himself on the closest shrub, and then sniffed the grass, stopped and pawed at the dirt. Marnie turned away with a shiver as the men loaded the fallen officer into the van. Beside her, the detective looked down at Tater, who was digging.

"What have you got, pal?"

The dog ignored him and continued to paw at the soggy earth, kicking dirt back onto the detective's shoes.

Nudging the psychic, he asked, "Marnie, what's he doing? Has he got something?"

Squatting, she discovered a black object poking up through the earth, and she tugged Danny's sleeve. He crouched, and their eyes locked when they realized the dog might have found evidence.

The detective pulled a bag out of his pocket as she nudged the probing pooch away from the hole. Sliding his hand into the baggie, Danny wiggled the pup's treasure, loosening the surrounding earth, and retrieved the muddy item from its grave.

Holding up the see-through pouch, he inspected its contents. "Hmm ... It's a heel from a woman's shoe." He held it out for her to examine. "Do you recognize it?"

"No. I don't wear heels like that often, and when I do, I don't traipse around the front yard. Besides, that's Christian Louboutin. I would never spend that much on a pair of shoes."

"What?" He frowned.

"Only Louboutin has legal rights to use red soles on black shoes. That heel leather is black, so it must be Louboutin or a knockoff."

He wrinkled his brow. "Okay. I'll take your word for it. It doesn't look like it's been stuck there for long, does it?"

"No, but no one has been around here in heels in a long time—not since July, anyway, when I had a bridal shower. I can check with my girlfriends, though." She shivered again and looked up, frowning at the inclement weather.

"This hasn't been here since July. We had a lot of rain in August and September. The leather would be in worse shape. I'll send it to the lab and check it for prints," he said, pocketing the evidence.

Tom was behind them when they stood up. "Whatcha got?"

"A heel," said Danny, pulling the bag from his pocket.

"Really?"

"Yeah. It's Looo-booo-TANH, according to Ms. Reilly," he said, smirking and walking away.

The psychic glared after him and then turned to her friend, who was scratching Tater's ears. "What the hell? One minute I'm Marnie, the next I'm Ms. Reilly." She had deepened her voice, mimicking the detective. "That guy pisses me off!"

"I think someone has a little crush on Detective Gregg," he teased.

Face reddening, she protested, "Excuse me? No, I wouldn't give Detective Stick-up-his-butt the time of day. What's his problem?"

"C'mon, Marn. You know better. Two bodies within twenty-four hours, and one of the deceased is a cop." Exasperated, he ran a hand down his face. "Look, go inside, and I'll come in before I leave. Make some coffee and tea. We've got wet people out here, and they're going to be in the cold for a while longer." He nudged her toward the house.

"Are you kidding me? Go make tea and coffee? You're such a dick!" she spat, storming off with Tater in tow.

Danny returned a moment later and nodded his head toward the woman's retreating form. "What's with Madame Séance?"

"Are you serious? Two dead bodies at her house ... The two of you are ... forget it. Geez!" Throwing his hands in the air, he cursed under his breath as he ambled down the road. "Maybe I'll get peace on the bridle trail," he muttered.

"Hey, Danny!" Rick Price walked toward him with a bundled tent in his arms. "The guys are buttoning things up, and then we'll head over. I doubt we'll get much. This sleet will have frozen the tire tracks by now."

The detective gave a resigned nod, and under the sickening yellow glow of a streetlight, he watched freezing rain slash its way to the ground. "Why isn't Mother Nature cooperating? You think it's a woman thing? Ha-ha!"

"Yeah. That's it. She's kicking our butts tonight for something we don't even know we said or did. It's only for tonight, though. Tomorrow, she'll be fine. Women, hey?" Rick snickered and left to catch up with his crew.

Raking fingers through his wet hair, Danny grumbled about the weather as he trudged through the frozen mud. He started up the front steps, then changed his mind, clomping down to the slick cobblestone walk.

"I don't have the patience for Madam Séance," he groused, trekking to the rear of the property to search for undiscovered clues.

The detective paused near the back step to pull on a pair of gloves and spotted Marnie through the kitchen window. She was wearing a pair of blue plaid pajama pants and a New York Mets T-shirt. He nodded his approval and glanced up at Officer Weaver, who stood guard at the back door.

"Ha-ha! Look at that. Madame Séance is a Mets fan."

The cop grinned. "Ha! You think that's a good thing? I like the Yankees."

Danny waved him off with a chuckle. "Overrated and overpaid!"

"Any news?"

"Not yet. We're heading out as soon as we've checked on tire tracks Keller found in the forest. You should keep watch from the kitchen when we leave. It's too cold for anyone to be outside tonight."

"I won't argue. My sock warmers quit working twenty minutes ago."

Marnie pulled the boiling kettle from the burner and filled a teapot, popping on the lid to steep. As she got her teacup out of the cupboard, she caught movement and a beam of light in her backyard. Squinting, she peered through the window for a better look and recognized the man directing a flashlight. His huge shoulders gave him away, and her heart skipped a beat as she followed his steps. Closing her eyes, she admonished herself.

Why does he have to look like that? It's so inconvenient. He's the most interesting man I've met in a long time and, just my luck, he's annoying. Thanks for that, Universe. Are you testing me again?

She stood at the drainboard, drinking her tea, telling herself how inappropriate it was to find the detective attractive. After all, he was there investigating a murder, and now, with Officer Webb's death ... well, words like improper and untenable came to mind.

Reaching to turn off the light over the sink, her back straightened when she saw a glint in the ray of his flashlight. With a frustrated harrumph, her shoulders drooped because he didn't see what she saw shining up through the sleet-laden grass. She knocked on the window, waving her hand for him to back up. Not understanding her gesture, he shrugged. She crooked her thumb, pointing behind him, and the detective looked down and then back up—his hands out to his sides and a furrow on his brow.

Opening the door, she called, "Back up a bit. I saw something shiny in the grass."

"It's wet and icy out here. Everything's shiny," he barked, not masking his annoyance.

With an exasperated sigh, she said, "No. Back up. I saw a flash of red."

He walked backward, stopped, and glanced up at her.

"A bit more!"

He did and stopped.

Leaning out the door, she said, "Right around there. Shine the flashlight into the grass. Maybe I'll see it again."

He did as she asked.

"There! Right there! Officer Weaver, did you see it?"

The cop replied, "Nope. I didn't."

Danny let out a frustrated breath. He couldn't see anything either. Marnie went out onto the porch and pulled at her T-shirt, conscious of her wardrobe.

The detective palmed his face at her standing there in her pajamas. "Go back inside. There's nothing here."

She gripped the railing and walked down the slippery steps, pointing. "It's right there. See?"

Danny stepped back, examining where she was pointing. Dragging fingers through his mop, he sighed with frustration.

"Give me a glove," she said, holding out a hand.

He dug into his pocket and passed her one.

She stooped and plucked something out of the grass. He held out an evidence bag, and she dropped in a long, bright-red fingernail.

"Wow! That's like finding a needle in a haystack. Stick with me, and we'll see what else we can find."

Shivering, she nodded—her teeth clenched so that they wouldn't chatter.

"You're cold. Go back inside before you get wet."

She gazed into the dark green sky, a hand raised to shield her cheeks from the stinging sleet. "It's going to storm again. Hang on. I'll be back in a sec."

She left, returning moments later wearing a yellow rain slicker and a pair of bright-red Wellingtons. He turned away, grinning at her silly outfit. *She sure is different*, he thought to himself.

He regained his composure and pointed the flashlight to the ground. "Okay, I'll shine the light, and you keep your eyes out."

They walked the yard in a grid pattern, and thirty minutes later, they'd found nothing else.

Marnie gripped Danny's arm and pointed at the house. "The security cameras! Whoever killed Officer Webb is on the video! We need to get Tom. He knows the setup better than I do." Pulling his sleeve, she dragged him to the house.

Once inside, the detective called his partner, but the call went to voicemail.

"Tom isn't answering his phone. I'm going to look for him."

"I'll come too," said Marnie, worry etching her forehead.

"No. You stay here. I'll send an officer in to check the video."

"I'm coming, Detective. If Tom's hurt or in trouble, I want to be there for him."

He threw up his hands—he didn't have time to argue. "Fine. Come on, but you stay close, and don't wander off on your own."

"Where are you two going?" Carl watched their dripping forms pass in the hallway as he sat smoking his pipe by the fire, Tater asleep at his feet.

"Tom's not answering his phone. We're going to look for him. We'll be right back," she said, throwing him a stiff wave.

9:03 PM, The Bridle Trail

A crack, pop, and *thunk* to his left gave Tom a jump, and he swung his flashlight into the trees, searching for the culprit. A silver maple limb lay on the frozen earth, three yellow and orange leaves clinging to its branch. Directing the beam onto the sparse field opposite, he searched for the shadow he'd seen skulking in the forest moments earlier. "Lighten up, Keller," he said to himself. "It's probably a deer." *Or even better, my overactive imagination,* he thought.

Reversing course, he headed back to the house, stomping his feet to get feeling back into his toes. At the rustle of foliage and the snap of a twig, his head swiveled and his heart leaped into his throat. Goosebumps trickled up his back and prickled his scalp. With a shiver, he glanced at his phone to find he had no service, so he jammed it into his pocket and backed up the trail, chastising himself. He grew up here and knew better. The creaks and snaps were pines, maples, and birches protesting under the weight of ice gathering on their branches. But his self-castigation didn't stop there.

What the hell was I thinking? I should have waited for Danny. Wandering off without backup was stupid.

"Tom," whispered someone at the edge of the forest.

Spinning around, he reached for his weapon and jerked his head, turning left, then right, but no one was there. Soft, crunching footsteps in the woods approached the trail, and he shone the flashlight into the trees.

"Who's there?" he called out.

"Tom."

Common sense told him to run, but a blinding crack to his skull forced him to his knees. He teetered before collapsing onto the frozen dirt path, consciousness evading him.

Chapter Seventeen

9:23 PM, The Bridle Trail

Danny retrieved a raincoat, a radio, and fresh flashlight batteries from his car, and he and Marnie hurried up the road. They stopped along the way to ask a couple of officers if they had seen Tom. With a nod, one cop pointed to the trail, commenting, "Keller's cranky face was as red as a smacked ass."

"Ha-ha. Thanks guys," said the detective, setting off at a jog.

Marnie slip-slid behind him, cursing her rubber-soled Wellingtons and their useless treads. The bone-chilling wind changed direction, whipping the freezing rain into a face-on assault. They pulled up their hoods and collars to thwart the stinging attack on their noses and cheeks. Low rumbling thunder grew in the distance, letting the duo know the storm wasn't over. The next harbinger of foul weather announced itself with a bang, and the searchers flinched, feeling the boom under their feet. The warning that followed wasn't as subtle. A jagged bolt streaked across the sky, illuminating the path ahead. The flash delivered an electric *zip-zap*, the cracking of branches in the distance and the sweet metallic scent of ozone.

A *thwack-thud* followed by an *oof* found Danny turning back to help the psychic to her feet. With her hand in his firm grip, they navigated the slippery terrain. Above them, a blaze of lightning shot across the sky, revealing Tom's motionless body lying in the snow just off the trail. Their heads pivoted left at the snapping of a twig, and the detective pointed the beam of his flashlight into the forest, searching for immediate threats.

Heart racing, Marnie slid to a halt and dropped to her knees beside her lifelong pal, exhaling a sigh of relief. "He's breathing, but he's freezing cold," she said, squeezing his arms and legs, checking for broken bones. She ran her fingers through his black curls, looking for a head injury, and pulled away her hands, now sticky with blood. "Ah! Geez! He's bleeding, and look, he's been moved." Her eyes darted to the muddy drag marks on the ice-covered trail.

The detective freed his gun from its holster and cast the light along the pathway and into the trees. Following his lead, the psychic picked up her injured friend's torch and lit up the opposite side of the woods. Danny spotted movement in the distance but couldn't discern between human and wildlife.

Eyes on the forest, he radioed his team. "This is Detective Gregg. We've got an officer down. Call an ambulance. Kriss and Weaver cover the front and back of the house. All other officers and forensics should come to the trail. Now isn't soon enough."

He kneeled next to his wounded partner and checked his vital signs. He had a bloody gash on his temple—his breathing rapid, his pulse racing.

"Someone tried to pull him *into* the forest. That's his shoe over there," said Marnie, waggling a finger at the boot.

Two officers traipsed with caution down the treacherous path. Tony, the cop leading the way, called out, "Detective Gregg, we've got paramedics on the way, but the weather is slowing them down. The forensics guys said we could borrow a body bag and cadaver cart, though. They're coming right behind us. Doctor Price can check out Keller when he gets here."

"Thanks. I forget he's a real physician," said Danny, letting out an uneasy chuckle. "Can you guys check the path and forest on both sides? Whoever hit Tom may have left something behind. Watch your backs!"

Pushing himself to his feet, he analyzed the scene in every direction and was relieved to see the forensics team skidding down the frozen track. Rick was at the front of the pack, carrying a medical bag and a tent kit over his shoulder. He handed the bundle to Tony to set it up and instructed his team to get photos of the area around Detective Keller, the trail, and the wooded areas on either side.

Face grave, the doctor assessed the patient and tried to ease the heaviness of the situation. "I don't get to work on the living often, but I'll have a look." Cringing, he apologized. "Sorry, that was callous. Bedside manner is the reason I don't work with the live ones." He placed his bag on the wet ground and kneeled next to Tom, glancing up at the psychic, who was hugging herself and shivering. "Ms. Reilly, you should go home. An officer will escort you. Go. We'll take care of him." He pulled a pair of gloves out of his pack and nodded back toward the house.

"I'm fine. I want to stay. This is my fault. He wouldn't have been out here if it weren't for me." Eyeing Danny, she asked, "Can I stay?"

With a half-hearted nod, he turned to Rick. "There's a deep laceration on his head and a lot of blood." He held his flashlight on his partner's ashen face so he could be examined.

The forensics photographer lit up the woods with a flash of his camera as thunder growled and the storm closed in. Ice-laden tree limbs creaked in protest, their branches bending to meet the ground.

Danny crouched and asked, "What's the damage, Doc?"

"He's going to have a headache in the morning. My guess is somebody hit him with a rock. His pulse and heart rate concern me. We need to carry him out of here and settle him at the house." He snapped off his gloves and shoved them in his pocket. "I doubt the ambulance will arrive in the short-term. There are trees and power lines down in town, and the weather is getting worse, not better. We'd better get a move on. It's unconventional, but let's get him in a body bag to keep him dry. Then we can set him on the cart. At least he'll be warmer. We won't zip him in, of course."

Danny shouted out to the officers searching up ahead. "See if you can find the weapon. Could be a rock, but whatever it is, it will be heavy and have Tommy's blood and hair on it. Tony, we need a couple of officers down here to carry him out. Who's left up there?"

"Jalnack's in the house. Kriss is watching the front, and Weaver is out back. And there are two guys from Hudson Hollow on the road keeping the press away."

"Hmm ... Yeah. Okay. We'll make do with who we've got." The detective counted heads; lips pursed.

Marnie raised her hand. "I can help."

"He is not a small guy. Are you sure you can lift him?" asked Danny, staring at the top of her head.

With a determined glare, she straightened her shoulders, inching up to her full height. "*Well*, not by myself, smarty pants. But if all of you are helping, yes."

Before he could sling back a response, an officer rushed out of the trees carrying a worn duffel bag.

"Detective! We've got something!"

Danny took the tote, positioned his coat up over his head to shield the contents, put his flashlight between his teeth, and pulled the zip. It contained two coils of piano wire, energy bars, an old padlock with a key, bottled water, and an assortment of tools.

Zipping the bag, he uttered, "Jesus!"

Rain dripped down his nose, and he shivered, squinting into the depths of the forest. *Where did you go?*

Trees moaned under the weight of the ice, and the lightning bursts were more frequent as wind gusts slammed freezing rain into the team. The detective chewed his bottom lip, knowing he had to wrap up the investigation for the night before another accident occurred. He glanced down to see Rick and Tony finagling Tom's long limbs into a body bag, and it struck him as funny.

"Ha-ha. Oh, he's not gonna live this down," he said to himself, before shifting his attention back to the seriousness of the situation. "Okay, guys. We need to go. The sleet is coming down too hard and fast. The tent won't last much longer, and those birch and elm limbs are gonna snap. That silver maple over there looks ready to topple." His face pinched with the strain of the last few hours, but he knew his decision was best for everyone's safety. "Let's wrap it up. We'll come back as soon as the storm passes."

The detective scanned the faces of the team to ensure they had heard his previous order. A burst of lightning brightened the trail as he counted heads again, and he gritted his teeth. They were one person short.

He barked, "Where's Ms. Reilly? Where the hell did she go?"

Shrugs and an uncomfortable silence were the only responses from the team.

"Dammit!" He kicked the trail and turned in circles. "Where did she disappear to? I *told* her to stay close!"

Fears allayed; the psychic emerged from the forest, holding a flashlight under her chin. Her pajamas were drenched, and her coat was gone from her shoulders, but was wrapped around a bulky item she carried in her arms. Relief enveloped him, and he yelled at her.

"What the hell were you doing out there? Jesus, Marnie!"

She scowled at him through a curtain of water-soaked hair and shoved the bundle at him, dropping the flashlight to the ground.

"I found the weapon. The rock that hit Tom. I knew if we waited until morning, we might not find it." Tossing her head, her hair dripped with precipitation and her words with sarcasm. "You're welcome!"

"How did you find it?" His tone teetered between pissed off and thankful.

She stood on tip-toes with her lips to his ear. "Better not talk about my superpowers in front of the kids."

He jerked out a quick nod. "Yeah. Okay, then."

Stooping, she snatched up the flashlight and threw him a dirty look.

Rick stared at them; eyebrows raised. "You two finished there? Can we get moving? This weather isn't improving, and we need to get the patient back before it gets worse."

"Yeah, let's go." Taking a breath, he asked, "Can someone get Ms. Reilly a blanket?"

Tony dug through a kit and found one, unfolded it, and draped it around the psychic.

Satisfied she was protected from the elements, Danny walked to one side of the bag and motioned to the other men to fall in. "Marnie, you stay in front. Light the trail, and do not go off into the woods alone again."

"Sir! Yes, sir!" She saluted, turned on the flashlight and started up the path, slipping and sliding in her bright-red boots. Snickers, grins and amused head shakes came from the techs and officers.

Rick smirked and winked at Danny. "She's different."

"Yes, she is," he agreed, hiding his grin behind his collar.

Chapter Eighteen

10:22 PM, Marnie's House

Stepping out of the canopied forest, the rescue team was greeted by a bluster of north wind, biting at their noses as they made the slippery trek back to the house. The men trudged forward, struggling to keep their balance, half pulling, half carrying the cart over the rough terrain. Marnie announced ruts and bumps along the way and trained her flashlight on the icy path ahead, glancing back every few minutes to check progress. Static electricity ripped across the sky, and crashes of thunder roared, filling the valley with an ominous drum roll.

"Uh-oh!" said the psychic as her home came into view. "Power outage."

The men looked up to see darkened windows except for the flicker of flames from the fireplace on the first floor.

Officer Kriss eased down the steps, gripping the railing, and shone his MagLite on the approaching group. "Detective Gregg, do you need a hand?"

Danny shook his head. "No, thanks. Slow and steady will get us there. How long has the power been out?"

Kriss pulled up his collar around his ears and replied, "Half an hour. The ambulance is trying to get here, but the storm is slowing it down. That big old maple at the top of Creek Road split in half about thirty minutes ago. The guys are trying to move it. Good luck to them! It's enormous!"

"Aww! I love that tree!" Marnie dropped her shoulders and frowned.

With a side-eye and a grin at her sentimentality, the detective said, "I think we have a bigger problem right here. We've gotta get Tom up the steps."

They pushed the cart under the shelter of the eaves while they made a plan to get him up the slippery stairs. Rick zipped the bag up to his patient's chin, and Tony got foil emergency blankets from his car and covered him.

The psychic clapped Danny on the arm. "Hey, if you guys can wait a sec, I'll put down sand so no one falls!" Before he could answer, she inched her way up onto the veranda and disappeared into the darkness.

The detective watched her walk away, amused by and envious of her pluck. He dragged his hand down his face, wondering what else could go wrong. "Rick, can you take care of Tom? I mean, if the ambulance can't get here, is he in immediate danger?"

The doctor shrugged and tugged on his bottom lip. "He needs to go to the hospital. We can get him inside and dry, but he requires medical attention. We can't be too careful. Head injuries can be funny. His pulse and heart rate have dropped, so that's good, but … I will do my best." Concerned that the patient hadn't regained consciousness, he texted a doctor friend for advice, and she replied within moments with the best course of action.

◆

The detective stretched his back and neck, summoning the courage to call his boss with the grave news. Phone in hand, he stared at the screen and muttered, "Fuck it. Just make the call, you coward." He rang the number, and his superior answered on the first ring.

"Cap, Gregg here. Look, we've got a situation at the Reilly house out on Creek Road. We need an ambulance. Tommy got hit on the head with a rock. He's bleeding, and he hasn't regained consciousness. The ambulance can't get here because of the ice, and there's a big maple down, blocking the road. Do you have the pull to get a road crew to move the tree? A sander would help too."

He listened, hoping for good news. "Thanks. We'll get him inside and wait to hear from you. We don't have electricity, but we'll do everything we can. Rick's with us. He's a doctor. Well, sort of."

His boss told him to hang tight and that help would be on the way as fast as the weather would allow.

"Thanks again, Cap. Do what you can do. We've got officers on the road who will direct emergency vehicles.

Marnie returned with a bucket of sand and a large battery-operated lantern. She turned on the light and got to work, sprinkling the deck, the stairs, and the cobblestone walk. When she finished, she waved to the detective, who told his team to take their places, and they eased the stretcher up the steps. A crack of lightning hit close by; they all startled, jostling the cart.

"Jesus!" Danny flinched. "Give us a break! This is like a scene from a freakin' horror movie!"

A mournful howl echoed around them. The Border Collie peeked out from behind a curtain, his head raised to the sky, wailing *ahroo* in tempo with thunder booms and flashes. Carl appeared and pulled back the dog, though the wailing continued.

Opening the door, Marnie stuck her head in and called out to the healer. "Could you please hang onto Tater so he doesn't trip up the guys?"

"Yeah. Sure," he said, grabbing the pup's collar, holding tight as the men carried their colleague into the living room.

Lit by candlelight and a crackling fire in the grate, the coziness of the psychic's home bathed the crew in a soft glow of warmth.

The counselor tugged on the psychoanalyst's sleeve. "Would you light a fire in the downstairs bedroom, please? Tom can rest there until the ambulance arrives. I'll take care of the generator and make coffee for the guys. Would you mind?"

"Sure. I'll take Mister Fluffybutt with me so he can settle. He's not used to this many people in his house," he replied, disappearing down the hall, with the dog protesting all the way.

Snatching a shabby gray cardigan from the coat rack, Marnie pulled it on, rolling the cuffs. "Guys, please make yourselves comfortable. I'll get everyone food and coffee as soon as I get the power back on. Detective Gregg, there's a generator in the cellar. Could you help me, please?"

"Yeah, sure," he said, following her through the entryway and down a corridor.

Marnie took a flashlight off the shelf above the cellar stairs and switched on the light. They descended the narrow steps to the smell of must, sawdust, and earth. The concrete floor was clean except for a daddy longlegs curled up in a death pose at the base of the stairs. As they walked further into the room, the detective noted three large doors and eight small, rectangular windows set in the fieldstone walls, and a closed hatchway at the far end.

Marnie led them to the front of the basement, where a large generator sat. A wide silver ventilation pipe curved up and outside, pink insulation stuffed around the hole.

"I don't know if the battery is dead, but we may need to swap it. I bought one last week," she said, pointing to it on a bench next to the machine. "Fingers crossed." She clicked the power switch, and it purred to life, the lights flickering on.

With a fist bump in the air, she said, "Excellent! Let's get back upstairs and check on Tom."

She pivoted and bumped into Danny. They stood toe-to-toe, and a wave of emotion washed over her as she looked into his tired eyes.

"Detective Gregg, are you okay?"

He ran his hands up her arms and gazed into her eyes—the corners of his mouth lifting when he noticed a smattering of tiny freckles on the bridge of her nose.

"Yeah, I'm feeling out of sorts. Like I can't get warm. It's a soaking cold that seeps into your bones. Know what I mean?"

"Yeah, I've been feeling it all day," she said, trying to take a step back, but he held tight.

She shifted, eyes darting to the exit. "We need to check on Tom."

He turned his head toward the stairs, then back again, and stepped closer. The heat between them brought a blush to her cheeks, and she looked down so he couldn't see.

"Marnie, I need to apologize to you again. I'm sorry I yelled at you earlier. Those things you said to me ... you rattled me, and you *know* you did." He glanced up for a moment—hiding the feelings bubbling up in his eyes. He put a hand in his pocket and drew out the tiger with the glistening green eyes. "Mentioning this … well, no one else knows about it. You knocked the wind outta me."

She looked down at the trinket and nodded. "I'm sorry for blurting out all of that, but your wife and mother have been pestering me all day."

He laughed and put the totem away. "Ha-ha! I think I used to call it nagging." He rubbed his big hands up and down her arms, leaned forward, and kissed her forehead.

Her eyebrows shot up, and a lopsided grin appeared on her reddening face. "What the heck was that?"

He winked and nudged her toward the cellar stairs. "Call it a thank you for reminding me what it's like to have a strong, bossy woman around. My mother and wife may have suffered from depression, but on good days, they were unstoppable. The cocktail of medications required … they both despised the effects, especially not feeling emotions. They got tired, and I couldn't help them. A team of doctors couldn't either."

"I don't understand depression. I've not experienced it, but I can sympathize, and because I have spent the day with them bossing me around, I can empathize with you." She took his hand and led him to the stairs. "C'mon. Let's check on Tom."

A phone was ringing when they reached the top, and Carl appeared, holding it out. "It's Kate again. She keeps calling your cell."

Marnie took it and held it to her ear. "Hey. I can't talk right now. Tom's been attacked. Can I call you in the morning? Hello? Kate?" The psychic looked at the phone screen, checking the service. Full bars. She held it up again. "Are you there?" A burst of static erupted from the earpiece, and she winced. When the noise cleared, she put the call on speaker.

"Oh, my gosh! Is he badly hurt? Will he be okay?"

"I hope so. They're looking after him now. We're waiting for an ambulance, but the roads ... Kate? Where are you? It sounds like you're in a tunnel or something." Taking the phone off speaker, she held it to her ear again, listening. "Okay. Be careful out there and text me when you get home. What? I can't hear you. Call me tomorrow when the storm is over." She disconnected, staring at the fire in thought.

"Everything okay with your friend?" Danny cocked his head, eyebrows raised.

"Yeah, she was at a party in town that ended early because of the weather. She was walking home, and her phone kept dropping out."

"She's in town? Huh. The coverage there is usually good. There must be a lot of ice on the towers. We're out here in the middle of nowhere, and I have full bars. Well, except down on the bridle trail." Eyebrows knitting together, his steel-blue eyes darkened with doubt.

"Are you always this suspicious of people?" She narrowed her eyes.

"After the day I've had, yes. I suspect everybody," he said, stalking off to check on his partner.

Chapter Nineteen

11:10 PM

Marnie ducked her head into the downstairs bedroom. Tom had regained consciousness, but the huge gash on his temple, ashen skin, and glassy eyes told her he was not okay. He lay on the bed in wet clothes, arguing with Rick, who was urging him to get into something dry and warm.

He sat up, wobbling with dizziness. Shutting his eyes, he rested his forehead in his palm. "I'm fine. Besides, I have nothing else to put on."

"You can't sit there like that. You're in shock. Wrap a warm blanket around yourself until the ambulance gets here." Rick opened the cedar chest at the foot of the bed, pawed through it, and tossed a quilt at the patient.

Danny grabbed the top doorjamb and leaned into the room. "Listen to the doctor."

Marnie huffed out a breath, pushed her way in, and opened the closet to reveal a rack, shelves, and drawers full of clothes. She pulled out a pair of jeans, socks, a T-shirt, and a sweater. She threw them onto the bed next to her injured friend.

"You'll have to go commando, but you can change into these. Stop arguing. I'm going to the kitchen to get you a hot drink."

With a childish pout, he scowled at the clothes. "I am not wearing women's stuff."

"Hop to it, Thomas Michael Keller. Those are my father's—not mine. Stop being a baby, or I'll have to find you a binky. Move it!" she ordered, shooting him a stern glare, before stomping out the door, and hovering in the hallway, listening.

The men burst out laughing.

Tom's bottom lip made another appearance, and he gave his colleagues a blank stare. "What's her problem?"

His partner shrugged. "She has a point, but I don't know where she'd find a pacifier on a night like this. I suggest you do as you're told, or Ms. Reilly will come back in here and yell at you again."

Rick snickered, and Danny turned to the door, only to see the psychic glowering. Face devoid of humor, he pivoted to Tom.

"C'mon, man. Get changed," he said, handing him the T-shirt before looking back at Marnie, who nodded her approval and sauntered off with a satisfied smirk.

Once she was gone, the detective asked, "Did you see who hit you?"

"Nah," he said, pulling off his one wet boot and soggy socks. "Where's my other shoe? Jesus!" he whined.

"It's in an evidence bag. Someone tried to drag you into the forest. Your boot was lying on the bridle trail. Forget about it. What did you see?" Danny studied his partner's drawn face, who was now pulling off his shirt, revealing red welts on his back.

"Shit! You got hit with a stun gun."

"What the hell?" said Tom, twisting to see his back in the mirror on the closet door. "Holy crap! Rick, were these on Wilder, too?"

The doctor examined a series of small, paired circular reddish spots resembling burns on the patient's neck and back. "Don't know. I haven't read the autopsy report. I got called out again when we delivered the body to the morgue. It's been a busy day, guys. I doubt they have even gotten to Wilder. We've got a backlog from that fatal freeway accident yesterday. Give me a sec," he said, stepping into the hall with his phone.

"What *can* you tell me?" asked Danny, leaning against the wall.

Reply muffled as he pulled the shirt over his head, he said, "Someone said my name; I turned around to see who it was, and then I'm on the ground—I can't move and my head's spinning. I'm lying there—sleet's hitting me in the face, and someone whacks me on the head. BAM! Lights out."

"Okay. The voice. What did it sound like?"

"Hoarse. It was a husky, croaky whisper. That's all I've got." He held up his hands, a look of defeat clouding his face.

"Hmm." The detective dragged out the word, giving himself a moment to think. "Was it a man or a woman?"

"Dear God, I hope it was a dude, or I will never hear the end of it!" He grimaced and tugged at the jeans, trying to get comfortable before easing up the zipper. Commando wasn't for him—too dangerous.

"Let's get you that hot drink. Are you okay to walk out to the kitchen, or should I bring it here so you can rest?"

Tom wrestled himself into the sweater, shaking his head. "Nope. I'm good. But don't let me faint when we walk out there, huh? I've been embarrassed enough for one day." He managed a frail smile and took a step forward on his stockinged feet.

Thinking about the body bag, Danny decided now was not the time to agitate. There had been enough humiliation for one day.

"No problem, buddy. I've got your back, and speaking of that, why did you go out there without backup?"

Giving his partner a dirty look and a headshake, he replied, "Because I was trying to get away from Madame Séance and Detective Stick-up-his-butt. You two have a thing goin' on, and that's obvious to everyone. Pull your head out of your ass, and do something about it, or don't. Whatever." He walked away, muttering something indiscernible.

"She called me that?

"Yeah, and she's got a point."

Danny halted, grabbing his partner's shoulder. "Wow! Why would she say that?"

Shaking off the hand gripping his shirt, Tom replied, "One minute it's Ms. Reilly. Next, it's Marnie. Then you're back to Ms. Reilly again. Geez! Make up your mind," he griped, rolling his eyes and stomping away.

"Huh," he said, shrugging off the comment, and turning to the doctor, who appeared to have finished his call to autopsy.

Rick stuck his phone in his pocket and nodded. "Yeah. Same spots are on Wilder's neck and back."

The detective groaned, running a hand through his hair. "Geez!"

The forensics doctor and the detective located Tom seated at the kitchen table with Tater's chin resting in his lap, the canine getting an ear scratch.

Danny nudged him and said, "The marks on your back are like welts found on Wilder, and they're probably from a stun gun."

Tom clenched his jaw in response.

Marnie stirred a pot on the stove, listening, but pretending she wasn't. "I took chicken soup out of the freezer. It'll be ready soon."

Tony and Jalnack milled by the island, enjoying the aroma wafting from the copper kettle.

"Stun gun or Taser?" asked Jalnack, doing some stirring of his own, knowing Rick hated when they confused the two.

The doctor side-eyed the cop but didn't bite. Instead, he complimented the cook. "That soup smells terrific."

"Five minutes and we'll see if it tastes that way," she said.

A raging gust of wind whirled around the house, whistling through the eaves, rattling the casement windows, and clattering debris and freezing rain against the panes. A deep, resonate rumble thrummed in the distance, and Tater perked up his ears, letting out a growl, followed by two quick barks. The lights flickered twice, and the counselor's home plunged into darkness. Only the flame of the burner and the fire in the living room lit downstairs.

"I'll get the candles," called Carl from his comfy chair by the hearth.

The dog whimpered, grumbled, and growled, poking his head out from under the table.

"Shhh, boy!" said Tom, grabbing his collar and pulling the dog closer.

"Dammit!" Marnie clanged the pot against the counter as she moved it off the fire and turned the flame up so she could see. "The generator may need that new battery after all. Detective, can you please help me again?"

The Border Collie's bark softened to a mumble, but his amber eyes were like saucers and his head pivoted from the rain-streaked windows to his mistress.

"Yeah ... sure ... got a flashlight handy?"

"Yup. There's one here in the drawer."

The canine squirmed free and bolted to the back door, standing on his hind legs, stretching his body to see out the glass. His bark frantic and the snarl on his muzzle, vicious.

Crossing the room and gathering the dog into his arms, Tom did his best to settle him. "Calm down, Tot. Shush!" The dog's scruff bristled, and he grumbled, jerking his back end to escape.

"Tater, stop!" Marnie stepped around the island with a flashlight. "It's only the wind, buddy. Everything is okay."

The psychic and detective descended the cellar stairs again and hurried to the generator.

"Brrr ... it's cold down here," she said with a shiver. "Let's check it first and see if it shut itself off."

With the flick of the switch, the machine whirred to life.

"Thank God for small favors." She did a little dance and clapped her hands together.

"Mhmm. What I'd like to know is *how* it switched itself off."

"It resets if overloaded."

"Hmm. Okay."

Puzzled by the detective's response, Marnie followed his gaze and let out a gasp. The hatchway door stood open. She looked at Danny, eyebrows raised. He put a finger to his lips, pulled his gun out of his shoulder holster and crept toward the opening, glancing left, then right. Marnie trailed inches behind him, her hand on his back.

They reached the top step and looked out into the yard, but nobody was there. The detective back-tracked, grasping Marnie's hand along the way. She jerked free and started back up the stairs.

"Where are you going?" he hissed.

"To close the door."

"No," he said, his eyes locking on hers. "How many rooms are there down here?"

"Three—not counting this space." She pointed in the general direction of the closed doors. "The wood room, cold storage, and my dad's workshop. Why?"

"That door was shut earlier. Now it's open. Where did they go?" he asked, cocking his head.

"Where did who go?" She wrinkled her nose, then her eyes widened when she understood his question. Hand covering her mouth, she glanced sideways. "Leave it open in case we have to run?"

"Yeah," he whispered, grabbing her hand again, and pulling her back into the main room.

He nudged her. "Go upstairs and get backup."

"No way. I'm not leaving you alone. Look what happened to Tom." She took her phone from her pajama pocket, checked there were bars, typed SOS and sent the message to her injured friend. It worked. Seconds later, they heard chairs scrape across the floor, followed by a rush of footsteps stomping toward the cellar door. Jalnack and Tony clambered down the stairs, their guns at the ready.

Danny pushed her forward. "Go upstairs. Now!" he barked, fixing her with a steel-blue glower.

Without a word, she tore up the steps, bumping into Tom and Tater at the top.

He peered over her shoulder. "What's going on down there? What's with the SOS?"

She hustled him away from the door, catching her breath and pushing her heart back into her chest. "The hatch was open. It wasn't when we turned on the generator earlier, but it is now. They're checking it out."

"I'm going down," he said, trying to weasel past her.

"No, you're coming to the kitchen with me, and you are going to have some soup. You look like you're going to fall over."

"I need to help," he said, grabbing her shoulders and moving her aside.

She crooked an arm through his and wrenched him back. "Well, how about if you and Tater go to my office and watch the security footage? No one has checked that yet. We might see whoever has been roaming around my house tonight, wreaking havoc on all and sundry. Please. Then I'll bring you something to eat."

Defeated by her logic, he allowed her to lead him to a tidy workspace filled with a desk, an office chair, bookshelves, a file cabinet, and a printer sitting atop a credenza. The loveseat opposite the workstation was littered with tattered tennis balls, a chewed stick, and a stuffed sheep. An old, distressed leather satchel rested on a side chair to the left of the door. Through the bay window, they could see the outline of an old oak tree bowing to the storm.

"Pfft! Your computer's at the station. How are we going to see anything?" said Tom, pointing at the empty desk.

"Well, my laptop is in my briefcase, and if you remember, some bright spark of a detective advised me to add a backup. The same guy, I might add, didn't take his own advice when he wandered into the forest tonight *alone*."

Eyebrows up, he nodded. "Point taken. Is the password still the same?"

"It is. Sit. Watch and rest." She handed him her briefcase and left to attend to the abandoned homemade soup.

Halfway to the kitchen, a shot rang out, and she wheeled around, rushing to the cellar, and colliding with Tom.

"I'll yell if you're needed," she said, yanking open the door and clambering down the steps two at a time. She hit the bottom in time to see a figure run up the hatchway, with Danny and Tony in pursuit.

"Oh, my gosh! Where's Jalnack!" she cried.

The firewood room was on her left, and she rushed through the door to find it empty. She moved on to the cold storage, where she found the cop leaning against the wall, holding his right arm, blood seeping through his jacket. She turned in a circle, looking for anything that would stop the bleeding, and snatched an old towel hanging from a peg, hurrying to Jalnack's side. Face pale, he cringed with pain before slipping down the stone wall, his backside settling on an upturned potato crate.

"It's okay. I'll tie this around your arm and go get Rick? What's your first name?" she asked, doing her best to comfort the wounded policeman.

"Sam."

His croaky reply caught Marnie off guard, and she stared into his face.

"That's my brother's name," she said, tying off the terry cloth. "How's that? Too tight?"

He nodded.

"Good." She patted his hand. "That's how it's supposed to be. I'll be back in a sec."

Scurrying into the kitchen, Marnie yelled, "Rick!"

Coffee cup halfway to his lips, he glanced up, a wrinkle between his brows.

"Please help! Jalnack's been shot. He's in the cellar."

The doctor slammed down the mug, sloshing coffee across the counter, and retrieved his medical bag from the kitchen table.

"I heard a bang but thought it was a limb breaking." He hurried to the basement with the psychic on his heels.

Tom met them in the hallway, but his friend pushed him back into the office. "Please check the footage. Find out who's doing this!"

They flew down the stairs, and she nudged the doctor toward the cold room.

With all the calm he could muster, Rick entered and said, "Sam, my man, what's happening? The lady tells me you got yourself shot."

Jalnack gave a feeble smile as the doctor sank to his knees beside him.

Once Marnie knew the cop was in good hands, she dashed through the hatch and peered out into the frozen yard.

Danny shouted in the distance, with Tony shouting in reply. Another shot rang out, and she heard the detective yell again—a distinctive "fuck" followed by "son of a bitch." She held her breath, waiting for a reply. A moment later, the officer's voice echoed. "Gregg! Over here!" She exhaled and went back inside.

Rick and one of his crew were helping Jalnack get up the cellar stairs. Concerned for everyone's safety, she shut and locked the hatch. With a cautious glance around the open space, she turned and jogged upstairs, where she found Tom leaning against the office door, waiting for her.

"Marn, you need to see this."

Chapter Twenty

11:48 PM

Marnie carried a steaming bowl into her office, handing it to Tom. "Eat the dang soup!"

His bottom jaw jutted out, and he accepted it with a grumble. "Argh. I don't feel like it. My head's swimmy and my stomach's churning." Sniffing the contents, he scrunched his face, puffing out his cheeks. With a convulsive gag, he handed back the bowl. "Oof. I'm gonna hurl on your desk." He closed his eyes and breathed through his mouth, his Adam's apple bobbing for air.

She wrinkled her nose at the prospect of half-digested pot roast and pie on her keyboard and took it back, setting it on the corner of her desk. "Fine! How about a mug of broth?"

Shaking his head, he blew out his cheeks. "Ugh. No."

She side-eyed him, knowing the point was moot. He was as stubborn as she was.

Danny and Tony appeared in the doorway, both winded and soaked through.

"You two got anything?" Teeth chattering, the detective ran his fingers through his hair, water dripping down his arm into a puddle at his feet.

The psychic gasped at the sight of them. "Goodness! You're drenched! I'm sure there are more things in Dad's closet. C'mon! You know the way!"

"Tell me you've got something, and I'll get into dry clothes, but if you've got nothing, I'm heading back out there." He clenched his jaw and hooked his thumb toward the door.

"We've got something. Now, go." She shooed him toward the hall.

Grinding his teeth, his steely blue eyes turned to ice. "You know what, Ms. Reilly, Marnie, whatever the hell your name is. I'm heading of this investigation until someone above me tells me I'm not. Show me what you've got."

Squaring her shoulders, she climbed up on her chair and looked down at him. "I'm above you, Detective. Go change. Then you can see. Tom's a detective, too. He's managing the footage, and I'm in charge of the health of everyone under my roof. Go. Change. Now!" She stepped off her chair, pushed the men out, and down the hall to the spare room.

Sliding open the closet, she took out socks, jeans, and shirts, tossing them on the bed. Tony was smaller than the detectives, but the well-worn clothes would do. Danny frowned, holding up the pants.

"How tall was your father?" he asked, assessing the length against his own long legs.

"Six-foot-five and a bit. Those will do—at least they're dry. They might be loose in the waist, but they'll fit."

His phone rang. "Hey, Cap, you got my message?" He listened. After a long pause, he grimaced. "Shit. That's not good. We've got another officer down. Jalnack got shot in the shoulder. He's doin' okay. The bullet went straight through, so that's good. Tom seems better, but he looks like shit." He listened again. "Yeah, okay. There's nothin' we can do until it's cleared. Keep me posted, will ya? Thanks, Cap. I'll check back soon." He disconnected.

Face pinched, he chucked the garment onto the quilted duvet. "This is fucking wonderful. There are trees down on the highway. The ambulance can't get through, and we're not goin' anywhere. There's nothing they can do at this point. We're gonna have to go get the Hudson Hollow boys and bring them back here. They've been out there a long time."

Marnie suggested, "The forensics guys are warm and dry. Can't they go get them? That way, you and Tony can warm up."

Setting his jaw, he growled, "No, Miss Fix-it, they can't. Those men are my responsibility. I'll pick them up and then change."

She bit her bottom lip and shrugged. "Suit yourself. Go out there and catch your death of foolishness."

Hearing words from his childhood, he shot her a sideways glance. "What? Not your words, I'm assuming?" he asked, dragging knuckles across his stubbled chin.

"Well, you won't listen to me," she said. Tossing her hair, she leaned closer and whispered, "But maybe you'll listen to your mother." With a smug smile, she sashayed down the hall.

With shoulders drooping, he followed her to the kitchen, and Tony tagged along, shaking his head. As the trio trooped through the living room, they passed Carl and Tater, who were snuggled up together on the couch. The healer was snoring, and the canine opened one eye as they breezed by.

Entering the dining room, Danny asked, "Rick, can your guys go up the road and get the Hudson crew? There's a tree blocking us in, so we're stuck for the night." He ignored the smirk on Marnie's face. "Kriss is guarding the front and Weaver's out back. I need them to stay in place."

The doctor set down a coffee mug, rubbed a deep line on his forehead with his fingertips and heaved a sigh. "Yeah, no problem. We'll get the Hudson guys. It's worrisome, though. Jalnack's not doing so well."

Color drained from the detective's face, and his eyes darted between the back and front of the house. "Kriss is out front, right?" Racing to the door, he yanked it open.

The officer turned and nodded to him. "What's up?"

"Get in here!" the detective ordered, gripping the cop's sleeve, dragging him inside.

The policeman kicked snow and ice off his boots. "What's goin' on?"

Not answering, Danny stalked through the house. "Where's Weaver? He should have been in the yard when Tony and I ran up from the cellar. I don't remember seeing him. Where the hell is he?!"

Storming through the kitchen, he crossed to the door and peered out through the glass. Weaver was sitting on the back stoop, leaning against the railing. *Why is he sitting on the frozen steps?* thought the detective.

With a pang of dread, Danny pulled open the back door, and Tater made a run for it, bumping the cop as he bounded down the steps into the yard. Watching in horror as the policeman toppled, the detective inched forward, adrenaline raging. Weaver stared up at him, pupils enlarged, his severed throat wrapped in piano wire, and a pool of blood soaked the cedar decking around his corpse.

The canine raced to the fence line, barking with a ferocity Marnie had never heard. She stepped onto the porch, but Danny shoved her back inside and hauled the door shut with a bang, hurrying down the steps, shouting at the frenetic dog.

"Tater! Here! Now!"

The Border Collie skidded to a halt, dropped his ears, tucked his tail, and crept on his belly to the detective. Kneeling, he patted the dog's head, scratched him under the chin, and shook his paw. "You tried to tell us, didn't you, pal? You knew someone was out here. We'll listen to you next time." He stood up and peered out into the trees. A branch groaned, cracked and crashed to the ground.

"Dammit," he muttered, pivoting to the back porch where the forensics team huddled around the dead officer's body.

Danny stooped, gathered the wet dog into his arms, and walked up the back steps, weaving a path through the forensics team. He carried Tater into the kitchen so that he wouldn't further damage the crime scene and set the pup down.

With a hand covering her mouth, Marnie met his gaze, and he retreated a step. He'd never seen a woman consumed with this much anger. He thought that he'd seen it all. But with a second look, her aquamarine eyes gave her away—the reason for the fury. Just one glimpse revealed a beautiful soul who had suffered the loss of family and battled an abuser. This woman championed the mistreated, exposed impostors, adored animals, and loved with her whole heart.

The psychic dropped her eyes to her dog, sensing the detective was more like her than he would ever admit. *Stop it. He's a cop. Of course he can read people. But the way he was looking at me ... Hmm...*

Carl nudged the detective and gave a chin nod toward the psychic. "Uh-oh! She's pissed off. When she gets that look, it is game on. Second time I've seen it today. Glad it's not directed at me."

"You might see things clearer if you look closer," Danny snapped. Moving to Marnie's side, he said. "Hey, I'm sorry I yelled at Tater. I know it wasn't my place, but I didn't know if he could get out of the yard." He patted her shoulder, searching for forgiveness.

She shook off his hand. "I'm not upset about that. It's all the death … around me … my home… I don't understand how any of it connects. Why is this happening?" She searched the detective's face for an answer.

"I don't know. We're going to figure it out. But I need dry clothes. Then I'll be able to think straight. Now that the adrenaline has worn off, my teeth are chattering. We're here for the night, so can I use a shower? I think it's the only thing that will defrost my toes."

Marnie nodded. "Of course."

On his way to the bathroom, the detective stopped short to issue a warning. "Everyone stays in the house. No one goes outside without a partner, and if you must, watch your backs. I'm going to get changed. We need to pick up the Hudson crew. Kriss, you and Tony go as soon as he's changed."

Tom heard footsteps and poked his head out of the office as Danny stepped into the hall. "Are you coming in to look at this video?"

He stopped, considering the question. "Yeah. Let me change my clothes. I'm freezing."

"I'm sure Ms. Reilly can help with that," said his partner, adding a wolf whistle, and waggling his eyebrows.

"Weaver is dead! Focus on finding out who did it!" growled the detective.

The counselor appeared from around the corner, lips straight—eyebrows raised.

Tom winced, lifting a hand to his neck. "Sorry. I didn't mean any disrespect. I'm crap at dealing with shit like that." He stepped back into the office and sank into the chair, hitting play on the video. He paused a frame, sat up, and cocked his head. "Who the hell are you?"

Dry clothes in hand, Danny scowled at the closed bathroom door and the sound of running water.

"Tony must be in there. I'll wait for him to finish," he said, letting out a long breath.

"C'mon. You can use the bathroom upstairs. I've got heaps of hot water," Marnie offered, starting down the hallway, before turning back and seeing hesitancy on the detective's face. Taking another step forward, she waited for him, and with reluctance, he joined her.

"Don't worry. Ken's gone, and I'll stay on the lookout for things that go bump in the night." She winked and headed up the stairs.

He blew out a breath and followed her, his thoughts taunting him. *Spooks don't concern me, Ms. Reilly. Being alone with you does. God help me. You're a distraction.*

Chapter Twenty-One

November 18th

12:38 AM, Marnie's House

Tom's head thumped with pain as he watched the surveillance feed, trying to process the night's events. A missing piece of the puzzle nagged, but he found it difficult to recall specific details, so he took a pad of paper and a pencil out of the desk.

A timeline of everything I can recall might help, he thought. I remember being at the station and leaving to meet up with Danny at the Wilder house. And the guy at the gate telling us Mrs. Wilder is out of town, and nobody knows where she is.

He jotted bullet points of each recollection. The drive to the Reilly residence. The dinner that followed, and the questioning of Carl. Danny and Marnie's weird flirting. He struggled to write the memory of Webb's corpse, his nausea returning in a pulsing wave. His best friend's scream echoing through the valley, and her revelation about his partner's late mother and wife. He snorted as he wrote Madame Seance and Detective Stick-up-his-butt arguing, and thought, *get a room.* The last recollection was standing on the bridle trail, hearing someone call his name, and pulling his gun out of its holster. Pausing, he looked at the page and went white. Bingo!

He rested his head in his hands. "Shit! Where's my sidearm? It's not in evidence. They would have handed it back. Dammit!*"*

Leaping from his chair, he marched to the kitchen, where he found Rick Price at the table, drinking a mug of coffee, writing notes. The doctor frowned as the detective stumbled through the doorway and grabbed the back of a chair to steady himself.

Studying Tom over his glasses, he said, "What's up? You look green. Your head must be pounding up a storm. Pun intended. I've got some acetaminophen in my kit if you need it."

Mouth open, Tom stared at him for a second. "What? Oh, yeah, I could use something to kill this pain. Thanks." Scratching his five o'clock shadow, he gathered his thoughts. "Have you got my pistol? I know you've got my boot."

The doctor jerked up, tossing down his pen. "No. Shit! It wasn't at the scene. Danny's gonna lose it when we tell him."

"Yeah. I was thinkin' about Jalnack getting shot 'cause it's a different M.O. I mean, Wilder and the piano wire. Webb and Weaver too. Jalnack and a bullet didn't quite click, but now, it's making sense. He got shot with *my* weapon!" He sank into the chair, face drawn.

The doctor did his best to bolster the cop. "We gotta tell Danny. He'll be back in a few. Don't worry, man. It's not your fault. You got stunned *and* knocked out. It could have happened to anybody."

"No. It *shouldn't* have happened. I was out there without backup. I am *so* screwed. Can you get me those painkillers? My headache just kicked up a notch," he said, rocking his head in his palms and groaning.

●

Upstairs, Marnie veered left, and Danny turned right, and she stopped to see if he was following her.

"Where are you going?"

He pointed to the bathroom, walked in, and turned on the light. "Oops! Just a bathtub. I thought you had another shower!"

"I do. In my ensuite. This way," she said, disappearing around a corner.

He followed her down the hall and found her by a fireplace, adding pinecones to glowing embers. They snapped and sizzled and sparked to life.

"Let me get it going again," he said, setting the clothes on the bed, before moving the screen and adding two logs to the grate.

"Thank you. I love a fire at night. It makes me feel snug as the proverbial bug," she said, rubbing her hands together, chasing away the chill slithering around her.

Turning around, he admired the room. Neither feminine nor masculine—its muted green curtains and duvet cover, timber floors, and oak furnishings oozed warmth. Against the back wall stood a queen-size sleigh bed with hand-carved acorns and oak leaves etched into the headboard and the foot. A highboy, dressing table, chiffonier, and cedar chest all sported similar designs. The hearth was book-ended by an old rocker and a chintz-covered club chair. Beyond the open curtains, wind-lashed tree limbs reached out, tapping at the panes, causing a shiver to race up his back. He shuddered, happy to be inside.

"The dressers and bed are your father's handiwork, I assume?"

"Yup. He was a brilliant craftsman and made most of the furniture in the house."

"Hmm … where's the ensuite?" he asked, looking uncomfortable standing in her bedroom.

"Oh. Sorry. Through here." She crossed the room, nudged open a door, and flicked on the light.

His jaw dropped when he entered. This was the biggest bathroom he had ever seen outside of a swanky hotel. Her shower was large enough to accommodate five people, and with water spigots at several levels, it offered a full-body water massage. The upper half had clear glass, while the lower half was frosted for privacy. He eyed a soaking tub big enough for two *tall* people. Scolding himself for allowing his mind to wander, he turned his attention to the marble-top vanity with its two basins and loads of counter space. Oak cabinets sat under the sinks, and another sat between the tub and shower. The tiling was simple—cream with little mahogany diamond accents.

Marnie stuck her head in the door and hit two more switches. "Overhead heat lamps and under-floor heating. You'll be warm in no time." She backed out and returned to the fireplace.

"Is there a trick to the shower?" he called out.

"Nope. Turn on the taps and you are good to go. Towels are in the tall cupboard."

"Okay. Thanks. I'll be right out, then it's all yours. You must be cold too. You're still wearing your pajamas. Aren't they wet?"

"Nope. I'm okay," she said, dropping into the club chair.

Shutting the door, he discarded his wet clothes and found a lush, fluffy towel in the cupboard. He turned on the faucet and stepped inside, allowing the water to pound his back, easing the tension of the day.

Concerned he would come out of the bathroom smelling like the hostess, he sniffed a selection of shower gels, choosing one smelling of lime and ginger. Another smelled like Marnie—fresh linen and grapefruit, and he wrinkled his nose at the third—heavy and floral. He couldn't imagine her using it. The scent didn't suit her. She wasn't flowery. She was...

"Lord, what is wrong with me?" he said, hanging his head. "Stop thinking about her."

Settled by the fire with Tater at her feet, Marnie began reading an old mystery novel about a group of people isolated on an island with a killer on the loose. Thinking it best not to fill her head with more gore and death, she set the book aside on the arm of the chair.

The bathroom door clicked, and the detective appeared with a towel around his waist, a cloud of steam following him.

Caught by surprise, his cheeks reddened. "Oh. You're not downstairs. Uh ... I forgot the clothes," he said, crossing to the bed, scooping up the garments and making an awkward retreat.

"I told you I would protect you from ghosts," she called after him, a giggle bubbling to the surface.

Head against the back of the chair, she muttered, "Did you see that, buddy? Detective Stick-up-his-butt works out. How is this fair? He's in there, draped in nothing but a towel, and my home is a crime scene. Just my luck." Eyes to the ceiling, she added, "Are you punishing me for something, or being a funny guy?"

Tater sneezed, startling her, and she laughed, scratched his ears and returned to her book.

When Danny re-emerged, he was dressed in jeans, a long-sleeved navy-blue Henley shirt, and a pair of white socks. Nose in her novel,

Marnie pretended not to watch him as he pulled on his shoulder holster, put his gun in place and combed his wet hair with his fingers. He returned to the bathroom and came out with a pile of wet clothes.

"Detective, you can toss those in the wash, if you'd like. We can throw Tom and Tony's in, too. The laundry room is on the left at the end of the hall."

"Yeah. Thanks. That's a good idea. I'll run down and check with the guys."

When she heard his feet on the stairs, she put down the paperback and took her robe off the peg on the door. Entering the bathroom, she discovered Danny's tiger on the vanity with his wallet, keys, loose change, and his badge, and his wet boots were on the floor. She carried all his things to the highboy, and on a second trip, she deposited his boots by the fire and returned to have her shower.

Fifteen minutes later, she opened the door to find the detective adding a log to the grate and chatting to her dog. Wearing a white terry bathrobe and a towel wrapped around her head, the psychic's face shone pink from steam and her toenails sparkled bright red. The crimson nail polish was unexpected, and he grinned.

"What?" she asked, looking at herself in the mirror over the dresser, feeling self-conscious.

"Nothing. You surprise me sometimes."

"I don't get it." She shrugged and shook her hair free of the towel, moved to the highboy and opened a drawer.

"It's nothing. I came back to get my things and to throw the clothes in the wash. We'll have to remember to put them in the dryer."

"I'll do my best to remind you."

She got pajama bottoms and another T-shirt out of the dresser and tossed them on the bed. She turned, with fists on her hips.

"Well, Detective, are you going to stand there watching me, or will you be a gentleman and turn around?"

"Oh, geez. Sorry. I'm going. So sorry!" Flustered, he left, shutting the door.

Wrinkling his brow, he mumbled, "Wait ... why am I embarrassed?" With a sigh, he leaned against the door, only to find it hadn't latched, and he fell backward into the room.

"So, you *are* going to watch," said Marnie, roaring with laughter.

Tater hopped up, waving his tail, a smile on his black and white face. His mistress pulled her robe tight, and scurried to help, but the detective jumped up, red-faced, and stalked out, slamming the door. At the sound of his feet galloping down the stairs, she burst into a fit of giggles, which made the dog woof and wag his hind end.

1:20 AM

Tater followed his mistress downstairs and curled up in a dog bed next to the hearth, covering his nose with his tail.

Carl dozed in a chair beside the fire, his pipe slipping from his hand. Marnie took it and placed it on a tray on the mantel. She grabbed a blanket from the back of the couch and laid it over him, tucking it over his socked feet. The healer stirred, smiled in his sleep, and pulled the blanket up to his chin.

The psychic backtracked and peeked in on Jalnack, who rested in the spare room with Officer Kriss watching over him.

"Do you need anything?" she asked.

"No, thanks. We're fine," replied the cop.

"Okay. Let me know if you do," she said, turning away and leaving the door ajar.

Following voices to the kitchen, she found Danny, Tom, Rick, and his team of three, Tony, and two officers whom she hadn't met yet were at the table drinking coffee. Their attention turned to her when she entered the room and went to the cupboard and pulled out a can of cocoa.

"Would anyone like some?" she asked, waving the container of hot chocolate.

Everyone declined except Danny. She eavesdropped as she warmed up milk, hearing small bits and pieces of their conversation. From the specks of information she gathered, she concluded that whoever had whacked Tom had also taken his gun, and it might have been used to shoot Jalnack. Stomach in knots, she knew she was picking up on her friend's anxiety. So, she chased away the doom and gloom with a dollop of whipped cream on the steaming chocolate.

The psychic set down a mug on the table in front of the detective, and he said, "Thank you" and put an arm around her waist, as if it was the most natural thing to do. The corner of her mouth quirked up, and he yanked his arm away, realizing what he had done. Tom and Rick shot her a look. She responded with a shrug, disappeared behind the counter, and opened the refrigerator.

Calling out, she asked, "Can I get anyone something to eat?"

"What's on the menu, Marn?" asked her friend, craning his neck and peering over the island.

"Soup, stuff to make sandwiches, pie, ice cream, fruit, leftover pot roast, bacon, and eggs. Uh ... cheese and crackers. What do you feel like?"

"Something to stop this headache would be good. You don't have a potion, do you?"

"Not for the headache you've got. If it was tension, I could help. What about the pain medication they gave me when I sprained my knee? I never used it. I'll get it, and Rick can check it out for you." She opened a cupboard, pulled out a bottle, and handed it to the doctor.

Rick inspected the label. "If you aren't allergic to acetaminophen or codeine, this is fine."

"Give me." Tom waggled a hand across the table.

Marnie brought him water, and asked, "How about some food? You don't want that on an empty stomach and coffee."

"A sandwich sounds great. Whatever you make is fine," he said.

She made a big platter of sandwiches and placed it and a plate of cookies at the center of the table.

"It's after one and I am exhausted. Make yourselves at home. There's another spare room down here next to my office, and there are three upstairs. Sheets and extra blankets are in the linen press in the upstairs hallway, too. I will see you gents in the morning. Shout if you need anything."

A chorus of "goodnight, Marnie" filled the room as she left them. Passing through the living room, she added wood to the fire, laughed at Carl snoring away in his recliner and peeked in on Kriss and Jalnack one more time. Kriss was asleep in the chair, and Jalnack was awake.

"Can I get you anything? Water maybe?" she asked.

He nodded, and she returned to the kitchen.

"The patient requested water," she said, filling a glass at the sink. "Rick, could you please check on him? He looks uncomfortable."

"Yeah, sure. I'll come with you. Can I give him these?" The doctor held up the prescription bottle.

"Of course. There's Valium and antibiotics in the cupboard, too. They might be out of date, though." She headed back to the stairs.

"Excellent. I'll give him some painkillers and antibiotics. That will help in the short term." Rick pulled back a sidelight curtain and peeked out. "The sleet is still coming down. It looks like Superman's palace out there."

She peered over his shoulder and out the window. The thunder and lightning had stopped, but freezing rain still fell. The ice accumulation, while dangerous, painted an eerie and beautiful picture, and she walked away, hoping the danger stayed outside.

Chapter Twenty-Two

1:32 AM, Marnie's House

With Tater on her heels, Marnie climbed the stairs, keeping watch for unwelcome visitors. Prickles raced across the top of her head, and she dashed to her room, slamming the door. The psychic was aware the solid oak wouldn't keep out spirits, but the forceful bang comforted her inner control freak.

Embers glowed in the grate, and she tossed in three pinecones to get the fire going again. *Sizzle. Snap. Spark.* She added two seasoned logs and stood back, waiting for them to catch. Trembling, she pivoted to the cedar-lined chest at the foot of the bed, opened it and took out a worn, wool navy-blue cardigan.

"Hello, old friend," she said, draping it around her shoulders.

The chill running through her was as much from the tragedies of the past few hours as from the relentless crackling of the ice-laden trees outside her window. Flinging back the covers, she climbed into bed and turned off the light, with her dog snuggling up on the rug next to her.

"Night, buddy," she said, resting a hand on the Border Collie. She drifted off to sleep, wrapped in her father's favorite sweater and with her loyal friend by her side.

2:58 AM

Tossing and turning—her sleep was haunted by memories of the day, her tragic past, and unsettling premonitions. She struggled in her slumber, calling out to Kate before she was startled awake.

"Marn. You're talking in your sleep. Wake up!" said Tom, shaking her shoulder.

Bolting upright, her eyes darted around the room. "Where's Kate? What's wrong? Did she call again?"

Tater sat on the bed next to her, peering into her face. With his snout, he nudged her under the chin before giving her nose a lick.

With one knee on the mattress, Tom said, "You were shouting. We could hear you all the way downstairs." Rubbing her shoulder, he sat and wrapped an arm around her.

Jerking away, she threw off the covers. "Something's wrong. Has she called again?"

"Hey, it's fine. It was a dream. Do you want water or something stronger?" he asked, squeezing her arm.

"No, I don't want a drink!" she said, shrugging off his comfort. "I want to speak with Kate! Something is wrong. She's in trouble. I need to call her." She pushed away her friend and swung her feet to the floor, finding her way to her dresser where her cell sat in its charger.

"It's three in the morning. You'll wake her up. C'mon. Think it through," said Tom, switching on a bedside lamp.

Danny appeared in the doorway as the psychic searched through recent calls, and crossed the room in two giant steps, snatching the device out of her hand.

"Give that back!" she said, grabbing at air.

He held it behind his back, his eyes meeting her glare. With a sigh, her tense shoulders dropped in surrender.

"Marnie, you were dreaming. Take a breath. Tell us what you *think* has happened. C'mon, sit by the fire and talk to us." Hand under her elbow, the detective led her to the rocking chair.

Inhaling, she closed her eyes, searching for her center. Exhaling, she settled onto the wooden seat. "It was a vision. I know when something bad happens. I can feel it. Kate is not okay." Her voice trailed off, and she stared into the fire.

Tom sat on the cedar chest, and Tater lay down—his head in his lap. "A lot of shit's gone down today. I'm not surprised you had a bad dream."

Danny took the club chair opposite the psychic, leaning forward, elbows on knees. "He's right. Wilder's death brought up the past. Add Webb, Weaver, Tom getting whacked, and then Jalnack's shooting … I think we're all gonna have nightmares for a while. Be rational and…" Cut off by the shrill ring of the phone still in his palm and he stared at it.

Marnie reached out to take it from him, but he answered it before she could get it.

"Hello?" He listened. "Yeah, she's right here," he said, handing over the device. "I think it's Kate."

"Hi. Is everything okay?" Voice shaky, her eyes filled with tears as she listened. She stood and paced—her arm wrapped around her waist. "I can't get there tonight. The roads are closed, and there's a tree down. I'll be with you as soon as I can. I am so sorry." She pressed the phone tighter to her ear and looked at the ceiling, trying to prevent tears from spilling down her cheeks. "Okay. I'll be there tomorrow. I promise. Be safe."

Tater hopped off his perch, pawed her leg, and gave her knee a nose bump. She set her phone on the mantel before crossing to a window and peeking outside.

"C'mon, boy. I'll take you for a wander," she said, stooping to rub his ears, planting a kiss on his head. "Lovely boy. Let's go out." Grabbing a hoodie from the closet, she headed for the stairs.

Danny opened his mouth to say something, but Tom stopped him, raising his hand. "Leave her for a minute."

He gave a curt nod. "Okay, well, one of us needs to go outside with her. You or me?"

"You go, but don't pester her. She'll talk when she's ready. I've gotta go lie down. My head is killing me," he said, walking into the hall.

"Yeah. Okay. Go rest, and I'll ... Hey, Tommy, how can she get there's a problem with Kate, but not sense the danger all around her? I don't understand how it works. How could she not know all of this was going to happen?" He put both of his hands up, sucked in air, and blew it out again. "Don't answer that. I'd rather not know." He picked up his boots, stalked past his partner and stamped down the stairs.

Danny found Marnie in the foyer, clipping on Tater's leash as Rick slipped into his coat, ready to go out with them.

"Take a load off, Doc. I got it," said the detective, sitting on the steps to put on his boots. "Where are Frick and Frack?" he asked, peeking around the wall into the living room.

"Ha-ha. The Hudson Hollow guys are unpopular. I get it. They don't play well with others, including me. Except Joan. She's a nice gal. Made me a coffee this morning. Anyway ... Beck's getting something to eat and Hall's in with Jalnack. Tony, Kriss, and my guys are at the table playing cards. They can't sleep, unlike Carl, who snores through anything," he replied, kicking off his boots. "Three murders in twenty-four hours—that has to be a record."

"Yeah. Creekwood doesn't see this level of violence," said the detective, getting to his feet and grabbing his jacket from the newel post.

"Not in over sixty or seventy years. Maybe longer. Anyway. The pup needs to pee," said the doctor, glancing at Marnie, who had a hand on the doorknob.

Tater barked and tugged at his lead, adding a whimper to define the urgency of the mission.

"Okay, buddy. We're going," said the psychic, heaving open the front door and bracing against the wind. "Well, it's turned to rain, and it's warmed up a bit, which means I'll be able to get to Kate in the morning. When can I get my car back?"

The detective said, "I'll take you. Your vehicle is still in the forensics bay, and since my best guys are here with me, I doubt they've processed it. Anyway, whatever happened to your friend could connect to all of this. Best I have a word with her, too, don't you think?" He saw her posture tighten, readying for an argument, so he added, "That's a rhetorical question and is not up for debate."

"I'm not debating. Someone attacked her on her way home, and she's upset. A couple of guys grabbed her bag, threatened her with a knife, and pushed her around. I can't imagine how it could connect."

"Stranger things have happened, Ms. Reilly. You never know until you ask, and let me make myself clear. I *will* ask."

His authoritative tone irked her, but too tired to argue, she spat out, "Whatever."

Marnie and the dog stepped off the veranda, and he pulled, his nails digging into the ice.

"Tater, slow down! It's slippery. I'm gonna fall on my ass. Easy, buddy. Heel!" She gave his lead a tiny yank, and he fell into step. "Good boy," she said, patting his head.

The Border Collie sniffed around the front lawn, lifting his leg on each shrub and tree in his path.

Hands in his pockets, Danny watched Marnie, her eyes intent on a stand of pine trees, and he wondered what was occupying her mind and how her gift worked. Did she hear spirits, too? Or only see them and feel them? Then he pondered whether she could read minds, and how worrisome it would be if she did.

She sensed his eyes on her, glanced back, and frowned. "What?"

With a wry smile, he angled his head. "Don't you read minds, Ms. Reilly?"

"Only those worth reading, Detective."

"Ouch! But since you know other things, I thought maybe you could."

"No, Detective. I don't read minds. I read body language, though, and I sense that you're judging me because you don't understand. When this is all over, I'll serve you a big scoop of ice cream with your humble pie."

With a huff, she wheeled around and followed her dog as he moseyed his way across the lawn. Every now and again, his ears would perk up, his nose would twitch in the wind, and he would stand at attention, fluffy tail waving.

Danny blew out a puff of steam in the frosty night air and noticed snowflakes dotting the canine's rump. Thinking the roads would be a mess in the morning, he focused on the bright side of the situation: the shift in seasons brings change.

Completing his mission, Tater kicked back ice and dirt, and Marnie patted the dog's backside, brushing away the snow.

"The first snowfall of the season brings hope and a new chapter," she said.

As they walked up the steps, a snow owl landed on the railing and hooted.

The psychic grinned and greeted her old friend. "Well, hello there, Francis. Lovely to see you. It's always a good omen when you turn up."

Pulling a face, the detective said, "Huh. I thought owls were a bad omen."

"You would," she said, as she pushed open the heavy door and slipped inside.

He felt the sting of her comment like a cold slap. Following her into the house, he wondered if she was this bristly with others.

They took off their coats and boots in silence and found Carl standing by the fireplace with a steaming mug.

He held up the cup. "I made a fresh pot of coffee if anyone is interested. Is it calm out there?"

"It's snowing and Francis is back. No doubt he's out hunting for small rodents." She scowled at the detective before disappearing upstairs with Tater trotting behind her.

"Piss her off again?" asked Carl.

"Yeah. She snapped at me when I asked her a simple question."

"Well, I know Marnie and I would guess it was not that you asked. It was *the way* you asked that pissed her off."

"Shut up, Parkins," growled the detective, stomping off to the kitchen for a coffee.

Chapter Twenty-Three

7:13 AM

Marnie awoke to a dog staring into her face and the delicious aroma of fried maple bacon. Stomach growling, she sat up and gave the pup a cuddle before falling back onto her pillows. Outside the window, the early dawn's pink sky boasted clouds spilling huge flakes. She closed her eyes, thinking back to five-year-old Tom Keller knocking on her door, and inviting her to go sledding on the hill behind her house. Mid-recall, an actual rap disturbed her memories of a simpler time and drew a *woof* from her fluffy-tailed companion.

"I'm awake," she called out, swinging her feet to the floor and searching for her robe. Plucking it off the foot, she put it on as the door opened and Danny entered, carrying one of her big breakfast cups with a matching saucer. The canine jumped down, planting himself between the detective and his mom.

"I thought you might like tea while you get ready for the day. Do you want me to take out the pooch? He must need a tree or a shrub by now."

A peace offering, she thought with delight. "Thank you."

"Is that for the tea or the walking service?" he asked, showing off his dimples.

"Uh … both," she said, noticing he had on his own clothes. "You remembered to put the stuff in the dryer, I see. How is everyone this morning? Are the roads open?"

"Yeah. Jalnack made it through the night. And he and Tom caught a lift to the hospital around five-thirty. The forensics guys are doing their thing now, and Carl and Officer Davis are downstairs cooking breakfast. Oh, the electricity is still out, and I swapped the battery about an hour ago. Anyway, I'll leave you to it."

He set the cup and saucer on the highboy and moved toward the door.

"What time is it?" she asked, looking at the flashing clock on her bedside table.

"Just after seven. If you shower and dress, I'll take you to see Kate. I have to wait around for Rick and his guys to finish anyway," he said, backing out of the room. "So, Tater's coming with me, and we'll see you downstairs. C'mon, pal. Wanna go out?"

The Border Collie stared at the detective before side-eyeing his mistress.

She gave his rump a pat and ruffled his coat. "Go with him, boy. It's okay." With a gentle coax with her toe, he slunk across the room with his tail between his legs and his ears glued to his head.

Danny squatted and called him. "Come on, buddy. Let's go for a walk."

The magic word: *walk*. Tater perked up his ears, gave his tail a wag, and trotted over to the detective, who accompanied the canine downstairs. The psychic grabbed her tea and followed them, stopping at the top and breaking into a grin when she heard him talking to her dog.

"Don't be afraid of me, buddy. I'm one of the good guys. How 'bout you tell your mother that?"

With a bark, the deal was done, and she could picture them, paw in hand, shaking on it. When she heard the door open and shut, she continued down the stairs, her mouth watering from the smells wafting from the kitchen.

7:20 AM

"Good morning," said the psychic, popping her cup into the microwave. "Still snowing, huh?"

"It was blizzarding when I drove in," said Joan, passing Carl a stack of plates to set around the table.

"Are you here to babysit?"

"I got a call to come over when the roads opened. Well, we're..." the woman's voice trailed off.

"You're short-staffed, thanks to me." Marnie sighed, glowering at the crime scene tape flapping in the squall outside the window.

"No. Well, yes. But I'm here because we need to move you and Tater to a safe location. We knew the men wouldn't convince you, so they sent in a family friend."

"Uh ... No ... I am not going anywhere. I'll lock up the house and turn on the alarm. Hell, I'll even get Dad's gun out of the safe if I must."

"The events of last night should be enough to convince you. Don't be stubborn. We both know your father wouldn't want you to take unnecessary risks. Forget that damn Reilly pride."

Rolling her eyes at Joan's *mom* tone, she retrieved her hot tea.

"Don't dig your heels in. I can't be here tonight. Michelle and I have plans," Carl added, opening the silverware drawer.

"This discussion is over!" she growled, sidestepping Danny and her dog, who were back from their jaunt. "I'll feed you in a bit, buddy," she muttered, stalking out.

The pup's smiley head swiveled between his new friend and the healer.

"I don't know what you eat, pal, but I bet Carl can hook you up."

"Yeah. I'll get it. Want some tuna, Tot?"

The clever canine lifted his paw in thanks.

The detective turned to Joan with mild amusement. "I'm guessing from her brooding exit you didn't convince her to leave, eh?"

"Good luck with that plan. She's not budging. Obstinate, just like her father." The cop sighed and plated up some food, setting it on the table.

Danny drummed his fingers on the counter, wondering if her stubbornness was insurmountable, before a plan of action took shape. "Carl, do me a favor?"

Narrowing his eyes, he asked, "How much trouble will I be in?"

"I won't lie to you. She's gonna be pissed, but I don't think we should care about that, considering the alternative. When she comes downstairs, you run up to her room and put a bag of her stuff together. You know her better than me. Joan, you go with him. Make sure you get what she'll need for two or three days. Whatever she wears for work, too. You'll also have to sneak out the dog's stuff. Then, throw it in the cargo of my Jeep. It's unlocked. Okay?"

"Pfft! Are you kidding me? No way! Do you have any idea how angry she'd be if I helped you?"

Danny swung around to his colleague for backup, and she set a stern gaze on their quarry.

"You *will* help me. It's that or Marnie hangs around here and gets dead," Joan said, thrusting a dish of scrambled eggs, bacon, and toast at him.

Carl took the food, groaned, and caved in to her reasoning. "Fine. Okay. None of this was my idea, though. You make sure you tell her that when she starts throwing things."

7:33 AM

Silverware on pottery and gongs from the backyard wind chimes were the only sounds in the kitchen as the cops and healer dug into their meals. But curiosity got the better of the detective, and he broke the silence.

"She throws things?" he asked with a chuckle.

Stretching his lips into a grimace, Carl replied, "Yeah, and that's the least of your worries. She's taken a swing at me once or twice *and* connected. And you know, she broke Ken's nose—not that he didn't deserve it. Marnie is not a violent person, but if you push the wrong buttons ... Holy shit! Look out!"

The policewoman agreed. "Ha-ha! She is feisty. Her dad told some tales." She turned at the sound of heels on timber.

"My father told stories about what?" asked Marnie, sauntering in with Tater, his snout in the air. Yum! Bacon.

Danny raised his eyes, appreciating her outfit of faded jeans tucked into tall black boots and a charcoal hip-length V-neck sweater with a bright red scarf. Little silver hoop earrings and a touch of makeup complemented her ensemble. While her green eyes were puffy from tears and lack of sleep, she looked pretty. *Stop it. Be a professional. You cannot think about her like that,* he thought, admonishing himself.

"Well, he told me about you getting stuck in that big old oak out front. He said he had tried to help you down. Pleaded with you for hours, but you refused. You kept telling him you would come down when you were good and ready. As the story goes, you waited up there until it got dark on that humid summer night. He believed you might sleep in the tree. But then you surprised him, and crept out on the branch, swung onto the porch roof, climbed down the trellis, and sat beside him on the porch. He said it took you that long to figure out how to get down without help, but you wouldn't admit it," said Joan, her laughter cutting the tension.

The dog settled beneath the table as Marnie filled a plate and joined the others. Placing a paper napkin on her lap, she snuck a crispy rasher to the pup. "That's my father's version. The truth is different. There were baby birds in a nest, and I was waiting for their mother to come home. I climbed down as soon as I saw her land on one of the higher branches. I'd seen a cat hanging around the tree earlier in the day, and I didn't want it to eat the babies."

"Did you ever tell your father that?" asked the policewoman.

"Nope. He liked his version, but truth comes in varying editions, depending on the storyteller. I was being stubborn, but not for the reasons he thought. Abandoning the hatchlings was out of the question." She picked up her fork and dug into her eggs.

Danny grinned. "You would have been a handful."

"Nope. I had a mind of my own, and I still do. I am not going to a safe house or whatever it is you have planned," she said, crunching a piece of bacon, the corners of her mouth lifting in a satisfied grin.

The detective picked up his coffee, gulped the last of it, stood, and took his plate to the sink.

"Thank you, Joan, for the lovely breakfast. Can you two please excuse me?" He shot a knowing look at his co-conspirators.

Carl and the officer scraped back their chairs, put their dishes on the washboard, and chattered about the snow accumulation as they darted from the room.

Marnie raised her eyebrows as they scarpered. "What's that about?"

"I want to chat about today." He paused in thought. "Tom's truck is here. Would you mind driving it to the hospital for him?" He held out the keys, jangling them like bait.

"No, not at all. I want to see Kate, anyway. He can drop me home after," she said, taking the keys, not masking her smugness.

"Thanks, but he won't be going home. They want to keep him for observation. So, I'll meet you at the hospital and give you a lift. Okay?"

"Well, if he's staying, I'll keep his car. That shouldn't be a problem, right? I'll pick him up in the morning, and he can drop me here on his way home." She averted her eyes, focusing on her food and thinking. *Don't give him control, Reilly. And don't look at him. He'll flash those dang dimples.*

"Nuh-uh. He wants it there in case he's released early. I'll bring you back. It's not a problem." He peered out the window, telling himself, *Don't look at her. She will wrap you around her finger if you let her.*

"Hmm ... I'd be more comfortable taking a cab."

Thinking fast, he said, "So you're leaving Tater here alone then, is that right? Rick and his team will finish soon, and there won't be any cops around today. We're short-staffed. They've reassigned almost everyone except two uniformed officers arriving early evening. Your cameras will monitor, but that's it."

Her head shot up. "The security footage. We never finished watching it."

"Sure we did. Tom and I watched it after you'd gone to bed."

"Did you see what he and I saw? Was it Wilder's wife?" Her eyes widened, and she scooched to the edge of her chair.

"Nope. I don't think so. She's out of town. It can't be her."

"Was it a woman?"

"Nah. Didn't look like it. We viewed it three or four times. The figure was too bulky, and the feet were big. It has to be a man. From what I hear, Wilder's wife is small. The words the gatekeeper used were 'petite and lethal.'"

Frowning, she stuck out her bottom lip. "Huh. Ominous description. That sounds intriguing. Does she have a boyfriend?" she asked, her head swiveling at creaks on the stairs and a door slam.

He shrugged. "Don't know. We haven't done much investigating yet. We'll start looking into things today."

Carl breezed in, kissed the top of the hostess' head, and gave the detective a wave. "Okay. I have grocery shopping to do before I pick up Michelle at the airport. Talk to you later."

"I'll call you after I've seen Kate. Say hey to Michelle, and thanks for staying with me."

"Anytime, Sunshine. Catch you later, Detective." He gave a thumbs up and left.

Chapter Twenty-Three

After he was gone, Marnie asked, "You don't like him much, do you?"

He held up his hands. "I don't know him. I can see how he could be useful, but I question his sincerity. Anyway, let's clean up the kitchen and go."

"Dang it! I wanted to ask him to watch Tater this morning."

She jumped up and hurried to the door. When she yanked it open, the taillights of his truck disappeared in the flurries.

"Shit!" Storming into the kitchen, she cleared her dishes from the table.

"We won't be in the hospital long. He should be fine in the truck," said the detective.

"We'll take him to the morgue to hang out with Doctor Markson. He loves Mr. Fluffybutt. I need to talk to him about something anyway."

"Okay. I'll take the bait. Why do you need to speak to the medical examiner?"

"Oh, it's about a woman I met on Friday night. She was upset about her husband's death. I want to see if she's been calling. I doubt he'll give me an answer, but I can ask." Gathering up condiments, she shrugged and put them away.

"Please tell me this isn't connected to what's been happening here."

"No, he was ninety-two, but the wife suspected foul play because a few psychics told her some bullshit," she said with an exasperated sigh. "I spoke to her grandson. He thinks she's calmed down since I talked to her, but I want to make sure without interrupting the family."

"Okay. I don't understand, but that's not unusual for conversations with you." He rinsed off a plate, passing it on to her. Snarling, she placed it in the dishwasher.

"Careful there, Ms. Reilly. Your face could freeze that way," he teased.

"Blah, blah, blah, blah." She made a mouth-flapping sign with her hand.

"What are you? Four?" he asked, shaking his head and chuckling.

Sticking out her tongue, she giggled.

Chapter Twenty-Four

8:03 AM, En route to Creekwood Hospital and The Morgue

Tongue hanging out and tail at attention, Tater stood on the passenger seat, watching flurries of big white flakes spiraling through the air before meeting their untimely demise, splatting against the windows.

Marnie pushed the dog's tail out of her face and switched the radio from hard to classic rock. Pumping the brakes twice, she checked the touchiness of her friend's tires. Experience told her black ice lurked beneath the slush and snow, waiting to fishtail the vehicle.

Three car lengths behind the psychic, Danny turned up his two-way multi-band, twisting a knob to clear the static. He kept a close eye on the surrounding traffic. A niggling twang grumbling in his gut kept shouting that whoever was after the psychic might T-bone the truck at a cross-section or cut her off and force her into a telephone pole. But when he saw her taillights come on and off in rapid succession, he felt better.

"Okay. She knows enough to test the brakes, so maybe she's watching for a road rager too," he said.

🌢

8:28 AM, Creekwood Hospital

Arriving at the hospital's visitors' parking lot, Marnie got out and clipped on the canine's lead before letting him out the driver's door. The frisky pup bounded into the snowy banks, plowing his nose through a drift, barking with glee to be free.

Pulling into a spot two spaces down from the psychic, Danny cut his engine and got out of his vehicle. Phone to his ear, he trailed behind, holding up two fingers to let them know he would join them inside soon.

With a thumb up to the detective, the psychic gave the dog's tether a tug. "C'mon, buddy. Get a move on. Let's go visiting."

Tater trotted to her side, stopped to pee on a pole before falling into step on the path to the morgue.

8:35 AM, The Morgue

The foul scents of spoiled cabbage, rancid garlic, and formaldehyde hit the psychic's nose as she walked through the heavy steel door of the morgue.

Standing in the entry and shielding her nose with her scarf, she called, "Hey! Uncle Giles. Gawd! I don't know how anyone could get accustomed to this stench."

The medical examiner appeared around a corner, pinching half a plain doughnut between two fingers. "Ha-ha. I prefer this to the perfume counter at the mall. Hungry? I have a box ... minus one, in the back."

Scrunching up her nose, she gagged at the thought. "No, thank you."

Giles Markson was a medium height man with sensible loafers, gray wool trousers, a white lab coat, and half-moon glasses perched on the tip of his nose. His snow-white sideburns, mustache, and beard were crowned by a freckled scalp.

"Hello, my little friend! You've got snowflakes on your bum. Ha-ha," he said, offering an ear scratch to his goddaughter's sidekick, and the dog offered him a paw and tail wag.

"He-he. He's been playing snowplow in the drifts.," said Marnie.

Giving the pup one more pat, he held out his arms. "Come, give an old man a hug and tell me about what happened last night. Your aunt and I have been worried sick."

She wrapped him in a tight embrace and planted a kiss on his ruddy cheek. "First, I'm okay. Second, I'm wondering if Tater can stay in your office for an hour or two? I have friends in hospital and I want to visit them, but I didn't want to leave him at home or in the car."

"Of course. He's always welcome." Hearing the big door slam shut, he looked beyond his goddaughter. "Detective Gregg, how can I help you?"

With a wave, Danny said, "I'm with Ms. Reilly, Doc."

Giles nodded and turned back to Marnie. "I tried calling, but the phone must be out. I keep misplacing your cell number, as you know. Your parents will be worried sick. I bet your mother is chatting up a storm?" said the doctor with a knowing arch to his eyebrows.

Ignoring his comment about her family, she said, "The detective is leading the investigation and keeping the boogeyman away."

"*Boogeyman*? You should take it more seriously. I've seen Mr. Wilder and the officers. This isn't a game. Why don't you stay with Aunt Janet and me? We would love to have you," he said, giving her shoulder a squeeze.

"You can't have dogs at your apartment, remember? We got into trouble the last time. Thank you, though. I appreciate the kind offer." She crouched, taking off the dog's leash and handing it to her godfather. "Now, little man, you stay here with Uncle Giles while I go visit Kate and Uncle Tom. Deal?" she asked, putting her hand up in front of him. He slapped her palm with his paw and consented with a sharp bark. "Done!" she said, tugging one of his ears and standing. "Thanks for watching him. We won't be long."

"It's always a pleasure to have breathing company. Take your time. Tater and I have heaps to catch up on."

Treacherous terrain lay between the morgue entrance and the main door of the hospital. Last night's storm had created an ice rink on the pavers, and Marnie held her hands out, trying to steady herself.

"Holy crap. This is precarious," she said, taking tiny steps, trying to remain upright.

"Somebody better get out here with salt or sand. This town can't afford a lawsuit," said Danny, grabbing a telephone pole to right himself.

Marnie reached out a helping hand but lost her balance when her boot heel skidded on the ice. Flailing to stay on her feet, she grasped the detective's arm, which knocked them both off kilter, and they crashed to the snowy ground—arms and legs tangled.

"Oof!" said Danny, banging his chin on her skull.

"Ow!" cried the psychic, as her brow cracked against the detective's kneecap.

Winded from the impact, they sat dazed on the ground before untangling their limbs with ungraceful awkwardness. Scooching on her backside, she searched for a way to pull herself up, but Danny laughed at the silliness of the situation. She joined in until the detective gasped; his eyes trained over her left eye where blood seeped from a split. Frowning, she touched her forehead, feeling the stickiness of blood on her fingertips.

"It's not too bad," he said, scooping up a handful of snow and squeezing it tight. He bum-shuffled to her and held the ice to her wound.

A bout of dizziness took hold, and she clamped her hands around his, clinging tight as a wave of nausea crashed over her and she feared she might pass out. The detective pulled a handkerchief out of his pocket with his free hand and gave it to her.

"Thank you," she said, moving his hand away. She dabbed her injury with the hankie, checking the fabric for blood. "Ah, geez," she gulped. Stomach churning, she sucked in a breath, exhaling once her tummy stopped flip-flopping.

"Head wounds always bleed a lot. Let me see," he said, placing a thumb under her chin, inspecting her pupils for concussion. "We'd better get you checked out. You're going to need stitches, I think."

She jerked out a nod and tried to stand up. The detective steadied himself on a park bench, stood, and offered her a hand. Grateful for his help, she accepted and got to her feet. Clinging to one another, they slipped and slid their way to the main entrance of the hospital.

"You okay?" he asked, not masking his concern.

"I've got a hard head. I'll be fine," she said as they entered the automatic doors.

Marnie recognized the nurse standing behind the emergency room desk and waved. They had met a few nights ago at Station Hall. But here at the hospital, the woman appeared composed and in control.

"Hi, April," she said, crossing the lobby.

"Ms. Reilly, how lovely to see you again," she said, forcing a smile. Shoulders taut, she didn't make eye contact.

The psychic caught on and played along. "I've had a minor accident out there on the ice. I don't know if stitches are necessary, but if you could have a look, I'd appreciate it."

The nurse straightened her uniform and relaxed—happy that her secret was safe with the counselor. "Let's see what we have here," she said, shooting a glare at Danny as she escorted Marnie across the tiled floor to a chair.

"Detective Gregg and I are here to visit friends, and we slipped on the ice. It's pretty bad out there. We stopped at the morgue first, then came around the side. Someone should get out there with salt," she said.

The nurse remembered Helen, the elderly woman from Friday night, and Marnie's promise to visit the morgue.

"I'll call grounds right away," she said, returning to her station to phone maintenance.

"What was with the dirty look she gave me?" asked Danny.

"I'll explain later," she said, holding a finger to her lips.

April returned, handing Marnie a form to fill out. The detective sank into the chair next to her and did what any good investigator would do. He peered at the paper while she filled in the spaces, memorizing the details.

Document completed, she got up and returned it to the nurse but glanced back. "Did you find out anything interesting, Mr. Nosy?"

"Ha-ha. I didn't know your birthdate, so that's new," he said, taking out his notebook and jotting down the fresh intel.

"How long is the wait?" asked the psychic.

The nurse replied, "There is only one patient ahead of you. And by the way … thank you for your discretion. I don't want anyone here to know about my personal problems."

"Of course. I understand. It's hard to keep secrets in this town. We'll talk more tomorrow morning."

"Eight AM. I *will* be there," whispered April as a light flashed on her console. She raised her voice and said, "The doctor can see you now."

She escorted the patient and detective down the hall to an exam room, placed the form into a horizontal file hanging outside the exam room, and knocked.

A disheveled thirty-something man with mussed blonde hair and tired blue eyes opened the door, picked up the document, and welcomed them in.

"Hi. I'm Dr. Ward. Please excuse me. My shift was supposed to end many hours ago, but the roads … Anyway." Setting aside the document, he said, "Mr. and Mrs. Reilly?"

Danny held up a hand in protest. "No. God no! I'm Detective Daniel Gregg. I was with her when she fell."

Insulted by his outburst, she shot him a dirty look. "He did this to me," she said, sticking out her tongue when the physician turned away.

Narrowing his eyes, the doctor appraised the detective. "I see. Would you be more comfortable if Mr. Gregg waited outside? I can call security if you wish."

"It's Detective Gregg, thank you, and she and I *both* fell on the ice. I hit my chin on her head, and her brow bone connected with my knee. We were trying to hold each other up. I didn't hit her on purpose. I even held snow on it to stop the bleeding." Turning to her, he said, "Tell him what happened."

With a coy smile, she replied, "Yeah. It's true. We visited the morgue and slipped coming around the building. We've asked the nurse to advise someone about the ice."

"Gotcha. Let me have a look at that laceration. Can you hop up on the table for me, please?"

The detective tried to help Marnie, but she pushed him away and got up on her own as he stepped back in surrender.

"So, you've been here all night, Doc?" asked Danny.

Inspecting the wound, he said, "Yeah. I got here around noon yesterday for a twelve-hour shift, and then the storm broke. No one could get here, so here I am. This doesn't look too bad. I'll clean it up and glue it shut. Can you lie back on the table for me, please?"

"Sure." She scooted around and lay down while Danny leaned against a wall and watched the doctor at work.

"You have a scar here below the wound. Childhood injury?"

"Mm-hmm. I fell when I was a kid. We thought there was a monster in the forest, so I took off running with my best friend. I tripped over a huge log and smacked my head on a rock. He stopped to help me up, saw the blood, and was certain the beast had gotten me. Oh, goodness, he and I used to get up to some interesting adventures," she said, laughing and recalling the memory.

"Are you and he still friends?" asked the doctor.

"We are. I'm here to visit him and another friend. Kate Parish came in last night, and Tom Keller arrived early this morning with one of his colleagues. Officer Sam Jalnack? Any chance you know how any of them are doing?"

"Of course. Yes. I looked after them. Kate Parish, you say?"

"That's right. Sorry for putting you on the spot. I know you can't say anything."

"Okay, Marnie. That looks pretty good. You've got bruising, and it will get worse. You might have a scar, but who's going to notice it when they're looking at those big green eyes? Besides, it will give you another story about a monster of an ice storm," he said, helping her sit up.

Danny checked his watch. "Can we go now? I've got a killer to catch."

The doctor's eyebrows shot up, and he turned to the detective. "A killer?" Then it clicked. He glanced back down at the form, noting the address. "Of course, this was all over the news last night. That reporter … What's her name? The annoying one," he said, snapping his fingers to divine a moniker. "Carrie Sutherland! She was outside the house."

With a grimace, he replied, "Yeah, we tried to stop that. We didn't want to scare people."

"She's a nuisance. The way she sensationalizes trauma is disgusting. Her van was out front last night, lying in wait, but they left around four this morning, right before your officers arrived. Swear to God, journalists should have to take an oath that forces them to a higher standard," said the doctor. "I'm sorry for ranting, but everything streams so fast these days."

Danny puffed out his cheeks. "Pfft! Tell me about it."

Marnie hopped off the table and stood next to the detective, nudging him with her elbow. "We ready?"

"Yeah, I want to have a quick word with the doctor about Tom and Jalnack," he said, examining her wound and the swelling and bruising surrounding the laceration. "Can you wait for me outside?"

"Yes," she said, narrowing her eyes and backing out the door.

Danny joined Marnie after a few moments, sidling up to her in the waiting room. "Okay, Ms. Reilly, let's go visiting," he said, stopping and crooking his arm, waiting for her to join him.

She got up, ignored his gesture, and strode off to the elevators.

Shrugging, he followed her. "You know where we're going?" he asked.

"Mm-hmm. I enquired while you were interrogating the doctor," she said, flashing him a dirty look.

"Okay, you wanna tell me what your problem is? What's with the stink-eye?"

She halted and spun around, right eyebrow raised. "No. God no!" Turning on her heel, she stomped off.

"Hey, I clarified that there's nothing going on here." He waved his hand between himself and her. "I'm the lead on a murder that involves you, and I can't let anyone think there's a personal bias. Sorry I said it that way, but that's the way it is."

Tossing her ponytail over her shoulder, she stopped in front of the elevator. "Whatever," she replied, poking the 'up' button several times and heaving out a breath. Punching it two more times, she thought, *I wish this was your face.*

"I don't understand why you're so mad," he muttered.

Jaw clenched, she said, "Well, you're an idiot. You made it sound like there's something wrong with me. How could anyone ever have an interest in damaged goods like Marnie Reilly? That's what it sounded like. What man in his right mind would be interested in her? It made me feel … oh, never mind." She looked past him and stepped onto the elevator.

"Look, Marnie…," he said, catching the door with his shoulder.

"Stop talking, Detective," she said, watching the floors click by on the lighted panel above the doors.

Chapter Twenty-Five

9:33 AM, Creekwood Hospital

Marnie and Danny stepped off the elevator on the fifth floor, and a nurse glanced up from her work before glaring at the clock on the opposite wall.

"Visiting hours start at ten. You'll have to come back," she said.

The detective pulled back the bottom hem of his navy wool coat, revealing the badge on his belt. "Detective Daniel Gregg, Creekwood PD. I need to see some patients. One of my officers and a detective are here. Sam Jalnack and Tom Keller. You have a Kate Parish here, too. She was the victim of an assault."

The nurse held her ground. "I can confirm they are here, but that doesn't change visiting hours. My patients need their rest."

"Ma'am, I understand all the rigmarole, but this is important. Are you telling me you want to hinder an investigation?" Clenching his jaw, he narrowed his steely blue eyes.

"Officer, I don't bend to threats. You can see my patients at ten. Are we clear?"

"Yeah. Not a problem, ma'am. We've got a suspect on the loose who's killed a citizen and two cops, and he's injured two more, but hey, you don't want to help, no worries. Caring for them is your domain. I get it, but, lady, I'm here to protect them! And you too, for that matter! Tchah." Waving her off, he took his rage to the waiting room.

Oh-faced, Marnie muttered, "Uh-oh." But never one to back down from tackling a righteous battle, she stepped up to the counter, where the nurse's back greeted her. "Hi. Hello," she said, and was met with an over-the-shoulder glower. "Look. It's been a long night. He's trying to do his job, and I need to see my friend. I'm sure Kate is a mess. She called me crying at three this morning, but I couldn't get to her because the roads were closed. She doesn't have any family here—her parents live out of state. Please! Detective Gregg was protecting me, and a deranged killer murdered two of his officers. He's responsible, and more importantly, he feels accountable. Officer Jalnack was shot while trying to apprehend an intruder in my home, and Detective Keller was hit on the head and tased. We would appreciate your help, ma'am."

The nurse considered the psychic's pleading face and gave in. She sucked on her cheeks and tapped her keyboard. "Fine. Ten minutes. Kate is in five-oh-three. Detective Keller is in five fourteen, and Officer Jalnack is in surgery. He'll be in recovery in a few hours." She peered at Marnie over the top of her glasses and nodded toward the detective. "He didn't have to be an arrogant jerk."

"With all due respect, you weren't much better. And let's face it, being an asshole is the only way sometimes. I think you know that," said Marnie, cocking her head.

"Yes, well, I was only doing my job. Please be quick and do not upset my patients." The nurse turned away, busying herself with paperwork.

"Thank you," the counselor replied, snapping her fingers to get the detective's attention and jerking her head for him to follow her.

Mouthing "really," he jogged to catch up to her.

"How'd you manage that?" he asked, looking back at the nurse's station.

"I have my ways, Detective." At room five-oh-three, she halted, and Danny plowed into her. "Watch it!" she said, glowering. "This is Kate's room. Tom is in five fourteen, and Jalnack is in surgery. I'll meet you in Tom's room after I've seen Kate."

"I'm coming with you."

"Suit yourself," she replied with resignation, and pushed open the door.

His mouth dropped open, and his eyebrows shot up. *Huh. She didn't argue.*

●

9:40 AM

Long, stringy sable hair framed a pale, delicate face resting on a pillow. With shallow breaths, Kate Parish slept, her eyelids fluttering. Marnie crossed to the far side of the bed and picked up her friend's hand. "She looks weak ... Poor kid ... I hope there isn't a mirror handy. She'll be mortified by those raccoon circles and that waxy complexion. Gawd. She's always perfect. I've never seen her look so fragile."

"Hmm ... Looks like she had a rough night. I'd think she would be happy to be alive, rather than worried about her appearance," scoffed Danny, his gut twisting as he studied the woman in the hospital bed.

The counselor flashed him a glare as the door swung open, and the doctor from the ER entered.

"Oh. Wow. How did you get past Nurse Ratched? Did your badge do the trick?" Dr. Ward asked.

"Nah, Ms. Reilly has a way about her, Doctor. Mind control or voodoo," Danny said with a wide, teasing grin.

"I explained the situation, that's all," she replied, cheeks burning.

The doctor glanced between them, and before an uncomfortable silence could fill the void, he turned his focus to his patient. "She'll be okay. Mild contusions, a bullet graze on her left arm, and a traumatic amputation of her left ring finger. Surgery was required, but the other digits were saved."

"You called the station when she came in?" asked the detective.

"Yes, sir. We called as soon as she walked in and told us what had happened. The police took her statement before the surgery. She told them that her assailants had taken the finger to steal a ring. Her mother's diamond, she said. She kept asking us to check her pockets, thinking it was there. We had to tell her the ring *and* the finger were gone."

The psychic looked down at her chum's gauze-wrapped hand. "Oh, Katie. What have they done to you?"

Leaning on the bedrail, Danny asked, "Any other injuries, Doc? Did you do a rape kit?"

Marnie's jaw dropped at the thought, and she placed a hand on Kate's shoulder, hoping her sixth sense would deliver insight. Sometimes psychometry worked, and often it didn't, but she had to try. Closing her eyes, she focused her energy, hoping the men wouldn't notice. *That's weird,* she thought. *Kate, what have you been up to?* Unable to decipher the vision, the psychic pulled back her hand, hoping she had her wires crossed. Then she scolded herself for breaking her own rules. *Reilly, you shouldn't have done that. You know better than to invade someone's privacy.*

"We offered to do an examination, but she declined and grew agitated when we asked a second time. Since there were no visible signs of rape, we let it go. She was in shock, and we didn't push her because saving her fingers was most urgent," said the doctor, writing a note in the patient's chart.

"Okay. You said something about a bullet graze. Did she say anything about that?"

"Yeah. She said she was walking down High Avenue and that she ran when two men yelled at her; they fired a shot. It scared her, so she stopped running because she didn't want them to shoot again. I overheard her telling the police that she had only one direction to go, straight, because there were no alleys or laneways. The streets were empty, and there was no one to help, so stood still and took her chances."

"Is that right? Hmm ... What tool was used to cut off the finger?" asked Danny, scribbling in a notebook.

"We can't be certain. It's a clean cut. Wire snips are a favorite among thugs, but this is not a crude cut."

The detective pointed to the unbandaged hand. "Funny, there are no defensive wounds."

"That's not unusual. People become submissive so they won't suffer harm. I've seen men bigger than you with none. It is often a case of fight or flight. She tried flight, and they shot at her. Perhaps she isn't a fighter and believed she could talk her way out of trouble. She looks the type. Beautiful, slender ... you know what I mean. She may have believed they would take her handbag and run for it."

Dr. Ward finished hypothesizing and glanced over at Marnie, whose death stare could have bored holes into Danny's skull.

The detective paid no attention to her anger, pushing through with his investigation, his eyes meeting hers with a dismissive squint. "Would Kate fight back? You know her better than we do."

She clenched her fists at her sides—her green eyes flashing. "No, Detective, she would not. She is diplomatic, calm, and, as a lawyer, she uses words, not her fists."

"So why didn't you call her yesterday instead of Bennett?"

"David and his father have been my family's legal counsel for years. Besides, I never said Kate is a good lawyer," Marnie said through gritted teeth.

The patient stirred, opening her eyes.

Kate Parish pushed herself up and pressed the button to incline the bed. With a longing look at her left hand, her eyes pooled with tears.

Pulling down the side rail, Marnie sat, giving her friend a hug. "I'm sorry it took me so long to get here."

"You did your best, Marn," said the invalid, crying into the crook of the psychic's neck, clinging to her.

The detective and doctor stepped back and gave them some privacy.

Danny asked, "You play racquetball, Doc?"

"I do. How'd you know?"

"I thought you looked familiar. I play at the courts over on Bay Road."

"Of course. I've seen you there. Hey, you're good and quite fast for a guy your age and size."

"Yeah. Not bad for an old, fat guy."

Cheeks reddened, Dr. Ward held up his hands. "No. No. Sorry. That's not what I mean. You look fit, and not at all old. You're a decent racquetball player. I didn't mean to insult you."

"Ha-ha! I'm messin' with you. It's been a long night. I'm trying to relax a bit."

Marnie cleared her throat, getting the men's attention, and they took a step closer to the bed. "Kate didn't give a description to the officers last night. She fell asleep but would like to do it today. Could you arrange that?"

"Yes, of course. I'll call the station now and get someone over here. A description would help," he said, taking his phone from his inner coat pocket.

"Uh. You can't use that in here," said the doctor, tipping his head toward a sign on the wall.

"Tchah! I've never understood that rule. What's my phone going to interfere with?" He hung his head, then scoped out the room, searching for anything that his mobile would send wonky.

"The courtyard is down the hall."

"Argh! Okay," said Danny, yanking open the door, letting it thump closed.

Turning back to her girlfriend, Marnie said, "Would you like me to go to your apartment and get you some things?"

"That's unnecessary. I won't be here too long. Dr. Ward, may I go home today?"

"No, ma'am. I'm afraid we'll keep you here a while longer to monitor your hand for infection, and you're still in shock. You don't experience something like last night's events and get over it."

"Are you sure you don't want me to pick up your things? It's no trouble," the psychic asked, needing to help her friend—an unhealthy byproduct of her profession.

Voice trembling, Kate replied, "No. I'm fine. Don't go out of your way."

Marnie moved off the bed and gave Kate's arm a soft rub. "I'm going, and that's final. I'll get you some PJs, your bathrobe, and your cosmetics. You'll feel better in no time."

"You can't. They stole my keys and my handbag. I can't get into my place." The injured woman broke into a sob, covering her face with her wounded limb.

"That's okay. I'll go see your super. He'll let me in, or I'll call a locksmith. If I have Detective Gregg with me, there won't be a problem," she said, sitting again.

Kate dropped her arm—her face scarlet. "No! Stop being Miss Fix-it! I don't need rescuing!"

Setting her jaw, Marnie wrinkled her brow, and got up from the bed, looking back. *Her shock is worse than I thought.* "Okay. I didn't mean to upset you. If you need anything, all you need to do is ask."

"I won't. Now, please go," Kate ordered, pointing to the door.

Marnie fell silent and backed away, her thoughts running into one another. *Huh. That's odd. She always expects me to take care of her.*

The doctor ushered Marnie into the hall, calming her with a shoulder pat, trying to explain. "Anger is a part of shock. She'll come around and will probably want help. But when a person has been violated, there's a sense of being out of control, and she's trying to take back her power. Telling you *no* is all part of it."

Nodding, she blinked back tears. "Yeah, I get it, but Kate's never snapped at me like that. It was strange. After a car accident last year, she called me to bring her stuff. I thought…" Her words trailed off when she saw Danny coming down the hall, a carry-out cup in each hand.

Eyebrows knitted together, he asked, "Everything okay? You look upset. What's happened?"

The doctor replied, patting the psychic's shoulder again. "Kate snapped at her."

Danny glanced between the man's hand and face, and then back to the fingers resting on the psychic's shoulder. Dr. Ward dropped his hand and stuck it in his lab coat.

Offering the counselor a steaming Styrofoam cup with a tea bag tag hanging over the side, he said, "Oh. Well, under the circumstances … tension, the injury, all that. She'll cool down."

Shaking out her arms like a swimmer warming up, she stretched her neck and exhaled before grabbing the cup and taking a sip. "I'm good. Thanks for that. Let's drop it and go see Tom." She started down the hall, paused, and glancing over her shoulder, asked, "Are you coming?"

Danny shook his head and chuckled. "Women…"

The other man laughed. "Yeah. Can't live with them. Can't shoot them."

With a smirk, the detective patted his sidearm. "I'm thinkin' about it."

Danny pushed open Tom's hospital room door to find Marnie already sitting on the patient's bed, eating a cup of red Jello.

The patient paced in front of the windows, huffing and puffing. "Break me outta here, would ya?"

The detective pursed his lips and gave his head a shake. "No can do, partner. That's up to the professionals. Besides, you might be safer here. Someone ratted about your gun, and Cap is pissed off. A uniform from Hudson Hollow told their commander, who called the superintendent, who chewed out Sterling. I spoke with him a few minutes ago about an identikit for Kate's attackers. He tore strips off me and told me you're going to have another asshole when he gets here." Rubbing the nape of his neck, he twisted his mouth into a grimace.

With a hand to his forehead, Tom stalked the room like a caged cat. "Aw, shit! Why the hell would they do that? It would have been better if I'd told him. Or you had. Dammit! What's goin' on? Cops are supposed to have each other's backs."

"Calm down," said Danny, crossing the room and pushing his partner into a visitor's chair. "He got ambushed and needs to blow off steam. I'll fix it."

Sinking back, Tom drew circles with his index fingers on his temples. "We should have called him last night."

"I've already told him the Hudson crew were on the road and that they don't know shit. Look. We were careful about what we said in front of them. We got this." Turning to the counselor, he said, "You'll help me cover his ass, won't you?"

"You want me to lie?" she asked, quirking the corner of her mouth.

"No. Just stretch the truth to help a friend."

She shrugged, got up from the bed, and draped an arm around her pal's shoulder. "Yeah. Okay."

Danny held out his hands. "There! You see? All we gotta do is tell the captain I was right behind you. I thought someone was following us, turned around, and Marnie was there. I asked her to go home. She argued with me; you got too far ahead. Then … uh … she and I heard a scuffle, and when we reached you, you were out cold."

Tom's eyes rolled back, and he groaned. "Well, that's one hell of a spin. Are you serious? That's how we're gonna handle it?"

"Yeah," said the detective with a determined nod.

The psychic wrinkled her nose. "I'm not sure I like the fact that I was sneaking around in the forest, following you guys, but anyone who knows me would buy that. I am curious by nature," she said, mischief twinkling in her eyes.

"Ha-ha! There you go, Tommy. She's willing to take one for the team," said Danny, tapping her jaw with a fist.

In return, she punched him in the arm, harder than intended.

"Hey! What the hell was that for?" he said, sulking and rubbing his arm.

"If you want to tell people I behaved like a petulant child, I'll act like one. I'm unpredictable and disobedient. I'm getting into my new role." Sitting on the edge of Tom's chair, she looked up at him and winked.

"And precocious. Don't forget that," said her best friend, giving her a tight squeeze. "Yeah, we can sell that. Our guys won't be a problem. Thanks, Danny."

The counselor turned to him, raising an eyebrow.

"You too, Marn. Thanks for having my back—again." Pointing to her forehead, he frowned. "Hey, what happened there?" Leaning over, he kissed her injury.

"Mr. Chuckles over there kneed me in the head," she said, smirking and getting up. Sauntering toward the door, she added, "I need more tea. Do either of you want anything from the cafeteria?"

"Hey, it was an accident!" said the detective, throwing out his hands.

"You asked me to lie. I need to practice." She winked and opened the door, leaving the men to talk about her.

Turning to his partner, who was trying not to laugh, Danny said, "Man, I don't get her. One minute she's sweet. Next, she's angry. And then she's all ... smart-ass. What the hell?"

Keller flashed a cheesy grin. "I think she has a little crush on you." He pretended to toss his hair, mimicking Marnie's husky tone. "You're so tall and handsome, Detective. I can't help myself."

Danny threw a pillow at him, trying not to grin. "No, she doesn't," he said, considering her behavior for a moment. And he thought, *does she?*

"Oh, that's crap! I've watched the two of you sparring for the last few days. Of course she does, and you have one on her. Except yours ain't so little. Yours is huge, my friend. Ha-ha!"

Tom threw back the pillow as their boss walked in.

"Good to see you're feeling better, Detective Keller," growled the captain, his massive shoulders filling the doorway.

Peter Sterling was a barrel of a man with white hair, shocking blue eyes, a square jaw, and hands the size of a grizzly bear's paws. He appeared taller than his five-foot-eight-inch stature, and his foghorn voice scared everyone, including the superintendent.

"Nice to see you, sir," said Danny.

"Good morning, Cap," said Tom, standing too fast, and grabbing the foot of the bed to catch himself.

The captain's booming voice was more of a roar this morning, as it often was when protocol wasn't followed to the letter of the law.

"Oh, please. Tell me what's good about it. When I heard from Hudson Hollow that you had allowed your firearm to get into the hands of a suspect, well, I was ready to chew nails and spit rust. I called your partner and read him the riot act, and I'm here to kick your ass so far into next week that..."

Marnie returned, and the grizzly stopped short. He pointed at her, raising his white caterpillar eyebrows. "Who is this?"

"I'm Marnie Reilly, sir. Hello," she said, holding out her delicate hand to the bear. "Thank you for allowing your officers to watch over me. You don't know how grateful I am. Please accept my regrets and condolences for Weaver and Webb's deaths."

He pulled down the hem of his jacket and straightened his tie. "Thank you. Please don't fret. They were doing their job." Clearing his throat, he glowered at the detectives.

"Sir?" she said, taking a brave step forward.

He turned back, his keen eyes studying her.

"Last night was all my fault. I mean, Tom's gun, sir. I followed him. Uh ... them ... uh ... the detectives. My curiosity got the better of me. I should have stayed in the house. I am so sorry for the trouble I caused."

When she stopped to take a breath, he patted her arm.

"Go on, Ms. Reilly," he said with compassion.

Danny stepped forward, a hand between the psychic and his boss.

"Uh ... Marnie, you don't have to do this."

"It's okay. It *is* my fault," she said. "Detective Keller didn't see me, and he kept walking. Detective Gregg and I were arguing when we heard a scuffle up ahead. He told me to stay close to him, and we ran to Tom. I take full responsibility, sir." She softened her brow as Captain Sterling searched her countenance for sincerity.

He looked from the counselor to the detectives and laughed, pointing at her. "Do you believe this? This woman is protecting you two." He patted her shoulder with a firm slap. "Ms. Reilly, can I ask you a question?"

"Yes, sir."

"Are you stupid?! You must be to get involved in a police investigation and to run around in the woods at night when a killer is on the loose?! You risked your life and the lives of my officers! I have a mind to lock you up!" His face turned several shades of red during the outburst—settling on pink when the tirade subsided.

She stepped back, eyes narrowed, and her fists clenched.

"Uh-oh," said Tom, nudging Danny.

She regained her step, her jaw taut with determination. "Captain Sterling, shouting won't change what happened. I have apologized and have admitted responsibility for my actions. If you think for one minute that I would ever put anyone at risk on purpose, you are crazy! It was an accident, and I'm sorry! And no, sir, I am not stupid! Are you?!"

As their boss folded his arms across his chest, the detectives braced for an explosion, but it didn't come. Sterling turned to them, jerked his head toward her, and laughed again. "This one's got spunk. I like her. We need to recruit her. She had me shaking in my boots." He pivoted back to the counselor, jabbed a sausage-sized finger in her face, and growled, "Don't ever yell at me again. We clear?"

"With all due respect, sir, you bellowed at me first, and you called me stupid. No one should call anyone such a thing. It's disrespectful." Shoulders squared, defiance and mischief gleamed in her green eyes.

Dumbfounded, Tom and Danny watched the exchange, and the latter thinking, *gutsy lady.*

Sterling and Marnie locked eyes—neither willing to back down. The captain cocked his head and squinted, intrigued by the strength in her eyes.

She held his gaze—fists and jaw clamped, thinking to herself, *I am not looking away, even if I have to spend a night in jail.* Then she thought of Tater and, as she was about to make amends, he broke the standoff, turning to the detectives.

Captain Sterling grumbled, "Ahem ... All right, then. Gregg, I'll expect your report before your shift ends and organize a new firearm for Keller. He can't be without one. It's the law." Eyes trailing back to the psychic, he said, "Madam, a pleasure doing battle with you." With a stiff salute, he walked out.

Collapsing against the wall, Marnie heaved out a trapped breath. "Holy shit! I thought he might arrest me."

The detectives roared with laughter, and Tom crossed the room, picked her up and swung her around, hugging her until she squirmed away.

"That was gold. Oh! My! God! I've never seen anyone win in a stare-off with him. Ever!"

"Well, let's not do that again," she said, twisting her ponytail before eyeing Danny, and adding, "What now, Detective?"

"Well, Jalnack is still in surgery. We've visited the patients, and you've battled Sterling and won. Should we go to Chinatown and find you a dragon to slay?"

"Ha. Ha. Can we leave, please? I need air. Hospitals smell funny." She wrinkled her nose, gave Tom a hug and made a move for the door.

"Yeah, you go on ahead to the morgue. I'll be right there. I need a word with my partner."

With a wave, she was gone.

"Okay. Here's the plan. Joan Davis and Carl packed up a bag for Marnie and threw in Tater's stuff, too. It's in my vehicle, so I can get her to a safe place tonight. How do I handle her?"

The corners of Tom's mouth lifted as he thought about how stubborn his best friend could be. He didn't want to laugh, but he knew it would be impossible to convince her to leave her home if a stable environment wasn't on offer for her and her Border Collie.

"Take her home with you, my man. Who's gonna look for her out in the sticks? You know she won't stay at a motel or hotel. Not with Tater, anyway. Since Creekwood PD doesn't have a safe house, there aren't a lot of options. Talk to Captain Sterling, though, and tell him what you're planning. We don't need more trouble. Know what I mean?"

Danny screwed up his face, doubtful the plan could work. "My house? You think she'd go home with me?"

"Yeah, I do. She'd stay with me if I wasn't stuck in the hospital. Make it her idea, though. Play her. She's smart, but you can finesse her." He sat back down in the visitor's chair. "Hey, do you think you could bring me a steak sandwich and some fries before you head home tonight? I can't eat the shit they serve here."

"Yeah. Of course. I'll see you later when I come back to check on Jalnack."

As he reached the door, Tom called out, "She likes steak. Rare steak and mashed potatoes. Promise her dinner, and she'll be hooked. Oh, leave the skin on the potatoes and mash them with butter and cream. Good red wine. Marnie doesn't drink wine from a box. She's a snob. Australian Shiraz or Oregon Pinot Noir are her favorites. And be nice to Tater—he is the way to her heart. He likes tuna and sardines. Feed them, take care of them, and you'll be home free."

Danny pulled a face. "I want her to stay at my place until we catch the psycho. You make it sound like I want to get her into bed."

Tom tipped his head. "I didn't suggest that. Are you feeling guilty?"

"I don't want to sleep with her," he growled and stomped out.

"Sure, you do," said the patient. Then he pondered, *how do we catch a psycho?*

Chapter Twenty-Six

10:55 AM, The Morgue

"Thanks so much for the tea, Uncle Giles. You do not know how much I am savoring the calm of your office. I never would have imagined finding a morgue relaxing. Ha," said Marnie, settling into the visitor's chair with Tater curled on the floor beside her.

Leaning back in his chair, the medical examiner set his cup on a coffee-stained toe tag atop his gray metal desk. "I find it comforting most days, dear. Now, that may sound odd to most, but I think you can understand. Helping people is what we do. Living or dead. The two of us assist them in moving on."

"Hmm ... I never thought about it like that, but I can't disagree. We *do* make a difference."

"Indeed," he said, craning his neck when the outer door squawked open and banged shut. "And so do the police. Speak of the devil. Here's Detective Gregg now."

"Gee, Doc. I didn't realize my reputation was that bad," said Danny, winking.

"Ha-ha. No, my goddaughter and I were patting ourselves on the shoulders, feeling proud about our chosen professions. You're one of the good guys, too."

"Well, that's nice to hear," he said, squatting and snapping his fingers to get the dog's attention. "Come here, pal."

The Border Collie rose with a huff, and ambled over, tail tucked, head down and ears drooping.

With his mouth shut tight and his amber eyes wary, the canine allowed the man to scratch his ears. But when the detective asked, "Want to go for a drive?" the dog bounced forward, his ears perked, and his backend waggled with gusto.

Marnie laughed. "He's a tough one to win over. Ken kicked him once or twice, so he's careful. People must earn his trust. Especially men."

"I will never harm him," said the detective, stroking the top of the pup's nose with his knuckle. "How 'bout we get some lunch? I know a diner where the owner will let him sit with us."

"Uh, sure., but it's only eleven," she said, consulting her watch.

"That's okay. I'm hungry and could use a strong coffee. Want something to eat?"

She nodded and pushed herself out of the chair. "Yup. I can always fill my face."

"Good. Let's go. I've had enough death in the last twenty-four hours." He faked a shiver. "Doc, do you want to join us?"

"No, thank you. My beautiful wife packed me a lunch, and I am hoping it's leftover spaghetti and meatballs."

Marnie excused herself. "I'll be right back. I need to use the ladies' room," she said, getting out of her chair and walking through the swinging doors to the back of the morgue.

Giles stood and gave the pooch a pat before giving Danny's shoulder a firm clap. "Time for me to get back to work. I trust you will look after my goddaughter."

"Yes, sir."

"Stay out of trouble," said the medical examiner as he walked away.

Left alone with Tater, the detective greased the wheels, so to speak. "Want to come to my house, buddy? It's a big log cabin on a lake. I've got a fireplace you can curl up beside, and we can hike and run. Hey, pal, how does that sound?" He clipped the dog's lead onto his collar and patted his rump. "We can be friends, can't we? How 'bout I get you some tuna?"

The dog thumped his tail on the floor.

"Ha-ha! You understand every word, don't you, boy?"

The dog smiled, adding a bark to confirm as his mistress returned.

"What's going on in here? The knucklehead is grinning like someone mentioned tuna," said Marnie, gathering up her coat and bag.

"What?" said Danny, squinting and shrugging.

With a wry grin, she reached for her dog's lead. "Let's go."

11:10 AM, Leaving the Morgue

"I can't believe it's still snowing," said the psychic, slipping on her gloves.

A flurry of flakes skittered through the air on the wake of a biting north wind before melting on the wet pavement. While the roads were better, the now-salted sidewalk was a slushy mess, making Marnie wish she'd worn her unfashionable rubber boots.

"It seems too early for snow, but the months and years run together the older I get," said the detective, opening the car door for his passenger. Adding a cheesy bow, he motioned her into the vehicle with one hand and took her dog's lead with the other as she stepped up. He waited for her to get organized, then slammed the door shut.

"C'mon, buddy. I've got the perfect house for you," he said, going around the back to the cargo, where Tater jumped in and turned in a circle before resting his chin on the seat back.

When Danny turned on the engine, Marnie leaned forward and switched on the radio.

"Can I change the station? Do you like country music? I'm a sucker for a twangy tone."

"Sorry. Gotta have the police radio on when I'm on duty. It's the law—or so Sterling tells us. And yes. I like country music."

"Cool," she said, folding her hands in her lap. "So, where's this diner?"

"It's a few blocks up from the station. Best club sandwich and fries in town."

"Ooh ... That sounds good," she said, hugging herself to warm up.

Chapter Twenty-Seven

11:23 AM, Ryan's Diner

"Giles Markson is your godfather, eh? How did that happen?" asked Danny.

"He and his wife Janet were close friends of my parents. As the story goes, on the day I was born, Dad got stuck in weather in Lake George, and they were afraid he wouldn't get home. Anyway, Aunt Janet and Uncle Giles took Mom to the hospital and picked up my brother from school. They stayed with her until my father arrived. I was born during a blizzard."

"Ha! That makes sense," said the detective, chuckling.

"What's that supposed to mean?"

"Uh ... You can be ... umm ... blustery. Ha-ha." He paused before adding, "I have to tell you. Back at the station yesterday when you said, 'Here comes the storm,' you freaked me out. It was like you knew what was coming. The word *prognosticate* comes to mind."

"Oh. That. Well, I can't help what comes out of my mouth sometimes, as you know."

"Hmm ... the stuff with my mother and Sarah."

"And others," she said with a side-eye.

"Yeah. So, they made the doc and his wife your godparents for getting your mother to the hospital?"

"That's part of it. After I was delivered, Mom was resting, and Aunt Janet took my brother to the cafeteria. Uncle Giles wasn't hungry, so he wandered off and found Dad looking at me through the window and thought there was something wrong. He went into the nursery to check. I wasn't breathing, and Dr. Markson, caretaker of the dead, resuscitated me."

"Holy shit. Wow! You died?"

"Yup."

"And that's why he's your godfather. He saved your life."

"Yep. And dang it. I forgot to ask him about Helen's husband, even though he won't tell me anything. I'll text him Michael's number. He's the grandson, and he can handle it however he wants. I'm sure Uncle Giles will call and smooth it over."

"Well, don't worry about it now," he said, turning on the indicator and slowing the vehicle to a stop at the curb. "We have arrived."

Marnie looked up at the sign. "Ryan's Diner. I know this place. I've been here with my father. We had breakfast before a fishing trip."

"You fish?"

"Not in a long time, but yeah. I even bait my hook," she replied, removing her seatbelt.

She is more interesting by the moment, he thought.

Getting out of the vehicle, they opened the back for Tater, who trotted alongside and kept checking out Danny, who was holding his lead.

The counselor said, "I think he likes you now. He keeps looking up at you. Did you bribe him with food?" She paused on the pavement. "Are you sure it's okay for him to go inside?"

"It'll be fine," he said, opening the door to the jangle of a bell, which made his dimples appear.

A white-haired woman behind the counter smiled and waved when they entered.

"Danny! Give us a hug!" She jogged across the room and wrapped her arms around him so tight it looked like his eyes would pop out. Stepping back, she spied his guests. "Now, who's this lovely lady?"

"Gram, this is Marnie Reilly and Tater," he said, before adding, "And this is my grandmother, Margaret Ryan."

The counselor offered her hand. "Hi. It's nice to meet you, Mrs. Ryan?"

"No. No. Any friend of my grandson can call me Gram, and with a name like Reilly, we're practically family," she said—her Irish brogue strong.

Before the counselor knew it, the older woman had thrown her arms around her, squeezing with all her might, then stooped to greet the pup. "Hello, little fella," she said, ruffling his fur. "Now, off you go. Grab a seat before the rush starts," she said, scurrying back behind the counter.

"Wow! She's energetic," said Marnie as they made their way to a table.

"Ha-ha. She's been that way as long as I can remember. It's hard to keep up with her," said Danny, pointing to a booth near the back. "This is my table. Gram keeps it open for me most days."

"So, you're spoiled? Hee-hee."

"Not at all. We take care of each other."

They sat on opposite sides, and her dog jumped up on the bench seat next to the detective.

"You cheeky boy. Hop down. Floor, mister," said his mistress, containing a laugh.

Tater turned in a circle, bumped Danny's chin with his nose, and jumped down, sitting next to the table.

Impressed by the dog's obedience, the detective grinned. "I can't believe him. He understands every word."

"Yes, he does. Did you know the Border Collie is the smartest breed? Very intelligent and they can reason. Not many can do that. Fun fact: this little monster can open doors. And Tom taught him to get him a beer out of the fridge. Ha-ha."

"Here we go," said Gram, returning with menus and handing them to the diners. She asked Marnie questions about Tater, and the detective studied his guest as she chatted to his grandmother. She had a beautiful smile that lit up her face when she laughed. And her gorgeous eyes were on the light green side of aquamarine, with little gold flecks. She was easy to look at.

"What will you have, son?" the older woman asked, but he wasn't listening—he was staring at his dining companion. "Danny, over here," she said with a snap of her fingers. "It's not polite to stare. What can I get you, dear?"

Cheeks reddening, he pondered the menu to cover his blushing face. "Uh ... the usual, please. Can I have a strong coffee, too?"

"One coffee and a club sandwich coming up. What would you like, love?" she asked, turning to her grandson's friend.

"I'll have the same, thank you."

"Don't you want to try the Reuben? It's the best in town."

"Ah, yes, thanks. I haven't had one in years," she said, shivering and putting her hands under her legs on the red leather seat.

"Are you cold, darlin'? Danny, get over there and warm her up," said his grandmother, elbowing his shoulder.

"Umm ... We're not together ... as a couple. It's not like that," he said, squirming.

"Ah. Well. Bloody shame," she said, trudging away.

The detective's face reddened again, and the psychic snickered at his discomfort. Bringing her hands back up to the table, she fiddled with a sugar packet and watched people entering the restaurant and wandering to their seats.

Filling the uncomfortable void, the detective asked, "Are you still cold? There is a draft from the back door. It's creeping across my neck."

"I'm okay."

Reaching across the table, he brushed her hand with his thumb. "Whoa. Icy. Give me," he said, laying his hands palms up. With hesitation, Marnie placed hers on top of his, which were calloused and warm, and they dwarfed hers.

He clasped them together and joked, "There we go. A hand sandwich. Want mustard and chips with that, ma'am?" Laughing, he added, "Gosh, your hands are small."

"Gee, your hands are ginormous!" she teased, pulling away and looking anywhere but at him.

"So ... Ms. Reilly ... to cut the awkward silence, tell me about you and Kate when you were kids. Did you get up to trouble?" He leaned his elbows on the table, hands clasped under his chin.

Eyes twinkling with mischief, she said, "Oh, you know the usual teenage debauchery. Like terrorizing her neighbors with ding-dong ditch or hanging out in her room and talking ... mostly about whatever boy she was obsessed with. Sometimes we'd go to my house, and in winter we'd skate on the pond out back, go sledding, or watch movies. Every so often in the summer, if my brother and Tom weren't around, we'd go skinny-dipping in the pond. Umm ... We both loved listening to music, singing, and dancing. She enjoyed shopping and going to the mall at Hudson Hollow and still does. I didn't and still don't. The library was one of my favorite haunts, but she would only come with me if a cute boy was going to be there. We've always been different. She's a girly girl. I'm a tomboy. Not much has changed."

"You say you went skinny-dipping?" he said, feigning boredom.

"Out of that whole little preamble of my teen years, that's all you heard?" she said, giving his arm a playful slap. "It is true. Men do only retain information they want." Squinting, she gave him a sizing-you-up gaze and added, "I bet you were a stuck-up boy in high school. You were a football player and, what, prom king, right?"

"Nope. I was a shy, studious, and serious geek, and only played sports to keep my old man happy. My high school dating history is all but nil. It's a tragic story."

She wagged a finger. "Ha-ha! You are a terrible liar, Detective."

He flashed a smile, his dimples on display. "Yes, ma'am. All-State in football, basketball, and baseball. And stuck-up prom king. That's me."

"Hmm ... I'm not sure about all of that, but at least part of it is true." Shifting in her seat, she stretched her neck and shoulders and was happy to see their food was on the way. "Yay! Here comes your grandmother."

Gram bustled over to the table with two cups of coffee and two plates balancing on her inner forearm. Setting down the food and drinks, she said, "There we go. How's that for service?" She wiped her hands on her apron and pulled a bottle of ketchup and a vinegar cruet from the pocket, setting both between them.

"Wow. This looks amazing," said Marnie, eyes wide, admiring the plate overflowing with steak fries, an open-faced Reuben, and a sliced dill pickle. "Thanks for the suggestion."

"With a name like Reilly, it had to be corned beef," said the woman, pinching her grandson's cheek before scurrying back to the kitchen.

Tater sat up—nose in the air. His tail thumped as drool dribbled from his mouth.

"Can he have a fry?" asked Danny.

"Hmm ... Why not? Only one, though."

The dog took the tasty morsel in a gentle bite and lay back down beside the table.

"He's great," said the detective.

"Most of the time," she agreed, stroking the collie's back.

The proprietor returned with a raw beef bone on a plate. "Can the wee one have this, or perhaps he can have it later?"

The dog stood, eyes like saucers, and watched the platter, his body wagging at the beautiful sight before him.

"Aw, thanks for thinking of him. He can have it now." Marnie accepted the dish and passed it to Danny. "Here. You want him to be your friend. This should help. Make him work for it, though."

He took it from her and turned to Tater. "What will you do for the bone, pal?"

The canine barked and bounced forward, waiting for a command.

"Tater, sit!"

The dog sat, but his owner interrupted before he could be rewarded.

"Too easy! This is a Border Collie. Raise the bar, will you?"

"What do you mean?" he asked.

"Ask him to shake."

"Okay. Tater, shake." He put his hand down and waited for the dog to lift his paw, but he didn't. The clever canine stood up and shook his body as if he were getting water off his coat. Danny and Gram burst out laughing.

"Now, that is smart," he said, grinning and handing over the bone to the grateful pup, who settled under the table and chewed.

Gram returned to the kitchen, and Danny and Marnie ate in silence. When they finished their sandwiches, they sat for a moment, looking out the window. The detective was thinking about how best to broach the subject of her safety.

"I was thinking. Do you and Tater want to come to the station and have dinner with me tonight? I know an excellent steak place."

"Detective, I know you are trying to keep me safe, but what will we do while you're writing reports and investigating?" she said with a sigh.

Glancing outside, he tried to come up with a solution. "You and Tater could stay here with Gram until I finish, and then we can have dinner."

"Okay, we could for a few hours, and we could have dinner with you tonight, and then what? Tater and I get stuck in some sleazy motel room with a cop guarding the door? C'mon, Danny, that's not okay for me or the knucklehead. He needs a run, and I want to curl up next to my fireplace, sip wine and read a book or watch television."

He dropped his head to his chest and fiddled with the sugar packet. When he lifted it, he met her gaze with a dimpled smile.

"Well, you called me Danny and not Detective. That's a start, so here's the plan. Don't get mad; just listen. Gram has an apartment upstairs with a fireplace and heaps of books. There's a fenced yard out back. You and Tater could play fetch while I'm at the station. When I finish my report, I'll stop by the grocery store for steaks and something for Tater, and we can go to my place, and you can crash with me. I have a spare room, a lake, a fireplace, and a security system. You'll be safe." He stopped and took a breath, waiting for her to respond, but she was staring past him. Glancing back, he wondered who was haunting her today.

She shivered, then her eyes met his, and she gave a solemn nod. "Yes. Okay. We can do that, but I have appointments tomorrow, and I can't let people down. Can we pick up a few things at my house, please?"

"Not a problem. How 'bout you tell me what you need, and I'll have Joan and another uniform pack you a bag. Will that work? I don't want you going back there tonight." His blue eyes pled his case.

She sighed and gave in. "Fine. Make sure Joan is safe, though. Don't send her out there with a wimp. I'll write you a list of things to add to the bag you already have in your trunk." She furrowed her brow, wincing with pain. "Ow! Damn glue. It pulls when I do that."

"You saw that, huh? Sorry. I didn't think you'd come with me," he confessed.

"I'm not a fool, Detective, and I don't want to die. If Tom wasn't in the hospital, we would have stayed with him. When I thought we would end up in a sleazy hotel, I wasn't comfortable. Let's face it. That's the norm, isn't it? I was angry and felt misplaced. All the crap at my house. Ken, Tom, Jalnack, Webb, Weaver, and now Kate's been attacked too. It's all a bit much, don't you think?" she said, her gaze meeting his as she picked up a sugar packet, tossed it in the air, allowing it to drop between them.

He reached across the table and placed his hands over hers. "It's gonna be okay. We're gonna catch this guy, and everything will go back to normal."

"No, Danny. Things will never be normal again. My home will never feel safe again. We can wash away the blood, but the memory will still be there. Whenever I go into my backyard, I'll see Weaver's dead body bleeding out on the porch. Every time I come home, a vision of Webb and his blood pooling on the deck … that will haunt me too. Those police officers' families will never be the same, and Ken's wife doesn't even know she's a widow. Perhaps with time, things will get easier. A new version of normal will emerge, but some things have changed forever." She looked past him. Her eyes filled with tears, and beneath his hands, her fingers curled, her nails biting her palms.

Quirking up the corners of his mouth, he concurred. "Yeah. I know. It's something stupid cops say to make people feel better. It works sometimes." He stood with a sigh and said, "C'mon. We'll get you and Tater settled, and I'll go catch a killer."

Chapter Twenty-Eight

Danny said goodbye to Marnie and Tater at the gate to Gram's tiny backyard. He waved to the duo playing fetch with an old tennis ball and dodging muddy patches of melted snow. To be fair to the Border Collie's skills, *catch* was more accurate because each time the psychic would throw, the dog would lob the fuzzy toy back with his nose. *What else can this pup do?* he wondered, getting into his vehicle.

12:50 PM, Creekwood Police Station

Sitting at his desk, Danny sifted through forensic data and crime scene photos before tapping out his report. He hated desk work because it pulled him away from investigations. But he knew that if he didn't do things by the book, the captain would come down on him like a sledgehammer.

He let out a harrumph when he discovered the search warrant for Wilder's house wasn't approved. Then he cut Judge Lawrence some slack. She was as overworked as he was, so he continued, jotting notes and tacking up pictures on the whiteboard in front of him. It would be referred to as the murder board for the remainder of the investigation. The detective stared at the evidence, then looked away for a beat before turning back, absorbing the detail.

A clearer picture emerged, and while the pieces had been coming together in his mind, the visual helped connect the dots. He sucked his bottom lip and tapped his pen on his desk as he studied the details. His gut told him they were close, and he always trusted it.

He filed paperwork with the armory for Tom's new firearm and called his partner, but his phone went straight to voicemail. Then he remembered the regimented nurse he had dealt with earlier. *Hmm ... Maybe she took away his phone.* Pulling on his jacket at two-fifteen, he attempted a stealthy exit.

"Gregg!" Sterling's booming voice echoed through the squad room.

Wincing, the detective halted and pivoted. "Yeah, Cap?"

"My office. Now!" roared the bear, lumbering back to his twelve-by-twelve cave.

With a grumble, Danny crossed the squad room in five big strides, gave the door a knuckle rap, and entered, but didn't sit, hoping for a quick getaway. "What's up?"

"Tchah! Take a seat," growled the commanding officer.

He shut the door and settled into an uncomfortable visitor's chair, scrunching up his long legs so his knees wouldn't hit the desk.

"You seem relaxed for a man who has two cops' deaths on his head. Two more cops injured and a dead victim sitting in the morgue. Get your head in the game," said the captain, face drawn and sallow.

"I'm focused, sir. I've been writing reports, chasing the search warrant for the Wilder home, and replacing Tom's gun.

The paperwork is ready. I was on my way to the hospital to get his signature," he said, shifting in his chair and leaning his elbows on the desk, trying hard not to glare at his superior.

"You got the board started?" asked the boss, glancing down at a list on his desk.

"Yes, sir. So is the case file. I've put everything we've got on the board and in the file. I've got copies here, too." He held up a thin blue folder as proof.

Ticking off items from the page in front of him, the boss said, "Okay. Well done. You need to speak with the uniforms. Get them to press their ears to the ground. I want you at the three-thirty briefing, then go home and get some sleep. You look like shit! I don't want mistakes made because you're tired. No excuses." He sat back, dropping his pen on the blotter.

"Okay, Cap. I want to run something past you," said Danny, leaning closer. "We need to arrange a safe place for Ms. Reilly. I can't help feeling she's in danger, considering everything that's happened. Someone was trying to get into her house. Two cops are dead. Two are in the hospital. The common denominator here, sir, is her."

The captain grimaced, shaking a sausage-sized finger. "That one ... Let me tell you, she can take care of herself. She's gutsy, but yeah, she should be someplace safe. Put her in a motel with an officer at her door," he said, resting his chin on his barrel chest as he fiddled with a letter opener.

"Sir, I think anyone watching us would know where she is, especially with an officer standing guard. She has a dog, so she can't stay at a motel, and I don't want a cop injured or killed. Whoever we're dealing with wouldn't hesitate to take out another." He shifted in his chair, straightening his back.

"Who do you think we're dealing with, and what does a pet have to do with it? It can go to a kennel. You got something goin' on with Ms. Reilly? Are you letting this get personal?" Captain Sterling narrowed his eyes, propping his arms on his desk.

"Okay, first, I don't know who we're dealing with, other than they don't care about human life. Second, the dog has everything to do with it. He's her only family, and she would go nowhere without him. Her parents are both dead, and her brother was FBI. He got killed in the line. Plus, if we'd listened to Tater—that's his name— last night, Weaver would still be alive. Third, Ms. Reilly needs our protection. Have I got something personal going on with her? Sir, I think you know me better than that. Some get to me more than others. I admit it. But keeping her safe is my job. Serve and protect, Cap. That's what we do." Danny pressed his fingertips on the desk, his steel-blue eyes holding his boss's gaze.

"Yeah, okay," he said, waving his paw. "Serve and protect. I got it. What's your plan?"

"Well, the safest place I know is my cabin. It's secure and the last place anyone would look. She can crash in the spare room. Tom can stay with her during the day so I can investigate, and I can monitor her at night. We can keep hours down and make sure she's secure. Nobody's gonna get into the cabin."

"You think she'll go for it?" The captain frowned, considering the detective's plan.

"Yeah, if she can be somewhere that her pup can be with her, she'll agree."

"Her pooch a guard dog?"

"No, sir. But he's intelligent, loyal, and crazy protective of his mistress."

"Okay. If she says yes, I won't argue. Make sure Keller has a firearm by day's end."

"Done!" Danny pushed back his chair.

"Where is she now?"

"The second safest place in town. My grandmother's diner."

Sterling grinned. "Ha-ha! Well, nobody's brave enough to take both on, are they?"

"No, sir." He stood up to leave.

"And Gregg?"

"Yeah?"

"Ms. Reilly is, well, she's an interesting woman. Keep it professional. Are we clear?" he said, standing to make his point.

"Crystal. Thanks, Cap. We're gonna get this psycho. I'll keep you posted."

"Go away."

"Yes, sir. I'll be back by 3:30 for the briefing."

With his back to the cold granite wall outside of the station, he called Marnie with an update.

"Hello, this is Marnie Reilly."

"Hi, it's Danny." He cringed. He'd made it personal. *Shit.*

"Hello, Detective."

"How are things over there?"

"Tater's tired out. Well, sort of. He's asleep on the hearth, and I'm reading. Your grandmother has quite a library, and she keeps trying to feed us. Ha-ha!"

"Yeah, she does that. I'm going to see Tommy, then back to the station at three-thirty. Will you be okay to leave there around five?"

"Yup, has Joan picked up my things?"

"Not yet. I expect her back soon, though. He looked at the sky to check the weather. Low-lying clouds veiled the sun, foretelling more snow was on the way.

"Good. See you soon then, and send my love to Tom, please."

"Yes, ma'am. Catch ya."

They both clicked off.

2:30, Margaret Ryan's Apartment

Marnie dropped into an overstuffed chair next to the fireplace, her thoughts still with the detective. The prospect of spending the night alone with him caused her stomach to flip-flop, and she frowned. *Hmm ... Is that my stomach or...*

Approaching footsteps broke her daydream, and Gram walked in with a plate of cookies and a steaming china teacup.

"Was that my grandson?"

"Yes, it was. He's picking us up at five o'clock."

"He has grown up to be a fine man." Pride glowed in the older lady's eyes as she set down the snack on a coffee table.

"Yes, ma'am. Are those peanut butter?" asked Marnie, helping herself to a biscuit.

"Uh-huh. I can tell when someone's trying to change the subject," said Gram, sitting in the club chair next to her, casting a knowing look at her guest.

The psychic bounced a leg and took a bite of a cookie, averting her eyes to her dog asleep on the hearth. "I'm not changing the subject. These are my favorite."

The older woman tittered, sensing Marnie's discomfort. Then she said, "My grandson smiled and laughed today. It's been a long time since he's done that. He tries to go along with the mood, and he's always generous and careful not to show his sadness. People don't see it because he doesn't allow them to. He's an excellent actor. Puts on a show for others, but today, he wasn't performing. He looked delighted with your company. When my Danny smiles, it lights up his whole face. It's you and Tater that brought him joy. Be gentle with his heart. He has a big one, but he's known a world of hurt."

"I know a bit about that. We spoke about his mother and wife," said Marnie.

"He talked to ya about Sarah and my Carol? He doesn't speak about them to anyone. How?" Gram asked, staring into her company's green eyes, seeing and sensing a kindred spirit. "Ah! You've been chattin' with them, haven't ya?"

"Uh … sorry?" She stooped and patted the pup's head, hoping to avoid the conversation, but she could see the older woman was a keen one and wanted answers.

"You heard me! Don't go tryin' to pretend. You know what I'm talkin' about," she said, moving to the hearth—her eyes never straying from her guest.

"What?" said the counselor, tossing up her hands.

"Are you goin' to sit there pretendin' that you aren't gettin' a bit of help from spirits?" she asked with a tip of her head.

"Um … uh … Well," she said, looking into the older woman's bright blue eyes. And then she saw it. A familiar spark only another psychic might see. *Well, I'm not getting out of this,* she thought. *Time to fess up.* Nodding, she said, "You could say I receive divine guidance. Don't you?"

Gram's eyes sparkled. "I do, yes. Some of us get more help than others, though, and you're one of the special ones, aren't ya?"

"Yes, ma'am, I am. And so are you."

Gram laughed, neither admitting nor denying. "Have you got my Carol with you now or Danny's darlin' Sarah? I can't see them, but they talk to me. I'm hearin' nothin' now." She stared at her with anticipation.

Marnie scanned the room, turning her head left, then right. "Neither is here now. I've got my dad with me, though. He's been trying to tell me something for days, but I don't understand. I can't quite connect with what he's showing me."

"Well, keep with it. It will be clear when it's supposed to be. Divine timing, divine guidance, and divine intervention will help you, my dear. Do you read the tarot?"

"Yeah. Do you?"

"From time to time. Danny gets upset when he sees the cards out, so I keep them in a box up on the mantel. Ever since he saw his mother's death in the cards and then Sarah's, he wants nothing to do with them, so I tuck them out of sight." Gram tapped a wooden box with carvings of angels.

The psychic's mouth popped open. "He *saw* that. Hang on ... He told me he didn't understand and seemed incredulous of my clairvoyance, yet it has been around him his entire life." She threw up her hands, shaking her head.

"He often disregards his own gift to cover up his fears. My Danny is as talented as they come, but he will never admit it. He believes he switched it off a long time ago. It scares him. We often deny what frightens us most. When he tells me he has a gut feeling about somethin', I know he's still connected. It's why he's such a brilliant detective, you know. We won't let him know that, eh?" Her eyes twinkled, and she offered a conspiratorial wink. "Do we have a deal? Between us, eh?"

"Yup," she said, a wry grin curling the corners of her mouth.

The smile disappeared from Gram's lips, and she cocked her head. "I'm hearin' a lot of chatter. Do you hear it too?"

"Mm-hmm. There's been a buzz in my ears for a few minutes now."

"Let's sit quietly and see if we can make out what they're tryin' to tell you."

"Oh, I know they have information. If they would all stop talking at once and let one clear voice come through, I'm sure we could figure out who the killer is."

Gram settled into the armchair, remaining on the edge of the seat. "Just be careful it isn't the devil in your ear. He'll mislead you."

"Ha! I don't believe in the devil, but I believe in evil. It was very much alive and at my house last night," said the psychic, taking a sip of tea.

Chapter Twenty-Nine

4:15 PM, Rocky Roadhouse Parking Lot

An old brown Chevy Impala, covered in mucky slush, sat in a closed-for-the-season ice cream parlor's parking lot around the corner from Ryan's Diner. The vehicle was parked with strategic placement so the driver had a vantage point of the upstairs windows and front entrance. Three fresh takeout coffees sat on the dash, the heat rolling off, keeping the windshield clear.

Spying between the front door of the restaurant and the apartment above, nothing gave away Marnie Reilly's location. Is she downstairs enjoying a slice of pie and tea or above sitting next to the fireplace, whose chimney coughed smoke into the frigid air? The car's occupant checked the surrounds to see if anyone was watching, but no one was. This was Creekwood. The land of boring, unobservant passersby. Although the gals at the coffee counter would be huddled, buzzing with excitement and fear after last night's murders at the Reilly house.

Adjusting the rearview, the driver glimpsed a shocking self-reflection in the mirror. Dark circles, untamed hair, a coldness in the eyes looking back. Seething with inner hatred and a death wish for the psychic, dark thoughts festered, urging a plan to evolve.

"Work the problem. Find a solution. You've been in tougher spots and finessed your way to victory. Do it again. Think."

Marnie has police protection. How do I get close to her? A twenty-four-hour diner was a tactical move. Well played, Detective Gregg.

Placing Ken in the shed after he was dead was an error. Even a rookie wouldn't believe he was killed there. The lack of blood screwed us. Novice planning, but out of my control. Last night didn't pan out either. That damn dog is a nuisance, and Marnie is too smart. Framing her would never have worked. She's got security cameras everywhere. I can't believe cutting the power didn't create the chaos intended. But how was I to know she had a generator?

She'll be at work tomorrow. Perhaps an opportunity will present itself unless the detective convinces her to close the office. That's doubtful. She gets off on helping pathetic people. Angel of mercy, my ass! She's addicted to fixing the unfixable. It builds her up and makes her feel better about her own tragic life.

A shadow crossed by the window above, and the driver hunched to see out the windshield, but no one peered out and the curtains remained closed.

Where are you, Marnie? I've got time to kill, and speaking of … murdering the cops was never a part of the scenario, but they were in the way. It had to be done. Shame about Detective Keller. It would have been satisfying to string up that smart-ass. Forever the protector. Then there's Kate … God! I'll deal with her later. She's safe in the hospital … for now.

Focus! Clear your head and don't make errors. Ugh. Leaving the duffel bag near the bridle trail was stupid, but the cops won't track me through fingerprints on the bag or its contents. Ha-ha! Anyway, it doesn't matter. Piano wire, chain mail gloves, and all the supplies I need are in the trunk. I'll stop at the army surplus store and pick up a new holdall.

Maybe no one will be at Marnie's house tonight. It's an unexpected hideout. The cops were there earlier, but no one was an hour ago. I doubt they'll let her go home. I can get into the house, light a fire, and settle down for the evening. Light a fire? No, that's a terrible idea. They would see smoke pouring out of the chimney. Damn it! The security cameras will be on! I can't risk it! I need Plan B. Checking into a motel is out. Where will I find a warm, dry place to sleep? Think!

Then, an idea came together. The engine roared to life as the notion emerged as an effective strategy. Marnie's previous residence on Creek Road was vacant, with a rental sign in the front yard.

"Her old house is perfect! But first, I'll pull around the block and wait for her to come out, then I'll follow to see her next move. They might put her up in a hotel or a motel. That would be ideal. I could get to her easier at the latter, but either way … Then again, she could stay here. Hmm … That would be unfortunate. There are too many people coming and going. I'll tail her, think about my next step, and then get settled in for the night. A good night's sleep will help me think."

Checking the rearview mirror, an evil smile and soulless eyes stared back.

Chapter Thirty

4:57 PM, Ryan's Diner

Danny pulled up in his Jeep outside the diner at five as a dusty old cruiser with huge tires pulled around him and did a legal U-turn, parking across the street. *I've seen that car before. But where?* he thought. Turning off the engine, he racked his memory. It was a popular older model he could have seen anywhere. Its low-riding trunk and lack of rust made it distinctive, though. After all, an early-nineties car should be rusty. Here in the mountains, winters were rough on vehicles. But maybe it wasn't local.

"It'll come to me," he muttered, opening the driver-side door. When he turned around to get a look at the driver, the sedan was gone, its tailpipe puffing smoke a block away. "Huh. Coincidence? Probably not."

The bell above the diner's door rang as he pushed his way through, and the detective glanced up with a grin. *An angel got its wings,* he thought to himself, scanning the restaurant, searching for his grandmother.

"Hey, Dorie! Is Gram upstairs or in the kitchen?" he asked a waitress.

"Hi, Danny. She's upstairs fussing over your girlfriend," said the server with a wink.

"Not my girlfriend," he growled, running up the apartment stairs, taking two at a time. He was greeted by a bark and a flurry of dog nails on hardwood floors, echoing through the stairwell.

Tater scooted to a halt, and his ears drooped when he saw who was visiting, and he backed away, side-eyeing his mistress.

Dropping to one knee, Danny held out his hand so the dog could sniff it. "Hey, pal. How ya doin'?" The pup wiggled his backend, and a silly, happy warble escaped his throat. "Hey, you're happy to see me this time. Let's find your mom?"

The dog trotted alongside the detective, nudging him with his snout before running ahead to Marnie and Gram, who were in a deep fireside chat. Then he disappeared down a dark hallway, nose to the floorboards, on a mission.

"What are you two gabbing about?" Danny interrupted, raising his eyebrows.

"We're conspiring to fix the world," replied his grandmother, patting Marnie's hand as she stood to give her grandson a hug.

The Border Collie returned, zipping into the room with the old tennis ball in his mouth. He scooted to a halt on the timber floor and threw the spit-laden orb at the detective.

"Don't throw it back, or the game will be on, and he is not a quitter," said the psychic, jumping up and snatching up the ball, grimacing at the squishy, muculent mess.

Tater tipped his head, stared at the object of his fixation, and bounced back and forth—waiting.

"No! Down. We will play later. Now, lie down." She pointed her finger at him, and the pup followed her command, dropping to the floor with a grumble.

"Spoilsport," said the detective, bumping her shoulder.

"I'm not. He's obsessive and will drive us all nuts." She bent and scratched her dog's ears, and he looked up, flashing a smile. Then, with a muttering mumble, he put his head down between his paws and flopped to his side.

"You ready to go?" asked Danny.

"Yeah. You said 5:00, and it's 5:01. I'm ready. Let me get my coat," she said, leaving the room.

"Where are you goin' now?" asked Gram.

"Home. They're coming to the cabin."

"Oh, are they now?" she said, clapping her hands, eyes twinkling.

Sighing, he looked up, wondering why she was making it into something it wasn't. "I told you. It's not like that. I cleared it with Captain Sterling. I'll protect her through the night, and Tom Keller will watch out for her during the day. Tater can go to work with her, so it's fine. If we both need to be out, they can come here, if that's okay. And you're being nosy." He leaned down and kissed her cheek.

"It's fine with me. She's a lovely girl, and no one could get past those stairs without someone knockin' them on the head with a fryin' pan. Ha-ha!"

Marnie returned with her coat and the dog leash, setting the jacket on the back of a chair, and stooped to clip on the dog's lead. The detective picked up her coat from her and held it out. With a funny grin, she accepted his help. *I can't remember the last time a man did that. Then again, he pulled out my chair last night,* she thought.

While her back was turned, Gram poked the detective's side, approving his chivalry and his choice of recipient. Pursing his lips, he thought to himself, *Mind your own business.*

Marnie swung around, frowning at him. "Who?"

With a wrinkle across his forehead, he asked, "Who what?"

"You just said 'mind your own business,'" she said, raising an eyebrow.

"No, I didn't."

"You did. I heard you."

"I didn't *say* it; I *thought* it, and it wasn't directed at you," he said, eyes narrowed.

"Ahh ... you *thought* it," she said, evading eye contact. "Shame on you. You shouldn't be thinking that about your grandmother."

"Don't change the subject, Ms. Reilly," he growled.

"Ready to go, Detective? I am." She grabbed Tater's lead and headed to the door. She stopped halfway and turned back. "Gram, it was lovely to meet you. Thank you so much for your hospitality." She gave her a hug and raced to the door.

"See you soon, Marnie." The older woman gave her grandson a nudge. "Go after her."

Marnie skipped down the stairs and out the front door, with the dog leading the way. When the little bell over the door tinkled, she glanced up and smiled. *There you go, Weaver. The first one was for Webb; it's your turn now.*

Outside, Tater sniffed around and raised a hind leg on a mailbox before burying his nose in a drift of snow. He lifted his head when Danny walked out, and he and the psychic laughed at his snow-covered snout.

With a hand at the center of the psychic's back, the detective urged them along. "Come on. I've got groceries in the car, and it's a bit of a drive out to my place." He opened the cargo door and called the Border Collie, who jumped in, turned in circles and sat as the detective lowered the door. He walked around the car and opened Marnie's door for her.

"Thank you, Detective." She stepped up and in, happy that some men still had manners.

He walked around to the other side and climbed in as Marnie turned to check on her dog, whose head popped up over the seat, a guilty look in his eyes.

"Where are the groceries?" she asked.

"In the back." He hooked his thumb toward the cargo.

"Way in the back with Tater?" she said, eyes wide.

"Shit!" He got out, grabbed the food, tossing the bags on the back seat.

"Ha-ha! Never leave Tater to guard the groceries. He will gobble up everything. He'll even eat the vegetables," she said.

"How'd you know they were back there? The same way you knew your bag was?" asked Danny with a sideways grin.

"No. I looked back because the silence was suspicious, and I knew it involved food. He loves to eat."

The detective smirked, remembering his conversation with Tom. "I hear Tater's not the only one."

With a playful punch, she asked, "Hey, who's been telling stories?"

"We both have our ways of finding out information. Although my sources are breathing."

"Not what I heard," she said, throwing out her hands.

His head swiveled, eyebrows raised—knowing her informant was his grandmother.

Laughing, she banged her hand on the dash. "You gonna get moving, or are we gonna sit here all night?"

"I'm goin'," he said, starting the engine and chuckling.

5:15 PM, Driving to The Cabin

Danny observed Marnie out of his periphery all the way home. They listened to the police radio and said very little during the journey. His mind raced, knowing that she and his grandmother had spent the afternoon together. Curiosity and concern took over his thoughts. *What did they talk about, and how much did my grandmother share?*

The psychic spent the drive studying the detective, too. When she wasn't pondering what he was thinking, her mind wandered back to her conversation with Gram. Shifting in her seat to say something, she changed her mind, deciding some things were better left unsaid. With her head pressed against the window, she let her mind drift back to the earlier chat. *Hmm ... He gets divine guidance, too, even though he pretends not to understand it. Why would he do that?* Then she worried whether the detective's cabin was as safe as he believed it to be. She knew anyone sick enough to do the things that were done last night wouldn't let a few locks stop them.

Danny pushed a remote over the visor, and the gate to his road sprang to life. Marnie peered out at the thick, dark forest surrounding them.

When they pulled up outside his house, the automatic security lights lit up the gravel driveway, and the detective jumped out and ran around to open her door.

"Wow," she said, getting out onto the crushed white stone path. "This is beautiful. Have you been here long?" she asked, looking beyond him to a lake and breathing in the scent of pine.

"I've owned the land for a long time but only started building the cabin after Sarah died to get my mind off my woes. I finished the cabin about six months ago."

Going around the Jeep, he let Tater out before meeting Marnie on the passenger side, where he handed her the lead and a key.

"Go on up. I'll put the truck in the garage and get the groceries."

She took the key and moseyed up the wide front steps to a massive veranda, where a dozen Adirondack chairs and pine tables clustered around the deck. A handcrafted fireplace adorned the far corner, a rustic bench swing hung nearby, and the water was so close that you could almost touch it.

She put the key in the lock, turned the knob, pushed open the solid oak door, and reached for the wall switch. Her eyes widened, and her jaw dropped. This was not what she had been expecting. The thick natural beams of the vaulted ceiling were astonishing—even to a carpenter's daughter. She gazed up at the mezzanine in wonder, appreciating the detective's craftsmanship. The cabin was homey, with its rustic decor and inviting energy. A fieldstone fireplace occupied most of the east wall. The sheer size of the firebox astounded her—she was certain she could stand up inside of it. The furniture was a mix of overstuffed pieces and chunky wooden handcrafted tables, chairs, and bookcases. One wall held a built-in bookcase filled with paperbacks, hardcover books, and knick-knacks, and a huge pool table took up the far end.

"Now, this is our kind of place, hey, Tater?"

The dog waved his tail, waiting for permission to proceed. She clipped off his lead, releasing him to wander and snuffle, which he did before settling underneath the pool table.

Marnie was trying to figure out where the kitchen was when Danny came through the door with the groceries and her bags.

"Let me help you," she said, crossing the room and taking her luggage from his arms.

"Thanks." He glanced around his home with pride. "You like it?"

"It's lovely. Gorgeous!" she said, her eyes landing once again on the fireplace, and she imagined a roaring fire, an adult beverage, and a book.

"Not too manly? Ha-ha! Women always tell me it's too masculine, and it needs a woman's touch."

"Well, those women might want to change it to suit their tastes, Detective. Ever thought about that? It could be *their* touch that's missing?"

"I don't know why they'd want to change a thing," he said with half a shrug.

"Or you?" she asked.

His face broke into a wide grin, knowing she was right. "Ha-ha! Shut up and help me carry this stuff into the kitchen."

He pushed the wall under the mezzanine with his foot, but it wouldn't budge. "Hey, Marnie, could you give me a hand? See that notch? Can you tug it toward you, please?"

She did as instructed, and the wall folded back like an accordion, and Danny walked through, turning on a light and setting down the bags on an island.

"Damn tri-fold door," he said. "I thought it would be practical, but it isn't. You can separate the two rooms to make it cozy, or you can open it up when you have a party." He folded the door against the far wall, opening the downstairs up into one grand room.

Marnie twirled, taking in the enormous space. "Okay. I'm in love."

Danny smirked, cocking his head.

"With your home, Detective, and this kitchen is ... well ... I am lost for words. If I had to describe my perfect kitchen, this would be it."

"You ain't seen nothin' yet, ma'am," he drawled. "Check this out." He sauntered through the room and switched on another light, revealing a wall of glass overlooking the lake and the back veranda. "Watch this!" He turned the door handle and folded up the glass wall. "Ta-da! Another tri-fold door. This one I like."

With a look of sheer joy, she clapped her hands and admired the view. "Oh, how lovely!"

She joined him out on the veranda, listening to an evening opera of birds and the chattering of squirrels. In a clatter of dog nails, the Border Collie burst into the room. The adventurous canine had slipped unnoticed into exploring the cabin, and he had found treasure. Racing through the kitchen, he stopped short and dropped a big leather slipper at Marnie's feet.

"Tater, you thief!" she said and bent to pick up the slipper. "Sorry, Danny. He steals things for comfort, like my shoes. He wouldn't damage anything, though. Well, he would rip up a tennis ball. I'm so sorry." Pivoting to the dog, she said, "Naughty! Don't do that again."

"That's okay. He must have been checking out the new digs. Its mate is in my bedroom. Were you hunting, pal?" he asked, crouching to scratch the dog's ears.

The pup looked up and put his paw on the detective's leg.

"Is that his 'feed me' face?"

"Yup. That's it," she said.

He ruffled the thick white fur on the dog's shoulders, then tugged on one of his black ears. "Okay, well, let's get dinner going. But first, I'll run upstairs and change. Back in a tick."

The detective strolled away with his slipper, chatting to the curious canine, who followed him. While they were upstairs, Marnie unpacked the groceries, putting the perishables in the refrigerator before going to the foyer to get the dog's bowls and mat.

Danny and Tater came down the stairs to find the psychic searching the room for her luggage and the pup's paraphernalia.

"Um ... where'd the bags go?" she asked.

"Oh, sorry. I dropped them into your room," he said, pointing upstairs.

"Thanks. Which one is mine? I need the knucklehead's stuff."

He nodded toward the stairs. "End of the hall. Last door on the right."

"I'll be right back with bowls and kibble."

Marnie meandered down the hallway, wondering which door was his. Aha ... the door on the left had a light on, so she took a peek. *Hmm ... Detective Gregg is a tidy monster.* The furnishings were beautiful. A king-size bed with a carved headboard, covered with a patchwork quilt, sat opposite a fieldstone fireplace. The nightstand on the left side of the bed held a lamp and his sidearm. The tall dresser nearest the door held a picture of a woman she guessed was his late wife.

"Stop snooping, Reilly," she whispered to herself as she backed out of the room and crossed the hall. She opened the door to find her bags inside. This bedroom was beautiful, too, and the bed looked so cozy and inviting. She puffed out her cheeks and thought, *Gosh, I'm tired. I could curl up now and sleep until morning.* Coaxing herself to stay awake, she rifled through the luggage and totes. With her pup's supplies in hand, she hopped down the stairs, finding Danny and Tater in the kitchen.

"Here we go, little man. Food for you!" she said, before turning to Danny. "Where can I put his bowls?"

"Wherever you think he'll be happiest," he said, glancing around the kitchen. "His stuff is near the back door at home. He might like them in a similar place here."

He notices the small things, she thought, setting down the mat. Grateful to be here rather than at a motel, she appreciated the detective's kindness.

Danny placed a tin of fish on the counter and dug through a drawer for a can opener as she filled Tater's water bowl. "It comes on good authority that Mr. Smiley likes tuna," he said, opening the can.

"Hmm ... would that informant be one Thomas Keller?" she asked, grinning.

"The one and only."

"Ha-ha! Thank goodness there's only one of him," she said, drizzling the brine on Tater's kibble before dumping the fish into the bowl. Then, she placed the food and dish of water on his mat.

"Can I help you with dinner?" she asked, peeking around him, placing her hand on the small of his back as she tried to see what he was preparing.

"How 'bout you go relax and I'll take care of this?" he suggested, finding it difficult to focus on the task at hand with her distracting him. Albeit a pleasant distraction.

"Sure?" she asked.

"Yeah, positive." He nodded.

"Okay. Shout if you need anything," she said, walking into the great room and spying a stereo. "Do you mind if I put on some music?"

"That would be great," he yelled.

She switched on the radio, sank into the big comfortable couch, and fell asleep to the music of Cole Porter.

Maps of Danny's Property and Cabin

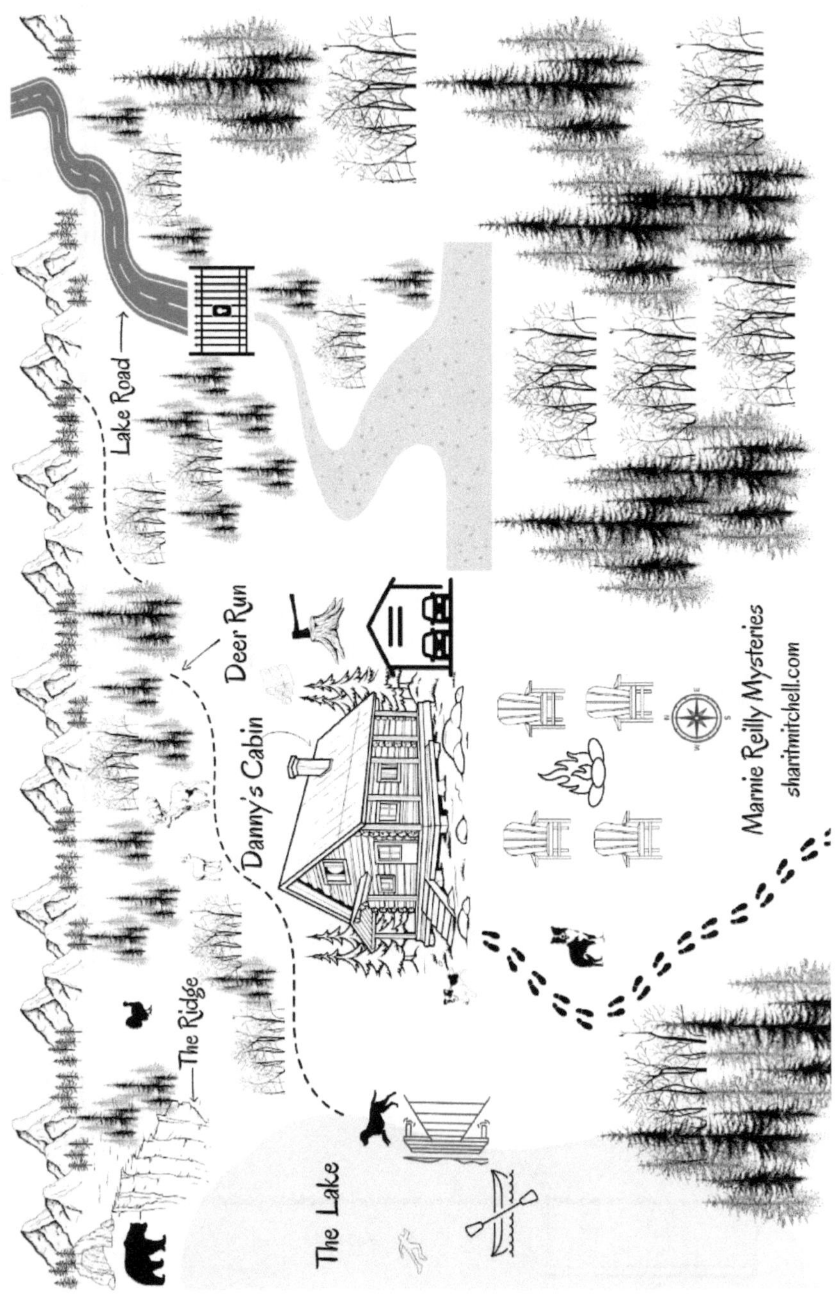

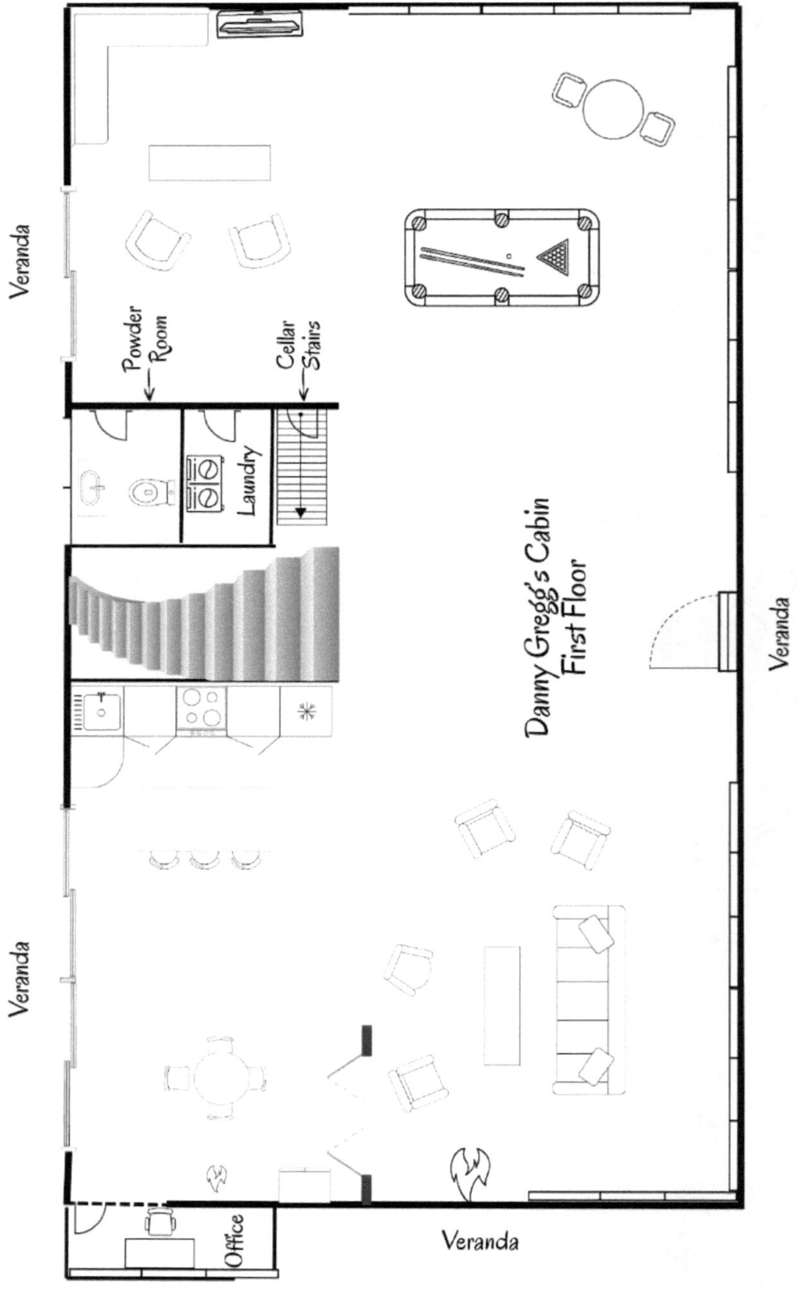

Veranda
Powder Room
Cellar Stairs
Laundry
Danny Gregg's Cabin
First Floor
Veranda
Veranda
Office
Veranda

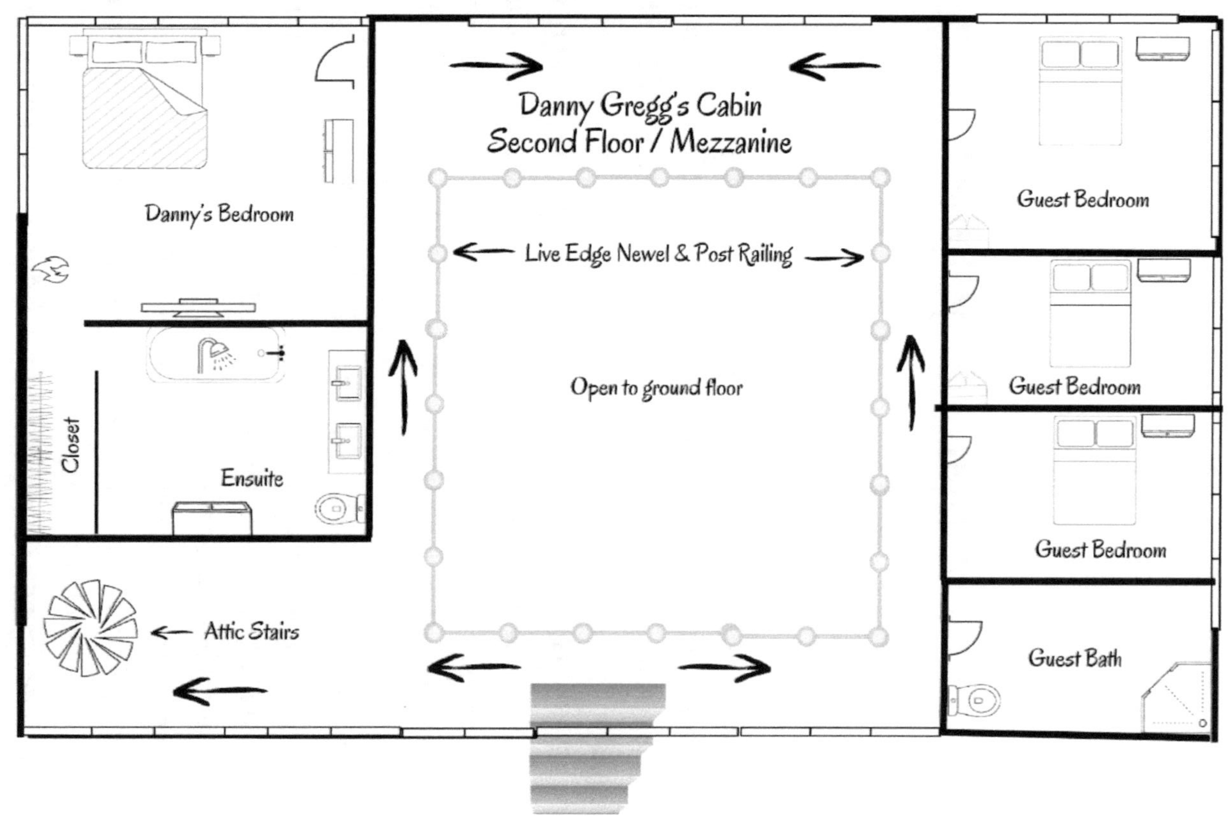

Danny Gregg's Cabin
Second Floor / Mezzanine
Live Edge Newel & Post Railing
Open to ground floor
Danny's Bedroom
Ensuite
Closet
Attic Stairs
Guest Bedroom
Guest Bedroom
Guest Bedroom
Guest Bath

Chapter Thirty-One

6:23 PM, The Forest off Lake Road

Snapping twigs followed each step. Stealth was impossible in the dense forest surrounding Danny's property. Homes were sparse, with only one other in the area, three miles back and devoid of people.

The lake is on my left. If I backtrack one mile, I can get to the water's edge below the ridge. I have wasted time. Think. You know these woods. Looking up at the night sky and down at the snow-covered ground confirmed west. *Follow the deer tracks to their watering hole.*

The lake's pebbled shore was the most navigable path, but even that was treacherous with its uneven terrain, slick boulders, and gaping ankle-breaking crevices. Around the next bend, lights shone above, and a log lodge took shape in the darkness.

Impressive. Detective Gregg has built himself a fortress. Hmm ... How do I get up there without them seeing me? I could cut the power, but I would have to get close enough, tripping the security system if he has one. Of course he does. What if I crawl on my belly and get tight to the foundation? Perhaps the lights aren't motion-activated. Ha! I am not that lucky.

Looking up from the lake with the front floodlight to map the structure, three rows of lit windows bathing the exterior in a soft yellow glow. Ground floor, second floor, and an attic. Squinting revealed a basement level with windows in the stone foundation. *How does a detective afford a house like this? Is he a dirty cop?*

I shouldn't have hiked around this damn lake. Now I've got cold, wet feet. What was I thinking? My spare socks are back at the car. Why didn't I bring them? Staring into the inky darkness, a course of action took shape. *I have to get up on the back veranda and see if she's in there. Marnie was with the detective for most of the day. He must have brought her home. I can't believe I lost them in town. That stupid woman stopped at the yellow light. Why do people do that? There was more than enough green left in that yellow. Shush. Shush. Let it go. It doesn't matter. I caught up with them.*

The rigorous trek up the bank and through the trees triggered the sensors. *The* back veranda, the deer run, and the nearby shoreline lit up like a Christmas tree.

Dammit! Stay low. Keep to the shadows.

Above, a door slid open, and the detective appeared on the porch. He scanned the forest, peering into the darkness before going back inside.

That was close. It's a good thing there is a lot of wildlife out here. He will assume a raccoon or a deer wandered by.

6:33 PM, The Cabin

"Hey, Marnie, wake up. Dinner's ready." Danny gave her shoulder a gentle shake, a line appearing between his eyebrows, wondering why she looked so angry while she slept.

Her eyes were slow to open as she stretched and yawned. "Sorry, I didn't mean to fall asleep."

"Don't worry about it. It's been a rough couple of days. Come on out to the kitchen. The steaks are done. Hungry?"

"I think so. Give me a sec to wake up. Where's Tater?" Eyes darting around the room, she searched for her dog.

Danny nodded to the fireplace where the canine was curled up on the hearthrug, sound asleep.

Covering another yawn with her arm, she joined her pup and put out her hands, fingers wiggling at the warmth of the flames. "I didn't even hear you start that."

"I came in after I turned on the potatoes to see where you were and got it going then. It always makes the great room cozier. I went overboard with the size of the cabin. It was never supposed to be this big. I kept building because it kept me busy and it didn't allow me time to feel sorry for myself." Pride filled his face as he looked up at the rafters.

"It's lovely—even when the fire isn't lit. It feels homey, doesn't it, buddy?"

The Border Collie lifted his head in agreement, stretched, opened his mouth wide and released what Marnie called a blurble. It sounded like an underwater scream to the untrained ear.

"Ha-ha. That's a distinct noise," he said, holding out his arm. "May I escort you to dinner?"

"Why, yes, thank you, sir. That would be divine." Her faux southern accent drew a chuckle from the detective. "Yum. It smells good." She said, inhaling the aroma of dinner as they walked to the table.

The fieldstone fireplace in the kitchen snapped and popped—adding warmth and intimacy to the dining area. Marnie wrapped herself in a hug as she admired the table Danny had set with blue stoneware plates and bone-handled flatware.

"I got the cutlery at an old restaurant auction a few years back. When I started building the cabin, I searched for different things and found these at an estate sale. And I go to flea markets every now and again to see what cool stuff is around. My garage is full of things I need to refurbish. I keep telling myself that's what weekends and retirement are for."

The table was clever. Four old oak wine barrels covered by a wide tongue-and-groove oak plank. The stools were wooden quarter casks with bright-red cushions on top. Marnie ran a finger over the stitching of the runner, thinking about the quilt on her bed at home. Both made with a loving hand and a person with an eye for detail.

Almost reading her mind, he said, "That belonged to my mother. It was worn in a few places, but I didn't want to throw it away, so I asked Gram if she could make something from it. As usual, she amazed me. She made that and placemats, too."

"Detective, you are a lucky man," she said with a wistful smile.

He opened his mouth, then hesitated. After a long pause, he said, "Marnie, let's get the name thing sorted. I'm Danny. No need for the formalities, huh?"

She nodded and concurred with half a shrug. "Okay. That may be tough to do. We flip-flop between professional and personal, *and* when you irritate me, Detective Gregg comes out, and when you try to put a distance between us, you call me Ms. Reilly. It's something we both need to work on, wouldn't you say?"

"Yeah. I guess it's tough when I am also supposed to be protecting you. We can be professional and friends, can't we? You and Tom do it. Anyway, at least I know now what you call me when you're pissed."

His dimpled smile made her laugh, and as she opened her mouth to respond, the lights on the veranda switched on. The psychic gave the glass doors a long sideways glance, and the detective gave her arm a reassuring squeeze.

"I think we may have company. There's an old bear that wanders through the woods. He should be in hibernation by now, though. It could be raccoons, but they're too small to trigger the lights. Or wildcat or deer. That happens all the time. Don't worry. No one's gettin' in here. We're locked up tight as…" his words drifted off, and he followed the psychic's gaze to a faint shadowy figure a few feet away.

"Danny, someone *is* out there. It's not a bear or a cat. You've gotta trust me on this. The glass. Is it tough? Will it break?" Her eyes darted from the door back to the detective.

"We're fine. Hunters are out there shooting sometimes, so safety was always a concern. Don't worry. All the windows are bulletproof, and the locks are strong too. No one is getting in here," he said with reassurance. "C'mon. Let's eat."

Marnie dropped onto a stool with a sigh when the outside lights turned off. The detective relaxed a bit, too. She glanced back to the corner, and then her eyes followed him as he crossed to the oven. He took out a tray with two giant mitts, grabbed a bowl off the counter, and set both on the table. Marnie's mouth watered as she stared down at the roasted vegetables, mashed potatoes, and two enormous New York strips.

"Wow! That looks yummy!" She pulled up her shoulders, and her face beamed.

"This one right here is your steak. Tommy tells me you are a carnivore in the extreme. It's rare—bloody and still mooing. That right?" he asked.

"Yup, thank you!"

"Mine is well-done. I could use it as a hockey puck. But hey, you enjoy your bloody mess over there." He settled onto his seat, cut into his steak, and took a bite. "Perfection, if I say so myself."

She laughed, tasting her steak, and savoring the seasoning. "Also perfect," she said. But before she could help herself to the veggies, her head pivoted as the floodlight came back on. Their eyes shot to the veranda and then to each other.

While his eyebrows knitted together, and his jaw clenched, Danny stayed in his seat. "It's gotta be the bear. Has to be. He's the only thing big enough to turn those lights on."

The detective watched the tri-fold doors for a minute, and when the lights flicked off once again, he scooped a big dollop of mashed potatoes onto Marnie's plate.

"Now, this mash is special. Old Irish recipe. Try it," he said.

She took a mouthful and allowed the flavors to mingle on her tastebuds. "Hmm ... Interesting. You left the skins on. Yum. I taste butter, not margarine. My favorite. And you added cream, not milk. Umm ... But there's something else. Hmm ... What is that flavor?" She took another bite. "Is that Dijon mustard?"

He threw up his hands—his mouth wide with surprise. "How did you get that? Yeah, it is. No one ever guesses that."

Marnie pointed an accusatory fork in his direction and quipped, "Ha-ha! *Irish* recipe? Isn't Dijon *French*?"

"You got me. It is French, but a half-Irish, half-Scot, New York-born American made the potatoes." He grinned and took a bite of his.

"This is a perfect dinner, Danny. Thank you." Marnie raised her wineglass, and he did too, and they clinked.

Chapter Thirty-Two

7:38 PM, The Cabin

Danny picked up the wine bottle and poured, but nothing came out. "Want me to open another? Or are you ready to turn in?"

"Mm … Yes. And yes," said Marnie, taking the last sip from her goblet, tossing her napkin on the table and getting up to clear the dishes. "I can't decide. The last twenty-four hours have been … uh …"

"The word you're looking for is *stressful*," he offered.

"Yeah. Between the murders and the chatter in my head, it's been a bit much."

"Is that why you were scowling?"

"I beg your pardon?"

"When I woke you. Your face was all scrunched up like you were mad at somebody."

"Oh. That. Spirits natter at me in my most vulnerable moments, like sleeping or when I'm relaxing in a bubble bath. That's when my mind is clear, so they come knocking. Anyway. I'll tell them office hours are over before I fall asleep tonight."

He pulled a face. "That works?"

She wagged her head, but before she could respond, Tater pranced into the kitchen.

"He'll need to go out before bed. I'll get his lead," she said, herding the dog to the door.

"Hang on a minute. I'll go with you." He scooted past her and jogged upstairs, returning with his sidearm. "Let's all go."

Giving him two thumbs up, she agreed, "I won't argue."

Marnie put on her jacket, fastened the pup's lead, and waited while Danny switched on two more outside lights. He peeked through the blinds and opened the door. Stepping out onto the porch, he reached for the psychic's hand, guiding her to stay behind him.

"Let's make this quick, huh?" he said as icy fingers raced up his spine. He patted the canine's back and glanced down. The Border Collie was not smiling. His mouth was shut tight, and his intelligent eyes intense. "Has he got a bead on something?"

The psychologist shrugged. "It could be a rabbit or an opossum."

The detective scoped out the surrounds and said, "Yeah. We'll go with that."

They walked down the steps and into the snowy front yard, where the dog sniffed around and dug at the earth before peeing on a big pinecone. He snuffled a bit more before kicking back dirt and nudging his mistress with his nose.

"He's done. Let's go inside," said Marnie, gazing into the darkness.

"Ssh. Ssh." Danny cocked his head, listening. Thinking he'd heard something, he mouthed, "Go," and she ran up the steps with her dog. He raced behind them, pushing them through the door, and locking it. Stalking around the ground level, he checked the doors and windows and pulled the shutters tight. Taking a keyring from his pocket, he unlocked a drawer in the table by the fireplace, took out another handgun, and loaded a magazine.

Passing it to the psychologist, he said, "Call it a hunch, but I'm guessing you know how to handle one of these?"

"It's been a while, but yes."

"Great. Come with me while I check the cellar. I can't remember whether I locked the outside door. Tater needs to stay here, though. I don't want him running out if it is open. Are you with me?" He held out his hand, and she grasped it.

When they reached the door, the detective pressed an ear to the wood before easing it open and flicking on the light. They tiptoed down the steps and approached the hatchway, both breathing a sigh of relief. The position of the deadbolt and the slide lock confirmed their security, and on inspection all windows were closed; their latches locked.

Returning to the great room, they found the dog scratching the bottom sill of the door.

Danny wiped a palm against his forehead and winced. "Does he need to go out again?"

With a slow turn of her head, her eyes traveled around the room, settling on Tater. "No. He's caught a scent. His scruff is up too."

"I'm calling the station. There's not much they can do. We're too far out, but at least I'm telling them what's happening. Would you call the sheriff with your phone?" he asked, grabbing the landline from its cradle. But he set it down again, the hair on his neck standing on end. Marnie appeared transfixed, and he waved a hand in front of her face.

"Hey, what's happening?" he asked, squinting at the space that had her attention, and the vague outline of a person took shape, standing between him and the psychic.

"Divine guidance … uh … a message. It's my dad. He's been with me since yesterday, but I don't know why. It's unusual for him to turn up like this, but when he does, I pay attention. He says we're safe here. He's not worried, but he wants you to get a fire going in every fireplace. Do we have enough wood inside? Never mind. He says you do. He wants you to keep them burning all night. Can you do that?"

"Yeah, of course. What's your father's name?"

"Colin."

He gave a quick nod. "Okay. Don't worry, Colin. How 'bout you make yourself at home and keep us company?" he said, leaving to gather firewood.

Tater clawed at the base of the door again and whined like he knew who was on the other side. Marnie grabbed her phone and called Tom. Was it him outside the cabin or someone else? He answered on the first ring.

"Hey, Marn. What's happening with you and your bodyguard?"

"Are you still at the hospital?" she asked.

"Nope. They freed me. I'm on the road. I had to stop at the station to pick up my sidearm. Where's Danny? I need to talk to him."

"He's in the cellar getting wood. I'll have him call you back."

"Yeah, thanks. Hey, are you okay?"

She frowned, weighing up whether to ask him to come to the cabin. In the end, she decided that putting him at risk again was unnecessary.

"Yup. We're locking up for the night. The outdoor lights keep coming on and off, but Danny said it's a bear." She looked at her father, who shook his head. "Have a good night. Take care of yourself."

"Yeah. See you tomorrow and don't forget to leave that message. It's important."

He stared down at his phone and chewed the inside of his cheek. *She would tell me if something was wrong, wouldn't she?*

Marnie closed her eyes, hoping to conjure up an image of whoever was outside the cabin. *Hmm … There's no way it's Carl. He doesn't know where the detective lives. Is it too late for Gram?*

Jolted from her thoughts, she dropped her phone when a ferocious bark echoed off the beams. Eyes wide, she froze. The scruff on Tater's neck bristled as he howled and growled, scooting backward.

Danny rushed in with two full totes of firewood, dropped them, and raced to the dog. Picking him up, he patted his back and carried him to his mistress. "It's okay, boy."

Marnie took hold of the collar when Danny set down the pup.

"I'm going upstairs to look out the big window. There's a bird's-eye-view of the property," he said, running upstairs to the catwalk above the great room. He scanned the surrounds but couldn't see anything or anyone lurking in the darkness.

Jogging down the steps, he shrugged. "Doesn't look like anyone is out there. I checked out back too. Nada!" He picked up several of the logs he had dropped and hauled them to the fireplace, putting two in the grate and two on the hearth. "Hey, Marnie, can you help me tend the fires? It will be quicker if we work together."

"Sure," she said. "I'll add fuel in the kitchen while you light the one upstairs."

"Done. I'll get the one in my room and meet you back here in ten minutes," he said, grabbing a full carrier and trudging upstairs.

Marnie carried a canvas tote into the kitchen, stacked seasoned logs on the hearth and threw another onto the fire. She stirred the embers with the poker until flames danced in the grate.

"There you go. Do you think the boogeyman is going to come down the chimney?" She peered over her shoulder at her father, and his response was a tight-jawed *dad* look. "Okay. Sorry. I won't make jokes."

$$\blacklozenge$$

8:28 PM, The Great Room and Attic

"We should be good for a while," said Danny, dropping the empty bag by the fireplace. "Is he okay?" he asked, chin-nodding at the dog, whose nose was pressed against the bottom of the door, sniffing from one side to the other.

"I don't know. He must smell something. Does anyone up here have a cat?"

"Maybe, but they wouldn't let them outside with all the wildlife. It's probably a raccoon."

"Hope so," she said, staring past him.

Danny shivered, flinched and jerked around as Colin Reilly reached out, his hand hovering over the detective's shoulder.

"Uh … my father wants to know if you have an attic," said Marnie.

With a stiff nod, he picked up his gun, and they dashed to the mezzanine and then up a spiral staircase to a hatch in the ceiling.

He pushed it up and pulled on a string, switching on a light, and they crept up the remaining steps. Marnie held on to his belt and walked in step behind him. At the top, they saw a man peering into the window. The psychic gasped a startled scream, and a clipped bark from the dog echoed below, followed by the harried clatter of nails.

The detective hurried to the window, pulled the shutters closed, locking them before rushing to check the dormer windows. Tater bounded into the room, looked up and broke into a frantic bark.

Danny looked up and cussed, "Son of a bitch. The skylight's open."

Grabbing an eight-foot stepladder, the detective climbed up to pull it closed as a hand appeared and struggled to yank the window from its hinges. Marnie held tight to the side rails, eyes shut tight.

The detective grasped the man's hand and twisted with all his strength, then smashed the intruder's wrist hard against the roofline. A pain-filled howl pierced the air, and retreating footsteps resounded above them. The detective slammed the skylight and latched it. Climbing down, he stopped four rungs from the bottom when he saw the psychic standing there, clinging to the rails with her eyes closed tight.

"Archangel Michael, lend us your army of angels. Thank you, Universe, for leading us to safety and surrounding us with your divine light of protection."

She opened her eyes, backed away, and looked up at Danny. In that moment, he saw Marnie Reilly for who she really was—a spiritual counselor—a woman of faith who was certain that divine guidance would deliver them into the folds of safety and away from the evil man who hunted them. He leaned down and kissed her forehead. Stepping off the last rung, he hugged her close and turned his gaze to the glass above. The intruder had returned and stared back at him. Danny drew his gun from his waistband and aimed it at the skylight as the Border Collie bounced back and forth, growling and barking at the boogeyman above. And then the face in the glass disappeared. The detective's eyes followed the sound of the heavy footsteps across the metal roof. Tater sat and watched the skylight for a moment, and when satisfied that the danger had passed, he settled his back against the legs of his mistress.

Danny stepped back and swept a tendril of hair from Marnie's eyes. "C'mon. Let's go downstairs and check in with your father."

Taking her hand, he led the way, the dog trotting behind.

8:52 PM, The Great Room and Kitchen

Tater settled on the hearthrug, put his head between his paws, grumbled, and closed his eyes. Marnie fell onto the couch with a long sigh and stared at the fire.

"Are you okay?" asked Danny, picking up the phone.

She gave a tight nod. "Yeah. My father's gone. His visit must have been a warning. Thank goodness we're here with you and not at home."

"Mm ... I'm sorry you had to go through that ... the guy on the roof. I watched the rearview mirror all the way home and didn't see anyone behind us. He must have had his headlights off." Taking a breath, he added, "Anyway, I'm gonna call the sheriff and let him know what's going on."

Danny provided a detailed report to a sheriff's deputy before hanging up the phone and dropping onto the couch next to the psychic. She scooted closer to him and rested against his shoulder. He eased his arm around her, ignoring his captain's earlier warning. *If Tommy were here, he'd give her a hug. Why can't I?* he thought. *And it feels right to comfort her after the ordeal in the attic*, he reasoned as the counselor snuggled closer, draping an arm across his chest. He relaxed, allowing his head to sag into the cushions as he mulled over the case. *C'mon, put the pieces together.*

Marnie jerked upright and turned to him—her green eyes wide. "How did someone get through the gate? Does the fencing go all around the perimeter?"

"Ah ... It's not the grounds that people can't get into; it's the cabin. I installed the gate as more of a deterrent, but of course they can get onto the property. A fear of getting lost in the woods discourages most, though. Besides, the road is private, and only folks who live down here have permission. There are 'posted' signs all over the place, but those only keep out honest people. Most of the property owners only come up on weekends to hunt and fish, or they live up here during the summer months. With Thanksgiving a few days away, maybe some families have come up to celebrate," he said. "I don't know, but whoever is out there must have walked around the lake for miles. But let's not think about it, huh? The sheriff will be here soon," said the detective, giving her a reassuring squeeze.

"Danny, I think you should call him back."

"Why?" He sat forward, studying her face.

"Whoever we're dealing with has piano wire. They could stretch that between trees or across the road and take off somebody's head if they're driving an all-terrain vehicle. You need to warn him."

He nodded in agreement and got up to make the call, followed by another to his captain. Images of the dead law enforcement officers drifted into his memory. Then he thought about something that had happened earlier in the day.

After hanging up, he said, "Hey, Marnie? This afternoon, when you heard me tell my grandmother it was none of her business? You know, when I thought it, but you believed I said it?"

"Yeah," she said, looking away.

"Can you do that on purpose?"

She scrunched up her face, assessing him with wary eyes. "What?"

"Can you get into someone's head on purpose?" He cocked his head, eyebrows arched.

"Uh ... I don't like where this is going. And no, Detective, I can't do it on purpose. I can't switch it on and off, and I will not try to get into a killer's head. No way. No freaking way!" She jumped up from her comfy seat and stood by the fire, eyes blazing.

"Okay. You're back to 'detective,' are you? Yeah, well, I thought it might be worth a try, Ms. Reilly. Tchah!" he shouted and stormed off.

She collapsed into a chair and allowed the crackling logs to soothe her as she considered what he had asked. *Can I get into the killer's thoughts? I guess it's possible, but why do that? I don't want his sick thoughts floating around in my head. Gawd!*

Jumping up from her seat, she stomped into the kitchen, where he stood near the fire, sipping red wine. He turned when she stalked in and set the glass down on the table.

"Want some?" he held up the bottle as a peace offering and waggled an empty glass.

"No, thanks. I drank too much earlier. I have to work in the morning." She wasn't expecting him to be cordial. *Why is he being nice?*

"Okay. Look, I'm sorry I asked you to, well, get into his head. I'm trying to put this all together, and it's frustrating me. Forgive me?"

"It's okay. It's not the dumbest request I've ever had," she said, shortening the distance between them.

"Oh, yeah? What's the silliest?" he asked, brushing another tendril of hair away from her eyes.

"Well, I have had people ask me to talk to dead pets. Lottery numbers—now that's a popular one. I had a woman ask me if I thought she could get away with killing her husband. I called Tom on that one. Then there is my favorite. Drumroll, please. It has to be the people asking me to channel Jimmy Hoffa because they want to know where he's buried. Can you imagine how many times I've gotten that one?" she said, palming her face.

Danny stared at her straight-faced. "Seriously, where is he buried?" He grinned and gave himself away.

"I don't know," she said, laughing.

The shrill ring of the phone made them both jump and woke the Border Collie. Tater ambled into the room, grumbled and lay down near the glass doors before flipping onto his back, legs splayed.

"Hello?" said the detective, picking up a pen from a notepad on the counter, ready to take notes. But he laughed and put the phone back in the cradle. "Well, whoever our visitor was, a very pissed off black bear escorted him out of the woods. That means if he's the guy who took Tommy's gun last night, he's tossed it. We would have heard gunfire otherwise. The Sheriff's Deputy had on his night vision goggles and saw old Percy, the black bear I was telling you about, running through the woods with a man struggling to stay ahead of him. He heard an engine start on Lake Road but couldn't get a license plate or model. Not unusual at that distance. They've got cruisers out looking, and if someone pulls off the road in either direction, they'll get him. He told me there's some piano wire strung up out there, too. He and a few of his guys have put crime scene tape over what they have found. I'll have to go out there tomorrow morning and cut it down." Pouring a bit more wine into his glass, he picked it up and swirled the contents.

"So, we can get some sleep then?" said Marnie, dropping her head to her chest, pretending to snore.

"Yes, ma'am! You're tired, huh?" he asked.

"Mm ... I'm a lot of things. Wired. Relieved he's gone, and worried he'll make his way back," she said, breathing out a final shiver and relaxing her shoulders.

"I get it. Let's chill out for a while," he said, snapping his fingers as a thought popped into his head. "Hey, we didn't have dessert."

Eyes bulging, she groaned, "Dessert? Are you still hungry?"

Making his way to a cupboard, he pulled out a bag of marshmallows, holding it up. "I can always eat toasted marshmallows. Are you in?"

"Hell yeah!" she said, grabbing the package, and jogging back to the living room with Tater scrambling behind her.

Danny got two skewers from a drawer and joined them.

"Yum. I can't remember the last time I had toasted marshmallows. I would have been a kid. This is a rare indulgence." She grinned at him as he offered her a skewer.

"Well, I don't like admitting this, but ... I eat them more often than I would like people to know." With the corners of his mouth turned up, he placed one on a stick.

They got comfortable on the floor next to the pup and put their treats in the fire.

"Now, this is nice." She leaned against the coffee table and popped a gooey roasted confection into her mouth.

"That's funny. I would have expected you to like the burned ones. Interesting! I didn't think you would be patient enough to sit there and turn one over the embers like that."

Side-eyeing him, she asked, "Are you calling me impatient, Detective?"

"Ha-ha! Yeah, I think I am."

"Huh, well, I suppose I can be sometimes, but not when it counts. A toasted marshmallow takes time. The best things in life do."

"Hmm ... divine timing, Ms. Reilly?" he said, smirking.

"That's right, Detective."

She grabbed a throw cushion off the couch and tossed one to Danny, taking a second for herself. She lay back and stretched out her legs.

"Comfy?" he asked.

"Yup. I could fall asleep right here," she said, sighing.

He tucked his cushion behind him, mimicking her. With a playful slap, she laughed, and he caught her hand.

"You know, this is inconvenient," he said, his eyes dropping to their intertwined fingers.

"What's that?" she asked.

Clearing his throat, he said, "You. Me. This."

"Whatever do you mean? I do not know what you're talking about."

He sandwiched her hand between his and shot her a grin. "You know, you can be quite irritating."

"Yup."

Chapter Thirty-Two

"Yeah. So, what do we do? You know, about this thing between us?"

"Divine timing, Detective. We wait and see," she said, snuggling into his shoulder.

"Wait and see? Huh. I would expect a more profound answer from Madame Séance."

"Shhh," she whispered.

The detective sighed and laid his head on hers. Cuddled close, they fell asleep listening to the crackling of the fire.

Chapter Thirty-Three

8:58 PM, A Field Lane off Lake Road

With the engine idling and the headlights off, the man who had frightened the bejesus out of Marnie and Danny a half an hour earlier sat in his car, hidden from sight. Tucked behind tall, dead grass on a farmer's field lane, he opened his duffel, searching for a pair of dry socks.

Damn bear. He surprised me, but he shouldn't have. Black bears will roam for another few weeks. I am not thinking straight. If I had remembered, I would have been prepared. It's a shame we tossed Keller's gun into the forest. And where did those cops come from? I can't believe the detective called the sheriff. What a pansy-ass. The piano wire I strung up would have slowed them down. He-he.

Friday night was supposed to be Marnie's last. I should have grabbed her when she was running or gone into the house and taken care of her and that fucking dog. We turned the alarm off. I should have done it then. It wasn't clever trying to frame her for Wilder's murder. It wasn't worth the risk. I should have taken her out. It was a stupid miscalculation.

He put his feet up on the bench seat and removed his boots, rolling off the wet socks, which he hung over the passenger-side seat back.

Muttering to himself, he said, "Next time I won't walk through water over my ankles. Or I'll buy hip waders. I should have been prepared. Why wasn't I? I know these woods better than anyone."

Turning up the heat, he put his numb feet near a vent, his boots under the other, and assessed his wound. *Gawd! My wrist hurts. It's only a sprain and a graze. I don't think it's broken, but it could be a hairline fracture. Just what I need. Two bad arms. Jesus!*

They saw me through the skylight. Did they see enough to give a description, though? Did she recognize me? I doubt it. She screamed, so I've got her scared. I want her to be terrified.

I'll sit here until the shift change. Those bozo cops will be tired and cold. They'll want to go home. Dumbass local yokels. I'll make a break for it when the graveyard crew are busy getting their coffee and doughnuts. That will give me time to disappear. I've gotten good at that over the years. I'll go dark for two or three days and come back when they least expect it. The element of surprise.

Next stop, Hudson Hollow University Library. I'll get cleaned up and go there. It's open twenty-four hours and has computers. The local newspaper had little about last night's events. Maybe the television station website has a report. I'll look through the newsfeeds, and if all else fails, I will hack into the police department's server. Ha! They can't hide information from me.

I need to get a hunting rifle to come back and kill that damn bear. One bullet right between the eyes. Then, I'll skin him, gut him, and leave the carnage on the detective's porch. That'll send a message.

Hmm ... I wonder whether the detective plays chess. The diner was strategic. Or was that just luck? Marnie's sharp. She doesn't play chess, though. She gets most of her ideas from the voices in her head. Clever girl. She knows things she shouldn't. It's irritating. I'd like to smack the voices out of her head. She thinks she's smarter than everyone else. Divine guidance. Pfft. She's a little smart-ass, like Keller. That's another one. I'll take that asshole out, too, and Kate. She's not so bright, that one. I'll never understand how she got through law school. Must have been her pretty face. She won't mess with me again. I've got that little bitch right where I want her. I have secrets about that one—and her family. She won't say anything.

It wasn't lost on me that the chimneys were all smoking. How did they figure that out? How did they know I would've tried that? I could've gotten down a chimney, like Santa Claus. The image made him laugh. *More like the Grinch. I wouldn't steal presents, ornaments, or food, though. I would take Marnie's life, and the detective's, and that fucking dog's too. Food. Hmm ... I am hungry.*

He grinned at himself in the mirror, and dead eyes and an evil smirk looked back. Giving the chimney another thought, he reconsidered the concept. *Eh ... I wouldn't fit, and he is smart enough to have bat and bird grates installed.*

With a shrug, he peered out of the window. The snow-covered ground and howling wind reminded him of a time long ago when he played in this forest. This place he knew like the back of his hand— where he'd hunted deer, rabbits, and foxes, and killed a neighbor's dog, burying the beloved pet so no one would know. He thought about another slaying and laughed—not because the murder was funny. But because law enforcement couldn't pin it on anyone. And he knew the truth, and he would reveal it when appropriate.

Chapter Thirty-Three

It was revenge. Jealous revenge. Fuck them all. No one cares about me.

He checked his watch. *Midnight. Time to make a move.* He popped a couple of pills, swallowed them dry, and turned over the engine. Leaving the lights off, he cruised out of his hidey-hole and onto Lake Road. The snow had stopped, and the moon was high. *I don't need the lights until I get to the main road.* The coast looked clear as he drove away from Marnie, the detective, and Tater.

Chapter Thirty-Four

November 19^{*th*}

5:26 AM, The Great Room

Danny woke up with the strange sensation of being watched. He opened one eye, startled to find Tater standing over him, staring into his face. Then he remembered last night and chastised himself. *You're an idiot, Gregg. What were you thinking, cozying up to a victim? Oof. I had better not refer to her as that out loud. She'll implode.*

He wiggled his fingers to relieve a tingling numbness prickling his left arm and tried to move, but he was pinned. Marnie's head rested on his chest, and her arm slung across his torso. He hated to disturb her. She looked so peaceful. As he tried to pull his arm free, though, he noticed she was smiling, and he laughed.

"Trying to make a run for it?" Her eyes were still closed, and a wide grin spread across her sleepy face.

"How long have you been awake?" Chuckling, he yanked his arm, and her head fell back onto a cushion.

"A few minutes. I was waiting for you to notice the knucklehead was staring at you. It's creepy, huh? He does it to me every morning."

A car door slammed outside, and they both jerked. The detective jumped up, grabbed a cushion off the floor, and threw it onto the couch. The psychic sat up, looked around the room, then down at her watch. Five-thirty. Tater barked, trotted to the door, sniffing and whining.

"Is it normal for people to come calling this early?" she asked, standing and stretching.

"Not usually. Could be the sheriff. He has access to the gate in emergencies. Might be him." He crossed to the window, opened the blind, revealing frost-covered glass.

Footsteps crunched on the steps, and a key rattled in the lock. They turned to one another—eyes wide. She grabbed his gun off the coffee table and rushed across the room with it. He pushed her to the hinge side of the door, and she grabbed the dog's collar and held onto him. The door opened, and the detective's partner strode inside.

"Morning, children. Uncle Tom is here with doughnuts for everyone." His face fell, jaw slack, when he saw the gun aimed at his chest.

Danny's shoulders dropped, and Marnie let out her breath. The intruder feigned shock, thrusting a pink box toward his partner.

"Don't shoot. I've got a jelly doughnut." He grinned and waggled the carton, snickering at the state of the room. "Cozy little campfire you got over there. Get much sleep?" he teased before disappearing into the kitchen.

The culprits looked at the floor near the fire, where cushions and a blanket were strewn about.

"Where did that blanket come from?" she hissed. Eyes blazing, she poked Danny in the stomach.

"I covered you up when you fell asleep and lay back down to have a chat with Tater." Throwing up his hands, he continued, "I planned to wake you up to go upstairs, but I fell asleep, too."

The early morning party crasher stuck his head into the room. "Shall I make some coffee while you two get your story straight?"

"Shut up, Tom!" they said in unison.

He laughed and ducked back into the kitchen, and they followed.

"Hey, Marn, why'd you call me last night, and why didn't *you,* Daniel, call me back?"

Danny scowled at her, wondering why she hadn't told him. "I didn't get your message." Realizing that the scowl may have been unfair, he shrugged. "Besides, we had a bit of excitement here last night."

"So, it would seem," his partner responded with a wry grin.

Marnie punched his arm. "Not that kind of excitement, Thomas. I called to see if it was you outside last night. But I didn't say anything because you'd just got out of hospital, and I didn't want you to get hurt again. Anyway, he was here. He tried to get into the cabin."

His eyes grew wide, and his jaw dropped. "Are you shittin' me? How the hell does he know about the cabin?"

"I don't know," said Danny. "My post office box is the address I use for most things. The only way to find my physical address is to follow me, or through a property search or maybe voter registration. Who would go to that trouble? It's public record, but still. Don't you have to sign for that kind of information? We gotta go to the courthouse today and see who's been poking around." He picked out a jelly doughnut from the box on the counter, took a bite, and smiled. "Just what I needed. Thanks, partner."

"No worries. You need security cameras. I know you're in the boonies, but it might be a good idea."

Wrinkling her forehead in thought, Marnie said, "Hmm ... I was thinking ... It may be a stupid question, but could you get his prints? You know, from the skylight?"

Danny caught her face in both hands and kissed the crown of her head. "You are brilliant! Yes, we can. Tom, do you have a kit in your truck? We can dust for prints before we head to the station?"

His partner did a double take. "You're kissing her now? Okay, that's new," he muttered. "Anyhow, yeah. We can try. Got a ladder?" he called over his shoulder as he went to the door.

With a yipe and an ahroo, Tater galloped after him.

"You need to go out, Tot? Come on, buddy," he said, spotting the lead hanging on a peg of the coatrack. He clipped it onto the Border Collie's collar and opened the door. "The leash is striking against the decor, Detective. And the leggy blonde ain't bad, either!" he said, doing his best Groucho Marx impersonation, and with a laugh, he tramped out.

With a snicker, the counselor said, "He's a comedian. Now, if you don't need me on the roof, I'll get ready for work."

Danny didn't respond as he watched her climb the stairs. *I don't think I can handle another night alone with you, Ms. Reilly. That would not be a good idea at all.* Snatching up his coat, he joined his partner outside.

5:55 AM, The Roof

The men carried a ladder from the garage to the section of roof where the skylight protruded, setting it against the eaves.

"How much information are we sharing with Marn? Are we safe to talk in front of her or are we taking the clandestine route?" asked Tom.

Danny considered the question, then said, "Let's not scare her. Until we have a clear picture of what and who we are dealing with, we'll keep it to ourselves."

"Okay, well, we can discuss what I need to tell you on the roof. She won't hear us up there."

"Yeah. And I need a favor. If we don't close this today, you need to chaperone tonight. I can't be alone with her again."

"Uh … Okay. Listen, I wanted you to call me back last night because…"

The detective's phone rang, and he stared at the screen, holding up an index finger. "Hang on. I've gotta take this. It's Sterling. Can you go up and get the prints?"

"Yeah. Sure," he said, handing over the pup's lead and slinging his kit over a shoulder and climbing the rungs, his breath billowing in clouds around him.

"Good morning, Cap."

"Is Keller with you?"

"Yes, sir. He's up on the roof pulling prints from the skylight. It's worth a shot, huh?"

"Has the sheriff's department provided new information?"

"No, sir. I'll call them as soon as we get off the phone."

"Keep me informed."

Before Danny could reply, his boss hung up. Not wasting time, he called the sheriff's direct line, receiving voicemail. He left a message, calling Rick as soon as he disconnected.

"What the H E double toothpicks are you doing calling me at this hour? I haven't had my coffee yet," said Dr. Price, heaving a sigh.

Chapter Thirty-Four

"Sorry. Just checking in to see what time you'll be in. I gotta swing by."

"The usual time. Uh ... seven-thirty."

"I'll see you then."

Tom clambered down the ladder, his face bile-green.

"Oh, man. I nearly lost my coffee up there. I have never had an issue with heights, but that ... ugh." He stooped, hands on knees. "Argh. I'm gonna puke."

Danny jumped out of the way, minding his leather boots. "Head wounds take time to heal. Go on inside. I'll put away the ladder and be right there," he said, clapping him on the shoulder.

"I won't argue. Here are the prints," he said, tossing the kit to his partner, who handed over the dog's leash.

"Thanks for that."

Waving a hand, he replied, "Yeah. C'mon, Tater. I need hydration."

6:28 AM, The Kitchen

"Are you feeling better?" asked Danny.

"I am, thanks. I drank two glasses of water and the end of your ginger ale," said Tom, belching as he poured a coffee.

The men turned, hearing Marnie's footsteps, and she appeared in the doorway a moment later, Tater prancing by her side.

Danny's gaze swept over her, from her sparkling green eyes to her charcoal sweater dress to her tall polished black boots. He admired her simple and elegant style and the way her gray silk scarf draped around her neck, concealing the scar. Her strawberry blonde hair was up, revealing her slender neck and showing off two tiny silver hoop earrings. As he appreciated her understated makeup, he realized he was staring again, and diverted his eyes to the countertop, hoping that no one had noticed. But Tom had and nudged him with his elbow, adding a wink and a smirk to agitate. Jaw clenched, he frowned.

"I would give my left arm for a cup of tea. You wouldn't have any by chance?" she asked, catching the tail end of their boyish exchange, offering them a judgmental eye roll.

"Yes, ma'am. We made you a pot. It's on the table, and the doughnuts are over here," said the detective, shoving his tormentor as soon as she turned her back.

Beaming with mischief, his partner shouted, "Hey! Why'd you push me?"

"Are you two four?" she scolded. Bowing her head, she hid a grin. She was accustomed to her friend's silly antics but wasn't sure the detective appreciated his partner's whimsy. What she also knew about her childhood buddy was that he used comedy to deal with fear and trauma. The counselor composed herself and asked, "Danny, do you have a teacup?"

Tom choked on his coffee. "Danny? So, you're using first names now? Ha-ha! How things change in one night."

"Zip it, Keller," she said.

Ignoring him, the detective pointed at the sideboard.

"Yeah. There are some in the cupboard over there."

When she turned, he sneered at Tom, giving him a sharp shoulder nudge.

"I saw that," she said, holding up the china. "Is it okay to use this one?"

"Yeah. That's fine." He gave his partner another shove when she was distracted, pouring her tea. "Knock it off," he whispered between gritted teeth.

Topping up his coffee mug, Tom got back to business, addressing his colleague. "Hey, I need an hour of your time today. I did some digging last night. Serious stuff." Turning to his friend, he added, "So, kiddo, you're with me today, huh?"

"Yay, I'm a lucky girl. I got to hang out with Abbott overnight and I get Costello all day. Should be a hoot." She bumped him with her hip as she set her tea on the counter. "Any chocolate doughnuts?"

"Yup. I got you two." He pushed the box to her. "Can you grab me a bear claw, please?"

Danny and Marnie exchanged glances and burst into laughter.

Mouth falling open, he asked, "What did I miss?"

They filled him in on the black bear story, and they all shared a chuckle.

Forehead creased, Tom said, "Thank Christ for Percy, though, right? I know nobody can get in here, but shit. We're dealin' with a psycho. All joking aside, we need to have a serious discussion. Full disclosure on what we've found. There's a lot to go through. Wilder, Webb, Weaver ... Who's next? This loon doesn't care who he takes out. He's killin' cops. A sane person doesn't run around doin' that crap." He puffed out his cheeks, exhaling for effect. "The three of us. Well, four of us," he said, looking down at Tater, who was eyeing his pastry, drool puddling around him. "We gotta stick together. We'll run over to my place today. I'm grabbin' some stuff, and we're all gonna hunker down tonight."

The partners had hatched their plan before Marnie came downstairs. Danny knew they needed a chaperone tonight. Last night he'd crossed a line, and he did not want to tempt fate twice.

"I agree," said the detective, turning to his houseguest. "You okay with that?"

"Sure. As long as no one goes outside to check the noises after midnight, we're fine," she warned, shaking a finger.

The men's wrinkled brows told her they didn't understand.

"That's how it happens in horror movies. The hunky all-American guy always gets his macho on, goes out on the porch to see what some noise is and wham!" She slammed her hand hard on the counter, and they both jumped. "His head's gone, or a pitchfork gets shoved through his chest. That's where it always starts," she said, giving a knowing nod.

Tom shivered. "Please tell me that's not a premonition, Oh Great Oracle of the North." Raising an eyebrow, he added, "By the way ... which one of us is the hunky, all-American guy?"

"I'm just sayin'. No macho bullshit. With you two locked in a cabin for the evening, there's bound to be some childish show of bravado. If I see a hint, I'll shoot you both. I won't kill you. But I will make sure you can't run around outside like idiots."

The detectives burst into laughter, and Marnie blew raspberries, tromping upstairs to get her bag.

Making his way to the great room, Danny asked, "Hey Tommy, where'd you get a key for the cabin?"

"It's the one you keep taped to the bottom of your desk drawer," he responded, following him.

"That's for emergencies only."

"I called Cap last night to let him know I'd been sprung, and he asked me to drive out this morning to take over babysitting duties. *Soo* I stopped at the office to get a notebook and my new sidearm and looked at your desk. And as any detective worth their salt would, I asked myself, what would my partner do? Would he keep a key and gate remote for the cabin in his desk drawer? I checked the drawers and found the remote, but no key. I turned the drawer upside down, and voila!" He finished with a hand flourish and a toothy smile.

"You could have called. You could have knocked. Knocking is good."

"Yeah. I could have, but you two wouldn't have jumped up and gotten all jittery about gettin' caught doing whatever it was you were doing." He waggled a finger at the area of the floor where the cushions and blanket were when he arrived.

From the stairs, the psychic responded to the accusation. "We were sleeping. That is all," she said, giving his arm a playful pinch as she walked past him.

"Jesus, what is it with you two today? I'm bruised and battered, and it's only seven. You're brutal."

"I am vicious only when someone irritates me."

He rubbed his arm and curled his lip. "Well, we'll send you outside tonight if we hear any strange and obnoxious noises. They don't kill the heroine in horror movies. You can beat him to death."

The detective growled, "This isn't a horror movie. Don't joke like that. I'm goin' to get ready for work." He stalked off, his feet heavy on the treads.

The friends shared a look. "He's under a lot of stress," said the psychic. "And last night was pretty frightening. The guy on the roof. Geez."

When the detective was out of sight, Tom turned to Marnie. "C'mon! What's goin' on with you two? He won't answer me straight, but I know you will."

"Nothing. I mean, it's obvious there is something between us, but we haven't crossed the line. He's not an idiot, and neither am I. We fell asleep by the fire. That's it."

"So, you *do* have a thing for him?"

Lolling her head, she said, "Look at the man. What woman in her right mind wouldn't? I think my friend Ellie would take a second glance, and she's gay. He's tall and built like a freaking Greek god. Top it off with gorgeous eyes and great hair. And he smells like the forest in spring, and that smile is amazing. Men who look like that don't deserve to have dimples, but there they are. Two of them. One on each side of that handsome face. He's gorgeous, funny, kind, and intelligent. Oh! And he can cook. So yes, there's something there. Happy?"

A bit surprised by her outpouring of information, his eyebrows shot up and his mouth tightened into an odd smirk. Pointing above them, he grinned. "Well, not sure I'm happy about it, but he might be."

Marnie looked up to see Danny leaning on the upstairs railing, looking amused. Face bright red, she grabbed her bag and coat, leashed Tater, shoved past Tom, who was roaring with laughter, and stomped out.

The detectives heard her exasperated cry of, "Argh, men!" and both burst out laughing.

"Tonight should be fun," said Tom with a snicker.

"That's enough. I think you've amply embarrassed her for one day, don't you?"

"Nah. I haven't picked on her this much since we were kids. Anyway. We need to talk. Like now."

"We'll make it a priority when we get home," Danny replied, holding the door for his partner to pass.

Tom shrugged in surrender. "It's important, but if you want to wait..."

Map of Marnie's Office

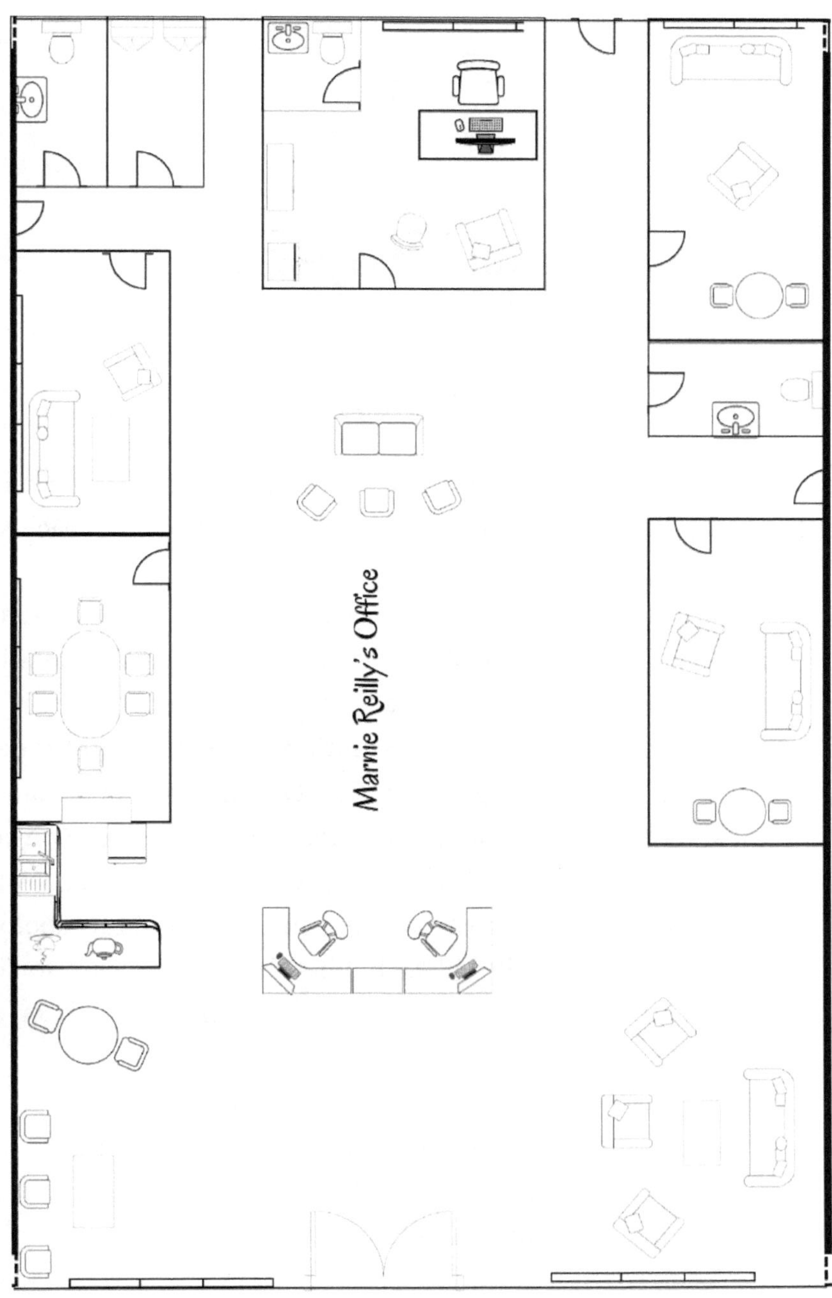

Chapter Thirty-Five

7:20 AM, In Tom's Car on the Way into Town

Marnie sat in silence, listening to Tater's peaceful snoring from the backseat. She didn't look at Tom or speak to him until they reached the outskirts of the city.

"You are an asshole. I can't believe you let me rant like that with him standing there. You should've given me some sign he was listening." Waving him off, she glared, her face still red.

"Hey, I didn't know he was there until you finished your tirade. Not that I would have stopped you. You two have somethin' and I think it's great. I can't imagine how long it's been since you've had sex, and I don't think he's been with anyone since Sarah. You and Danny are two of my most favorite people. It would be cool if you got together. You might kill each other, but hey, at least you'd die happy." With a cheeky grin, he asked, "Seriously. Has it been a year? Two?"

"What?" Face scrunched, she shook her head.

Deadpan, he asked, "When was the last time you had sex?"

"You are infuriating. I will not tell you that. Jesus, Tom. Get a filter," she said, pushing his shoulder.

"You know, I *will* ask you guys not to have sex tonight. Someone always dies when people are screwing around in horror movies, so do me a favor and don't. 'Cause it's the funny guy who gets impaled first, you know?"

She shot him a dirty look and turned her attention to the sights outside her window, muttering, "Asshole."

7:43 AM, Creekwood PD, Forensics Lab

Detective Danny Gregg navigated the backstreets of Creekwood, dodging rush hour traffic and potholes. With the new evidence of fingerprints in his hand, he stopped at the forensics lab before heading to the squad room.

Dr. Rick Price was at his desk, arguing with his computer, a takeout coffee cup resting beside his elbow. He glanced over his readers and grunted, "Morning."

"You look like hell," said Danny, dropping the envelope on the specialist's desk. "We've got more prints."

"Can you come back later? I'm smashed and need to follow up on some things," said the doctor, taking off his glasses and tossing them on his desk. Rubbing his blurry eyes, he sighed.

"No sweat."

"And next time, bring me a coffee. I'm empty." He picked up a cardboard cup and threw it in the bin, spilling over with similar containers.

"You got it. Catch ya."

"Yeah," said Rick, poking at his keyboard, scowling at the screen.

●

7:50 AM, Marnie's Office

"This walkway is like a wind tunnel," said Tom, pulling open the door for Marnie, allowing her to escape the chilly gust ahead of him.

"Brr. Morning, Andrea," she said to her assistant as she set down her briefcase and unbuttoned her coat, hanging it on the rack inside the office entrance.

The practice was in an older building in downtown Creekwood. Its floors were polished hardwood with cozy scatter rugs of muted greens dotting the space. A soft mahogany leather couch, a coffee table, and two comfy armchairs sat to the left of the entrance, with a curved beverage station on the opposite wall. The counselor's office sat at the center back, with two meeting rooms on the left and two on the right. The office was bigger than she required, but she had plans for growth.

Busy making a pot of coffee, the office assistant waved. "Good morning." Then she frowned when she spotted her boss's sidekick. "What are you doing here? Looking for doughnuts?" she teased, but catching sight of the dog, she swooned. "Yay! Tater's with us today. Come here, boy! Did you have a lovely weekend playing in the snow?" She stooped to give him a pat, but he didn't sit still long before running into his mistress's office to curl up under her desk.

Pulling a face, Marnie asked, "Haven't you heard the news?"

"No. Did something juicy happen?"

The counselor's mouth dropped open. "Are you serious? Were you out of town?"

"Yes, ma'am, I was. I had a wonderful ski weekend in Killington with Richard. The snow was terrible, but our room was divine. He has a friend you should meet. Nothing to look at, but quite nice and funny, too. A bit like Detective Keller," she quipped, squeezing his arm.

Tom jumped back. "That's it. Pinches, pokes, punches, raspberries and now insults. I'll have you know I was voted 'Cutest Boy' in my graduating class. Marnie will confirm, and by the way, our Ms. Reilly doesn't need to be fixed up. She's got herself an admirer," he teased, bowing with dramatic flair.

Andrea clapped her hands with excitement. "Oh, do tell! A new man? God, how long has it been?"

The counselor glowered at the pair. "Wow! What is wrong with you? People have died, and you two are inquiring about my sex life!"

"Or lack thereof," Tom muttered with a wink.

"People died? What the hell? Who?" Andrea reached out to grab Marnie's arm but missed as the psychic crossed to the door and peeked out.

"Tom will catch you up. I've got an appointment." She walked past him, leaned in, and whispered, "Expect payback for the 'lack thereof' comment, you big jerk."

He feigned terror, backing away, running into Andrea, who gave him a shove when he stepped on her toe.

"A guy can't win with you two around," he said, dropping onto the visitor's couch, his bottom lip protruding.

"You'll trip over that if you're not careful," said the counselor, opening the door again to greet her new client.

8:00 AM

"Hi, April. Come on in. We'll go into the consulting room on the left. Door's open. Make yourself comfortable, and I'll be right there. Can we get you a coffee or tea?"

"Coffee with one sugar would be nice, thanks," the client said over her shoulder.

To her assistant, Marnie asked, "Could you please bring us strong tea, coffee for April and some water?"

"Yeah. Be right there," she said, filling the kettle. When the counselor was gone, she glanced at Tom. "Okay, Keller. Give me the down and dirty of weekend events."

And the detective did just that, leaving out some of the gory bits.

8:45 AM

Marnie popped her head out of the room and found Andrea huddling with Tom on a mahogany leather two-seater sofa near the kitchenette.

"Psst! Can you bring us more coffee and water, please?" she asked.

The assistant gave her a thumbs up, held up tissues, and the counselor nodded.

"Toss it," she said, catching the box midair, before returning to her session, shutting the door.

"I can't believe police officers were murdered. Right on her doorstep. Gawd! She must have the most overdeveloped coping mechanism on earth," said Andrea, wringing her hands.

"We know she does, and she's more worried about the families than she is about herself. Classic Marn," said her friend, making the psychic's tea exactly as she liked it and placing it on the serving caddy her assistant was putting together.

Andrea poured a coffee and added, "Well, we'll have to keep an eye on her. I hate it when she gets stressed."

"Me too. Need help carrying that?"

"Nah, I've got it," she said, knocking and entering the meeting room with the tray of hot and cold beverages, and setting them on a glass coffee table. She looked at her manager with bug eyes as if to say, "Tom filled me in" before backing away, mouthing, "Holy shit." Marnie nodded and turned back to her client.

●

9:35 AM

Marnie exited her office with her client, whose red, puffy eyes spoke of an emotional session. They stopped at Andrea's desk and booked another appointment before the counselor walked the teary woman to the door and handed her a key.

"Please call if you need anything, April. Are we all set?"

"Thank you. Yes. I'll be at my brother's house in Hudson Hollow for the foreseeable future," she replied, throwing her arms around the psychic. "I am so glad you were at Station Hall on Friday night."

"Me too. And let's celebrate that you have a safe place to heal. See you on Thursday," she said, patting the woman's back and opening the door.

"Eight sharp," replied the nurse, strolling out with a wave.

"Looks like that went well," said Andrea, handing her boss a fresh cup of tea.

"Oo. Thanks. I think it did. She's coming back, so that's a good sign."

"Hey, what was that key for?" asked Tom.

"None of your business, Mr. Snoop," replied Marnie, wrinkling her nose up at him.

"Not for your old house, is it?" he asked.

Pursing her lips, she said, "No. It's for a storage unit. We keep a few so that people can stash their stuff if they need to disappear." She looked up from her appointment book. "Why would you think it was for my old house?"

"It's up for rent again. I saw the sign yesterday and thought you might have the key. Mr. and Mrs. Hale gave them to you the last time, remember?"

"I didn't know that, but no." She thought about the house she had bought and fixed up with the help of her father and sold when she moved in with Ken. It was a lovely home for a time.

The bell rang, and they all directed their attention toward the door. Danny walked in, looked up at the jingling bell, and grinned.

"How are we all doing on this beautiful fall day?" He clapped his hands together and almost sang as he spoke. "It's brisk out there. Hey, where's Tater? I thought I'd take him for a walk to the courthouse."

The Border Collie trilled and scooted out from under Marnie's desk and into reception, his muzzle dusted with powdered sugar.

"Who fed him doughnuts?" Marnie glared at her friend and her associate. Both shrugged and faked innocence.

The assistant swept her eyes up and down the visitor's tall frame with appreciation.

Tom whispered to her, took her arm and led her across the office, introducing her to his partner.

"Andrea, meet Detective Danny Gregg, your boss's bodyguard."

The counselor rolled her eyes. "Pfft."

Her assistant held out a hand. "It's nice to meet you."

Taking her hand in both of his, he flashed his dimples.

"You too."

Half-turning to Marnie, then pivoting back, he asked, "Can I steal your boss and her four-legged friend for an hour?"

Her manager gave her no time to respond. "No, I have appointments today. I can't leave. We'll order lunch in and be ready to go at five."

All business, she leaned over Andrea's desk, studying her appointment book.

"Okay. Well, can the knucklehead take a walk with me? We'll go to the courthouse, stop at the diner, and pick up lunch for everyone on the way back," said Danny, bending to see if she would look at him.

Face red, she glanced up. "Fine," she said through gritted teeth. Retrieving the dog lead from the coat rack, she held it out to the detective, who was grinning from ear to ear.

He leaned close, grazing her hand as he took the lead and whispered, "You know, you're kinda cute when you're embarrassed. Red's your color, and you know, you smell like fresh laundry from the clothesline in spring."

"Go away, or I will do serious damage with my letter opener." She glowered, green eyes meeting blue steel.

He winked and held his hand up in surrender, and with a salute, he opened the door and left with the prancing canine.

The assistant crossed her arms and raised her eyebrows. "Wow! You spent the entire night with him and didn't sleep with him? Are you crazy?"

Marnie threw up her hands in exasperation. "There was a psycho running around outside the cabin. A murderous lunatic! How can either of you believe we were thinking about sex? You two are incorrigible!" She stormed off into her meeting room and slammed the door.

The agitators looked at each other and shrugged.

The secretary winked. "They thought about it, right? They may not have done it, but they were thinking about it."

"The words 'hot and bothered' come to mind. Ha-ha!" said the cop.

Andrea responded by poking him in the side.

Brow furrowed, he asked, "What was that for?"

"Marnie speaks to me telepathically. It was from her," she teased, and poured herself some coffee. "Want another cup?"

"Sure. Why not? I've got to stay alert. I don't know how we're gonna do it, but we gotta get that guy tonight."

"Any idea who it is?"

Tom blew on his coffee and shook his head. "I have suspicions, but nothing concrete. Danny told me Marn's father was at the cabin last night. Maybe the ghosts of the past will share their wisdom. Or the fingerprints we got this morning might tell us something. You never know until you find that one piece of evidence that connects everything."

"Fingers crossed," said Andrea.

"And toes," said Tom.

Chapter Thirty-Six

9:40 AM, Creekwood Town Square

Danny pulled up his collar, his watchful blue eyes scanning the streets for the dusty cruiser. He and Tater were on their way to the courthouse to see if anyone had accessed his property records. The small town buzzed with energy as people stopped for sustenance at their favorite vendors, whose carts took up residence on the pathways in the square. The detective searched for the roasted chestnut cart, even though he knew it was too early in the day.

Snow from the weekend storm still lingered, making a slippery journey for locals and the bustle of people who were visiting Creekwood for the Thanksgiving holiday. The Border Collie relieved himself at every lamppost and fire hydrant along the way—each scented with a special dog-blend fragrance from the neighborhood pooches. Laughing, the detective wondered when the pup's tank would be empty.

At the courthouse, the cop told a fib when the clerk advised dogs could not enter the courthouse. So, Danny crafted a quick-on-his-feet tale about Tater being a sniffer dog, new to the K-9 unit, and they were out for a test run. It got them through the door to the records without incident.

It took only moments to find what he was looking for. After all, he was a cop and accessed these files often. With the register before him, he stared at the page, scratching his head. With the logbook in hand, the detective asked the clerk, "Were you working when this info was requested?"

The clerk looked at the date and replied, "Yeah. I work every day."

Danny pointed to the name in the logbook. "Do you remember this guy?"

Shaking his head, the clerk said, "Nah. We get loads of people through here looking for information on houses that are going up for tax sale. I don't remember everybody. We can check the security footage, though." Hooking his thumb, he motioned to the video equipment on a low shelf behind the counter.

"I'd appreciate that." The detective reached down and gave Tater an ear scratch. "Here we go, pal. I love security cameras." The dog smiled at him and hit him with his paw. "Ha-ha! You're a lot like your mother, you know that?"

Running through the video, he found what he needed and asked the clerk if he could get a copy, handing him a thumb drive. The clerk nodded, fiddled with the machine, copied the file, and gave it back with a notarized copy of the register too.

10:33 AM, Creekwood Town Square and Forensics Lab

Danny strolled out of the courthouse with proof someone had been poking around his personal information. *It's about time we found two pieces of sound evidence. Now, if the DNA from under Tommy's nails and the fingerprints from the duffel and skylight shake something loose, we are off to the races. Fingers crossed, we have a match in the system,* he thought.

He and Tater made a stop at a coffee cart along the way, and their second stop was Rick's office.

"Got anything for me, Ricky, my pal?" asked the detective, offering his colleague a steaming fresh coffee.

The doctor looked up from the file he had been studying and took the cardboard cup, noticing Danny's wide grin. "Have you been drinking? Kind of early, isn't it?"

"Nope. But I am having an excellent day," he said, hitting the scientist on the back with a friendly slap.

"Yeah, I heard you were playing bodyguard for Ms. Reilly. Working well for you, is it? You sly dog, you," he teased. "Speaking of dogs, what's Tater doing with you?" He stooped and gave one of the dog's ears a gentle tug.

Ignoring the sarcasm, the detective said, "Yeah. Tommy is with Marnie at her office. I thought the pooch could use a walk, so he's helping me gather evidence. Got anything?" He sat down in a visitor's chair, and the pup took up station at his feet.

Rick peered at him over his reading glasses. "Well, there's something funny going on with the system. We got a couple of hits, but we can't access the details." His forehead wrinkled as he rubbed his jaw.

"Why not?" Danny leaned forward, his eyebrows knitting together.

"Well, you need to go a lot higher than me to find out who the fingerprints and the DNA belong to. If I can't access it, there's a security reason. It's unusual. I search shit for the FBI, ATF ... all the alphabet cops. This is the first time I've been blocked access," he said, puffing out his cheeks and leaning his elbows on his desk.

"Is there anything we need to do to get the information?"

"Leave it with me for a while. I'm gonna make a few calls and see what I can find out," he said, taking the lid off his coffee. "Spending the night with Ms. Reilly again?"

Distracted, the detective didn't answer right away. His mind raced with sound reasons Rick couldn't retrieve vital information. Shaking off the sense of dread that was building, he responded, "What? Oh, yeah. Yeah. Thanks. Call me when you've got something."

"No problem. Take it easy."

11:45 AM, Creekwood PD and Lunch Pick Up

Danny put his case files in his desk, locked the drawer and pocketed the key. *Let's see Mr. Smarty Pants get into my desk again,* he thought. He'd called the diner thirty minutes prior to arrange a selection of sandwiches and sides. His grandmother told him his order would be ready by noon, so he grabbed his jacket and snuck out before Captain Sterling could nab him.

Trotting down the stairs, he could hear Sergeant Lou Beaumont chatting with Tater. He'd left the pup with him because he didn't want his commanding officer to give him a hard time. Besides, Beau loved dogs and offered.

"This is the smartest pooch I've ever met," said the sergeant, clipping the lead.

"He's impressive, isn't he?" said the detective, face beaming.

"You can bring him back anytime. Heck, if Ms. Reilly ever goes away, I'll be happy to take him home with me for as long as she'd like. But, hey. Don't tell her I gave him a quarter of my liverwurst sandwich. I couldn't say no."

"Ha-ha! I get that, and I won't narc. Thanks, Beau. I gotta get to the diner to pick up lunch."

"Take it easy, Detective," said the cop. "Bye, Tater. Come visit again."

Zipping his jacket, Danny mulled over his conversation with the forensics doctor as he and his furry sidekick made their way to Ryan's Diner. *This doesn't add up. Who the hell are we dealing with? If Rick can't access the information, it can't be good. He has the highest clearance of anyone I know. Federal field agencies call him in all the time.* His stomach twisted in knots, and he let his mind go to places it shouldn't. He was thinking the worst when it could just be a system hiccup. But his gut told him it wasn't.

The detective believed bad things happened in threes, and he started a tally: Wilder, Webb, Weaver, Tom. *Two more.* Then he scratched the back of his neck and wondered if the guy at the cabin counted but decided it didn't. No one had been hurt, so he tucked away the thought until he entered his grandmother's restaurant, and a wave of impending menace took over his senses.

11:58 AM, Ryan's Diner

The bell above the diner's door jangled, but the detective ignored it as he gave a half-hearted wave to Gram, his eyes trained on the stairs to her apartment. Tater got distracted by a group of women sitting in a booth near the counter. They called him over, making a fuss and patting him, and Danny, impatient to get answers, gave a sharp whistle, and the dog obeyed, prancing to the detective's side.

"Here you go, love. I packed a lunch fit for a king, a queen, and their entire court," said his grandmother, setting a box on the bench.

"Thanks," he replied, before pivoting and taking the stairs to her apartment three steps at a time. He dropped the dog's lead at the entrance and rummaged through the bookcase, drawers, and cupboards, mumbling to himself. Then, swinging around to find the next place to hunt, he spotted Gram watching him from the doorway, her forehead crinkled with concern.

"What are you lookin' for?" Their eyes met, and the fear and panic she saw in her grandson's face sent a chill up her spine. When he didn't respond, she asked again. "Did you hear me, Daniel?"

Hands clenching his hair, he turned around. "You know damn well what I'm looking for. Where are they?" he said, dropping his arms to his sides.

Clasping her hands in front of her, she said, "It won't do no good lookin' at them cards. Go do your job and protect Marnie. Now, come downstairs, pick up your lunch and get back to her with Tater. She'll be frettin' after him by now."

"Where are the cards? I need to know what's happening. Is she going to be okay?" His voice cracked, and deep lines etched his forehead as he continued to search, peering inside cubbyholes and closets.

"Daniel, do you remember what I told you after Sarah died? When you do, you'll have your answer. Now, go do your job. Go on. The cards can tell what *could* happen. But you know that because you feel it in your gut, and it's clouding your judgment. You're a fine cop, and you have the power to protect Marnie, and she has some say in it too. That was taken away from you with your wife. Don't let it happen again. The two of you can figure this out without the tarot." With a firm grip, Gram took his arm, stooped and picked up Tater's lead, and escorted them to the door. "On your way!"

He searched his grandmother's eyes. "I don't remember what you told me, but you know what's going to happen, don't you? Tell me," he pleaded.

She handed Danny the leash. "I'm bettin' on you, Marnie, Tom, and Tater. Off you go."

Shaking his head and muttering, "She knows something," he jogged down the stairs with the pup, grabbed the box of sandwiches off the counter, and stormed out. The bell over the door clanged and tumbled to the floor.

With one arm around the carton of sandwiches and a hand tethered to the Border Collie, Danny trudged up the street, his brain working triple time. He peered down alleyways, checking for the Impala, asking himself probing questions. His nose caught the scent of roasted chestnuts wafting up from the square, and he stopped, lost in a blurry past, grappling for answers.

What did Gram tell me when Sarah died? I was a mess, and I don't remember. The funeral is a blur. Who was there? Why can't Rick access the prints? The clerk's records can't be right. A corpse can't sign a log. What am I missing? Jesus! Let me remember what my grandmother said.

A screeching yelp pulled him back from his thoughts, and with one hard tug on the lead, Tater was gone. Wheeling around, he saw a man wearing a ski mask struggling to hold tight as the dog squirmed and snarled. The detective dropped the box and lunged forward as the canine snapped twice at his captor and wriggled to free himself. Clamping his jaw on the snatcher's wrist, the pup broke loose and sank his teeth into the dognapper's ankle before racing back to the detective.

The man fled down the street and into an alley, and Danny took up the chase, shouting, "C'mon, Tater," and the dog darted after him.

On a side street lined with shops and vending carts, they lost their target, and Danny and his furry friend eased to a halt.

"I don't have backup, pal. Sorry. We're gonna have to catch him another time," he said, hands on his knees, heart thumping.

Picking up the dog, the detective snuggled him to his chest, and Tater bumped him under the chin with his nose. Gut churning, the detective considered Marnie's safety, and he knew they needed a better plan. He set down the dog, putting his collar back in place, and wound the lead around his wrist before calling the station.

The detective spoke with Captain Sterling as they returned to the place where the dog was abducted. A young woman stood on the sidewalk, holding the box of sandwiches.

She held out the carton. "Are you and your dog okay, mister?"

He looked down at Tater, catching his breath. "We're fine, thanks. You didn't, by chance, get a look at that guy, did you?"

"No, sir, he had a ski mask pulled over his face. Why would he be wearing that? It's not that cold out today." Pausing, she thought. "Oh! I bet so he could steal your dog, huh?"

"Yeah," he said, taking the sandwiches. He muttered his thanks and marched back to Marnie's office, a vigilant eye on Tater the entire way.

◆

12:20 PM, Heading to Marnie's Office

"You know, pal, that's the guy we saw in the security footage at your house the other night. I recognized his wonky gait," said Danny, glancing down at his fluffy sidekick. "We're gonna make sure nothing bad happens to your mom. You'll help me, right?"

The dog's rolling growl and *roo-roo* mumbles confirmed his commitment to keeping his mother safe. Danny shared his plan with the Border Collie as they walked back to the office, and the pup grumbled in agreement to each of his points.

Slowing their pace a foot or two from the counselor's door, the detective stopped and held up his hand to his fluffy co-conspirator. "We go in there and clear the place out. You with me?"

Tater high-fived him, and they stormed into the waiting room.

"Okay. This office is closed for the day. Time to go home," the detective ordered. "Where's Marnie?"

With a scowl, Andrea dropped her pen on her desk. "Excuse me. She's in a meeting and has two more appointments today. We can't just leave."

"Uh, yeah, you can. Reschedule. We're leaving in ten minutes." Pivoting to his partner, he said, "Tommy, have you got what you need from home? If not, go now and wait for us at your place. Let's go!" With two quick claps of his hands, he glanced over his shoulder at Andrea before turning back to his colleague.

With a nod, Tom replied, "Yup. I walked over while you were out and got a bag—it's in my truck. I had a patrolman outside the office the entire time." Pulling Danny aside, he whispered, "What's goin' on, man? You're scarin' me."

"Someone tried to steal Tater. The same guy who was killin' cops at Marnie's house on Saturday night. I recognized his weird, gimpy walk. It's the same. As for the DNA from under your nails and the fingerprints on the rock, the roof, and the gym bag, guess what? Classified. Even Rick can't access the information. Rick! He has FBI clearance, and he can't get in to see what kinda psycho we're dealin' with. The records on the cabin? You'll never guess who signed the register to get information about my home."

"Who?"

"Colin Reilly."

Tom pulled a face. "What? No way! Mr. Reilly died in a boating accident with a group of friends years ago. It isn't possible. I was at his funeral. No way! Besides, he would never hurt Marnie. He adored her."

"Yeah, well, we'll see. We need to go while we still have daylight. Andrea, please get Marnie. Now!"

The assistant jumped at his bellow, and having heard enough, she agreed the situation was dire. She knocked on the office door, entered, and backed out with her hands raised.

Marnie flew out behind her, green eyes blazing, and hissed, "What's with the ruckus out here? I've got people in my office. You can't storm in and think..."

The detective cut her off. "Someone tried to snatch Tater. The same guy who stashed Wilder in your shed on Friday and executed cops with piano wire on Saturday. I recognized him from the way he ran away. We gotta get out of here now. Right now! Get yourself packed up and let's go."

Carl emerged from the office with a small group of people following him. Forehead creased, he asked, "What's going on?"

Marnie kneeled on the floor, giving her pup a tight hug. "Little man, are you okay? Did that horrible beast hurt you?" She ran her hands over the dog, checking for injuries. The Border Collie panted, put a paw on her arm, nuzzled her ear and stretched his neck over her shoulder.

Eyes ready to spill over with tears, she looked up at the healer, her voice trembling. "Detective Gregg said someone tried to steal Tater out on the street—the same psycho who was at my place the other night. We have to reschedule, and could you please make sure that Andrea gets home? Will you do that for me?"

Before he could answer her, a short, pudgy woman with a large, pink birthmark covering the side of her face pushed her way in front of the psychic and pointed a chubby finger in her face. "More punishment will come your way. You shouldn't have gone against us. Unfortunate things happen to people who upset God's flock. We warned you."

Fists clenched, Marnie stood ready to defend herself. But Danny stepped forward. "Who the hell are you?" he growled.

The woman bobbed her head, offering the detective a snooty smile. "I'm Alice. I lead The Collective."

Face beet red, he stooped, his nose inches from the woman's. "Yeah, well, Alice, leader of The Collective, get the fuck out of here now, and don't you ever threaten Ms. Reilly again. Do you hear me? If I get the tiniest sniff that any of you are fucking around with her, I will take you down!"

Backing up with a gasp, the woman squawked, "I'm going to report you to your superiors." Fanning her face with her hand, she cowered into the protective circle of her coven of spiritual quacks.

With a menacing sneer, the detective loomed over the group. "Yeah, well, I'll do you one better. I'm gonna have a chat with the man upstairs and make sure he doesn't let you through the gates when your time comes. I go to see him most Sundays and talk with him every night before I go to sleep, so don't mess with me, lady. He's on my side, and I am quite certain that you are about as low on his list as anyone can get. And don't think I don't know what you've been up to. When I met Parkins the other night, I did some digging. I've seen the tapes of your performances. I know who you are. You piece of shit charlatans! Get out! All of you! Now!" Shoulders heaving, he pointed a thick finger at the door, readying to physically remove them if they didn't hurry their exit.

Huffing and puffing, they grabbed their coats, and deriding the detective with their spite-filled eyes, they filed out the door, nattering to one another as they went.

Carl, Marnie, and Andrea stood speechless.

But Tom broke the silence. "Holy shit! You scared the crap out of me! I've never heard you speak to anyone like that. Dang! I'm finding myself strangely attracted to you right now."

Danny rolled his eyes, and feeling an unusual weight on his leg, he glanced down. Tater leaned against him—a smile on his furry face. The detective bent to scratch his ear, and the dog put his paw in his new friend's hand, who laughed and kneeled, giving the pooch a hug.

◆

12:50 PM, Marnie's Office

Marnie and Andrea tackled the job of postponing appointments until after Thanksgiving, accepting the week they returned would be hectic. Lending a hand to kill time, Carl tidied the kitchen, waiting for the women to complete their calls.

Huddled in a meeting room, Danny filled in Tom on the failed dog-napping, as the Border Collie, having recovered from his attempted abduction, lay beneath the table with a stuffed, squeaky lamb.

"It happened so fast. One minute we're walking down the street. Next, I felt tension on the leash, and he was gone," said Danny, raking his digits through his wavy hair.

"I'll bet Tater got him good," said his partner.

"Yeah. He latched onto that asshole's wrist and shook before squirming free and taking a bite out of his ankle."

Giving the dog a pat, Tom whispered, "Good boy."

The men stood when they heard the bell over the door ring and stepped out. Captain Sterling had arrived with Officers Kriss and Tartetto, each carrying a box and rifle bags.

"Got any news, Cap?" asked Danny, crossing the office to the reception area with Tom lagging a few steps behind.

Sterling shook his head. "Not yet. We're still working on it. Whoever this man is, he is invisible to us. I handed it over to the

Superintendent and he called the feds, who aren't too interested in helping. Creekwood, New York isn't on their radar."

With a grunt, the detective asked, "That stuff for me?"

"Yeah. Where do you want it?" asked Kriss.

He tossed him the keys to his Jeep. "My car is right out front. Put that stuff in the cargo and please stay with it until we come out. Thanks."

"You got it," said the officer, following his partner out the door.

Sterling cleared his throat. "Detective, we will have a SWAT team around the cabin in about 40 minutes. He went for the dog; we have to believe he will try something again. If not tonight, then the next. You get Ms. Reilly home, lock up tight and don't come out. If the dog needs to go out, I recommend that you all wear the tactical gear in those boxes we brought to you. There's even a vest for the dog. Special model from K-9. I liberated it from stock." Winking, he gave a quick salute and strode out the door.

A lightbulb went off in the psychic's head, and she glared at Danny. "Did you use Tater as bait? Your boss just said the guy tried to get him. Did you have that planned when you picked him up today?" She stared up at him, her mouth agape, eyes shooting daggers.

"Honest to God, Marnie, I did not use him and never would. I wanted to hang out with him. The guy came out of nowhere. I swear to God, I would never hurt him." He laced his hand over his heart—pleading for her forgiveness.

She narrowed her eyes and studied his face. "I'm sorry for jumping to conclusions. This whole thing ... none of it makes sense. How can you protect us if we can't see him coming?"

"We don't need to see him, Marn. The SWAT team will. They have night vision goggles and all sorts of contraptions," said Tom, wrapping an arm around her shoulders.

Carl asked, "Is there anything I can do other than get Andrea home?"

"No, thanks. You've been great. I'll call you in a few days. I want to talk more about us working together—not with The Collective—only with you," she said, stretching to give him a peck on the cheek.

Turning to the detectives, he warned, "Keep her safe, or I swear to God, I will kick your asses. I don't care if you are bigger than me and I die trying."

"Great to see you, Carl. Be safe, big guy," said Danny, thumping him on the back, delivering a teeth-clattering jolt.

"Keep me updated, boss," said Andrea as she and Carl hustled out the door.

"I will. Thanks for everything," replied the counselor, checking her watch. "Can we stop at my house along the way? I have a few things I want to pick up. Please?"

"Yeah. How long will you be? We should be at the cabin before dark." Danny clenched his jaw and glanced down at his wrist.

"I won't be long. I'll run up to my room and grab a few things. We can get some food out of the fridge, too."

"Yeah. It's just after one. We're fine," he said, and his partner confirmed it with a nod.

She grabbed her bag, coat, and Tater's lead, and they all walked out together, locking the door.

Officers Kriss and Tartetto stood guard by the Jeep, eyeing the activity around them.

Kriss handed the keys over and said, "Do you want us to come with you?"

"Thanks, but no," said the detective.

"Call us if you need us. We're on duty until eleven," said Tony Tartetto as they walked back toward the station.

Danny opened the cargo door, got Tater settled in the back, and held the passenger door for Marnie. Tom gave Marnie a playful punch on the arm before getting into his truck.

"It's gonna be okay," he said.

Stone-faced, she gave a tight nod, causing her friend's heart to jump into his throat.

Chapter Thirty-Seven

1:33 PM, Creek Road

Marnie shivered as they drove up her street—not because she was cold, but because she couldn't bear to see her bloodstained deck again.

"Is Joan here?" she asked the detective.

"I'm not sure who's on duty," he said, shaking his head.

Coming around a bend in the road, the afternoon sun bathed the house in a warm glow. Melting snow and ice dripped from the eaves and trickled down the cobblestone walk. Two officers from the Hudson Hollow station loafed on the veranda. One smoked a cigarette while the other drank a steaming beverage from a thermos.

Parking at the curb, the trio got out of their respective vehicles, and the psychic rescued her dog from the cargo. She glanced up at the men on her porch and didn't like the vibe they gave off. Tater's mumbles and grumbles told her he agreed.

"Good afternoon, detectives," said one cop, smirking and nudging his workmate.

Tom's hands curled into fists in response to the smug greeting, but his partner brought him back from the ledge.

Danny pivoted, placing a firm hand on his chest. "Choose your battles, Tommy. This one ain't worth fightin', man. Go in the house and ignore them," he said, turning back around. "Beck. Hall. Any activity?"

"Haven't seen a soul. We don't expect any cops will be slaughtered on our watch," said Hall, a diminutive man with spiked black hair in his late twenties.

"Don't worry, Detective Gregg. We know what we're doin'," said Beck, who was the opposite of his partner with a face like a baboon's backside.

"It amazes me you both forget you were here on Saturday night when Officer Weaver was killed. Weren't you outside the house while the detectives were inside? Why didn't you see anything?" asked Marnie, raising an eyebrow, daring them to throw a barb.

Tater sniffed the snow and peed on a shrub, as dogs often do, before walking up the steps onto the veranda. He snuffled along the deck and stopped next to Beck, crooking his leg on his boot.

The officer jumped back, shaking his foot. "Hey, get that mutt off me!"

The detectives burst out laughing. Marnie, not having seen her dog relieve himself, took a step toward him, but Danny walked onto the porch, leaned in, and sniggered in Beck's ear. "Ha-ha! You think you're a big wheel. If you run around trying to be important and shooting your mouth off, dogs will piss on you."

Marnie dashed upstairs to her bedroom, packed a bag with her favorite sweatshirt, sweatpants, and cozy socks. She checked the bathroom next, ensuring she had everything she needed and tossed items in with her clothes. Hurrying downstairs, she found the detectives in the kitchen, gathering food and griping about the officers from Hudson Hollow.

"Have you got butter, flour, and baking stuff at your place? When I'm stressed, I bake pie or cookies," she said, taking her recipe box and a book from the shelf and shoving them in her bag.

"We should have that stuff at my place, but we'll grab what's here." Danny pulled open a door, checking the pantry.

Tom snatched grocery bags out of a drawer and started packing the items his partner handed him. While Marnie opened the freezer, retrieving berries and ice cream, placing both into a freezer bag. Then, she opened the fridge and got butter and milk.

"Okay. That's good. Let's go," she said, gathering up bags and heading for the front door.

As she touched the doorknob, a vision flashed, and she closed her eyes. With a breath in, she focused on the incoming message, knowing that sometimes divine guidance requires shutting out the world.

"Come on, Marnie. Let's get moving.," said Danny, nudging her forward with a gentle tap.

She shook off his coaxing, holding up a hand for the men to wait. *Come on. Speak to me. Tell me what I need to know*, she thought. A vision of a field played like a movie in her mind. A granite boulder … the fuzzy features of two people standing over Tom, and a life-or-death struggle that ensued. Releasing the latch, she wiggled her fingers, shaking off the energy, then said to the guys, "We need to go back to the bridle trail. Trust me, okay? There's something significant to see—something we missed."

Danny stuck out his bottom lip and shrugged. "Okay. I trust you. Let's put this stuff in the cars first," he said, following her out of the door.

The men exchanged questioning glances as they stepped outside.

1:53 PM, The Bridle Trail and Forest

Tater led the way with his nose to the ground—ears alert, glancing up only once when a gray squirrel chattered and raced across the crusty path. Marnie gave the dog's lead plenty of slack as they jogged up the trail. The detectives crunched through the snow behind them—their eyes darting between the trail and foliage.

The Border Collie stopped and stood stock-still—the fur of his fluffy white shawl ruffling in the *whoosh* of the bitter northern wind. With nose and ears twitching, his intelligent amber eyes scouted the area before his gaze locked onto a target up ahead.

He whimpered and bounded forward, pulling his mistress off the path and into the trees. She ducked and weaved between branches, and her boots filled with snow as she followed, trusting the keen sense of her dog. The detectives struggled to push through the thick branches, limbs pulling at their coats and hair.

Marnie whistled a shrill command. "Tater, stop!"

The dog halted and sat, looking over his shoulder at the psychic, who stood with her eyes closed, the wind rustling through her strawberry blonde bangs. When she opened them, Tater tugged at his lead, pulling her into a clearing, where he pounced on a patch of snow-covered ground and clawed at it with gusto.

Tom looked up—squinting. "That sun sure is warm once you're outta the trees."

"What the heck?" said Marnie, kneeling, inspecting where the dog was digging—holding him back with her forearm.

Grabbing Danny's hand, she pulled him closer and waggled a finger in front of her. He and Tom both crouched down beside her. The thawing snow in front of them showed a pinkish inkblot stain. Tater ducked under his mistress's hand, sniffed and scratched at the spot before they could stop him. When he picked up his head, he had something in his mouth, and Danny put his hand under the dog's mouth.

"What've you got there, pal?" he asked.

The Border Collie offered a playful growl and pranced away, ready for a game.

With her palm beneath the dog's muzzle, the psychic said, "Give it."

Wagging of his tail, Tater dropped the "toy" onto her mitten and sat back, tilting his head to the side. Danny took out a clear evidence bag from his pocket and put on nitrile gloves, and the counselor placed the item on top of the plastic.

The detective turned it over, revealing the finger of a glove, and inside was a flesh and blood digit. Grimacing, he placed it into the bag, and as he did, something dropped into the snow. Tom reached for the item and held it up, and the diamond ring sparkled in the afternoon sun. Eyebrows arched, Marnie and Danny stared at one another.

"Holy shit," she whispered.

The detective ran his knuckles along the edge of his jaw. "Yeah. Holy shit is right."

Chapter Thirty-Eight

2:13 PM, The Bridle Trail

Long shadows stretched ahead as Danny called Rick on their way back to the house. While Marnie and Tom heard the detective's side of the conversation, the doctor's was muffled.

"Hey, pal. I hate to do this to you, but you've gotta get back out to Creek Road. We found a severed finger and a diamond ring off the bridle trail near where Tommy got knocked out. The spot is marked with a gray silk scarf. We put some rocks around the edges to keep it from blowing away, and we tied blue nitrile gloves on the trees near the clearing. It's near a granite boulder. And I apologize in advance. We tried not to mess up the scene, but Tater was with us, and he dug for it."

He paused, listening to the forensic scientist's latest update, and his reaction of rolling eyes and undulating jaw muscles told the psychic and his partner there was no good news.

"Okay. We'll wait for the reports. I'm hoping the superintendent can get something done. Oh, there is some blood in the snow, but we believe it belongs to Kate Parish—the owner of the ring and the severed finger. It's possible that we missed other evidence. We'll leave the digit in Marnie's freezer and the ring on her island. We're in a hurry to get to the cabin before dark. You know about that, right? Cap would've filled you in on the SWAT team."

The detective took a breath, and hearing his colleague's comments, his steel-blue eyes watched the sun sink on the horizon.

"Okay, Rick, thanks. Get in touch when you're done, no matter what time. I want to know everything. The good, the rotten, and the nasty. Catch ya."

The foursome hightailed it to the house with the fresh evidence nestled in three ziplock bags—finger, glove tip, and ring. As they walked up onto the porch, only Beck was standing guard. His tiny cohort was missing.

"Where'd your buddy go?" Danny asked, eyeing the policemen.

The man sneered. "Inside taking a leak. I told him to piss on the furniture after what the little mutt did." He gave Tater a shove with the side of his boot, and the dog yipped, skittering sideways.

The detective wound up to throw a punch, but Marnie beat him to it. She slammed her fist straight into the jerk's nose, delivering a crackle of cartilage and the popping of bones. She winced, shaking her hand, before hauling back her leg and kicking him on the shin with a dull thwack.

"Whoa!" said Tom, pulling her away before she could do serious damage, dragging her and the dog off the porch. The psychic swung her arms—face red—lips snarling while her friend did his best to restrain her.

"Let me go," she growled, squirming loose. But he grabbed the hood of her jacket before she could charge up onto the porch.

With his hackles up, the Border Collie growled from the foot of the steps, but his uncle had a tight grip on his lead.

Danny pulled himself up to his full six-foot-five frame and loomed over the battered man's five-foot-ten paunchy form. The cop's eyes watered, and he grabbed his nose, blood oozing through his fingers as Hall returned, stopping in the doorway, mouth agape. The compact flatfoot clenched his fists and puffed out his concave chest.

"That's it. I'm callin' this in!" he said, reaching for his phone.

"Hey, pal, don't be a narc. Your partner slipped on the ice and bashed his face into the railing," said the detective, turning to his partner. "Tommy? Did you see him slip and fall into the railing?"

"Sure did. Marn, did you?" He poked her with his elbow.

She looked up at the uniforms and shrugged—eyes wide with innocence.

"No, I was walking down the steps when it happened. I had my back to him. Gee. Are you okay? That's gonna hurt like hell later. Better get some ice on that."

With a wink, she tossed her house key to Danny as she opened the back of the Jeep, shepherding Tater inside. Tom walked back to his car, chuckling at the memory of Beck's face when his friend smashed him in the face. Danny deposited the finger in the freezer and dropped the other two bags on top of the island before returning to the porch.

Cautioning the Hudson Hollow officers, he growled, "Anything gets messed up in that house, and you will both have me to deal with. You two bozos think about getting any revenge, and there's gonna be a big problem. Understand?"

They both nodded and turned their backs on him as he jogged down the steps.

He waved to Tom, got into the Jeep, and looked at Marnie.

"Ready to go?"

"Ready," she said, flexing the fingers of her right hand and inspecting the bruises coming up on her knuckles.

Danny laughed, leaning across the seat to examine her injury.

"Do you need some ice for that?" he asked.

"Nah, it'll be fine. This ain't my first fistfight."

She winked and stretched her arms in front of herself with a loud sigh. "It's Kate's finger. You know that, right?"

"Yeah."

The detective and Marnie drove in silence, the scanner chirping away. She could see his mind working, and she studied his profile, hoping that he would give something away.

Breaking the silence, he said, "Hey, remind me never to piss you off. I'm quite proud of the fact that I've never had my nose broken, and I'd kinda like to keep it that way, Slugger."

She grinned, a laugh escaping. "Hmm ... noted." Flexing her bruised knuckles, she frowned. "My fight-or-flight response is finely honed after a few years with Ken. I wish I hadn't reacted, but gosh. It felt so good to punch him. I've wanted to hit something for days. I guess I still have work to do on myself. Violence was never my default position until Mr. Wilder entered my world."

Lost in thought, the detective didn't respond. He searched his memory for the conversation he'd had with his grandmother, hoping it would reveal what was coming. *Which conversation, though? Gram said it was after Sarah died. Hmm ...* A frown wrinkled his forehead, and he pinched his chin. They had spoken about his late wife's death so many times. It was impossible to pinpoint one. With a deep sigh, he returned to the present.

He glanced at Marnie, who was resting her head against the window, then turned back to the road. Looking at her again, he started thinking about the video and the other evidence they had gathered. His steel-blue gaze shifted to the rearview to see if his partner was still behind them, spotting him six car lengths back. *Hello!* The dusty cruiser with big tires trailed at a slight distance. *There you are, you sneaky bastard. Do something wrong so I can pull you over and search your vehicle.* His eyes jumped from the pavement to the mirror and back again, and he gripped the wheel tighter as the Impala closed in on Tom.

Spotting a gas station ahead, he signaled to pull in, and his partner swung in behind. The other car kept going, but Danny got a look at the driver. He knew that face. He'd seen it last night and in the clerk's office earlier in the day.

"Is everything okay?" asked his passenger, leaning forward to assess his mood.

"Yeah. We need milk and eggs. You stay here and keep the doors locked," he said, getting out, tapping his knuckles on the roof.

Tom waved as he got out of his car, his boots crunching icy dirt and crushed stones as he crossed the gravel parking lot. "Yeah, I saw him," he said, answering the detective's question before he asked it. "That crappy sedan. He kept crawling up and dropping back like he was trying to see who was in front of him. I couldn't catch the plate, but I got a look at him when he drove past. There's something familiar about him. Can't place it, though."

"Yeah. I didn't get it either. He was the guy at the cabin last night. The creepy bastard was peering through the skylight, and he's the same guy in the courthouse video. Stay here with Madame Seance and don't scare her. I gotta get a few things to cover why we stopped."

He turned away and walked toward the little store, stopping short when his colleague called out.

"Hey! You don't have to protect her. She's a lot tougher than you think. Hell, she'd risk her life to protect us. Marnie's not stupid, you know. She knows something's up. We're standing right here having a serious discussion. Be straight with her. If she knows what's happening, she can prepare herself." He tucked his hands into his pockets and kicked at the gravel.

Danny gave a half-hearted nod and chewed the inside of his cheek, considering the pros and cons. "Yeah. You're right. Let's have that conversation with her once we get home. Anyway, if she's going to bake, we need milk and eggs. Back soon."

2:50 PM, Whitetail Junction Quickie Mart, Lake Road

Tom knocked on the driver's window of the Jeep, peeking in to see Marnie writing in her notebook. She ignored him, and he rapped again, but she didn't look up. He pressed his face against the glass and called her name. She reached across the seat and rolled down the window a crack. "Detective Gregg told me to keep the doors locked and not to talk to strange men."

With lips pursed, he motioned for her to roll the window down further. She did, and before he could speak, she said, "I've seen that car before. The one you two were talking about. It was near my office the other day, and I know I saw it outside Ryan's Diner. That's him, isn't it?"

He squinted in the late afternoon sun, half-nodding. "Yeah. We think so."

Twisting her mouth in thought, she said, "Okay, then. We know what he drives. Did you get the plate number?"

Hands in the air, he stretched his back and said, "Nah. I couldn't see it through the dust."

Danny returned with a bag of groceries and set it on the seat. Scowling at the pair, he asked, "What are you two talking about?"

"Before you jump down my throat, she's seen him, too. At work and outside Gram's. Haven't you, Marn?"

She nodded.

"Yup. Want his plate number?"

Tom's eyebrows shot up. "You got it?"

"Yeah. He drove right past me. Of course I did."

Danny took a pad and pen from his pocket, poised to jot down the number. "Give it," he said.

"Yes, sir," she said, ripping the page out of her notebook and handing it to him with a satisfied smile.

The detective leaned through the window, retrieved his phone, and moved away from the vehicle to make a quick call to Captain Sterling. When he finished, he turned back, rubbing his temples in thought before telling them about the conversation.

"He doesn't have news but will call back if there's an update. On a more positive note, I got a text from Lieutenant Allen. The SWAT team is at the cabin setting up. I warned them about the piano wire and hope that they've found it all. Anyway ... Let's get moving. Driving at dusk is a bitch—especially when you're trying to keep eyes on a tail."

The detective looked up the road, his hand shielding his eyes from the setting sun. He frowned at the flat and seamless slate gray clouds forming a ceiling above them. Tapping the roof of the Jeep with his left hand, he opened the driver's side door with the other. "We'd better go. We're burnin' daylight and there's a storm brewing."

3:03 PM, Lake Road

Drizzling rain dotted the windshield, the wipers leaving a half-circle smear of road dust on the glass. Marnie rested a shoulder on the door, watching for the brown cruiser in the mirror. Tom's flailing arm, gesturing toward the shoulder got her attention, and she tapped the detective's arm, but he was already looking at his partner in the rearview. The dusty sedan sat idle, hiding in a stand of pines, waiting for them to pass. The men both slowed down, observing the car as they drove by.

Danny turned on the headlights, spritzed the windshield and sped up the wipers to clear their view. He reached for his phone to call the Sheriff's office to give an update on their estimated arrival but jerked in alarm when it rang. Scowling as *unknown* slid across the screen, he grabbed it out of the console and pressed the speaker. Marnie sat up, wondering who was at the other end.

"Gregg," he barked, impatient with the anonymous caller.

The psychic's back stiffened against her seat, and she covered her mouth, muting a gasp.

An eerie rendition of "Hurt" played through the phone, breaking up as the line crackled.

"Who the hell is this?" roared the detective, and not waiting for an answer, he disconnected the call and dropped the device into the cup holder. With a reassuring hand on Marnie's knee, he said, "It's okay. I promise I won't let anyone hurt you—not you, not Tom, not Tater."

She faced him—eyebrows knitted together—mouth tight, eyes blazing.

"I know, and I won't allow him to harm you, either. I will kill the bastard with my own hands. Swear to God. I won't hesitate." She paused, bringing a palm to her forehead. "That damn song ... It causes a Pavlovian response every time I hear it. That stops now. Whoever was back there knows my history with Ken. I'm guessing Kate Parish is the source. But Wilder is dead, and no one will ever *hurt* me like that again."

With hands curled into fists and jaw clenched, she turned away, her eyes staring like lasers into the evening sky.

Worrying she would do something foolish, he said, "Marnie, you need to calm down. Every time I get angry, I make mistakes, so let's focus. Tell me more about you and Kate. I know about your childhood. Fill me in on recent stuff. Are you still close? How often do you see each other? That kind of thing."

"Hmm ..." she said, scooting sideways in the seat to face him. "I don't know where to start. When I was still in DC, she would come visit me often. We would hang out doing what young women do. But when I moved back to Creekwood, things changed."

Gathering her thoughts, she glanced back to check on Tater, who sat staring out the cargo window at Tom.

She returned her attention to the detective, adding, "She was absorbed with her career, and I focused on my father and my new house. Kate had her life, and I had mine, but we caught up quite a lot. When I met Ken, she was the only friend he didn't isolate me from. I'm sure she knew what was going on but said nothing. Not one word. I have always believed her father was a verbal and emotional abuser, so I guess she grew up in that environment, and it was normal to her."

"So, she liked Ken?" he asked.

"I don't know that she liked him; she never said either way. But maybe. She was the only friend who didn't help me escape. Tom was amazing, though, and he called so many people to help. It was humiliating, but it was what was needed." She paused a beat and said, "You're thinking I'm an idiot for staying as long as I did, but..."

He cut her off mid-sentence.

"No. No, I am not. Over the years, I have seen abusive relationships. It's horrible how it can tear someone down. Trust me. I don't think you're an idiot. I think you are intelligent and strong."

He gave her arm a squeeze, urging her to continue.

Dragging a hand down her face, she said, "Okay, so you asked about me and Kate. When I left Ken's, I moved into Dad's house. He left it to my brother and me. Anyway, she wouldn't come around— there was always an excuse. I'd call, and she'd be busy. That's been going on for a few years. We still catch up and talk on the phone, but she's been distant. I think I may have said some things about her not supporting me. But we'd still go out for lunch or dinner, sometimes to the theater or shopping. We both have busy lives, but she's not been present for a long time. I think I hurt her, and every time I bring it up, she changes the subject. She doesn't like confrontation, which is why she isn't a successful lawyer and has never won a case. Arguing is not her forte."

"But she called you when she was in trouble. She must feel close enough to do that."

Marnie nodded. "Yeah, she knows that I'm always there for her."

"Is she always there for you?" he asked.

"No. I call Tom. He's a smartass, and he loves to joke around, but he's my rock, and has been since we were five. I'm his, too. If you were to ask me who my best friend is, it would be him ... and then Kate."

"Why didn't Tom go see Kate at the hospital? I asked if he had, and he told me he hadn't. What's goin' on there?" Danny asked.

"They are so different—like chalk and cheese. He hasn't forgiven her for not helping me when I left Ken. His loyalty to me may be part of the problem. I caught them having a tiff last Thanksgiving. Neither would tell me what it was about—they both clammed up. Why are you asking me these questions? You have a reason."

She touched his arm, and stared at him until his eyes met hers, before moving to the rearview mirror.

"You haven't seen her much lately. She's dropped off the grid, so to speak. You only catch up in public places. And yesterday morning she didn't want you to go to her apartment to get her things, something she had asked you to do a year ago after she'd had an accident. What kind? Did she give you details?"

Marnie turned to see what was interesting to him in the mirror and saw Tom's headlights—nothing else.

"Uh ... Car. I didn't question her. Why would I?" she asked, furrowing her brow.

"Describe her physical appearance."

Screwing up her face, she said, "You saw her yesterday."

"Yeah. Lying on a hospital bed. Humor me."

"Well, Kate's small. Five-four and while she didn't look it today, she is beautiful. The type of woman men stare at when she walks by.

She's always been the pretty one. Guys flock to her. I think Tom had a crush on her in high school but doesn't pay much attention now. It's possible they were fighting about that. Maybe he bruised her ego."

She glanced at Danny, who nodded, his attention on the road, mulling over the information the psychic shared. The hum of the tires filled the silence, heavy with thoughts of what the night would bring.

Chapter Thirty-Nine

4:13 PM, Widow's Watch Hollow (off Lake Road)

He sat in the woods, knowing they'd seen him, but he didn't care. They wouldn't be around long enough to be a worry. No doubt they called the sheriff. Again, it didn't matter. He'd take care of them, too. *Dumbass local yokels. They are no match for me. I have talked my way out of more trouble than most could ever imagine. Ha-ha. I have created more chaos, too.*

Inspecting the oozing bite marks on his hand, he swore. *That little mutt broke the skin, and it fucking hurt. My ankle is sore too, but at least my boot protected me. I cannot believe I screwed that up. It should have been easy. Take the dog and string it up at the cabin. Marnie would have fallen into a thousand pieces. It would have killed her.*

Hmm … The sky is ominous. Snow could complicate matters. Then again, it helped me Saturday night. It slowed down extra cops arriving to search the forest. It could assist me tonight, too. Rolling down the window a crack, he breathed in the scent of pine, stirring memories he kept locked away. The clouds above hung low and unbroken, a dull pewter dome. And the air felt suspended— expectant, holding its breath, gathering strength to release its fury.

He looked in the back seat and smiled at the hunting rifle and knife lying across the leather bench. *Guns may be out of sight, but spotting a hunter's vehicle is easy. They should know better than to leave a loaded firearm inside with boxes of ammo. A locked door is not a deterrent. And the hunting knife was a piece of cake. Shame about the guy lying in the woods. If he hasn't regained consciousness, his family will miss him as soon as the sun goes down. Either way, it will keep local law enforcement busy for hours—taking a report or organizing a search party.*

Last night's encounter with wildlife raced through his mind as he placed antibiotic salve and a fresh dressing on his wound. *That bear had better stay in its cave tonight. I'm ready for him. It's gonna be a cold winter. A fur coat would be nice.*

Snickering, he opened a can of beer, drank it down, and tossed the empty into the backseat. *Where's the sheriff? How utterly disappointing. I was looking forward to a chase. They saw me, didn't they? Maybe not. What if they have forgotten me? It would not be the first time.*

Closing his eyes, the past played over in his mind. The taste of bitterness filled his mouth, and he gagged. *Gawd. When will it go away?* He couldn't wait for this to be over and looked forward to going home. A nice warm bed and a cozy fire were comforting thoughts. *Everything I have ever wanted is right there in front of me. Not long to go.*

Where's their backup? He finger-drummed the dashboard, searching for cops. *Someone must be coming. How many of them can I outsmart?* Tap. Tap. Tap. *After last night and this afternoon with that damn dog, they may believe I have given up. No, they know I am out here. Yes. They will expect me. I wonder if they will invite me in for dinner.* Considering the thought, he grinned and shook his head. *It's best not to believe you will be welcome. You never are.*

A battered and worn book of poetry sat on the seat beside him. Its cover secured with two strips of silver duct tape. Popping another beer, he flipped through the pages, finding his favorite prose, reciting it in his head. Interrupted by the ping of a text message, he tossed aside the tome and checked his burner phone. The message was clear, and he took a bottle of pills from his pocket, examining the label. *These don't help. They never have.* With a shrug, he swallowed three with a slug of beer and rested his head on the steering wheel.

Marnie looked nice today, all dressed up. She was like that the other night, too. She didn't recognize me, though. Kate didn't either at first, but Ken did. He nearly pissed himself. What an asshole that guy is. Was. He's in the morgue with his stupid head hanging off. Hmm. Kate. What was she thinking? Did she believe she could play her childish games with me? Why would she call Marnie and then fight with me about killing Tommy Keller? She lost her finger for being a silly little bitch. Ignorant woman. I cannot wait until people find out her dirty secret. Hmm. Secrets. The depths of the dishonesty and depravity ... Ah, well, when everything comes out, Ms. Reilly's little world will crumble around her. She's pathetic. How could she believe Kate Parish to be anything but treacherous? And what about me? What will be my penance?

Darkness settled in around him as he gazed out at the setting sun, skulking behind the clouds. The forest was his friend. It masked dangerous things, but none more deadly than him. He smiled and stared into the trees. *The woods are lovely, dark and deep, but I have promises to keep and miles to go before I sleep. And miles to go before I sleep ... in a nice warm bed.*

Chapter Forty

4:23 PM, The Cabin

A crimson cardinal and a banditry of black-cap chickadees scattered from their perches as the gate to the cabin jerked free and squeaked along its icy track. Frigid air filled the car when Danny rolled down the window, scanning the woods, searching for signs of the SWAT team. As a cop, he knew they should be invisible, but from a personal perspective, he wished he could see them.

He stopped on the road, with Tom easing his truck to a halt a few feet behind. Stillness surrounded them. Even the birds were silent, but the sun was almost gone, so they would be on their way home to snuggle up in their nests for the night.

Eyes closed, Marnie whispered, asking for protection for the highest good of all. None of what she said made sense to the detective, but he was happy for someone in the spirit realm to have his back. While her taut jaw, clenched fists, and tight shoulders delivered a vibe of distance and anger, who was he to judge? He'd known her for just a few days. For all he knew, this could be her default position. Stepping on the gas pedal, they propelled forward, and his partner advanced his vehicle at the same slow pace, each scouting for their colleagues.

The vehicles rolled to a stop outside the cabin, and Marnie opened her door, walked around the back and grabbed Tater's lead. To anyone watching, she appeared to be on a mission. She took the dog for a brisk hike down to the dock, glancing up at the slate-gray clouds. Danny checked the sky too, and hoped sleet wasn't on the menu tonight. Snow he could deal with, but no more freezing rain. Tom came up beside him and poked him in the ribs.

"You okay?" he asked.

"Yeah." Then nodding in the psychic's direction, added, "I'm wondering what's going through her mind. We talked a little about Kate, and after that, she clammed up. I think she was meditating. It's not like her *not* to talk. Is it?"

"Nah. That's pretty normal for her. She goes off into her own little world. Kate and I call it recluse mode. She cocoons. I don't know many people who are happy in their own company, but she's one of them. It's frustrating, but that's Marn. It's like she's recharging her battery or something. When she comes out of it, she's a whole new woman. Don't let it worry you." He grabbed a few bags and walked up onto the wide veranda.

"I need to ask you some questions about Kate," Danny said, but he stopped, realizing that Tom was already gone. He got the supplies off the back seat, dropped them on the deck, and turned as the psychologist and her dog strolled up the path.

Stopping to help with the groceries, she asked, "Do you think we could go for a quick run? The knucklehead and I are feeling cooped up, and we'd like to stretch our legs."

"It's getting dark, and we saw him back there. You know he's headed this way. Even with the SWAT guys hiding in the trees, we need to be careful. I *am* sorry."

Curling her lip, she picked up two bags from the back seat and trudged up to the porch and into the cabin. The detective gathered up the remaining groceries and followed her inside.

Tom yelled from the kitchen. "Hey, partner, will both cars fit in the garage?"

"Yeah, no problem. Let's go get them locked up now so we don't have to worry about it later. It's going to be dark soon. Marnie, will you be okay alone?"

"Yup, I'll take my stuff upstairs and change my clothes." Picking up her totes, she patted her leg, urging the pup to join. "Come, boy. Let's go get comfy."

Danny watched the duo climb the stairs, happy she hadn't argued about the run. Then, digging into his pocket for his keys, he said, "C'mon. Let's get the cars tucked in for the night."

"Yeah, I'm comin'. I'm watchin' a few of our guys out the window."

"How many did you see?"

"Six so far. That's not so good. If I can see them, he will too. This guy, man, he's got me freaked. He can take them all out. I sure as hell hope they have night vision goggles."

Snapping his fingers, Danny remembered his conversation with Sterling. "That reminds me. They do, so I'll have to take the lights off auto. I don't want them to be blinded if Percy roams through," he said, crossing the room to change the settings.

"Did you warn those guys about Ursus americanus?"

"Yeah, they have a tranquilizer gun with them. They don't want to hurt him, but they have to control the situation. I doubt he'll appear—it's too cold. He'll be snug in his cave ... I hope," he said, jiggling his keys and heading for the door.

4:40 PM, The Cabin

The detectives put the cars in the garage and Tom poked through a table of auction treasures, while his partner fiddled with outdoor light settings.

"That should do it," said Danny, wiping his hands on his jeans. "We won't blind anyone now."

"Ready to go back inside?"

"Yeah. Watch your step. It's murky out there."

After locking the door and pocketing the key, the men stepped with caution through the snow.

"We should have grabbed a flashlight," said Tom, eyeing the treeline as he walked up the steps to the veranda.

"I was thinking the same. But we're here." Opening the door, Danny yelled, "Hey, Marnie! Where are you?"

"In the kitchen, chatting with Tater," she said, staring into the dog's soulful eyes. "I'm sorry, mister. I want to run, too. If we're lucky, we can go in the morning. I don't have to work, and we can ask the guys to go with us, okay?" Tugging his ear, she looked up as the detective entered the room.

"We're going to get the fireplaces set and ready to light. Do you need us to do anything?"

She frowned, tipping her head. "What do you mean?"

He gave her a thoughtful look. "I'm not sure what I meant. I think I was checking to see if you're okay."

"All good," she said, unpacking the bags, searching for baking supplies. "I'm going to make a pie. Any requests? I need to do something before I jump out of my skin."

Tom's reply came fast. "Raspberry? Blueberry? I'm easy." He strolled in and wrapped his arms around her in a tight hug.

She struggled out of his grasp and turned to Danny with a questioning eyebrow raised. He shrugged.

"Raspberry will always be my first choice."

"Done!" she said and went to work as the detectives went off to the cellar to fetch firewood.

Chapter Forty-One

4:58 PM, The Deer Run

Lieutenant Allen checked his team's positions through his goggles before settling his backside into the crook of the branches of an eastern white pine. The first flakes of snow were falling, and a hush spread across the forest as night settled in.

The temperature had dropped five degrees in the last half hour, but the officers were accustomed to the climate. Most had lived in the area their entire lives. They knew long thermal underwear and woolen socks would cut the cold, so they dressed in layers, anticipating what the night held for them.

Through their radios and hand signals, the crew maintained constant contact, keeping one another apprised of movements and sounds. After all, a murderous madman had stalked the forest last night, and they were certain he would return.

Every creak of a limb and rustle of a fox stimulated a rush of adrenaline in the men. *Was the stirring in the brush a black bear or the guy who had slain their fellow officers?*

5:13 PM, Bearberry Ridge

A north wind whipped up, blasting him with an arctic gust as he snaked through a gully, taking a different path from the night before. With a shiver, he pulled up his shirt collar around his neck, wishing he'd purchased a warmer jacket and gloves at the surplus store he'd visited last evening.

The hunting rifle was slung over his left shoulder. A Buck knife was secured to his belt, and the piano wire and other supplies were in a knapsack, hanging over his other arm.

A throbbing pain in his right wrist nagged at him and caused a wave of nausea when he grasped a branch to gain footing. The tussle with the detective over the skylight window had left bruising and an oozing scrape on his forearm. But the twinging pain of the deep puncture wounds from the dog bites was the primary source of his discomfort. He prided himself on his strength, agility, and his capacity to push forward no matter what.

There is no time for pain or weakness. Suck it up. Complete the mission. Move on.

A loud sigh escaped his throat, and he ducked lower into the brush. Resting against a tree, he held his aching head as his damaged memory drifted back—cutting in and out of sequences, as it always did these days.

Shoving himself forward, he skulked in the undergrowth, thinking about an incident that should never have happened. *Why was I alone? Someone was with me when the day started. Where did they go? What am I forgetting?*

Another injury he had suffered was a blur, but he was certain Tom Keller was involved. *How did it happen, and when?*

A thicket of dry, wiry brambles made for a perfect rest stop and hiding place. He could see the cabin from there. A soft glow seeped through the unshuttered windows onto the snowy veranda. On the second floor, the detective carried something in his arms and disappeared into a room. A light flicked on, and a few moments later, plumes of smoke puffed up through a chimney, and he smirked.

They must believe I would try shimmying down the flue. Ha! Been there. Thought about it. It would be fun to see the horror on their faces if I did. Even I know I would never fit. Besides, I am not alone out here. I spotted the SWAT team when I arrived. Dark blue uniforms do not camouflage. They're hiding in the trees along the deer run, and there is one on the roof. Maybe two.

He stooped low, shielding himself in dead and dried bracken, waiting for one of them to slip up. And when they did, he would rush into the cabin. He *would* get in, and he *would* do what he came here to do.

I will make Marnie pay!

Settling his back against the trunk of a young white pine, he picked up a fallen branch and whittled, waiting for an opportunity to spring into action.

Chapter Forty-Two

5:33 PM, The Cabin

Feet propped up on the coffee table, Tom shouted, "Hey, Marn, we've got the fire going in here. Why don't you come in and take a load off so we can compare notes?"

"I'll be right there. I'm putting the pie into the oven. Hey. What do you guys want for dinner? I'm not all that hungry, even though I haven't eaten since that doughnut this morning," she said, standing in front of the open fridge, holding a brick of cheddar in her hand.

The detectives joined her, both leaning their elbows on the counter.

"I'm hungry," said Tom.

With a sideways glance, the psychic said, "Surprise. Surprise. How about I make a plate of munchies? Between the stuff we brought from my place and what's here, it should fill us up while we talk."

"Works for me," said Danny, turning to his partner.

"Don't suppose I have any say, huh?" he said.

"No," replied the psychic and senior detective in unison.

As the counselor performed the trivial task of putting together a platter of goodies, she allowed her mind to wander, poking with care at the delicate fabric between her world and the next—searching for answers, but her senses told her to be afraid of what her prodding would reveal.

The shrill ring of a phone snapped her back to the earthly plane with a jolt, and Danny snatched his mobile from the table. He excused himself only to return a moment later; the friends looking at him—hoping for good news.

Groaning, he said, "They still can't get the DNA or fingerprint records. They're workin' on it, but nothing yet." Scratching his stubble, his eyes wandered to the wine rack. "Who wants a glass of vino? One drink won't hurt us tonight."

"I'm in," said his partner.

"Why not?" said the psychic, nodding with enthusiasm.

He chose a bottle and set it on the counter. "Now, this is an excellent vintage."

Marnie picked it up, read the label, and hugged it. "Yum! Australian Shiraz."

"It's the same one you had at your place the other night. The informant over there by the window snapped a pic and shared it with me."

Not listening, Tom stepped away from the back door, his face screwed up in thought. "Somethin' doesn't feel right. Two of the guys are gone."

"It's always harder to see things at dusk. Besides, Tater isn't growling. If the guy who snatched him was out there, he would be," suggested Marnie, wringing her hands, and eyeing her Border Collie who was sleeping by the back door.

"Back in a sec," he said, leaving the room and returning with a radio. "Movement in the west made them change things up. The roof is a better vantage point. They've put a sniper and a spotter up there. I hope our psycho doesn't have night vision goggles." Muttering to himself, he wandered to the door before turning back. "We gotta talk." With that, he stalked away.

"Are you almost done there?" asked the detective.

"Yeah. I'll add a few more crackers so your sidekick doesn't die of starvation."

"Great. We need to compare notes. Full disclosure. What do each of us know about this case? I'm gonna get Mr. Doom and Gloom and be right back."

The kitchen timer buzzed, and Marnie pulled the pie from the oven, all the while pondering her value to the investigation. *Why do they think I can help? I have no idea what's going on. Other than someone wants me dead.*

The detectives returned with their laptops and briefcases. Tom set his computer on the kitchen table and opened it. "What's the password for your wireless?" he asked.

Danny ruffled through papers, biting his inner cheek. "It's sarah4ever. All lowercase. 'For' is the number, not the word."

"Thanks," he said, sneaking a glimpse at Marnie, who looked teary-eyed at his fidgety partner, who was avoiding eye contact as he moseyed out of the room. The friends heard the cellar door open and close.

"So, sarah4ever. How does that make you feel?" he asked.

She lifted a shoulder—eyebrows knitting together. "What? He loved his wife. He must miss her every day. Why would you think it would upset me?"

"I didn't say it would. But you answered the question without realizing," he said, looking down at his keyboard, typing in the password.

"I am not upset. Of course, he still loves her. She was probably the love of his life—to have that taken away would be, well, it would be soul-destroying," she said, turning away, busying herself at the counter.

His password wasn't what I expected, but so what? His wife's life took a tragic turn and ended too soon. Pfft. The only men I have fallen in love with have ditched me or beaten me and played mind games. It's good to know men like Danny exist. I can't imagine how wonderful that kind of love could be.

The basement door opened again and slammed shut, and the detective returned carrying a large piece of plywood. He pushed together two kitchen stools to balance it on, then rummaged through a drawer in the sideboard, retrieving tape and a marker. He sat, logged into his computer and glanced up. The friends had been watching him, and he knew it.

"Okay. Tommy, what have you got?" he said with a pen at the ready.

His partner cleared his throat. "Okay. Well, I did some digging yesterday from the hospital. To be honest, I contacted a few of our guys and asked them to get out their shovels. They told me you had started the paperwork for a search warrant for Wilder's house. Anyway, Wilder's wife was a new acquisition, so to speak. They'd been married about five months but had been together for about seven years. People saw her coming and going for a long time. Her name is Catherine. Now, no one knows where she is or who her family is, so I got to thinking and went back out to Wilder's place last night with the warrant you arranged." He paused, glancing at

Danny, whose face was red, right eyebrow meeting his hairline. "The warrant was sittin' on my desk when I went to the station last night, so I jumped on it. Why lose more time? That's where I was goin' when Marnie phoned, and why I wanted you to return my call and the reason I've wanted to speak with you all day."

"Why didn't you tell me that?" asked the psychic, frowning at him across the table.

"Need-to-know basis, Ms. Reilly. Why didn't you give Danny my message?" he asked, matching her scowl.

"Wait. Did you say seven years? He *was* cheating on me. I knew it. That bastard!" She slid back her chair with a huff and leaped to her feet. "He told me I was crazy, suspicious and clingy. I've never been needy in my entire life. Suspicious, yes. Crazy perhaps, but I have never clung on to anyone! And how does this happen in Creekwood without everyone knowing? Gawd! You fart and someone in Hudson Hollow knows about it before you do."

Tom scratched his head and pursed his lips. "Now that your outburst is over, can I continue?"

She narrowed her eyes and dropped into her chair, resting her elbows on the table with her chin in her hands.

"Okay, so we went to Wilder's. I couldn't find any pictures of the lady of the house, and the only sign that a woman had been living there were a few toiletries in the bathroom. No clothes. No shoes and nothing personal. It looked as if someone had searched his office. The safe was open, and his last will and testament was on his desk. Ripped in half and stabbed with a letter opener."

"Are you fucking kidding me?" growled the detective, jerking himself from his chair. "Were you gonna share this with me or what? Jesus!"

Tom lurched to his feet and stormed around the island, nostrils flaring and chest heaving, stopping inches from Danny. "I tried last night, but you didn't return my call. Then this morning, we were supposed to talk on the roof, but phone calls and *your* personal crisis..." He stopped himself. But jaw clenched, he squinted at the psychic, knowing his partner would get his point. "And how many times did I say it was important? Huh? You kept sayin', we'll talk about it tonight."

"That's enough!" Marnie held up her hands. "Okay. Testosterone check, boys. Chill out," she said, getting to her feet and squeezing between them.

Tater barked, and they all pivoted. The dog stared out the window, eyes on the forest, his fluffy scruff bristled. Letting out a soft *ahroo*, he paced back and forth, his mouth shut tight.

"Does he need to go out?" asked Danny.

"No, he sees something. Must be your guys," she said, hoping that was true. "He needs to be fed, though. Shall we take a little time-out? You two could add wood to the fires, perhaps. No pun intended. Go." With a wave of her hands, she shooed them away.

6:13 PM

"Have you two cooled off?" Marnie asked when the detective returned to the kitchen.

Nibbling on a piece of cheese, he said, "Yeah. I could have handled that better."

"You think?"

Chapter Forty-Two

"Hmm ... Has Tater been fed and watered?" he asked, changing the subject.

"Yup. Hey, Danny. That tiger you carry in your pocket. What's that about?"

He wrinkled his forehead. "That was an abrupt subject change, but okay. Um ... It's something I picked up when I was traveling years ago. I saw it and thought my mother would like it. It was a Mother's Day gift. She had it with her always, and when she died, I almost had it buried with her, but something told me not to, so I kept it. I carry it in my pocket to remember her."

She nodded. "Is 'You are the Sunshine of My Life' Sarah's and your song?"

"No. I gave her a music box one year for Christmas that played 'You Are My Sunshine.' It had teddy bears on it. 'Teddy Bear' was our song—Elvis's rendition. She always said I was her big bear, and she would sing the song to me. When she stopped singing it, I knew something was wrong. Anyway, that's it. That's the story. I bought the music box because of the bears, not for the song, so I'm not sure why she said that to you."

"She said that because you are—were—the brightest part of her life."

"Uh ... well ... thanks for making the connection. But most people think I'm a grumpy bastard."

"You are at first glance," she said, wrapping her arms around him, and while he wasn't expecting it, he welcomed the warmth, hugging her too. They were still embracing when Tom returned.

"Am I interrupting something?" he asked, backing away.

Clinging to the psychic, Danny held out an arm. "Nope. It's team bonding. Come here, and get in on this, big boy."

"Freaks. Can we get back to work?" he said, pushing past them, curling his lip.

●

6:33 PM

Ears flat and tail tucked, Tater grumbled and mumbled, nose nudging the doors as limbs swayed outside the window, tapping the glass.

"Should we take the Tot out before we get back to it?" asked Tom, tossing a pen on a pad and eyeing his partner and the psychic.

"Yeah. Then he'll be okay until morning," said Marnie, setting her wineglass aside.

Picking up his radio, he made a call to the men outside and received confirmation that the team would be alert.

"Okay, buddy. Let's get this over with," he said, scratching the pup's head.

The humans and the canine trooped into the living room for jackets and the leash.

"We go out as a team and huddle together," said Danny, handing out the tactical gear Sterling had provided.

He squatted down next to the dog with the K-9 vest, but the pup scooted away, so he handed it to his owner. She took it and sat on the floor, patting the timbers and clicking her tongue. The Border Collie ambled over and sat, eyes downcast.

With the last button snapped, she said, "You look tough, little man." Patting his rump, she took the lead Tom handed her and clipped it onto his collar. "Here we go. All set."

Tater tried to shake free of the vest and then gave in with an equine huff and a side-eye.

Stepping out into the chilly night air, Danny left the door ajar in case they needed to make a hasty retreat. Thick snowflakes drifted in slow, silent spirals, and the psychic shivered as a restless wind wound around them, carrying a bite that warned something was coming. She peeked over her shoulder, certain an intruder was sneaking up, and a howl pierced the night. They all flinched, turning in different directions. Tater replied with a twitch of his ears and a whispered woof, his snout raised to the sky.

"Must be a coyote," Danny said, running his eyes across the landscape.

Tom nodded, but Marnie saw his jaw muscles clench and his Adam's apple bob.

"That was not an animal," she said, scanning the trees.

With his ears back and scruff bristling, Tater kicked back dirt and snow before releasing a sharp *yipe*.

"Let's get back inside. Now, please." Her eyes flicked between the dark treeline and the veranda, heart thumping. Then, she and Tater bolted for the cabin, snow scattering in their wake, and the detectives thundered up the steps behind.

Danny closed the door, locked it, and turned to Marnie. "Why did you say that wasn't an animal?"

"Because it wasn't. My brother used to make noises like that to scare us when we were kids. I know the difference between a wild animal and a person mimicking one. I've lived in the woods my entire life," she said, turning to her best friend for confirmation.

Tom nodded. "Yeah. I agree. That was someone trying to get a reaction, and it worked. We're all back inside, and I've got a case of the willies." He shuddered as he removed his vest.

The detective turned back to her. "Hey, have you picked up on your brother since his death?"

"Nope, and I don't go looking. If he wants to talk to me, I'm all ears. He and I argued right before he died. He may still be mad at me." She shrugged and trudged to the kitchen, feeling guilty for not sharing her earlier peek through the veil. *In my defense, I didn't discover anything useful*, she told herself. *But still, had the phone not rung...*

"You think that was him giving you a warning?" asked Danny, following her.

"Uh, no. You guys heard it, too. Got something you want to share, Detective? I mean, if you and Tom are clairaudient, it would be good to know," she said, waggling her eyebrows.

He leaned in—his lips brushing against her ear. "What did my grandmother tell you?"

With a coy smile, she side-stepped around him and opened the fridge.

"She told me you like to be well fed," she said, arching her brows.

"Careful there, Ms. Reilly. You're going to pop the glue stitch if you keep raising your eyebrows like that."

He sidled up beside her and brushed her bangs off her forehead, inspecting the cut and bruising, but she squirmed away, checking the fridge for more snacks, even though the plate was still ample with treats. The detective stepped away, resigned to his grandmother's lack of discretion and Ms. Reilly's ability to weasel out of answering a question. He retreated to the windows, joining Tater, who was grumping at snapping branches outside. Danny dismissed it as being one of their guys but leaned closer to the windows and cupped his hands for a better look only catching Tom's reflection as his colleague returned to the kitchen … and someone was following him. Wheeling around, he saw his partner but no one else.

"What's up, man?" asked Tom, sneaking a glance behind. "You look like you've seen a ghost. Marn, you see any spooks in the room?"

She looked up and smiled. "My dad. He's standing right behind you."

He spun around, arms windmilling. "Jesus! Don't do that to me. You know that freaks me out! Gawd!" He quivered and pulled his shoulders close to his ears.

She giggled and winked at her dad, and he wagged his chin at the detective, who was staring *at* him. *Hmm … Gram was right. He can see spirits.*

Chapter Forty-Three

7:03 PM, The Cabin

"Okay, Tommy, shoot," said Danny, sliding out a chair, settling at the table.

"Hang on," said his partner, chewing a mouthful of cheese and cracker. "Uh ... where was I up to? That's right, Ken's will. Anyway, it's there on the desk, ripped in half and stabbed. It's brutal. Oh, and there's dried blood on the floor in the conservatory and tipped over furniture. There wasn't any attempt to clean it up. Not that you'd get that out of white marble. Blech! Anyway, there was a struggle, and it looks like the kill spot."

"Impaling the document certainly sends a message," said the counselor with a shudder as she hung the dishrag on the side of the sink.

Her friend agreed. "Yeah, it does. Anyway, I read through it, and it was surprising to see that Wilder hadn't updated his will in a long time. He left quite a lot to charity, but most of his estate goes to ... drumroll, please ... one Ms. Marnie Sophia Reilly." He finished with a tap of a pencil on his wineglass.

She shot around the island, her mouth forming words that would not come out. With a hand on her forehead, she sank into a chair, closing her eyes.

As a trained detective, Danny knew that shock and fear look much the same, and Marnie's expression showed a bit of both, but her gaping mouth gave her away.

Tom put a knuckle to her chin and closed her gob, which led to a glower as she stared into space. Giving her shoulder a reassuring squeeze, he said, "I know, kiddo. I couldn't believe it. I read it three times. He's got a new wife, and she isn't in it. Maybe he never got to it. Who knows, but here's the kicker. It's the house, land and a few other properties he has around our fine town, and some out of state. He's got thirty-eight million sittin' in the bank and a lot of assets: stocks, real estate, a collection of vintage cars, and a Humvee in the driveway. You name it, he had it—and not much debt at all."

"I feel like I'm going to throw up," she said, putting her head down on the table, rolling it back and forth.

Danny got up and paced between the table and the back wall. "Did you have any idea he named you in his will?"

Eyes rolling, she lifted her head and pointed at her face. "Does this look like a woman who knew something like that?"

"No. Not really," he said. Taking another bottle of wine from the rack, he unscrewed the cap. "I need a drink." He leaned against the counter, poured, and swirled the wine around the glass. "If he's just married, why would his wife kill him? But who else could get that close to Wilder to take him out?"

"Uh ... I can think of thirty-eight million reasons his new bride might off him," said Tom, raising his eyebrows.

"Guys. Dad's trying to tell me something." The psychic watched the spirit and nodded as his message became clear. Her mouth formed an O, and she slapped her hand on her forehead. "Oh. My. God! You said his wife's name is Catherine?"

"Yeah. Why?"

She considered the name, smacked the table, rattling glassware, and startling the detectives. "Holy shit!"

Face scrunched, her friend asked, "What are you going on about?"

Jaw dropping, she said, "Catherine? C'mon, guys! Connect the dots! Danny was on the scent earlier today. Remember?"

With blue eyes sparking, the detective snapped his fingers, making the connection. "Got it! Kate is sometimes short for Catherine."

Marnie flung out her arms. "There you go! That's why she didn't want me to go get her stuff and why her finger and ring were in the forest. She was not walking home from a party, and two men on the street did not ambush her." Frowning, she added, "By the way, Hudson Boulevard has plenty of alleys to duck into. I know. I walk that way to the library. And petite makes sense, but lethal—not so much." Pausing to consider, she changed her mind. "Then again, maybe it does."

Tom stood, crossing the kitchen to the bottle of wine. He filled a glass and held it out to her. She accepted it and took a long drink. He poured another for himself and did the same.

Clicking her tongue on the roof of her mouth, the counselor considered Kate's story again, and the pieces fell into place. "That bullet graze on her arm is from either you, Danny, or Tony shooting at her out in the forest. You guys are her alleged attackers. And she tried to kill Tom on the bridle trail." Stopping mid-sentence, her eyebrows knitted together as she rearranged her thoughts. "Wait. She's not strong enough to drag him. So, the guy on the roof, the one who grabbed Tater, helped her. And remember, her phone kept cutting out. She was down there trying to cover her ass, pretending to be a damsel in distress. Give me a break!" Catching her breath, she said, "Now. What else haven't you shared with me about the video from Friday night?"

Danny steepled his fingers, recalling the grainy footage. "We saw Carl first, then a man and what looked like a young man or a boy helping Ken Wilder walk through your backyard. I'd say they were carrying him because the drag marks were minimal. That 'boy' could have been Kate."

The best friends agreed.

Scratching his head, the detective asked, "Who knew about the piano wire?"

The psychic thought about the conversations she had had with friends. "Carl, of course. He was my therapist. Uh ... Tom and I told Kate as well. Some people in The Collective, like Alice, knew too. That's it."

Hearing a throat clear, Marnie twisted in her seat to see her father shaking his head. She scoured her memory, and what she remembered made her feel ill. She mouthed a name, and the spirit nodded. Danny saw it too and waited for the psychic's reaction. Green eyes wide, she covered her mouth with a hand.

"Holy shit! This is *sooo* bad." Scooting back her chair, she went to the doors and peered out. Tater whined and hit the glass with his paw, and she gave his ear a gentle tug before returning to the table. Her gaze met Tom's, and his stomach dropped.

They had grown up together. He knew her better than anyone, but the fear he saw in her eyes felt like a gut punch, and he sucked in a breath. *What the hell? She's not afraid of anything. Well, almost.* "Marn, what are we dealin' with?" he asked, voice quaking.

Hands trembling, she said, "It's a *who*. We're dealing with Sam."

Brow in a deep furrow, Danny screwed up his face. "Hang on! I'm confused. Why are you afraid of Jalnack? He's in the hospital. What am I missing?"

"Come here," said Tom, hugging the psychic, resting his chin on top of her head. "Not Sam *Jalnack*. Sam *Reilly*, her brother."

"Back up. Didn't you tell me he's dead?" the detective asked, dragging his hands down his face.

"Yeah. That's what we were told. But we never bought it. A body wasn't found at the scene. The Feds said the explosion at the meth lab—the one Sam was investigating with the ATF and DEA—incinerated him. Marn pestered the FBI until they threatened to arrest her. She asked too many questions. I tried too, but it almost got me fired. Do you remember when I was in the doghouse a few years back? That's what it was about. We pissed off the Feds," he said, waving a hand between himself and his friend.

Squeezing his eyes tight, the detective pursed his lips. "That's why we can't access the prints and DNA." His eyes flicked between his partner and the psychic.

The pals nodded.

"Okay, you two. Tell me about the infamous Sam Reilly."

Tom held up a hand. "Hang on. We need to fill in the guys out there that they're not dealin' with Joe Schmoe. They have to know that a trained killer who knows this forest better than anyone is out there with them. He grew up in these woods and knows every tree, rock, cave—he knows everything. They are not up against a local yokel having a shitty week. We're dealin' with an assassin with a personal grudge." He looked at his friend for confirmation, and she nodded.

"So, he wasn't just FBI," said Danny, sighing and turning to Tom. "You said he was brilliant. That he could debate anyone. You told me he was a good guy."

The corner of Tom's mouth lifted, and he diverted his eyes. "No. Well, yes, I might have said that. I was thinking past tense, as when we were kids and, you know, the whole thing about never speaking ill of the dead. Once he went into the FBI, he changed. Hmm … It was before that, but he got worse. In fact, I didn't like him at all in the end. He could be mean when we were young, but it was different. Sam did stuff that an older brother would do. He teased us, roughed us up, and stuff like that, but when he came back after his first year, he was brutal." He nudged Marnie. "Tell him what he was like."

Wringing her hands, she hesitated, not wanting to say negative things about her brother. With a sigh, she dropped her head, recalling memories of childhood. When her tear-filled eyes met Danny's, she said, "He was different. Rough. Insensitive. The sibling wrestling matches were violent. I thought he didn't realize his strength, but deep down, I knew he meant to hurt me. When we were teenagers, he and Tom were joking around once, and I was terrified he would break his arm, so I hit my own brother with a baseball bat, fracturing his radius. When I looked into his eyes … well, if looks could kill, I'd be dead. My parents weren't home, so we had to take Sam to the hospital, and he swore and threatened us the entire way. We knew he wouldn't tell how it happened because my father would have throttled him if he found out. We had to make up a story about falling from a tree out back."

Danny leaned forward in his chair. "Where was Kate when all this stuff was happening? Was he mean to her, too?"

"No, Sam always had a thing for her. He was a few years older, so they didn't date that I remember," said his partner.

Marnie confirmed, "She liked him, too. She used to tell me how lucky I was to have a big brother, and she would follow him around. He liked the attention."

Danny asked, "What were you two fighting about when he died?"

"The house. He wanted me to move out so that he could have it. My dad left it to both of us. Sam was angry he had split his estate. He thought he should have gotten it all." She sat down and rested her head in her hands.

"Did you know about this?" he asked his partner.

"Yeah, I knew. I called him and tried to calm him down, but it only made things worse," said Tom, patting the psychic's back.

"We need a description. Do you have a picture?"

"Not with me, but plenty at home," said Marnie. "He looks like a male version of me, but a few inches taller and he's wiry. His hair is darker blonde with more red than mine. Mom always said he had an aquiline nose. And a strong jawline. I'd say square. Gray eyes. Oh, his nose has been broken once or twice."

"Okay. That helps. Tom, you get on the radio, and I'll call Captain Sterling."

7:25 PM

Tom relayed the potential danger to the SWAT commander, pacing between the glass door and the island. But he wheeled around as

Tater lunged at the glass, teeth bared, snarling at pounding footsteps thundering across the back deck. Stifling a scream, Marnie flinched, shattering her wineglass against the table edge, then raced to her dog, grabbing his collar. She pulled him into the center of the room, and Tom checked the lock with a hard twist and pulled the shutters tight.

Danny jogged into the room, sidearm in hand. "Everybody okay?"

Eyes wide, Marnie dropped to her knees beside her dog, who was still barking. "That was an uneven gait. Clop-clip-clop-clip. Heavier on one foot." Burying her face in the Border Collie's neck, she cooed, "It's okay, buddy. We're safe. Nobody is going to hurt us." He licked her ear and nuzzled his nose into her neck, as if reassuring his mistress, he would protect her too.

"So, it's the same guy from your house and today, then," said the detective, squatting beside them, patting the canine's back. "Don't worry, pal. We're gonna solve this soon." He stood and offered a hand to the psychic. "Come on. We've gotta talk."

"Let's go in by the fire, and we'll bring the wine," said Tom, getting another glass from the rack and grabbing the bottle by the neck.

Snuggled up on the couch with a blanket, a comforting beverage, and her dog at her feet, Marnie shut her eyes and tried to tap into her brother's energy. But Tom broke her concentration, plopping down beside her, giving her shoulder a gentle bump.

Danny settled into a chair opposite. "Does Sam play chess? I mean … is he a strategic thinker? Can he read our next move?"

Bottom lip out, the psychic shrugged one shoulder. "Uh … yeah. He *was* a federal agent. And yes, he played chess with my father. He is book smart and street smart. I believe my brother is strategic and tactical, which is a deadly combination. And I guarantee he is ten steps ahead of us. He's probably hacked into the police database."

"Really?"

"Oh, yeah," said his partner. "This is a mission for him. He won't stop until it's done."

"Which means what?"

"My brother wants me dead. Isn't that clear?" said the psychic.

"Do you think your father knows? Is that why he's here?"

"I guess. He's been with me since Saturday. He's here now. We can ask him." The psychic leaned back and looked up at her dad, who lingered behind her.

Colin Reilly nodded and dotted her nose with a finger kiss. As he faded away, the air stirred with a cool hush, and embers rose like fireflies, dancing above the grate before vanishing up the chimney.

Eyeing Danny, she said, "You saw that, right?"

With a hand over his mouth, he muttered, "Yeah. I saw it."

"Saw what?" asked Tom, his head toing and froing like a pendulum between the psychic and his partner.

The radio squawked, and Tom rushed to the kitchen, returning moments later, face pinched. "They had him. He was on the veranda, and then he disappeared into the trees. He was right there, and they let him get away. What the hell do we do now?"

Mouth twisted, Danny pointed at Marnie. "It's time for divine guidance. Madame Seance is gonna do what she does best."

Chapter Forty-Three

Squeezing her eyes tight and sighing, she said, "And what exactly is that?"

"Talk to the spirits. Get us as much advice as you can. That's your superpower, isn't it?"

"I wouldn't call it that, but … If I do it, you need to be quiet. And no making fun of me, Thomas."

"Swear to God, I won't," he said, running a finger over his chest, drawing a cross.

"Fine," said the psychic, settling in the lotus position on the floor in front of the fire. She shut her eyes, hands resting on her knees, palms up, and with three cleansing breaths, she bowed her head. *Okay, folks. Tell me what I need to know. And Mom, if you can hear me, I hate to bother you, but I need help.*

Tater moved from his spot under the coffee table and lay down facing her, resting a paw on her knee. Retreating to comfy chairs, the men switched their phones to silent, waiting for direction from the other side of the veil.

Tears streaked Marnie's cheeks, and her lips moved with soundless words. Back rigid and arms fluid, her eyelids fluttered, and her head tilted—listening to the hushed chatter of spirits and guides.

Danny's phone vibrated, and he tip-toed to the kitchen, returning minutes later with an update. Pulling Tom aside, he whispered, "The guys tried to track him and heard a car engine start up and dirt kicking back. He took off again. They've closed the roads. He can't get back to town without getting stopped."

"Pfft. Sam will get wherever he needs to get. He's resourceful. He's going to finish his mission or die trying."

"We need eyes on her house," said the detective, straightening a wool blanket across the back of the chair.

His partner snapped his fingers. "Her old house. We've gotta monitor it, too."

"He's headed there now," said the psychic, her voice ringing clear.

The men whipped around at the sound of her voice. With shoulders squared and fists clenched, she stood by the fire, her green eyes the most beautiful shade of aquamarine. The tears were gone, and she lifted her chin, jaw set with determination. "We have to stop him."

"On it," said Danny, making a call to his captain.

Tom grabbed the radio and asked the lieutenant to come to the cabin.

When each had finished, they shared a look, knowing what the other was thinking.

Slapping his partner on the back, Danny growled, "Let's get the bastard!"

"Right behind you."

"I'm coming too," said the psychic.

Shaking his head, Danny disagreed. "No. You are staying here. I will not have you in harm's way."

A knock at the door drew one return rap from the detective. When three thumps came back, he opened it.

"Hey, Lieu," he said, stepping aside to let him in. "Marnie, this is Lieutenant Allen. He's going to get one of his guys to stay with you."

"I'm going with you!" she said, cheeks flaming red. "If you're going after my brother, I want to be there."

Locking eyes, the detectives debated the situation in silence.

Relenting, he said, "Okay. You stay in the car and don't get out for anything. Do you hear me?"

"Fine. We will," she said, shoulders drooping.

"*We?* Pfft. Tater's not coming."

"Yes, he is!" Narrowing her eyes, she dropped a hand onto her hip.

The lieutenant cut in. "She and the pooch can ride in the van. They can see out, but no one can see in. She'll have a few control guys in there with her. It'll be fine," he said.

Holding up his hands in surrender, Danny gave in. "All right."

She pulled on her boots and jacket and clipped on the Border Collie's lead. Then she handed the men their vests and riot helmets. "Don't forget these."

"We'll see ya soon, Marn," said Tom, taking the equipment and chucking her under the chin before stepping out into the cold with Allen.

Danny fixed her with a stern glare. "Do not get out of the van." Then, his blue eyes softened as he moved past her, his hand brushing against hers. She caught it and gave his fingers a warm squeeze. He paused, glancing back with a dimpled smile. "See you soon."

"Be careful."

7:38 PM, Lake Road, En route to Creek Road

"We should expect the unexpected," said Tom, checking his second magazine before tucking it into his pocket.

"Ominous much? Elaborate, please," said his partner, switching on his windshield wipers.

"Look, I've known Sam Reilly my entire life. He never has just one plan. There is always a backup and a second, third, or fourth option for an operation. There was a time I considered the FBI and asked him a lot of questions. He couldn't help but boast about his special skills. His expertise is unconventional infiltration and extraction methods. He found himself in sticky situations where things didn't go to plan, so he had to improvise. Find another way to carry out the mission. Taking him down won't be easy. He's already figured out twenty ways to evade capture."

"Pfft. Thanks for getting my hopes up," said Danny, wishing he had a layout of Marnie's old house and a map of the woods beyond.

Chapter Forty-Four

8:08 PM, Glencrest Road, Creekwood, NY

Hide the car. Brush away your boot prints. Find a warm jacket. Food. Sam Reilly's mind jumped from one thought to another as he parked his car behind a dumpster at the animal shelter on Glencrest Road, which intersected with Creek Road. *I can walk through Flannigan's Woods to Marnie's old house. Why did the cops not have cars on the back roads and streets? Did they think I would take main thoroughfares? They should have asked my sister which way I would go. She could have given them a map. The road less traveled is always the way. Robert Frost knew what he was talking about. Ha-ha.*

The suspect scoped the terrain as he trudged through wet knee-high brush, searching for law enforcement behind every tree, boulder, and thicket. *They won't hunt me here. The lookout will be on the car. I wonder if Dad's truck is in the garage. Or did she get rid of it? Forget it. Going home would be a tactical error. I can return to Wilder's house. The key to his Humvee is in the cupboard. How many steps am I ahead of them?*

Snow flurried thick and fast, the storm blanketing ground hazards in a sheet of white. His boot caught on a root, and he fell forward, catching himself on the branch of a weeping willow, the drooping branches releasing a shower of crystalline powder on his head. The backpack dropped off his shoulder and landed in a drift at his feet. *Shit! All right. Calm down, Reilly. Rest and take your pills.*

He took a jug of water and a prescription bottle from the bag, downed three tablets, and drank half the liquid, returning the containers to his pack. Two whitetail deer wandered into view, and he watched as they foraged in the undergrowth for food. Stealth in his movement, he retrieved a pouch of trail mix from the front pocket of his duffle, opened it, and scattered the contents on the ground before tramping off to his next destination.

Ha! Try tracking me now, he thought, glancing back at the deer trampling his boot prints.

⬤

8:12 PM, Lake Road

Marnie and Tater rode in the back of the SWAT van with Officers Cheswick and Moore. They killed time explaining the equipment and trying to reassure her that everything would be okay.

When she could take no more chit-chat, she asked, "You guys don't know who you're dealing with, do you?"

They gave her a sideways look, turned to each other, and back to her, and shook their heads.

"My brother is a killer—a paid assassin. He's killed two cops and Ken Wilder in the last three days. Officer Jalnack and Detective Keller were lucky. Sam Reilly is evil, and I have that from the highest authority. He's the worst kind of human being you can imagine. Do not underestimate what he will do. I never will again." She scooped an arm around her dog and pulled him closer.

The officers stared at the psychic before Cheswick twirled his index finger next to his ear and rolled his eyes.

Squinting, she said, "I saw that, and I am not crazy."

Cheswick gasped, slunk back in his seat, and lowered the brim of his hat over his eyes.

8:18 PM, 508 Creek Road

Sam skulked out of the woods on the opposite side of the street, staying low and watching for cops. Once satisfied the coast was clear, he sprinted across the road, through the front yard, and up onto the darkened porch. He took a small leather case from his pocket, thankful he still had a set of lockpicks. The latch wasn't a complicated mechanism, and he got to work, opening the front door with ease, and closing it again with a soft click. He kicked the snow off his boots on the doormat and checked to see if the house had an alarm. Fabulous news for him. It did not.

Familiar with the layout of Marnie's old home, he prowled through the house in the dark. He dropped his pack and rifle on the floor and stooped to turn on the gas fireplace. Blue flames danced in the darkness—the flicker reminding him of an explosion and an all-consuming firestorm he had endured. An acrid taste filled his mouth as he pulled a stubby church candle and safety matches from his bundle and lit it before going to the kitchen.

He moved between rooms with ease, his cat-like vision one of his greatest assets. He also had the nose of a bloodhound and caught scents of lavender and tea tree oil as he passed by the downstairs bathroom. Its door sat ajar, and a nightlight flickered as he neared. *Motion sensor.* He reached inside and pulled it from the outlet, dropping it in the trash.

When he reached the kitchen, he rummaged through the pantry, pulling out a box of saltines and vanilla cream wafer cookies. Not his favorite, but they would do. He munched on a cracker as he opened the fridge, its tiny light illuminating the room. Peering inside, he was happy to see something more agreeable and took out a longneck ale. *How nice. The bar is stocked. Ha-ha.* He twisted off the cap, rested a hip on the counter, took a long swig, and contemplated his next move.

Think! Dammit, think!

A headache pounded in his ears, and with a hand to his temple, he pressed on the pain and focused on his current predicament. He had miscalculated at the cabin. The officers' movements appeared to have a pattern, but he read it wrong. He thought he had time to get in the back slider, but they had spotted him before he could jimmy it open. "Dammit!" he said, slamming a hand on the counter, wincing with agony.

That little bitch Marnie and her fucking dog. She slugged me with a baseball bat, and that mongrel bit me. And that mama's boy, Keller. I should've ripped his arm out of the socket when I had the chance. A stream of unfortunate relationships and decisions.

Chapter Forty-Four

Why the fuck did I trust Kate? I never say no to her. Argh! My head hurts.

What is my next move? Tomorrow night or early morning. They won't expect me right before sunrise. Pieces of a plan formed, then an inauspicious notion occurred to him, and the thought festered, and he frowned.

What if my sister knows what I am planning? Does she know where I am? Is she reading my thoughts the way she used to?

Fingers pinching and twisting his bottom lip, he glimpsed a clothesline through the window.

"Huh, that'll work!"

8:22 PM, Lake Road

The scanner crackled and squawked, spitting out clipped voices and coded messages as the detectives made the thirty-five-minute drive to Marnie's home. The latter searched the sides of the road to see if Sam Reilly had pulled off into the forest to observe and assess.

Danny had shifted his Jeep into four-wheel drive as soon as they pulled out of the garage. Snow was accumulating fast, and the roads were messy, with a heavy blanket of snow over black ice.

"Creek Road will be a mess. It's always the last one on the outskirts to be plowed," said Tom, remembering when they were kids, Marnie had been late for school quite a lot in the winter. Watching the rearview mirror, he could see snow dancing in the halogen lights of the van.

8:47 PM, 404 Creek Road

The police vehicles parked on the verge, blocking the driveway of the Reilly family's home. It was a quarter of a mile up from Mr. and Mrs. Hale's house, Marnie's previous residence. Danny and Tom exited the vehicle and put on their vests. The detectives read each other's minds; they had both trained for situations like this, but they had never been part of a live operation. Geared up, Captain Sterling waited for them at the curb.

He nodded down the road to the psychic's prior home. "We're all set up. Lieu contacted the Hales, and they are cooperating. They told us where we could find their hide-a-key so that we don't have to bust down the front door. There are signs Reilly is in the house. The team reported a flicker of light coming through the cracks in the blinds. We'll get him. He doesn't have a chance of escaping this time," he said, puffing out his chest and straightening the hem of his jacket.

Tom cocked his head. "Yeah, well, you don't know him, sir. If anyone can get out of a surrounded house, it's him." Eyes to the sky, he breathed in a lungful of air. Letting it out, watching the steam billow before evaporating into the night.

Danny clapped him on the shoulder. "I've got your back, and you've got mine. Let's go."

Marnie watched out the front window of the van as the detectives walked up the road. She slid open the side door and hopped out.

"Get back in there!" Danny's hushed command drew a scowl.

Tom took her arm, turning her back to the vehicle. "Get in the car. We aren't kids anymore. You can't hit him with a baseball bat and fix it."

She leaned up, kissing his cheek, and whispered, "That fireside chat I had earlier. There's something you should know. It's like we thought. He murdered my mother. Please be careful."

With a blank stare and clenched jaw, he gave her a tight hug. Then she turned, pecking the detective's cheek, repeating the message as Captain Sterling watched the exchange. Danny nodded his understanding, then pulled Marnie close and pressed a tender kiss on her lips. She stepped back, with fingertips to her mouth and a rosy glow on her face.

With a wink and a lopsided, dimpled grin, he said, "Please, get in the van."

Eyes twinkling, she stepped up into the vehicle.

Tom gave Danny a nudge. "Let's go, Romeo. We've got ass kickin' to do."

As the detectives strode off into the darkness, Marnie closed her eyes and asked her parents to watch over them.

9:13 PM, 508 Creek Road

Lieutenant Allen met Danny and Tom on the road outside of Hale's home. His team of ten officers was busy getting into position around the exterior of the house. Five were in the front; two covered the back door and three more positioned themselves along the property line between the backyard and the forest beyond. Gregg and Keller would offer backup if needed.

"Let my guys take the lead on this. We train for it every day," said Allen, handing the guys headsets so they could listen to the operation.

Danny checked his sidearm. "Copy that. We'll stand by to knock him on his ass if he gets past you."

The SWAT commander clapped his back. "Let's get this asshole."

The three men marched along the hedgerow leading to the yard. The detectives stationed themselves to cover the back gate in case their person of interest evaded the elite squad while Allen joined his team on the front porch.

Through the cracks at the edges of the blinds covering the front windows, the officers could see the flickering light of flames in the fireplace, but the suspect was nowhere to be seen.

"We're in," said the lieutenant as he unlocked the door, and the SWAT team rushed into the house.

"Clear" echoed through the earpieces each time the officers entered a room and there was no sign of the fugitive.

Sam Reilly was a skilled survivor, and as he sat in an attic window overlooking the backyard, he snickered at his own genius. A zip line made from stainless steel clothesline traveled from the attic window the length of the backyard and into the forest. He had attached one end to a ceiling joist and the other end to a huge sugar maple in the forest.

He opened his backpack, digging out gloves and a bundle of paracord. Zipping up his pack, he threw it over his shoulders. Then, sliding up the window, he peered out and grinned. No one was looking up. He swung his legs onto the windowsill, and with the cord in place, he pushed himself off the ledge, and zipped over their heads, plunging into the forest beyond.

"Son of a bitch! He flew right over our heads! Sam Reilly is running!" shouted an officer at the treeline.

In a clatter of commotion, the team set off in different directions—some through the yard, others racing to the bridle trail loop to cut off his exits from the forest.

Gunfire boomed, and Lieutenant Allen yelled through his headset. "Get him! He's running! He's in the trees!"

"Stop! Wait! Piano wire!" hollered Danny, racing to the veranda.

Tom grabbed his radio to remind and warn the team of the suspect's diabolical scheme.

The police, who were running into the forest, jerked to a halt, slowing their steps into the thicket. They were met by Sam's handiwork, a strategic web of piano wire woven through the trees on either side of his escape maple.

"Dammit! How the hell could he get away?!" The detective slammed his hand into the cedar siding.

Tom bit his lip and said, "I've been sayin' there is no way he's goin' down without a fight."

9:34 PM, 404 Creek Road

Speechless at being outwitted, the detectives and lieutenant jogged back to the Reilly house, where they found Marnie and her dog on the verge, chatting with Sterling. To be more apt, she was talking *at* their captain, her arms waving, finger pointing, eyes pleading.

"He's gone to the cave. I know he has," said the psychic, eyes blazing, shoulders taught.

Tom jumped in, rescuing his boss. "He has the forest strung up with piano wire. There's no way we're going in there tonight. We'll have to find another way," he said, a hand massaging his forehead.

She clenched her hands into claws. "Will someone listen to me? You don't have to go into the forest." She gripped her friend's hand. "We know this terrain as well as he does."

Throwing back his head, Tom said. "We can go *around* it. Can we use the boat?"

"Yeah. He's on the other side of the pond, and he may not know that we know how to get there."

Tom's face dropped—prodding his memory for the location of the cave resulted in a fat zero. "Marn, I don't remember the way. It's been years. I haven't been there since we were kids. Everything's changed. The markers would be different."

"*I* know where to go. And don't ask me how. I just do," she said, searching the men's faces for approval.

Sterling shook his head, his fleshy neck wobbling. "No. A civilian will not be involved in chasing down a suspect. I must draw a line somewhere."

She gritted her teeth, bristling at his dismissive and narrow-minded response. "Do you want to catch him? He hates me. I am the perfect bait." Pivoting to the guys for support, she continued, "Right now, he is trekking the edge of the pond. After that, he's got a five or ten-minute swim to the island. If he makes it, he'll be cold and disoriented. We'll catch him by surprise. I'll bet that he doesn't have a weapon with him. We can catch him unawares. Let's end this. Let's get him!"

Sterling locked eyes with the lieutenant, who confirmed Marnie's prediction. "Ms. Reilly is right. His rifle is on the floor in the family room, and there's a hunting knife in the kitchen."

"No one could survive the water this time of year," said Sterling.

"Someone with the right gear and proper training could," said Allen.

Chapter Forty-Five

In small and isolated towns like Creekwood, the cops don't always have the luxury of handling things by the book. Sometimes they lean on the guy who has the right tools to pick an antique lock. Or the librarian whose research skills match the guile of a seasoned agent. But on this particular night, it was a psychic psychologist who could read her brother's thoughts. She was sharp enough to sense his next move and reckless enough to follow him into the darkness, dragging along Detectives Keller and Gregg, and an astute Border Collie named Tater. And if all else failed, she was excellent bait.

9:45 PM, The Boathouse, 404 Creek Road

"So, tell me why the boat is still in the water," asked Danny.

"It's up on a hoist. I have a guy who comes over after Columbus Day to do whatever needs to be done to store it over the winter. Don't ask me what. I just know that in the spring, he comes back, checks everything, and it's good to go."

Tom laughed. "The guy's name is Bert Winfrey, and he owns the local marina. He and I have looked after the little boat since Mr. Reilly died."

"Uh ... does that mean there is more than one?"

"There was," said the psychic, quickening her pace to get away from the conversation.

Her best friend said, "It's the one her dad was on when he disappeared." Putting a finger to his lips, he ended the questioning.

His partner understood. "Ah. Bad subject."

They eased their way down the snowy, slippery path to the boathouse and creaked open the door. Marnie stepped in and turned on the flashlight they'd retrieved from the Jeep, and the detectives and dog followed.

"Will this decking hold all of us?" asked Danny.

"Yeah. Mr. Reilly built it, and it's maintained every spring," said Tom, jumping up and down.

"Jesus! Don't do that!" said the psychic, grabbing a pylon for support.

Tom shone his Maglite into the water below, and inky darkness glinted back. "I hope the water isn't frozen this close to land. If it is, we aren't goin' anywhere. Then again, our days *have* been above freezing, so we should be okay." He lowered the eighteen-foot Jon boat, and a splash echoed through the boathouse.

"Yes!" said Marnie, as she and Tater boarded, the dog's ears dropping when the boat wobbled.

Danny untied the bow and stepped on, holding a post to keep them in place while his partner slid the door open before boarding, and taking the wheel.

"Marn, can you get the stern line?" he asked, digging the key from his pocket.

Without answering, Marnie untied the rope and pushed off the back wall, the boat gliding forward.

"I hope it starts," said Tom, turning the ignition. With a stuttering put-put, the engine turned over. "Thank Christ for that!"

"They'll leave the sirens on for twenty minutes or so while we cross. I hope it covers the sound of the motor," said the detective.

"I'll keep the speed low to minimize wake, and we'll have to whisper. Sound carries out here."

"Holy crap. It's cold on the water," said the psychic, teeth chattering, clinging to her dog for warmth.

10:03 PM, The Island

Reaching the shore, the detectives jumped out and pulled the boat close to a decrepit dock. They tested their weight on the old cedar boards, bouncing from left foot to right.

"It could be worse," whispered Tom, tying off the bow while his partner secured the stern.

Danny offered Marnie his hand, and she held the dog leash in the other as she and Tater stepped off.

Stooping, she told the Border Collie to be stealthy, and his intelligent eyes said he understood. "Good boy," she cooed, patting his head.

"I know where we're goin'. It's all coming back to me," said Tom, leading the way, keeping the flashlight beam low and ahead of them as they crept up a frosty bank, peeking over the crest of a hill.

There in a snow-covered clearing ahead, they spotted Sam Reilly squatting at the entry to the cave, building a fire. Marnie handed Tater's lead to Tom.

"Don't do anything stupid," he whispered, but she waved him off, zipping her fingers across her lips, telling him to shush.

She clambered up the pebbly bank, thinking, *What the hell am I doing?* At the top, she brushed her hands off on her jeans and leaned against the trunk of a white birch. Taking a breath for courage, she waved. "Hey, Sammy Bear. Fancy meeting you here?"

Startled, his head snapped up, his face twisted into an unnatural grimace. "How do you know about this place?"

"Tom and I used to follow you here, and *you* brought us when we were little. Remember? I mean, how could you forget? Anyway, I knew you'd be here," she said, sauntering toward him.

He glared at her—his eyes bloodshot—his pupils dilated.

"So, tell me, brother dear. How did you get Kate to help you?" she asked, stopping, keeping a few yards between them.

"It wasn't hard. But she needed me more than I needed her. I've been back in town for, oh, about three months. She invited me to crash at her apartment if I promised not to tell you. You see. Kate had a plan. It started when you and Wilder got together. The little gold digger set her sights on him as soon as you welcomed her into his house. Come on. You know she always wanted what you had. She wanted his money, and he saw the value of a trophy wife. She is malleable. You are not. Poor little Marnie. He didn't want to marry you. All on your own still, huh? What a shame," he said, pouting and rubbing his eyes, mocking her as he had when they were children.

"The number of times Kate and I have laughed at you." A sardonic grin etched his face. "You never were too bright, were you, Squirt?"

"Well, they always said you got the brains in the family. And I was gifted," she said, walking further into the clearing. "But something has happened." She tilted her head, studying her brother. "What's goin' on, Sammy? There's something off in your head, isn't there?"

She paused, allowing the silence to grip him. Marnie knew that a lull in a conversation between them was unusual. As a child and teen, she was a chatterbox. This was unfamiliar; a moment of contemplation might unnerve him. After a moment, she clapped her hands—jarring his senses.

"Anyway, I hear Ken didn't update his will, and I get all his money, and you and Kate will go to prison. She can't contest because the marriage wasn't real, and the courts will see that. Your addled brain deceived you, didn't it?" Her hands rested on her hips, and her smirk broadened.

Sam leaped to his feet, sneering. "What are you talking about? I am your only heir, and I've got you where I want you."

Willing herself not to run, she said, "Well, you aren't my beneficiary because you are legally dead. Tom Keller is the sole heir to my estate. Anything happens to me, and he gets everything."

"Where is he now? You always got yourself into trouble, and that smarmy pain in the ass had to come to your rescue. Why isn't your little boyfriend here?" He scanned the surroundings, turning in a circle. The grotesque grin on his face sent a shiver up her spine.

Kicking at the snow with her toe, she said, "He's back at the house. They're organizing a search. I snuck off to the boathouse and got a head start on them."

"Ha-ha! Well, that was stupid of you," he said, pouncing forward, and pinning her down before the detectives could move. With his knees pressing her arms to the ground, he wrapped his hands around her throat. She struggled, twisting and jerking, and swiveled her head, biting into skin and drawing blood. He pulled back with a yowl and slapped her face.

Springing to his feet, Tom roared, "Get the fuck off her!"

"You're a dead man!" growled Danny, launching forward.

The detectives scrambled up the incline, halting when Sam pulled Tom's missing gun from his waistband.

"Uh-uh! Any closer, boys, and the blonde gets it!" He held the pistol to his sister's head and snickered. "Oh, lookee here. I dropped it in the woods but found it again! Take your sidearms out of their holsters and set them down. Now!"

"Snake! You're a snake," said Danny, inching closer.

"Ha-Ha! I'm a reptile with a firearm." The grin disappeared, replaced by a cold, unreadable stare. "Now, drop them." Clamping a hand around the psychic's neck, he squeezed, making her cry out. "What's wrong, Tommy? You want your mommy?"

"Snake! You're a snake." Tom said, his eyes darting beyond Sam.

Hidden from view by a felled tree, Tater belly-crawled across the snowy ground parallel to his mistress and her maniacal brother.

"Snake! You're a snake," said Marnie, twisting to free herself of her brother's grip as the white tip of Tater's tail poked up from behind the dead pine.

Squinting, Sam growled, "What the hell? Snake? What is wrong with all of you, you stupid bitch?" He slapped her face again and held the gun up at the detectives. "Weapons down, boys. Now!"

Danny and Tom laid down their pieces and backed away, holding up their hands in surrender and giving the psychic a nod.

"Tater! Attack!" she screamed.

The Border Collie dove over the log, landing on Sam's back and sinking his teeth into the murderer's arm. With a crackling crunch, the dog shook the limb like a rope toy. The man howled, dropped the gun and shielded his face from Tater's oncoming attack. Marnie balled her fists together, slamming them hard into Sam's chest and he rolled off her with a thud, with Tater still clamped to his wrist. She rolled away, scurried to her feet, grabbed the gun, and pointed it at her brother.

"Marnie! No!" Tom shouted as he and Danny raced into the clearing, stopping only to retrieve their guns.

Sam clenched his free hand and delivered a hard blow to the pup's snout. The dog yipped and released his jaw, but before he could scuttle away, Sam clutched his neck, squeezing tight. Tater struggled and whined—his legs flailing in panic.

"Let him go! Don't you kill my dog, you bastard! You killed our mother. Don't you take him away from me, too!" Marnie fired the gun in the air. "Die, you bastard!" She sprang forward, tears streaking her red cheeks.

Tater went limp in Sam's grasp, and he threw the dog to the ground with a sickening thud. The Border Collie lay motionless in the dirt, eyes closed, his tongue poking out of the side of his mouth.

The murderer struggled to his knees, but before he could stand, the psychic rushed him. He vaulted off a boulder, left leg extended, knocking the gun from her hand. Landing with trained precision, he swept his right leg behind hers, knocking her to the ground. She scrambled for the gun, but he snagged the collar of her jacket and wrapped his hands around her throat.

Danny raced to her, ramming his shoulder into Sam's face, forcing him off the psychic. She scooted out of harm's way, and the detective slammed his fist into the side of the assassin's head, driving him into the granite wall of the cave. The predator bounced back on his left foot and swung his fist at the detective, but he ducked and wrapped his arms around his attacker's legs, dropping him to the ground. The men clambered to their feet as Tom positioned himself for a clear shot, but Marnie beat him to it. She scooped up Sam's gun and took aim at her brother.

"Freeze, asshole!"

The detectives froze. Sam took a step, and Marnie fired a shot into the ground at his feet. She got him in her sights again—her green eyes trained on her mother's killer.

"She said, freeze! Asshole!" roared Danny, pushing himself to his knees. Getting to his feet, he yanked Sam's arms behind his back, forced him to the ground, and cuffed his hands behind his back.

Tom sank to the ground next to Tater, lifting the dog into his lap. His eyes filling with tears, he cried, "Oh, Marn. I am so sorry. I didn't think he'd get hurt." He buried his face in the dog's white shawl.

The detective grabbed the collar of Sam's T-shirt and lifted him to his feet. "You piece of shit!" he growled, before shoving and dropping him to the ground, sneering when Sam winced in pain.

He reached out to Marnie, pulling her into a hug, and cradling her head. "I'm so sorry," he said, tears stinging the back of his eyes, trying not to look at Tater's lifeless body sprawled in his partner's lap.

She pulled away from him and took a step toward her brother, kicking him in the stomach, which delivered a loud groan and "bitch" from his blood-streaked lips. With a shaky breath, she crossed to her best friend and kneeled beside him, a hand resting on his shoulder.

"Tom's sad. What do we do to cheer him up, buddy?" The dog opened his eyes, poked his 'uncle' in the face with his snout, and dragged a big wet tongue along his cheek.

"Oh. My. God. Tater! You're okay, pal," he cried, hugging the pup.

Danny, mouth open, struggled for words and laughed.

Marnie grinned, shrugging a shoulder. "My boy is smart, and he knows a lot of tricks. Tom knows how to get him to take a beer out of the fridge. Danny knows how to make him shake, and I can get him to play dead. That asshole wouldn't have let him go otherwise," she said, casting an icy glare in her brother's direction.

The detective squatted and snapped his fingers. "Come here, Tater Tot. You brave, intelligent little man." The dog ran to him, sat and nudged him under the chin. "I think I've won him over."

"His ears didn't droop, so that is a good sign," said Tom, getting up from his seat in the dirt, brushing snow and grit from his pants. "But Marn, I gotta ask. Freeze, asshole? Really?"

"Ha-ha! Hey, it's something I've always wanted to say."

The detectives laughed, and she sank to the snowy ground to give her furry hero a cuddle.

Stepping away, Danny called his boss. "Cap. We got him. Send a boat."

Chapter Forty-Six

10:43 PM, The Island

A whirl of flashing lights from a police skiff greeted the detectives, Marnie, and Tater as they slip-slid their way down the bank, making the quick journey to the decrepit dock. They were more than happy to leave Sam Reilly behind, handcuffed to a tree in the clearing, writhing in pain in the dirt and snow.

Superintendent Cafferty and the captain stepped off the boat first, with two uniformed officers following. Sterling stuffed his fat sausage finger into Danny's chest. "Where is he? Did he get away from you again?"

"No, Cap. He did not," said Danny, attitude sneaking into his tone. "I would appreciate if you could remember, he wouldn't be cuffed and ready to be taken into custody without the three, uh, four of us. Now, I think that Ms. Reilly and Tater deserve a thank you for assisting the police in apprehending a cop killer. Don't you?" Side-eyeing his partner and Marnie, he gave a lopsided smile.

His boss coughed his embarrassment into his fist and bounced on his toes. "I want that report on my desk tonight, Gregg. You too, Keller!"

The psychic leaned in, placing a gentle hand on the grumpy man's sleeve. "Sir, couldn't the detectives do their reports in the morning? We have some injuries to take care of, and it won't hurt my brother to sit in a cell overnight and stew. We haven't had a decent night's sleep in three days. With all due respect, sir, we caught the bad guy. Isn't that the most important thing?"

The captain's face burned red, and he puffed out his chest, ready to blast back when the superintendent extended his hand to the group.

"Thank you, Detectives, and you, too, Ms. Reilly. Go home and tend to those wounds. Work will wait until tomorrow." He stooped to give the Border Collie a pat. "Who do we have here? Are you a member of the K-9 unit? Ha-ha!" Cafferty scratched the dog's ears and ruffled the thick fur of his fluffy white shawl.

"That's Tater, sir. He's Ms. Reilly's, and he helped us in apprehending her brother, sir," said Tom, bending to give the dog a pat on his rump.

The superintendent lifted Tater's paw and shook it, and the pup rewarded him with a wet kiss to the nose. "Did you now? What a clever boy!" The super straightened and turned to Marnie. "I love dogs. I have two shepherds at home. They're retired police dogs. Don't you find that a house isn't a home without a dog or two?"

"Yes, sir. I agree one-hundred percent," she said, giving her boy's fluffy ear a tug.

The captain grumbled, clearing his throat. "All right. The officers will take the suspect into custody. Go home and rest up. But be in early to file your reports." He turned to Marnie. "Ms. Reilly, thank you for your help—ahem—and for Tater's assist, too."

Marnie stuck out her hand, offering Sterling her cheesiest smile. "My pleasure, sir," she said, breaking away from the group, walking to the water's edge with her canine cohort.

Settling on a boulder, she hugged her dog tight. "Man, Tater, I am so glad you remembered that trick. And isn't it ironic that Sam taught it to you when you were just a pup? Clever boy." She looked into his face, and he rewarded her with a lick from her chin to her forehead.

Danny and Tom joined them a few moments later, and she got up, dusting snow off the seat of her jeans. "Can we please get the hell out of here and go have a drink?"

"Yes, ma'am. Your place or mine?" said Danny with a wink.

Tom laughed. "There is no way I am goin' to Marnie's. Too much dead energy over there."

His partner stared at him blankly. "Who said you're invited?"

"You two need a chaperone, and I'm volunteering."

"Okay, guys. Let's settle this. I need a glass of wine, a shower, and another glass of wine, in that order. I don't care who comes along or where we go, but I am not going back to murder central tonight," said the psychic, eyes landing on each of the men.

Her friend shoulder-bumped Danny. "We'd better get her back to yours before she pulls a gun on us and says, 'Freeze, assholes!' I still can't believe you said that," teased Tom, giving her a playful push.

To his horror, she slipped, grabbing his arm, and they both tumbled down the hill, splashing headlong into the pond with a shriek and an "Oomph!"

Danny and Tater chased after them, and the detective scooped Marnie up, carrying her out of the freezing water, while the dog gripped Tom's sleeve in his teeth and tugged.

Sputtering and coughing, she collapsed in fits of laughter.

Tom stood up in ankle-deep water, rescuing his sleeve from the Border Collie. "I'm okay, pal. Let me go," he said, climbing out of the pond.

The dog bounded after him, shaking his coat and spraying everyone.

Still laughing, the psychic shivered—her lips turning blue. "Brr. Geez! That gives new meaning to 'Freeze, asshole!', eh?"

Hands up in fists, teeth chattering, and convulsing with cold, her friend said, "Does it ever! Gosh. I didn't think you'd fall. I'm sorry."

"Let me be clear. If either of you has a thought about pushing me in, I'll shoot you," said Danny, taking off his jacket and wrapping it around Marnie.

After retrieving blankets from the police boat, the detectives, Marnie, and Tater loitered on the dock, waiting for the officers to escort Sam Reilly off the island. Nearing the group, his eyes fixed on his sister.

He lurched forward, threatening, "You're dead!"

"Come get me," she said, poking out her tongue.

"In time," he said with a menacing grin.

The cops gave her a dirty look and hauled the killer off as he struggled to free himself from confinement.

"Let's go home," said Danny, offering the crook of his arm to the psychic.

"Best idea I've heard all day."

Stomach gurgling, Tom pushed them forward. "Move it! I'm starving!"

Chapter Forty-Seven

11:48 PM, The Cabin

A buzz of unsettled energy followed them into the cabin as they came to terms with the night's events. Danny built a fire and poked through the fridge for something to hold his partner until morning while Marnie and Tom raced upstairs for hot showers and a change of clothing. Even Tater looked for comfort, darting off, returning moments later with a big leather slipper. He settled on the hearth, using the detective's shoe as a pillow, and fell asleep, mumbling about his day.

The psychic jogged downstairs first, dressed in blue-checked flannel pajama bottoms and a two-sizes too big gray New York Mets hoodie.

"I can feel the stress leaving my body," she said, dropping onto the couch and stretching out her long legs, leaning back on a couch cushion. "Looks like the Tot has accepted you into the pack."

The detective nodded. "Ha-ha! He's tuckered out. Poor guy has had a tough couple of days."

A creak on the stairs announced Tom's entrance. "I need food and beer," he said as he hit the landing, wearing Creekwood PD sweatpants and a ratty red sweatshirt.

"I hate to do this," said Danny, "but we need to talk. We've got a report to write in the morning, and I don't know where to begin."

"Boo! Hiss!" said his partner. "Yeah. Okay. Let's get a snack and adult beverages first, then we can knuckle down."

November 20th

12:13 AM

With a mug of hot chocolate laced with a generous shot of peppermint schnapps and a package of shortbread, Marnie sunk into the couch cushions, propping her feet on the table. Tom chose a bag of corn chips, a longneck ale as his poison, a big slice of raspberry pie, and an overstuffed chair as his perch. The detective settled next to the psychic with a deli bag of pepperoni and a glass of Irish whiskey, neat. The Border Collie rested by the fire, his eyelids fluttering and legs jerking.

"This is an unpleasant subject," said Danny, setting his highball on the table, "but how did you know Sam murdered your mother?"

"Divine guidance," said the psychic, wrapping an arm through his.

"Your mother?"

"Yup. And thanks for giving me a nudge. You know, it's not always easy getting details from the other side. It's pictures and feelings, but seldom words or full sentences. Mom showed me memories."

"Ouch. That would have been hard," said her friend, hitting her foot with his toe.

"Nah. It was fine. A flash of a Volkswagen Beetle was all I needed to understand."

"Ah. That old chestnut."

"Someone want to explain it to me?" said the detective, sitting forward, nibbling on his dinner.

Pushing her mug aside, she said, "Well, Sam and I were both visiting Creekwood for the Fourth of July. Dad and Sam went to a ball game, and Mom and I went out shopping. When she and I got home, he was furious. He and Dad had argued about a sixty-five Volkswagen Beetle that was in the garage. It had been my mother's. She gave it to me so that I would have transportation and not have to take the bus every time I wanted to visit. Sam had Dad's old pickup—so they didn't think it would matter. But he was raging mad. He kept talking about the VW being a classic and how he wanted to restore it and sell it. The financial worth of the car was important to him—not the practical value of my having transportation. Anyway, he got on a rant about my folks favoring me."

Tom butted in. "They didn't. I'm not saying they didn't treat you differently, but it wasn't all good for you and tragedy for him. Your parents even knew when you were agitating, trying to get him in trouble."

Danny smirked at the thought of the psychic as an annoying little sister.

"Hell, yeah! Neither of us got away with crap like that. Uh … where was I? My mother told him they'd planned to give him something, too, and she got out her checkbook, wrote him a check for $500, and handed it to him. He threw it at her, grabbed his bag, and stormed out."

"That sounds irrational," said the detective, taking a sip of his whiskey.

"You think? Um ... A few days later, Dad and I came back from fishing. As we walked up through the yard from the pond, we saw Mom sitting on the back porch. What we didn't realize until we got closer was that she'd been shot. She was dead."

"Jesus!" Danny laid a comforting hand on her arm, his thumb brushing her fingers. "I'm so sorry, Marnie."

Tears threatening to spill, she cleared her throat and looked away. "Hmm ... Words aren't enough. Mom's death almost destroyed my father and me."

"And the community," said Tom.

The detective's eyebrows shot up. "How so?"

She turned to Danny. "My mom was the town judge. Everyone loved her. Uh ... Maybe not the criminals."

"Did you suspect your brother at the time?"

"There were whispers," said his partner. "My parents were friends with the Reillys, and they wondered. There were conversations, huh, Marn?"

"We all had our suspicions, but no proof. And I still think Sam had something to do with my father's death, too."

"You're not the only one," said Tom.

"Like I said before, messages aren't always straightforward, but I think my mother was trying to tell me Sam was angry with me for not sending out a search party for him. But I tried, just like I did for Dad. The Bureau—well, they wouldn't listen to me or didn't want me to know the truth. Sam was a rogue agent, and the government was trying to cover it up. Maybe they said he was dead because they set it up."

"Or maybe pieces are still missing," said the detective.

"Maybe," she said, shrugging and picking up her cocoa.

Tom sat up, took a slug from his beer, and added, "How are we gonna spin all this into an official account?"

"Shit. We can't include the information we got from Mrs. Reilly in the report. Sam's gonna have to confess," said Danny, running his fingers through his mussed locks. Getting to his feet, he added wood to the grate and gazed into the fire. "I can't say we got intel from a ghost. It won't go down well. I don't know how to make him talk," he said, wheeling around, looking for advice.

"I do," said his partner, standing, stretching his legs and back. "He thinks he's smarter than everyone. He is *counting* on it. Call his bluff. Make him uncomfortable. Take your chessboard with you and challenge him to a game. I didn't witness rational thought tonight. His brain isn't functioning the way it used to. Let him know you are as strategic as he is, and set up the board, figuratively and literally. We'll put the questions together first thing in the morning, and with Madame Séance's help, we can get divine guidance if we need it. It's all about strategy, and I think he's lost his marbles. You'll get him in about five moves."

Marnie agreed. "My brother is smart, but you, Detective Gregg, have your wits about you. He is lost in the weeds. I will not sleep well, getting over who and what he's become. He doesn't even look like the old Sam."

"No, he's aged. A lot," said her pal.

"Yeah, he has," she said, standing. "You guys need anything? I want more cocoa."

Marnie returned with a steaming mug, a longneck ale in her pocket, and the whiskey and schnapps bottlenecks clenched in one hand.

Setting down her hot chocolate, she added more schnapps and caught the detectives checking her pour.

She wrinkled up her nose and took a healthy sip. "Hey, I need this. I'm going to the hospital tomorrow to have it out with Kate. I can't believe she helped my brother. By the way, check the Humvee in Ken's driveway for blood. Those big tire tracks Tom found on the bridal trail may belong to it. When I called her earlier, she covered her ass, blaming everything on Sam. As she tells it, he went to the house uninvited. She was out, and he told the guard he was delivering a package from Saks for Mrs. Wilder, and the stupid ass let him in. When she returned, Ken was dead, and brother dear threatened if she didn't help him, he'd kill her too. So, she grabbed a change of clothes and brought them with her. They drove out of the service exit because there wasn't a guard there at the late hour."

"We're still waiting for the security footage from the gate," said the detective.

"Well, we need to review my video too because she said she let herself into my house, disarmed the alarm, and locked up without resetting. I didn't see any signs of her when I was watching. She knew Tater wouldn't bark at her because he always steered clear of her. That should have been a warning, huh?"

"Smart boy," said Tom.

"Ha-ha. She said her shoe broke on her way back to the car. I bet Tater could smell her on that heel, and that's why he dug it up. A familiar scent may have piqued his interest. Anyway, she changed clothes in the back seat and threw the stilettos in the trunk."

"We have a lookout on Sam's car. Someone will find it over the next few days, I'm sure," said Danny.

Marnie curled her legs beneath her, snuggling into the corner of the sofa with her mug. "It has been bothering me how she knew where the security cameras are located. I never discussed that with her. She's more cunning than I thought. I mean, she knew to cover her face. Then again, they left the heel and red fingernail behind. It will be interesting to hear what they were doing at the house on Saturday night."

Eyes bulging, Tom said, "C'mon, Marn, you know what they were doing! They realized your name was still in the will, and they went to your house to remove you from the picture. I know you don't want to think that about Kate or your brother, but c'mon. She wasn't a friend. She's been running around behind your back for a long time. Why do you think we had that fight last year? Please don't get mad at me, but I knew. I didn't know she'd married him, though. Plus, she hid the fact that your brother was in town."

"I don't know if it's true, but she said she lost her finger saving you. And I'm not mad. I'm too tired to be."

"I don't trust anything Kate Parish says, and you shouldn't either."

Danny stretched his back and yawned. "Are you two about done? I'm fallin' asleep. Let's go to bed so we can work on the questions in the morning."

"I'm going to sleep here by the fire with Tater," said Marnie, sliding to the floor and snuggling her dog.

The detective tossed three throw cushions to her and snatched a blanket from the chair. "I'll keep you and our little hero company."

With a snort, Tom said, "Have a good sleep. I'm going up to a warm bed."

Marnie called out. "Hey! Say goodnight to my dad. He was in the upstairs hall earlier."

The psychic and the detective shared a knowing grin.

"On second thought … the couch is looking pretty good," Tom said, dropping onto the sofa, pulling a blanket over his head.

Chapter Forty-Eight

Thanksgiving Day

2:03 PM, The Cabin

A fresh fall of snow blanketed the forest outside Danny's cabin, softening the edges of a chaotic month. At the window, he watched a family of deer making lunch of a cedar tree while inside Perry Como's dulcet tones drifted from the stereo. In years past, he wouldn't have put holiday music on so soon, but "No Place Like Home for the Holidays" felt right, wrapping the rustic home in the season's spirit.

Peeking in the oven, his stomach grumbled. The aroma of roasting turkey and homemade pies filled the cabin, and for the first time in a while, he relaxed. Sam Reilly was behind bars—never to be free again.

A robust ahroo from the great room told him company had arrived, and a knock at the door and the clattering of dog nails on timber confirmed his suspicion. Gram and Tom let themselves in, and Danny joined them as they removed their coats and kicked off their boots.

"Happy Thanksgiving!" said Gram, beaming at her grandson. Eyes twinkling, she clapped her hands. "The decorations are perfect, and that turkey smells like magic." With a scowl, she inspected the bruises on his face. "Goodness gracious. What kind of animal would do that? Tsk! It looks a damn sight better, but still. Hmph."

Tater pranced over to Tom, dropping a tennis ball at his feet. "Hey, Tot. How are ya, buddy?" he said, petting his back and fluffing his fur.

The dog wriggled around Gram's legs and nudged her with his nose. She ruffled his shawl and scratched behind his ears. "I've got a special present for the little hero," she said, handing a bag to her grandson. "I made him a batch of peanut butter bones."

Marnie skipped down the stairs—taking two at a time. "I thought I heard the door."

"You and my grandson are quite a pair with those shiners. That's a beautiful shade of purple, dear." She patted the psychic's cheek, frowning at the contusions, then wrapped her in a hug.

Tater woofed and scooted to the door, sniffing the threshold. The psychic and detectives eyed one another as the door pushed open. Rick Price entered—a bottle of wine in his hand. "I hear there's turkey on the menu today. My family deserted me for the comfort of the in-laws' house in Maine. I'm on call, so I couldn't leave. Room for one more?"

Tom shook the doctor's hand. "Yeah. It's always good to have someone around who knows how to carve up a cadaver. Ha-ha!"

"Geez, Thomas!" Marnie covered her face with her hands.

Danny closed his eyes, shaking his head. "You need a filter."

Another rap sounded on the door, and Rick swung it open.

Carl poked his head inside and waved. "Uh, Marnie invited me. Is that okay?"

"Yeah. Come on in. Dinner's almost ready," said Danny, striding across the room and shaking the healer's hand.

Pulling her aside, Tom gave his friend a hug. "So, girlfriend. How's the new living arrangement working for you?"

Gritting her teeth, she said, "I'm only here until I can find a new house. Mine is on the market, and I am never living there again. It creeps me out thinking about it."

Danny put his arm around her. "You could move in here, you know. There is a spare room."

Face reddening, she changed the subject. "Would anyone like a drink? We have hors d'oeuvres laid out on the island."

With a snicker or two, everyone adjourned to the kitchen.

"Oh! You two have been busy." Gram clasped her hands, admiring the homemade pumpkin and pecan pies on the sideboard and the trays of hors d'oeuvres on the island.

Danny shrugged. "Yeah, well, I've only checked on the turkey. Marnie's done all the hard work. She's brilliant in the kitchen."

Tom smirked, tipped his head, and opened his mouth to say something, but the psychic shoved a piece of cheese into his mouth before he could utter a word.

"Filter, Tommy!" said the detective, clapping him on the back.

Gram grabbed her grandson's hand and pulled him away from the others. "So, Danny, did you remember?"

He slung an arm around her. "I did. You told me I would meet a woman who is stronger than me and we would live happily ever after."

"I did, Danny. That I did."

They both turned to Marnie, who was chatting with Tater, and he was smiling up at her.

"And so it shall be," she said, patting his arm.

Chapter Forty-Eight

Danny nodded. "Yup. Marnie, Tater and me."

Gram's blue eyes twinkled. "And four or five great-grandchildren for me."

With eyebrows raised, he asked, "You know something I don't?"

"I might, Danny. I might."

Marnie held up a glass of wine. "Okay, what's everyone thankful for this year?" she asked, winking at the detective.

He winked back, and holding his tumbler of Irish whiskey high, he said, "Divine guidance."

-The End-

Epilogue

Saturday, November 28th

10:30 AM, The Cabin

Steam rose from the teacup as Marnie sipped a strong Ceylon dosed with half-and-half. Setting it aside, she picked up the newspaper, passing her eyes over the article one more time. A headline reading, *Creekwood Killer's Armory and Car Found*, blazed across the front page of a neighboring town's weekend edition.

"I. Am. Numb. And why so deceptive? It was one rifle, a couple of stun guns, and piano wire. Thank goodness this isn't the local paper," she said, folding it in half and slapping it onto the coffee table. "How many times are we going to have to see this crap?"

Danny shrugged. "The recovery of Sam's car behind the animal shelter and his weapons and gadgets is a big story to some folks."

"Pfft! Get a life," she said, curling her lip.

Tom kicked off his boots, adding, "C'mon, Marn. You know this will be a topic of discussion for years to come. The gals down at Drake's Drugstore are having a field day, spinning tales, their tongues hanging out, waiting for the next tasty morsel to drop."

The detective changed the subject. "Let's talk about something else. Thanksgiving was nice," he said. "I gotta ask. What is Carl's story? Why isn't he practicing anymore? I mean, you two have a strange relationship."

"That was not a well-crafted segue. But yeah, we do, and that's for another day, but I can tell you he is not what he appears. He's a victim of an unfortunate circumstance. You should ask him. It's not my story to tell," said the psychic, taking a sip from her cup.

"I've been tellin' you he's not a bad guy," said Tom, picking up the newspaper, before rolling his eyes and tossing it aside.

"Hmm ... what about The Collective?" asked Danny.

Marnie twisted her mouth and shut her eyes for a moment, opening them when she had an answer. "Well, I *feel* Kate believed they would eventually be blamed for setting me up. She knows they're a bit loony and have a weird vendetta against me. Although I just don't see Alice or any of that group stooping to such violent measures—except Grace Wilmot, but she's out of the picture."

Her friend agreed. "They're still angry with you for walking away and turning in their leader. Plus, you kick the crap out of them when you have a chance."

"Huh ... I suppose. They're probably struggling. Crazy Grace *was* their main money maker."

Cheeks reddened, Danny said, "I should probably apologize to Alice. My reaction to her at your office was a tad over the top."

"You think?" said the psychic, tittering. "Anyway, it's time to get off this morbid subject. We should do something fun. It's such a beautiful day. Let's get Tater from the back deck and go for a walk in the woods."

"Sounds like an excellent plan. Do you think he's tired of playing chase with the squirrels and cardinals?" asked the detective, grunting as he pushed himself up from his chair.

"Not a chance. That dog never bores of herding things," she said, tapping Tom on the noggin as she breezed past. "Come on, Keller. Get your boots on."

"I'm in for a jaunt in the forest. Cap had me sitting on my ass all week. Head injuries suck," he said, tugging on a shoe, hopping behind them.

"You fainted during roll-call," said his partner, quirking up the corners of his mouth.

Jaw tight, Tom retorted, "I passed out."

"It's the same thing," said the counselor, reaching the kitchen's glass doors.

"Women faint. Men pass out. There's a difference. Anyway, I feel fine now. Geez! We all pushed ourselves. Adrenaline is a magic elixir. It keeps you moving when all you should do is drop in a heap."

"Oh, I've done that. I had a good old cry a few nights ago," said Marnie, unlatching the lock, and pulling the bifold open. She clapped her hands together and called, "Come on, Tater. Let's go play in the snow!"

The pup pranced over, sat at the psychic's booted feet, and flashed a cheeky smile.

"We've all got different levels of PTSD goin' on," said Danny, stepping into the sunshine and ruffling the Border Collie's fluffy white shawl. "I have quite the view here, don't I?" Pivoting from the lake to the woods, he breathed in the crisp thirty-four-degree day and sighed. "Okay. Let's roll." As he turned to go inside, he noticed paper flapping in the breeze, sticking to a log with gray duct tape. "What's this?"

They all leaned in for a closer look.

"It's been ripped from a book," said Tom, running a finger down the rough edge.

Eyebrows up, the counselor gasped when she recognized the author. "That's one of our favorite poets. And when I say *our*, I mean my family."

In silence, they read.

Acquainted with the Night

By Robert Frost

I have been one acquainted with the night.
I have walked out in rain—and back in rain.
I have outwalked the furthest city light.

I have looked down the saddest city lane.
I have passed by the watchman on his beat
And dropped my eyes, unwilling to explain.

I have stood still and stopped the sound of feet
When far away an interrupted cry
Came over houses from another street,

But not to call me back or say good-bye;
And further still at an unearthly height,
One luminary clock against the sky

Proclaimed the time was neither wrong nor right.
I have been one acquainted with the night.

As a chilly breeze blew around them, they each considered the words and what they meant to them. The psychic was the first to comment.

"That's why Sam ran up onto the porch that night. He stuck this to the house and bolted."

"What do you think it means?" asked her best friend.

"It sounds like a veiled threat to me," said Danny, poking a finger at the page.

"Yeah, but he's locked up," Tom replied.

Marnie eased the note from the wall, took in a breath, closing her eyes. "Hmm ... Just like Carl, there's more to this story," she said, glancing up at them, her eyes the most beautiful shade of aquamarine the men had ever seen.

Acknowledgements

Without my dear friend Nik Ballingal, Divine Guidance would never have been published. But she broke her leg and required entertainment, so I obliged. Thanks for giving me a nudge, Nik, and for designing all my covers. I love your talent and you!

Frances, a ginormous debt of gratitude and miles of love go out to you for encouraging me to write the second edition. And thanks for listening to me whine about how hard rewriting and editing out redundant bits could be. One day we'll have cocktails in person and end up in fits of giggles, I am sure.

A huge thank you, loads of love, and tight hugs to my beta readers, Jane Hackett Backus, Wendy Flood, and Laurie Lashomb.

Jane, forever my teacher, thanks for catching my grammatical errors, spurring me on, and boosting moody moments that need a zhuzh.

Wendy, where would I be without my favorite eldest sister? I always need feedback from someone who isn't afraid to hurt my feelings. But yeah, you were right. Dinner needed to be a snack. Thanks for calling me out.

Laurie Lashomb, thanks, soul sister, for making editing fun with your commentary. When I see a note from you, I am never sure if I've made a mistake or if it's a funny observation. Wherever possible, I will always use the word tuque just for you—or fit lolly water into the story.

Chronicles of Crime, from the depths of my black heart, thank you so much for writing a back cover quote. Is it too early for a drink?

A shout-out to Tracy Brown, author of the Door to Door Paranormal Mysteries and The Bellerose Witchline series. Thanks heaps for your kind words about Divine Guidance, which are now inscribed on the back cover. Bejesus is such a fun word, isn't it?

Chuck Arndell, I didn't forget you. Many thanks for being my number one fan (except for Harper, of course). Your kind words and support are invaluable.

Harper, I greatly appreciate your expert guidance on the topics of mental health, veterans, firearms, and dog noises. I know you'll do a better job of keeping the Pawsome Foursome quiet in the future. Even though I now have to worry about your noise. Happy retirement, old dude. Have I mentioned recently that I love you more than pizza? Well, I do.

Big cuddles and ear scratches to my lovely distractions: Dougal, Callee, Midget, and Mags. You fill my world with unconditional love and make certain I am never late for dinner. Where would I be without my furry schedulers?

And to the Instagram Writing Community, I am grateful to have found a supportive village where my weirdness and dark humor are welcome—and encouraged.

Here's a challenge for folks who live in or are from my hometown of Ogdensburg, NY: a signed copy of the series is waiting for you if you can find all references to the Burg and surrounds.

Mom and Dad, thanks for the divine guidance and for being brilliant storytellers. I know you're standing over my shoulder.

To all the dogs I've loved before, Tater and Dickens are for you.

For Readers

Thank you for reading *Divine Guidance*. I hope you enjoyed the story. Please consider leaving a review on Goodreads, Amazon, or wherever you purchased the book.

The Marnie Reilly Mysteries continues with *Torn Veil*, *Fatal Vow*, and *Vacant Grave*. Book five in the series, *Devil's Dance*, is scheduled for a late 2026 release.

Website

Visit ShariTMitchell.com for short stories, recipes, and to learn more about her books. Sign-up for her newsletter for updates from Creekwood.

Social Media

Instagram: @sharitmitchell
Facebook: www.facebook.com/ShariTMitchellAuthor
Goodreads: www.goodreads.com/sharitmitchell

Book Club Contact Information

Book clubs can contact sharitmitchell@gmail.com with queries and requests.

Books in This Series

Divine Guidance, First Edition
Divine Guidance, Second Edition
Torn Veil, First Edition
Torn Veil, Second Edition (coming 2026)
Fatal Vow
Vacant Grave
Devil's Dance (coming 2026)

About the Author

Shari T. Mitchell is the author of the Marnie Reilly Mysteries thriller series, which includes Divine Guidance, Torn Veil, Fatal Vow, and Vacant Grave

Raised in Northern New York State, Shari's hometown and surrounds are the inspiration for her series' fictional town of Creekwood, New York—which is located somewhere in the Adirondack Mountains.

While Shari loves developing multidimensional characters with whom her readers can relate, her passion is plotting the twists and turns of a mystery. It feeds her analytical and creative mind.

She lives in North Carolina and shares her home with her partner in crime, Harper, and their crazy rescue dogs, Dougal, Callee, Midget, and Mags.

A thirty-plus year marketer, Shari loves spending time with her family, cooking, hiking, traveling, gardening, and reading. She is often heard chatting with her characters because they natter at her constantly!

Mystery is her favorite genre, having cut her teeth on Nancy Drew, The Hardy Boys, and Trixie Belden. Her favorite authors include Robert Frost, Agatha Christie, Mary Higgins Clark, Ruth Rendell, Michael Connelly, Jonathan Kellerman, Sue Grafton, David Baldacci, Louise Penny, Stuart MacBride, and Michael Koryta.